the blood of innocent be slain

wait to kill ... help me! I do not believe

I am to accept such inf...

... I pray infinite ... mercy on what remains

I am Dracul. The blood of

... and now I wait

whom I put my faith,

... did not, but if I a

Evil as I have becom

... exists as well, and th

... of my soul. I am the

... of innocents stains my

... kill him ... God, in wh

I do not believe in you —

... such infinite Evil as

... infinite God exists as

... mercy on what remains

COVENANT WITH THE
VAMPIRE

COVENANT WITH THE VAMPIRE

THE DIARIES OF THE FAMILY DRACUL

JEANNE KALOGRIDIS

Delacorte  Press

Published by
Delacorte Press
Bantam Doubleday Dell Publishing Group, Inc.
1540 Broadway
New York, New York 10036

Source for some of the information on the Dracul Family Tree is
Dracula: Prince of Many Faces by Radu R. Florescu and Raymond T.
McNally (Little, Brown, 1989).

Library of Congress Cataloging in Publication Data

Kalogridis, Jeanne.
Covenant with the vampire : the diaries of the family Dracul / by
Jeanne Kalogridis.
p.   cm.
ISBN 0-385-31313-6
1. Dracula, Count (Fictitious character)—Family—Fiction.
2. Vampires—Fiction.   I. Title.
PS3561.A41675C63   1994
813'.54—dc20   94-6049
                               CIP

Designed by Nancy B. Field
Manufactured in the United States of America
Published simultaneously in Canada

October 1994

10 9 8 7 6 5 4 3 2 1

BVG

For S.

ACKNOWLEDGMENTS

I am enormously indebted to:

My editor and evil twin, Jeanne Cavelos, for her saintly
patience, her constant encouragement, and her unshakable faith that
this overdue manuscript would someday materialize on her desk;

My agent, Russell Galen, for his exemplary professionalism and
his suggestion that I try my hand at historical fantasy;

My cousin, Laeta Kalogridis, whose painstaking edit of the
manuscript powerfully shaped this book for the better;

My dear friend, Kathleen O'Malley, whose comments had a
profound influence on how the tale was told;

Toby and Ilona Scott, who freely offered their expertise on
all things Roumanian;

Most of all, the two men whose constant love makes all effort
worthwhile: my father, Irwin, and my beloved husband, George.

DRACUL FAMILY TREE

VLAD THE IMPALER (Dracula)
(1431–1476)
m. Princess Cneajna of Transylvania
(suicide, 1462)

Mihnea "the Bad," (143?–1510)
m. Smaranda (no children)
m. Voica

Milos   Ruxandra   Mircea II
m. Maria Despina

Petru the Lame (?–1594)
m. Maria Amirali (no children)
m. Irina the gypsy

Stefanitsa   m. Maria, Circassian lady-in-waiting

Alexandru*   Maria*   Mircea (1590–1640)   Petru*   Elena
m. Elisabeth of Hungary

Maria*   Mircea*   Petru   Bogdan, first to take surname
"Tsepesh" (1616–1672)
m. Ilona

Elisabeth   Bogdan*   Radu Tsepesh   Milos*
(1647–1699)
m. Ana

Ana   Radu*   Petru*   Vlad Tsepesh
(1699-1724)
m. Catherine (no children)
m. Maria of Amlash

Vlad*   Mircea Tsepesh (1697–1750)
m. Suzana Rosetti (suicide, 1718)
m. Gavrila Radescu

Maria*   Ana   Mihnea Tsepesh (1721–1778)
m. Maria Tsamblac

Suzana*   Vlad*   Mircea   Alexandru Tsepesh (1760-1811)
m. Elena ?   (suicide, 1795)

Ion*   Maria*   Elena*   Petru Tsepesh (1791-1845)   Radu   Alexandru*
m. Vera Vitez

Stefan*   Zsuzsanna*   Arkady Tsepesh (b. 1820)
m. Mary Windham

Stefan George Tsepesh (b. 1845)

* Died in childhood or born afflicted with physical or mental deformity

The devil is an angel, too.
—*Miguel de Unamuno*

COVENANT WITH THE
VAMPIRE

The Diary of Arkady Tsepesh
{undated, on the inside cover in jagged scrawl}

God, in Whom I put no faith, help me! I do
not believe in You—*did* not, but if I am to accept
such infinite Evil as I have become, then I pray
infinite Good exists as well, and that it has mercy
on what remains of my soul.

I am the wolf. *I* am Dracul. The blood of
innocents stains my hands, and now I wait to kill
him . . .

1

The Diary of Arkady Tsepesh

5 APRIL, 1845. Father is dead.

Mary has been asleep for hours now, in the old trundle
bed my brother Stefan and I shared as children. Poor thing; she
is so exhausted that the glow from the taper does not disturb
her. How incongruous to see her lying there beside Stefan's
small ghost, surrounded by the artifacts of my childhood inside these crumbling, high-ceilinged stone walls, their corridors awhisper with the shades of my ancestors. It is as if my
present and past had suddenly collided.

Meanwhile, I sit at the old oaken desk where I learned my
letters, occasionally running my hand over the pitted surface
scarred by successive generations of fidgety Tsepesh young.
Dawn nears. Through the north window, I can see against the
lightening grey sky the majestic battlements of the family
castle where Uncle still dwells. I ponder my proud heritage,
and I weep—softly, so as not to wake Mary, but tears bring no
release of sorrow; writing alone eases the grief. I shall begin a
journal, to record these painful days and to aid me, in future
years, to better remember Father. I must keep his memory ever
green in my heart, so that one day I can paint for my yet-
unborn child a verbal portrait of his grandfather.

I had so hoped he would live long enough to see—

No. No more tears. Write! You will grieve Mary if she wakes to see you carrying on like this. She has suffered enough on your behalf.

The past several days have seen us in ceaseless motion, borne across Europe in boats, carriages, trains. I felt I was not so much retracing my journey across a continent as traveling back in time, as though I had left my present behind in England and now moved swiftly and irrevocably back into a dark ancestral past. In the rocking wagon-lit from Vienna, as I lay beside my wife and stared at the play of light and shadow against drawn blinds, I was riven by the sudden fearful conviction that the happy life we led in London could never be reclaimed. There was nothing to tie me to that present, nothing but the child and Mary. Mary, my anchor, who slept soundly, untroubled and unshakable in her loyalty, her contentment, her beliefs. She lay on her side, the only position now comfortable in this seventh month of her confinement, her gold-fringed alabaster lids veiling the blue ocean of her eyes. I gazed through the thin white linen of her nightgown at her taut belly, at the unguessable future there, and touched a hand to it, gently, so as not to waken her—moved to sudden tears of gratitude. She is so sturdy, so calm; as placid as a motionless sea. I try to hide my wellings of emotion for fear their intensity will overwhelm her. I always told myself I had left that aspect of my self in Transylvania—that part given to dark moods and despair, that part which had never known real happiness until I deserted my native land. I wrote volumes of black, brooding poetry in my native language, before going to England; once there, I gave up writing poems altogether. I have never attempted any literature other than prose in my acquired tongue.

That was a different life, after all; ah, but my past has now become my future.

On the rumbling train bound from Vienna, I lay beside my wife and unborn child and wept—out of joy that they were with me, out of fear that the future might see that joy dimmed. Out of uncertainty at the news that awaited me at the manor high in the Carpathians.

At home.

But in all honesty, I cannot say that news of Father's death was a shock. I had a strong premonition of it on the way from Bistritsa (Bistritz, I mean to say. I shall keep this journal entirely in English, lest I forget it too quickly). A strange feeling of dread overcame me the instant I set foot inside the coach. My mind was already uneasy—we had received Zsuzsanna's telegram over a week before, with no way of knowing whether his condition had worsened or improved—and it was not soothed by the reaction of the coachman when I told him our destination. A hunchbacked elderly man, he peered into my face and exclaimed, as he crossed himself:

"By Heaven! You are of the Dracul!"

The sound of that hated name made me flush with anger. "The name is Tsepesh," I corrected him coldly, though I knew it would do no good.

"Whatever you say, good sir; only remember me kindly to the prince!" And the old man crossed himself again, this time with trembling hand. When I told him in fact my great-uncle, the prince, had arranged for a driver to meet us, he grew tearful and begged us to wait until morning.

I had forgotten about the superstition and prejudice rampant among my uneducated native countrymen; indeed, I had forgotten what it was like to be feared and secretly despised for being *boier,* a member of the aristocracy. I had often faulted Father for the intense disdain he showed toward the peasants in his letters; now I was ashamed to find that same attitude aroused in myself.

"Do not be ridiculous," I curtly told the driver, aware that Mary, who did not speak the language, nonetheless had heard the fear in the old peasant's tone and was watching us both with anxious curiosity. "No harm will come to you."

"Or to my family. Only swear it, good sir . . . !"

"Or to your family. I swear it," I said shortly, and turned to help Mary into the coach. While the old man backed towards the driver's seat, bowing and proclaiming, "God bless you, sir! And the lady, too," I tried to allay my wife's curiosity and concern by saying that local superstition forbade night travel into the forest. It was at least the partial truth.

And so we headed into the Carpathians. It was late afternoon, and we were already exhausted from a full day's travel, but the urgency of Zsuzsanna's telegram and Mary's determination that we should meet the prearranged carriage propelled us onward.

As we rumbled past a foreground of verdant forested slopes dotted with farmhouses and the occasional rustic village, Mary remarked with sincere pleasure on the countryside's charm—cheering me, for I feel no small amount of guilt at bringing her to a country where she is a stranger. I confess I had forgotten the beauty of my native land after years of living in a crowded, dirty city. The air is clean and sweet, free from urban stench. It is early spring, and the grass has already greened, and the fruit trees are just beginning to bloom. Some few hours into our journey the sun began to set, casting a pale rosy glow on the looming backdrop of spiraling, snow-covered Carpathian peaks, and even I drew in a breath at their awesome splendor. I must admit that, mingled with the growing sense of dread, I felt a fierce pride, and a longing for home I had forgotten I possessed.

Home. A week ago, that word would have denoted London . . .

As dusk encroached, a lugubrious gloom permeated the landscape and my thoughts. I fell to ruminating on the fearful gleam in our driver's eye, on the hostility and superstition implied by his actions and words.

The change in the countryside mirrored my state of mind. The farther into the mountains we ventured, the more stunted and gnarled the roadside growth became, until ascending a steep slope I spied nearby an orchard of deformed, dead plum trees, rising black against the evanescent purple twilight. The trunks were stooped by wind and weather like the ancient peasant women carrying on their backs a too-heavy burden; the twisted limbs thrust up towards heaven in a mute plea for pity. The land seemed to grow increasingly misshapen; as misshapen as its people, I thought, who were more crippled by superstition than any infirmity of body.

Can we be truly happy among them?

Shortly thereafter, night fell, and the orchards gave way to straight, tall forests of pine. The passing blur of dark trees against darker mountains and the rocking of the carriage lulled me into an uneasy sleep.

I fell at once into a dream:

Through a child's eyes, I gazed up at towering evergreens in the forest overshadowed by Great-uncle's castle. Treetops impaled rising mists, and the cool, damp air beneath smelled of recent rain and pine. A warm breeze lifted my hair, stirred leaves and grass that gleamed, bejeweled with sunlit drops of moisture.

A boyish shout cleft the silence. I turned, and in the dappled light beheld my elder brother Stefan, a gleeful six-year-old, his dark, upslanting eyes ashine with mischief, his flushed, heart-shaped face wearing its wide imp's smile above a narrow chin. Beside him stood huge grey Shepherd, half-mastiff, half-wolf, who had grown from a pup alongside us boys.

Stefan motioned for me to follow, then turned and ran, Shepherd bounding joyously beside him, towards the heart of the forest.

I hesitated, suddenly afraid, but reassured myself we were safe so long as Shepherd accompanied us, for there was never a more fiercely loyal companion or protector; and somehow I knew, with a dreamer's certainty, that our father was nearby, and would let no harm come to us.

So I chased my brother, half-laughing, half-shouting in outrage at the injustice because his legs were longer and, being a year my senior, he could run faster than I. He paused to glance over his shoulder with satisfaction to see me outpaced before disappearing from view into the dark, glistening woods.

I ran, ducking as low branches reached out to scrape my cheeks and shoulders and sprinkle me with captured raindrops. The further into the forest I ventured, the darker it became, and the more my face was slapped by low-hanging boughs, until my eyes filled with tears and my giggles turned to gasps. I ran faster, faster, flailing at the limbs that now seemed ghouls intent on clutching me, but I quite lost sight of my brother and the dog. Stefan's ringing laughter grew ever more distant.

I continued, crashing through the woods in a dark panic for a dreamy eternity. And then my brother's laughter broke off with a thud and a short, sharp shriek. There came a heart-beat of silence, then a low, ugly snarl. The snarl became a roar, and my brother screamed in pain. I ran, shouting Stefan's name, in the direction of the commotion.

And froze in horror as I reached a clearing and in the sunlit mists that filtered through the trees beheld a ghastly spectacle: Shepherd, hunched over Stefan's still body, his mus-cular jaws clamped on my brother's neck. At my footfall, the animal lifted his head, rending tender flesh with sharp teeth as he did so. Blood dripped from his silvered muzzle.

I stared into his eyes. They were pale, colourless; before, they had always been the gentle eyes of a dog, but now I saw only the white eyes of a wolf, a predator.

At the sight of me, Shepherd bared his teeth and released a low, deadly growl. Slowly, slowly, he crouched—then sprang, sailing effortlessly through the air despite his bulk. Terrified, I stood rooted to the spot and released a wail.

There came an explosion behind me and a shrill yelp before me as the dog fell dead to the ground. I turned and saw my father. Swiftly he lowered his hunting rifle and hurried to Stefan's side, but all was lost: my brother's throat had been ripped out by the heretofore-gentle Shepherd. I walked for-ward to find the tree trunk over which Stefan had stumbled, and the rock on which he had struck his head.

And then, with the exquisite clarity that marks the most vivid, terrifying nightmares, I saw my dying brother.

The small gash on his forehead had bled profusely, but it was nothing compared to his throat, which had been so severely mauled that the skin had been torn away and hung from his neck in a bloody flap, revealing bone, cartilage, and glistening red muscle.

Worst of all, he was still alive and dying, struggling to expel a final scream, a final breath; his horrified eyes were open, and they focused on mine in a silent plea for help. Tiny bright red bubbles roiled up from his exposed larynx, each prismatically ashimmer with filtered sunlight, a hundred miniature rainbows dipped in blood. Nearby blades of grass bowed, laden with shining crimson droplets.

I woke from this terrible vision with a start as the driver reined the horses to a stop. I must have dozed for quite some time, for we had already made it through the Borgo Pass to the rendezvous point. Mary had apparently been sleeping as well; she seemed as disoriented as I for an instant, but we came to ourselves and gathered up our things as we waited for Uncle's caleche to arrive.

We sat no more than a few minutes before we heard the rumble of wheels and the thunder of hooves. Out of the forest mists the caleche appeared, drawn by four high-strung and magnificent coal-black stallions, who quivered, eyes and nostrils wide, as Uncle's driver climbed down to greet us. Old Sandu had died two years ago, and this was a new man, one I had never met, dark blond and bland-faced, of cold, disagreeable disposition. I did not inquire after Father, nor did the driver volunteer information; better to learn any bad news from family rather than this silent, unpleasant stranger. Soon our trunks were situated, and we were tucked with blankets into the caleche, for the night had quickly grown chill, and Mary and I rode in sleepy silence towards home. This time I did not doze, but used the time to reflect on the nightmare.

Would that it had been but a dream.

In fact, it was a somnolent memory, triggered perhaps by the familiar scent of pine. The terrible event had actually transpired in my fifth year, though in reality I had not ventured close enough to examine my poor, bleeding brother. In reality, I had fainted the instant my father sank to his knees beside his dying son and released an agonised scream.

Years later, when Father had recovered somewhat from the tragedy of Stefan's death (and from the guilt—oh, how he blamed himself for trusting the animal!), he spoke to me of what might have caused Shepherd's sudden viciousness. Stefan had stumbled, Father said, and struck his head, which had bled profusely. Shepherd had always been a good and loyal dog, but the smell of blood had caused him to revert to his predatory instincts, those of the wolf. The dog was not to blame, Father insisted; rather he himself was responsible, for trusting the animal to overcome its dual nature.

❉❉   ❉❉   ❉❉

The recollection of Stefan's death caused my sense of dread to increase until I became convinced that the very worst news awaited us at the end of our journey. Alas, my premonition proved correct. After an interminable ride on serpentine sand roads, we arrived at my father's estate very close to midnight, and together the coachman and I helped Mary from the caleche. (She seemed rather taken aback by the size and grandeur of the manor, a far cry from our humble flat in London. I suppose I have been vague concerning the extent of our family's wealth. What shall she say to-morrow when the sun rises and she sees the magnificent castle, dwarfing us?) I must admit that I took fright when a huge Saint Bernard bounded barking down the stone steps to greet us, but I forgot the dog when my dead brother appeared in the doorway.

Stefan stood, fringe of tousled jet hair against the translucent alabaster of his forehead, despite the passage of twenty years a small, solemn six-year-old, and raised his hand slowly in greeting. I blinked, but his spectre remained; only then did

I notice that the pale upheld palm and white linen of his torn shirt were stained dark red—in the gleaming moonlight, almost black—and realised that his hand was lifted not to greet, but to disclose blood.

As I watched, he stretched forth his arm and pointed, small fingers dripping blood and dew, at some object behind us. I glanced over my shoulder surreptitiously, knowing that Mary and the coachman did not share in this vision, and saw nothing but an endless forest of dark evergreen.

I turned back to see Stefan, moving down the stairs towards us, silently but emphatically gesturing towards the forest.

Abruptly dizzied, I let go a cry and closed my eyes. There are legends in my country of the *moroi*—the restless dead, doomed by secret sin or concealed treasure to wander the earth until the truth be revealed. I knew Stefan's brave young heart had held no sin, nor could I imagine he had possessed much by way of treasure; I knew this apparition was caused by nothing more than the stress of travel, and the fear of the news to come. I am a modern man who puts his hope in science rather than God or the Devil.

I opened my eyes, and saw, not Stefan, but Zsuzsanna in the doorway.

At the sight of her, my heart constricted with pain; beside me, Mary raised a gloved hand to her lips and emitted a low moan of grief. We both knew at once that Father was dead. Zsuzsanna was dressed in mourning, her eyes red and swollen; though she tried to smile, her fleeting joy at seeing us was overshadowed by an air of sorrow.

Ah, sweet sister, how you have aged in the few short years I have been away . . . ! She is only two years my senior, but appears fifteen. Her hair—like mine and Stefan's, dark as coal—is streaked now with silver at temples and crown, and her face is lined and gaunt. I knew grief had taken its toll upon her, and was stricken with guilt that she had had to bear it alone.

I rushed to her at once, crossing the very spot where Stefan's ghost had appeared not seconds before. She managed to limp down a step before I caught and embraced her on the stone stairs. Her attempt at cheerfulness crumbled entirely then, and we sobbed openly in each other's arms.

"Kasha," she repeated. "Oh, Kasha . . ." The sound of her pet name for me tugged at my heart. (It was our private joke; *kasha* is a type of gruel I keenly despised and was routinely served for breakfast by our old Russian cook. As a boy, I had devised all manner of ingenious methods for disposing of it and fooling Cook into thinking I had eaten it.) Zsuzsanna seemed so light in my arms, so frail, so bloodless, that in the midst of my grief for Father, I felt concern for her. Ever since she came into the world with twisted spine and leg and frail constitution, she has never been strong.

"When, Zsuzsa?" I asked, in our native tongue, without even realising that I was no longer speaking English—as if I had never left for London, had never forgotten for the past four years that I was Tsepesh.

"This evening. Just after sunset," she replied, and I remembered the dream I had had in the coach. "At noon he lapsed into unconsciousness and never woke. But before he did, he dictated this for you . . ." Dabbing at her tears with her handkerchief, she handed me a folded letter, which I slipped inside my waistcoat.

At that moment, the Saint Bernard trotted up the stairs to stand beside his mistress, and I involuntarily recoiled.

Zsuzsanna understood, of course; she had been seven when the incident with Shepherd occurred. "Do not be afraid," she reassured me, leaning down to stroke the beast. "Brutus is purebred and very gentle." (Brutus! Has she any inkling of the implications of that name?) She straightened and moved haltingly down the steps towards Mary, who had been waiting at a short distance to allow us our privacy, and said in English, "But I am being rude. Here is my beloved sister-in-law, whom I have never seen. Welcome." Her accent seems quite thick to me now, after years in London; I could see it took Mary slightly aback, for she was accustomed to reading Zsuzsanna's precise, poetic prose, and clearly assumed her spoken English would be as perfect as her written.

Despite my wife's awkward condition, she moved with far more ease and grace on the stairs, and hurried towards my sister so that she would not have to struggle far. Mary kissed her and said, "Your beautiful letters have already endeared you to me; I feel we have been close friends for years. How glad I am to meet you at last, and how sad of the circumstance!"

Zsuzsanna took her hand and led us into the house, out of the chill night air. In the main drawing room, weeping and sighing, she told us of the course of Father's illness and his final days. We conversed for at least an hour, and then Zsuzsanna insisted on showing us to our room—my old room—as Mary was clearly exhausted. I saw to it that she was situated, then left with Zsuzsanna to go see Father.

She led me out the east end of the manor across the grassy knoll to the family chapel—or rather, to what had been the chapel, for Father had been an outspoken agnostic who raised his children to be skeptical of the claims of the Church. Even before we opened the heavy wooden door, I could hear wafting out into the cool night air the sweet, wavering voices of women singing the *Bocete,* the traditional songs of mourning:

> *Father, dear, arise, arise*
> *Dry your weeping family's eyes!*
> *Waken, waken, from your trance,*
> *Say a word, cast a glance . . .*

Inside, the trappings of Christianity—the icons, statuary, and crosses—had long ago been removed from the altar, but could not be expunged from the walls, for every spare surface glittered with Byzantine mosaics of the saints; on the ceiling of the high domed cupola, from whence hung the huge candelabra, Christ Himself gazed dispassionately down. As I entered, I caught sight of my childhood favourites: Stephen, the martyr (whom I always identified with my brother), the calamitous fall of Lucifer from Heaven, the stalwart Saint George slaying the ever-hungry dragon.

The building no longer functions as mausoleum or church, but as a place where family members can seek solitude and reflection, and indeed, it still possesses an almost spiritual aura that invokes a sense of reverence and calm. Father had spent hours there in the grim years after his son's death.

We moved towards the front from the back, where engraved gold plaques marked where our ancestors rest in crypts built into the wall. So many generations of Tsepesh lie entombed there that the chapel can contain no more; a century and a half ago, a new burial site had to be constructed between the manor and the castle. I walked past the dead feeling their eyes upon me, hearing in the rustle of Zsuzsanna's and my clothing their whispered approval, and feeling the same curious hyper-awareness of time that I had experienced traveling— except that I no longer moved backward through the centuries but forward, emerging at that moment from my ancestor's loins, out of history, moving swift as Stefan and Shepherd towards my present. Towards my destiny.

Father lay, just as small Stefan had so many years ago, in an open burnished cherry casket near the altar, which was draped with a black cloth and lined with rows of glowing candles. Two large tapers burned in heavy brass candlesticks at either end of the coffin. At the head of the casket, on either side, two black-clad women stood singing to my father, reminding him of all he was leaving in this life, as if they sincerely believed he might waken, persuaded to remain on this earth. I hesitated several feet away, suddenly unwilling to confront the object of my grief in front of witnesses.

"Leave me, Zsuzsa," I told her. "Go and rest. You have taken care of him all these years; I will see him through the night." It is the custom of our land for the men to sit with the dead—to keep the *privegghia,* as it is called—I suppose out of the ignorant belief that the soul must be protected from those who would steal it. My father would no doubt have disapproved of following a superstitious peasant tradition, but at the moment, I wanted to honour him, to show my respect—to help, even though I had come too late for it—and I could think of nothing else to give him. He was a kind, tolerant man, and I know he would have allowed me this, with gentle, fond amusement.

At the same time, with the irrationality of grief, I was annoyed by the singing women. It was permissible for me to choose to honour my father by following a custom he disdained; it was not acceptable for strangers to do so.

Zsuzsanna offered no resistance, but lingered for a moment, studying me with eyes ashine with loving misery and candlelight. "One of the servants brought a letter from Uncle earlier to-night," she said, and, drawing it from where she had tucked it at her waist, unfolded it so that I might see. Written in fine, spidery script, it read (as best I can recall and translate):

My dearest Zsuzsanna,

By this letter, let me extend my most heartfelt condolences. I share deeply in your loss, for as you surely know, there was no one closer to me in all the world than your father. Without his brilliant and astute management of the finances and estate, I could not have survived, but to speak of the business aspects of our relationship seems to demean it, for it was far more than that. Although Petru was my nephew, I loved him as a brother, and you and Arkady as my own children. Believe me, while I have breath, you shall want for nothing, need fear nothing! You are, after all, the last bearers of the name Tsepesh and the hope for our proud family's future. If ever there is anything which you need or desire, please do me the honour of asking, and you shall have.

Greetings to our dear returned Arkady and his wife, and sincerest condolences as well. I trust their journey was a safe and comfortable one. A pity that the joy of their homecoming must be dimmed by tragedy.

I have hired mourners to sing the Bocete *for your father; please*

*do not vex yourself with arrangements. All will be cared for. With
your leave, I may come by to-night to pay my respects. It will be
quite late, and so I will not disturb you or the others, but merely
request that you leave the door to the chapel unlocked.*

Your loving uncle,

V.

I nodded to indicate I was finished. Zsuzsanna folded the
letter and replaced it, and we shared a look of understanding;
she had wanted to warn me that my privacy might be disturbed. And then she stood on tiptoe to kiss my cheek good-
night, first turning to face Father's casket for a reverent moment.

I stood, still and silent, listening to the singing, to her
shuffling, uneven footsteps against the cold stone, then the
creak of the iron hinge on the heavy wooden door as she closed
it behind her.

I turned to the women and said, "Leave."

The younger of the pair's eyes widened with fright, but
she kept singing as the elder, her eyes downcast with the same
slavish fear I had seen in the coachman, said: "Sir, we dare not!
We have been hired to sing the *Bocete,* and if the singing ceases
even for a moment, your father's soul will not be properly laid
to rest!"

"Leave," I repeated, too weary with grief to engage in an
argument.

"Sir, the prince paid us a generous sum. He would be
angered if we—"

"I hereby release you from your obligation!" With a
sweeping gesture so abrupt that both women recoiled, I
pointed towards the door. "If the prince becomes angry, he
will have to be angry with me!"

Black skirts whispering, the singers hurried towards the
door, glancing over their shoulders at me with looks of muted
terror.

At last I was alone. I drew a breath and stepped alongside

the casket to gaze upon my dead, beloved father. He was a tall, handsome man, but like Zsuzsanna, he had aged decades in the few years since I had departed; his blue-black hair, generously streaked with iron grey when I left for England, had gone entirely silver, and his forehead was heavily furrowed with care. His life had been marred by tragedy: insanity and deformity have plagued recent generations of Tsepesh, due to intermarriage among *boier* families. His grandfather, mother, and sister were lost to madness, another sister and two brothers to defects and consumption. Of his generation, only Petru and his younger brother, Radu, escaped the family curse and lived to adulthood. And then came Zsuzsanna's crippled spine and leg and subsequent spinsterhood, the death of his wife, the death of Stefan. I felt an overwhelming sting of guilt and sadness at knowing that my departure for England had no doubt added to his sense of loss. He had died without ever seeing a grandchild.

(Dear Unborn Child, how I wish you could have known firsthand your grandfather's gentleness, his kindness, the depth and constancy of his love. How he would have doted on you, his only grandchild, how he would have delighted in carving you wooden toys, as he did for me and Zsuzsanna and Stefan. To know his face, you need only look at your own father's; my sharp, hawkish features are his, as is my raven hair, though my eyes are hazel, a mixture of my father's green eyes, and the brown eyes of my mother. I wish I could tell you I had known your grandmother, but the only memories of her I possess are the stories relayed me by Father; she died shortly after I was born.)

I gazed down at his pale, waxen face with its sharp, pinched features. His eyes were closed, and I let go a solitary piercing sob at the realisation that I would never again gaze into those beautiful, intelligent green eyes again. I wept bitterly as I laid my cheek against his cold, unmoving chest and implored him like a child to open those eyes again, only once more, only once more.

I know not how long my anguish continued, only that after some time, I came to myself enough to know that something cold and metal scratched my cheek. I lifted my head and spied beneath it a large gold crucifix attached to a rosary which had been hung round Father's neck. Obviously, one of the superstitious servants or the *Bocete* singers had put it there, knowing full well that it would have offended Father deeply. In a fit of fury, I snatched it. The cord snapped at once, and the beads fell into the coffin and scattered on the floor. I flung what was left of it across the room; the crucifix struck the stone wall with a small clink.

I stood fuming for a moment, and then I calmed myself: whoever had done this had only done it from good intentions. Slowly, I retrieved the cross and beads, and slipped them into my waistcoat pocket, and then I sat on the wooden pew nearest the coffin and retrieved Father's letter, written in Zsuzsanna's bold, artistic hand. It read:

> *My dearest Arkady,*
>
> *When you read this I shall be dead. {Here there was a waterspot on the parchment, where the ink ran.} With my whole heart, I wish you, your wife and child could return to England to lead the life you have always wished to lead. But without you, your uncle is helpless, with no one to run the estate. You must take my place, and do whatever the prince bids, for the good of the family. It is unavoidable; nothing else can be done.*
>
> *No matter what evil may befall you, one thing you must always remember: that I love you with all my soul, and that your uncle loves you in his own way, as well. May this knowledge sustain you in times of future sorrow.*
>
> *Farewell! My love to you, and to the daughter-in-law and grandchild I shall never see.*
>
> *Father*

I sat mourning for some time. I cannot honestly say that my father's request that I take his place came as a surprise; Mary and I had been discussing it ever since the telegram from

Zsuzsanna had arrived. When I first left for England, I fully intended to return home at the end of my studies to assist Father in running the estate; but at the time, I had assumed that he would outlive Uncle and inherit the property, just as I expect someday to inherit it. In the intervening years, I grew accustomed to my new country, fell in love with an English girl, married, and entirely forgot my familial obligation.

I can forget it no longer. Our bloodline has faced a number of difficulties because of intermarriage; there have been deformed, sickly children, such as Zsuzsanna, and madness in our family, so that it dwindled over the centuries until only my father and his brother were left to carry on the name. Fortunately, Father married an outsider, a strong Russian-Hungarian woman, and both he and Uncle were kind enough to give their blessings when I announced my engagement to Mary. But when Uncle dies, I shall be the last male Tsepesh— or Dracul, to use the accursed name given us by the peasants. It is only fitting that I raise my children here and teach them to love this land as I love it, and as my father and his father, and all my ancestors loved it before me. We have held this land for almost four hundred years. I cannot abandon it; to sell it to strangers would be unthinkable.

Yet as proud as I am of my heritage, I feel an overwhelming sense of guilt at asking Mary to give up England and remain in this backward, isolated country. She insists that she has always known this would be the outcome, and that she is fully prepared. It does little to ease my concern. I cannot be happy here if she is not.

Still, in the gloomy, candlelit silence of the chapel, I swore a solemn oath—a deathbed promise to Father, if several hours too late: I would remain, as he bade, and take care of Uncle. Mary and I would raise his grandchild here, on the property he so loved, and I would not forget to teach that child of his grandfather and all those Tsepesh who went before him.

Thus I remained on the hard wooden pew, mourning my father where generations of Tsepesh had sat before me, holding vigil for lost loved ones. After some hours, I drowsed, and lapsed again into the anxious dream of my child-self, running through the forest after Stefan.

I was jolted awake by the sound of eldritch howling, uncomfortably close by. At that same instant, the heavy wooden door swung open with a groan, and I beheld, for the first time in years, my great-uncle Vlad.

(Dear Child, your great-great-uncle Vlad, who will have passed from this earth by the time you are old enough to read this, was a notably eccentric recluse. I suspect this was due to a mild case of the family madness. Vlad was an agoraphobe who rarely left the castle, and feared regular contact with anyone other than my father. For that reason, my father handled all business dealings of the estate, and most dealings with the servants. Yet V. was lavishly generous with us. He visited us upon holidays and birthdays and played the kind and interested uncle, showering us with gifts upon those occasions. He paid not only for my father's education, but for mine, as well, and saved Zsuzsanna's life by bringing in the very best physicians from Vienna when she was ill.

Unfortunately, my great-uncle's eccentricities led to many rumours among the servants, and among the superstitious peasants in town. These have caused a good deal of suspiciousness towards our family on behalf of the countryfolk; I'm sure you will hear of that, too.)

It was evident we both were startled by the other's presence. He lingered in the doorway a moment, a tall, hawk-featured, leonine-proud figure dressed in mourning. I must admit that, over the years, I had forgotten the oddness and severity of his appearance, and was at first intimidated by him, as I had so often been as a child; for he was ghostly pale (as befits a recluse), so pale it was impossible to tell where his skin ended and the thick silver mane on his scalp began. His long, drooping moustache and wild, massive eyebrows were the same hue. This exceptional pallour was emphasised by his black cloak and dark green eyes—arresting, ancient eyes, the colour of the forest, full of swift intelligence.

For a moment, I felt both drawn and repelled by the sight of them. But then they softened suddenly in recognition, and filled with an extraordinary kindness; and he was transformed from a fear-provoking spectre into the loving uncle I remembered.

I drew in a breath as I realised my childish prayer had been answered. I had forgotten the striking familial resemblance, but now I looked into my father's eyes once more. He spoke, and I heard my father's voice.

"Arkady," he said, "whose name means Heaven. How good it is to see you again, and how deeply I regret the conditions under which we meet."

"Vlad," said I, rising. "Dear Uncle." We stepped towards each other and clasped hands, then exchanged the traditional kiss on each cheek, a custom I had become unused to after years in London. He must be quite old, for as far back as I could recall, his hair had always been silvery white, and he moved with the deliberation of age—but his grip, though cold, was strong, belying his frail appearance. Through some miracle or the deception of my memory, he had not aged. We held hands and gazed into each other's eyes some time; I felt I peered into the souls of all my ancestors, now merged into one flesh.

"I apologise for disturbing you," he said. "I had not expected to find you here."

"It is no disturbance."

"And how is your dear young wife?"

"Well. Resting."

"That is good," he said gravely. "We must do everything possible to maintain her precious health, for the sake of the coming child." He glanced about at the still, empty chapel. "But where are the mourners? The ones I paid to sing *Bocete*?"

"Gone," said I. "I dismissed them. It is entirely my fault. I hope you are not angered, but I wished for silence."

"Of course," he replied, with great sympathy, and waved a hand to dismiss it. "But how you have changed since last I saw you; you have become a man. More than ever before, you resemble your father." He took a step back to better study me, and drew in a short, pained breath. "It's true. You have his face, his hair . . ." This was stated approvingly, then (surely I imagined this) his tone grew faintly disappointed. "But your eyes have something of your mother in them."

He held my gaze for a moment, then turned towards the coffin. A look of sorrow crossed his face as he sighed, "And here is our Petru . . ."

"Yes," I said, and retreated to the pew to allow him his moment of grief.

He raised a hand to his face as he closed his eyes, and said, with a grief so deep fresh tears sprang to my eyes: "Is there anything more horrible than death? More terrible than the realisation that he is lost to us forever?"

And then he lowered his arm, and approached the casket reverently; he took my father's hand, and in a low, impassioned voice, exclaimed: "Ah, Petru! Has your flesh grown so cold at last?" And he bent, raising the hand to his lips, and kissed it, saying, "At times, I feel I have walked too long upon this earth; too many times have I seen loved ones die, too many times kissed a dear dead face."

He tried to replace Father's hand with some dignity, but sorrow finally overwhelmed him, and he sank down to rest his cheek upon my father's chest, as I had, whispering all the while: "Petru! Petru! My only true friend . . ."

And he wept. I closed my eyes and turned away, for to witness his suffering was to add to my own; he looked so frail and pathetic bending over the casket that I could not keep from thinking that soon, all too soon, he would be lying in his own.

When at last he collected himself and rose, he gazed down on my father and proclaimed, with such forceful, passionate conviction that his voice rang echoing off the cold stone walls, and I knew it carried beyond the pale of death, so that my father and all my ancestors heard: "I swear to you, by the name Tsepesh, that your loyalty will not go unrewarded."

With that, he came and sat beside me, and we held vigil in silence. Soon afterwards, the wolves began to howl again, so nearby that I could not help glancing anxiously out the darkened window. Uncle saw and smiled faintly, reassuringly. "Do not fear, Arkady. They will not harm you."

But the sound settled deep into my mind, and after some time, I fell into the dream of Stefan and Shepherd once again, in the nightmare running through endless forest. Hours and hours I ran, screaming Stefan's name while wolves snarled in the distance; only then did I arrive at my ghastly destination to see my brother's bleeding body, and Shepherd, raising his dripping bright red muzzle to gaze at me . . .

Suddenly my father stood between us, his back trustingly towards the beast. He gripped my wrist and turned the tender inside of my arm outward. I did not resist; this was my father, whom I loved.

Trust me, he said. *No harm will come to you . . .*

Silver flashed in a gleaming downward arc from his upraised arm to my exposed flesh. I cried out, startled by the pain.

At the touch of a cold hand upon my shoulder, I woke gasping to find myself staring into white wolf eyes.

"Arkady," Uncle said sternly. "Wake up. You are dreaming."

I blinked, and the wolf's eyes became my father's, set in Uncle's pallid countenance. Outside, the darkness had eased to pre-dawn.

"I must return," Uncle said.

I rose and escorted him to the doorway, thanking him for sitting vigil with me, but he raised a hand to silence me, saying, "It is only fitting." He paused, and for the first time, I detected a trace of hesitancy in his manner. "Tell me, did your father ever mention to you the possibility of taking his place?"

"Yes," I replied. "It was understood. I had always intended to return to manage the estate someday; I would be honoured to do so on your behalf."

"Ah. Excellent. But let us not speak of business now while our hearts are heavy." He put his hands upon my shoulders, and we took our leave of each other in the traditional manner, then went our separate ways into the retreating night.

The renewed howling in the distance made me hasten across the dewy grass towards the manor. As I neared the manor's east entrance, I chanced to see a dark blur of movement low and to my left and froze in panic, thinking it was a stray wolf or perhaps even a crouching bear, running towards me.

It was neither. As I directed my sight toward the source of the movement and my eyes adjusted to the dimness, Stefan's small, bloodied form coalesced in the waning moonlight.

My dead brother stood at the far end of the east wing overlooking the forest between manor and castle; he raised a thin arm and gestured sweepingly at the tall pines.

Our gazes met. He regarded me with reproachful solemnity, no longer the grinning imp, his dark brown eyes—my mother's eyes—huge and almond-shaped, with a slight upward tilt, set in a child's head still too big for his bleeding body. Beneath his chin, a darkly glistening flap of skin hung down; moonlight gleamed off the whiteness of bone at his throat. He pointed with his forefinger again at the distant trees and silently stamped his foot in a characteristic gesture of impatience I had not seen in twenty years.

I emitted a soft bleat of terror, fell to my knees and covered my face. I remained there some minutes until at last I dared peer between trembling fingers.

Stefan was gone. I pushed myself to my feet, brushing away bits of damp grass that clung to my trousers, and hurried into the house.

And now I write. Everywhere I look to-night, I fear I will see Stefan—in the bed beside my wife, outside in the corridor. I know this apparition is merely the result of grief, yet I cannot free my mind from ruminating on the legends about the *moroi*.

What do you want me to find, little brother? What treasure lies hidden in the forest?

I have written this at feverish pace. It is yet morning, but the sun is high in the sky. Mary still sleeps, poor tired thing. I shall go lie beside her now, and pray I do not dream of wolves.

Zsuzsanna Tsepesh's Diary

6 APRIL. I write this after midnight—so I suppose it is really 7 April after all. I am so hungry for sleep, so weary. The day of Father's death I lay all night weeping; nor could I rest well the night after. Now that sweet sleep finally comes, I am wakened by Brutus' barking. He keeps lunging at the window. He is calm now, but if he does it again, I shall confine him to the kitchen before he wakes the entire house.

When first I opened my eyes and gazed over at the window, I thought I saw reflected there Uncle's face—but it was merely the lingering afterimage of a dream. Brutus was so agitated I finally went over and opened the shutters to investigate, and saw something crouched and grey running across the grounds: a wolf.

I had thought I would not be able to sleep after the fright, and would sit and write about Kasha and Mary's arrival, but exhaustion overtakes me again. To bed now. Sweet dreams, Brutus!

✠ ✠ ✠

The Journal of
Mary Windham Tsepesh

7 APRIL. This country is beautiful and wild and strange, like its people; and my husband's family, it seems, are the strangest of all.

I feel no small guilt recording such words. But I must ease the burden of this knowledge in some manner, and I cannot tell my good husband, and most certainly not his family. Yet as I begin to write, I am tempted to credit my uneasy perceptions to delusion, brought on by my condition. Perhaps all expectant mothers suffer such worries . . .

Nonsense. I have never been delicate, never subject to the maladies triggered by nerves. Arkady is proud of my level-headedness; and it is true. I come from a cool-blooded people. I love my husband for his warmth, his passion, his bold declarations which do not spring easily to my lips. Most times I envy those very qualities.

But his great-uncle and sister possess them to the degree of madness.

I can say nothing to my poor dear Arkady; he is heartsick enough over the death of his father. I am determined not to add to his grief, for I understand it all too well. I was orphaned at age thirteen. Four sisters and three brothers I have, yet we all grew up apart in the homes of distant relatives when Mother and Father died untimely in the fire. I have wanted for so long to belong once again to a real family that it brought tears to my eyes in London when I read the gracious letters from Arkady's father, sister, and great-uncle welcoming me into theirs. I felt honoured to be a part of a heritage that stretched back centuries; I felt blessed. I knew my children would grow up proud.

When at last I came to Transylvania, the lush beauty of the landscape charmed me, and the magnificence of the family estate quite steals my breath each time I focus my attention upon my surroundings. I can scarce believe I am a part of this, that I am now considered chatelaine of this vast manor built four hundred years before. As I write these words, I can lift my eyes and see through the open shutters ethereal clouds of blossom where cherry and plum orchards extend up the mountainside next to the prince's great stone castle, rising up against the backdrop of the Carpathians. Beyond the opposite window, quaintly costumed shepherds tend grazing flocks in the open meadow that borders the dense forest, a sight that must be no different from that viewed by this room's inhabitants in earlier centuries. Arkady says there is a vineyard, too, and when we rode from Bistritz, he pointed out his great-uncle's vast fields near the village in the valley, and said that come autumn, they would be golden with wheat. The Tsepesh estate feeds the entire town—quite generously, I should think, for the local peasants seem much better clothed and nourished than any I have seen elsewhere in this empire.

I am overwhelmed, and anxious to prove myself worthy to be part of the family. Another stab of guilt pierces me as I write these words, for they have required nothing of me, have done nothing save welcome me with open arms. When I met Zsuzsanna, my heart went out to her. She is so kind, and such a frail, lonely creature—crippled, as so many of the peasants seem to be. Arkady says it is because of their isolation and intermarriage, and one of the reasons his proud family line is in danger of dying out. I felt sorry for Zsuzsanna, alone now in this great, brooding house. I was sad for her father's death, but glad we had come. I believe nothing would make her happier than playing auntie to a horde of children (and nothing would make me happier than playing mother to one). She is something of a child herself, having been, like her people, isolated too long from outside contact. Although she is extraordinarily intelligent—she practiced English with Arkady "for amusement" before he left for England, and her letters to us prove she, like her brother, has inherited her poetess mother's brilliance with language—she is also resoundingly naive.

But the great-uncle, Vlad—

Of him I know not what to say, except that he frightens and disgusts and charms me. I do not want him near my children. Perhaps I shall have my wish, for he seems terribly weak and pale, and according to Arkady is incalculably old.

When we left Bistritz, I saw fear in the old coachman, and I see it daily in the eyes of my chamber-maid, Dunya. She and the other servants cringe when I or one of the other family members approach, and will not meet our gaze. After seeing the prince, I understand why. There is something terribly disturbing about him, something frightful. I cannot label it, for it has everything to do with instinct and naught with reason. Even the dog, Brutus, senses it, and flees the prince's presence.

But Arkady and Zsuzsanna do not. They look at him with such love, such devotion. They speak of him with a reverence others reserve for God, and they shrug off what they term small eccentricities. Vlad did not even attend the funeral, but no one took offense. It is as though he has them mesmerised.

Instead, he came the night after our arrival to Petru's *pomana,* a traditional "dinner for the dead," for which all the deceased's favourite dishes were prepared: *mamaliga,* a baked savoury cornmeal porridge topped with poached eggs, stuffed cabbage, and a chicken dish with a peppery red sauce. It was a small, sorrowful affair. In the cavernous dining-hall, Arkady, Zsuzsanna, and I waited, wistful beneficiaries of a surfeit of opulence, surrounded by hundred-limbed silver candelabra, a table service of pure gold, and the finest cut crystal whose every facet reflected a thousand shimmering tongues of flame. We were positioned at a long, heavy wood table that would easily have accommodated thirty, and at the hall's other end stood a second table of the same length but lesser height, which I assume was for the children. I could not help but think it sad that the family had been reduced to us three plus the uncle. Apparently I was not the only one to whom this notion occurred, for Zsuzsanna turned to Arkady and with wan, forced cheerfulness, said, "Do you remember, Kasha, when we were children and Uncle Radu came to visit from Vienna?"

My husband nodded as he said, in a voice still hushed by grief, "I remember. He brought our cousins with him."

"Six daughters," Zsuzsanna said, with a tremulous smile. Her large dark eyes glittered with candlelight and unshed tears. Apparently the *pomana* is supposed to be a happy event, the remembrance of what was good about the deceased's life, but she seemed teetering on the edge of an emotional precipice, uncertain whether to laugh or weep. "All of them so gay, so precocious! We sat with them at the little table there"—she pointed—"and they began to sing to the grown-ups. Do you remember?" And she sang a phrase of what sounded to my ears like a Transylvanian nursery song; her voice was clear and lovely. "And Papa led the grown-ups in singing the refrain back to them." She sang again, a single tear spilling down her cheek as she did so; at the end of it, her uncertain smile broadened. With the same emotional generosity that makes me love her brother, she turned to me and exclaimed: "I am so happy you have come! I have been sad that our family is so far-flung; but now we will have laughing children in these rooms again!"

Touched, I reached for her thin hand and clasped it. Before I could reply, Arkady turned in his chair and Zsuzsanna glanced swiftly at the entryway. I knew at once the prince had arrived, and I followed their gaze, eager to see at last the benefactor who has lavished so much kindness upon me and upon his family.

At the sight of him, I barely managed to restrain a startled gasp. His appearance was quite ghoulish. He stood in the doorway, a tall, stately figure who looked every inch the prince. But he seemed emaciated, half-starved, and so horridly white-skinned as to seem bloodless. By contrast, pale, worn Zsuzsanna appeared a blooming rose. My first impression was that he suffered from anaemia or some dreadful wasting disease. His complexion almost perfectly matched his silvery white hair, and in the wavering candlelight, his skin took on a strange phosphorescence. I fancied if we had blown out all the candles and sat in the dark, he might have glowed like a firefly. Yet despite his pallour, his lips were deep, dark red, and when they parted in a smile at the sight of us, beneath flashed overlong, sharp ivory teeth.

Amazingly, neither Arkady nor his sister seemed troubled by their uncle's strange appearance, or by his frighteningly magnetic eyes. Those eyes swept over me with such predatory keenness that I shivered, chilled as though a sudden draft had entered the room, and in my mind rose an unbidden thought: *He is hungry, terribly hungry.*

He said nothing, but stood still as a statue in the entry-way until at last Zsuzsanna cried: "Uncle! Uncle!" with such excitement and jubilation one might have thought her father had just returned from the dead. She struggled to push back her heavy chair, as though she intended to run to him like a child. "Please, come in!"

At her invitation he crossed the threshold into the room. Both Arkady and Zsuzsanna rose and exchanged kisses with him, one on each cheek. He lingered over Zsuzsanna, encir-cling her waist with his arms, and—

May God forgive me for evil thoughts if he be innocent, but I am not one given to fantasy or gossip. I know what I saw. She gazed up at him, her eyes ashine with adoration, and he looked down at her with clear, unmistakable hunger. I sensed an uncertain moment where he seemed barely able to control himself; and then he glanced up, saw my critical gaze, and his lips curved upward.

Under the scrutiny of those dark green eyes, I felt a sud-den confusion, as if my mind's grasp upon reality flickered for an instant like the candles. A fresh thought supplanted the old, but it seemed a stranger's, not mine: *Surely you are utterly mistaken. See, he merely loves her like a daughter . . .*

Those eyes tugged at me like the tide. I felt strangely

drawn, strangely repulsed. My heartbeat quickened—whether in excitement or dread, I am still undecided, and the child within me stirred. Instinctively, I put my hand upon my swollen stomach. At this, he moved over to me, took my other hand, and bent to kiss it.

His touch was so like ice that I fought not to shudder, and failed altogether when I felt his lips part and his tongue sweep lightly over the back of my hand, as if he were tasting my skin the way an animal might. He straightened, and again I saw a flicker of appetite in those snake charmer's eyes.

But you are mistaken . . .

"Dear Mary," he said, in thickly accented English, in a voice so lilting, so musical, so utterly charming that I melted at once, and felt a wave of enormous guilt that I could ever have thought such terrible things about a truly kind and generous old man. He looked at my belly, then, with the same craving—

Or was it rapturous love?

"Dear Mary, how good to meet you!" He still clasped my hand between his two huge cold ones. I wanted nothing better than to pull free, and wipe the back of my hand on my skirts, but I remained politely motionless as his gaze swept intently over me. "Arkady was right that you are so beautiful; eyes like sapphires, hair like gold. A jewel of a woman!"

I blushed and stammered awkward thanks. His words struck me as openly flirtatious, but Zsuzsanna and Arkady looked on with approving smiles, as if their great-uncle's behaviour were not that of a voluptuary, but perfectly appropriate. I decided that perhaps Transylvanian and British standards of conduct were quite different.

Having reached the end of his fluency in English—apparently his poetic compliment had been carefully rehearsed—Vlad switched to Roumanian, and Arkady translated: "How good to meet you at last, and thank you in person for the fresh joy you have brought our family. How are you feeling after your long journey?"

"Quite well, sir," I replied, and listened to the strange, sibilant sounds Arkady then used to relay my response to Vlad. I have studied some French and Latin, and could guess at some of the meanings. In fact, I did not feel altogether well, but was suddenly dizzy and wanted nothing better than to sit down.

"This is good!" Vlad remarked heartily. "We must take very good care of you and see that you are always well, for you are the mother of the Tsepesh heir."

For the rest of the evening, Vlad spoke mostly in Roumanian, and Arkady translated, though from time to time we dared communicate directly with each other in uncertain German. For convenience' sake, I shall record our conversation as if it had taken place entirely in English.

I thanked him for his kind letters, and we exchanged more gracious remarks, then took our places at the dinner table. The dog, Brutus, who had lain curled at Zsuzsanna's feet, growled most uncharitably at Vlad, then slunk out of the room and did not reappear for the rest of the evening.

Yet Vlad proved as charming as he was fear-inspiring. He made a small speech about his deceased nephew, so touching and clearly heartfelt that all four of us were moved to tears. Dinner was then served, during which each person relayed fond stories about Petru, and many toasts were made. I took only token sips of my wine, as drink does not agree with me generally, and even less so since I became with child—and it caught my attention that, during the toasts, Vlad raised his glass to his lips, but only pretended to drink. Nor did he eat, though he lifted his fork on several occasions. At the evening's end, both his wine and meal were entirely untouched. Even more amazingly, neither the servants nor the family seemed to notice. I felt certain the family simply tolerated this as just one more of the prince's eccentricities, but when I later timidly remarked about this to Arkady, he seemed to think I was joking: Of *course* Uncle had eaten dinner—he had seen him eat and drink with his own eyes!

This struck me as incredibly odd, but I said nothing more

to him about it, lest he think me deranged or fanciful due to the pregnancy.

Is it the beginning of madness to think myself the only one sane?

At one point during the dinner, Vlad drew out a letter for Arkady and seemed most anxious for him to translate it, as it was in English. Apparently it was from a British gentleman who had been planning, before Petru's death, to visit the estate. I thought the timing inappropriate, considering the solemn circumstance, but Arkady willingly translated it for him, then promised to help him later with a reply. Vlad turned smiling to me and said:

"You must both help me learn English!"

Flattered, I said, "And you must help me learn Roumanian."

No, said Vlad, that would not be necessary, for it was his intent, now that Petru was gone, to travel to England. Petru had felt tied to the land, he said, but as for himself, he was restless. Transylvania was a superstitious, backward country, and small, and the village was becoming an altogether lonely place now that so many of the peasants were leaving for the cities. He felt he could no longer rely on the occasional entertainment provided by visitors—who all told him stories of how the world beyond the forest was changing quickly, very quickly. "Better to keep up with those changes," said he cheerfully, "than languish in isolation here. Survival is for those who adapt to the demands of the times!" The move, he hastened to add, would take place in a year or so, after the child was born and old enough to travel. And by then he should be quite fluent in English.

"Well," said I, thinking that Arkady's progressive attitude was clearly hereditary, "certainly I should be most glad and privileged to serve as your instructor and travel guide. But as we shall be returning afterwards to Transylvania, it would benefit me to learn the language—"

"Ah," he replied, "but this is not my intent. I intend to

relocate, perhaps permanently, in England—though, of course, I shall return from time to time for nostalgic visits to the family estate—"

To tell the truth, my heart was already glad at the thought of returning home. But at this, Zsuzsanna leapt up from her chair in a fit of temper that startled us all. "I forbid it!" she cried, in a strange mixture of English and Roumanian, as if she could not decide whether she wanted Vlad or me to understand. (I write here what I gathered to be the gist.) "You cannot go! You know I am too weak to travel with you, and if you leave me, I shall die!"

He turned his head towards her swiftly. The candlelight caught his eyes so that they gleamed red, like an animal's, and for an instant fury contorted his sharp features so that I thought I gazed upon the face of nothing less than a monster. But he collected himself at once, and his tone was calm as he spoke soothingly. When later I asked Arkady about this, he said that Vlad reassured her that we would never leave unless Zsuzsa was strong enough to come with us, and that if she continued to feel weak, he would hire a doctor and make her well.

She burst into tears, and her voice shook as she said, "How can you think of leaving? Father is here. Stefan is here. All our memories are here."

He continued to speak comfortingly to her, and finally she calmed and retook her seat. The dinner concluded cordially and without further incident. But I was most disturbed.

I have seen how he looks at her, and she at him. She is desperately in love with him, and I fear Vlad is not above taking advantage of it. My innocent husband has no idea, and I do not know how to tell him.

The Diary of Arkady Tsepesh

7 APRIL. Damn the peasants! Damn them! Damn them and their superstition and stupidity all to hell!

I can scarcely bring myself to write about what has happened—it is too monstrous, too painful, too grotesque. Yet I must; someone must bear witness to the evil wrought by ignorance.

We buried Father yesterday beside Stefan and Mother in the family tomb, situated on the knoll between the manor and the great castle. I did not want Mary to attend, as she seemed wan and tired, and it was a cold, windy spring day. But she held firm, saying it was the least she could do for the father-in-law she had never met. The tomb impressed her deeply, and she paused to read the list of names on the outside wall of each person buried therein. Despite my gloom, I felt some distant pride at the lordly tomb and the fact that all, even the oldest entries—dating from the early seventeen hundreds—were legible, as they had been lovingly carved into the white marble, along with the dates, so that the name of the forebear would never be forgotten and lost to the ages. (Someday soon I shall show her the chapel, and the crypts dating back to the fifteenth century.)

It was a small ceremony at noon. We laid Father in a little alcove alongside Stefan and the mother I never knew. In accordance with his wishes, there was no priest, no reading of scripture or the burial service. The great door to the tomb was unlocked, and servants carried the coffin inside and set it to rest on a catafalque surrounded by lighted candles and decorated with fragrant white flowers. We followed and said our final farewells, then I spoke briefly, once again feeling the scrutiny and palpable presence of my dead ancestors; I half-expected to see little Stefan in the small gathering of mourners. Vlad did not come, which did not particularly surprise anyone, though he paid for an exquisitely engraved gold coffin-plate (that read: "PETRU TSEPESH, Beloved Father, Husband, and Nephew"), another pair of *Bocete* singers, and a beautiful cascade of red roses which adorned the casket and which we left in the tomb with Father.

The day passed quietly, and the next. Since my previous journal entry, Mary and I have several times discussed the conversation with Vlad and my remaining to take Father's place, and she has nearly succeeded in assuaging my guilt over asking my city-bred wife to spend the rest of her life in the wild Carpathian forest. Bistritz is the nearest post town, and hardly a replacement for London; to send or receive mail or to shop at the modest facilities there requires an eight-hour carriage ride (not to mention the return trip!) over winding mountain roads. During winter storms, we shall be effectively isolated.

Mary says it is of no import, so long as she can remain by my side. For my part, I cannot imagine what saintly deed I performed in childhood that brought the reward of such a wife.

The following day, Mary seemed physically drained, and remained in bed until late in the day. I rested and read an English romance from Father's well-stocked library and made the decision to go that evening to speak with V. Sadness still overtook me from time to time, but I knew that boredom was not the way to ease it. I wished to keep busy, and knew it would gladden my heart to accomplish that by doing something that would have pleased Father.

And so I set out shortly before sunset for the castle. It is hardly a fifteen-minute stroll up the gentle greening slope to the south, a mere stretch of the legs to a city-dweller. Sunlight filtered through the branches of tall pine to the west; the air was filled with subtle spring warmth and the sweet high song of birds. Despite the idyllic surroundings, a growing uneasiness crept over me, and it was not until I heard a dog's frenzied barking in the manor behind me that I determined its cause: I had altogether forgotten that wolves roamed at nightfall.

It was not so dangerous as in winter, when they grouped

in deadly packs, but the thought of encountering even a lone wolf caused me to hurry my pace. Nonetheless, I permitted myself a promised detour to the family burial place to spend a solitary moment with Father.

Yet, approaching the black iron fence, I could see through the bars a strange sight: the corpses of two wolves lying just inside the wide-open gate. I knew at once something was wrong, dreadfully so. I broke into a run and dashed through the open gate. The wolves lay on their sides next to one another, their eyes clouded with death; the skull of one had been shattered, and the other's belly was caked with dried blood. Clearly they had attacked some visitor here, who had shot them and fled, in his hurry failing to close the gate.

And more: I glanced up from the wolves to see that the door to the tomb had been unlocked, and stood open. Horrified, I ran inside; the entry to the tomb was blocked by yet another murdered wolf. I stepped swiftly over the body and hurried to the alcove where Father lay.

The tomb had been unlocked and entered, and Father's final resting place had indeed been violated. The beautiful red roses had been swept aside and were scattered everywhere upon the white marble floor. As for the coffin, the screws had been undone and allowed to drop where they had fallen, and the wooden lid pried off and propped against the nearest wall. The lead casing had been sawed through and peeled back.

Inside the casket, my father's corpse lay mangled. A thick wooden stake pierced his chest, as though driven in with a mallet. His mouth had been opened, and something white (I thought at first a handkerchief) stuffed inside; and his neck—

Oh, God! Stefan! Father!

The perpetrator of this vile deed had succeeded in sawing three-quarters of the way through his neck, but had stopped before the head was entirely severed. As Father had been dead two days, there was little blood, and his expression remained one of peaceful repose. But the weight of his skull, now detached from the front muscles of the neck, had caused the head to roll back slightly, and the chin to tilt upward, revealing the gaping crimson grin beneath his jaw. So deeply had the desecrator cut that I saw, embedded within the red and purplish mass of muscle and veins, his exposed spine. For an instant, it seemed as though I had been transported back two decades, to behold once more the flayed throat of my brother Stefan.

The shock provoked an overwhelming vision that I might have dismissed as a waking dream had I not been convinced by its vividness that it was real:

Again, my five-year-old self looked up at my father. I saw him clearly as the man he had been then, younger, black-haired; I saw, in the flickering candlelight, the love and misery in his eyes as he held my small, thin arm in his large hand. I realised he no longer stood in the rain-jeweled daylight forest, with the snarling wolf-dog at his back, but in a vast, dark place shrouded in wavering shadows. Silver glinted beside his face. I stared up, helpless as Isaac when Abraham raised the knife.

A sudden vise gripped my temples with such unrelenting force that I clutched my head; the image vanished at once, replaced by the compelling thought, *Surely this is madness.*

I sank to my hands and knees on the cold marble floor and emptied my stomach. I suppose I fainted, for I was quite mindless for a time. When I managed at last to rise on trembling, uncertain legs, I noticed on the floor beside me the implements of desecration, a heavy iron mallet and rusted steel handsaw, and some scattered heads of garlic; apparently the violator had dropped these in fright and fled before the task was done.

A new sort of insanity seized me, an unhappy combination of fury and hysteria. Had I confronted the perpetrator at that moment, I would easily have killed him with no more weapon than my hands. I knew I could not return to the manor —Gods, no! I have not spoken to Mary of this, nor shall I, for such a dreadful shock would surely harm her and the child. Instead, I ran like a madman up the southern slope, and arrived some time later, panting, at the castle's massive wooden door beneath the great stone arch. I was convinced only V. could help me; only V. would understand.

I threw myself against it and pounded wildly, ignoring the metal studs that cut my fists. When no immediate response came, I began shouting Uncle's name.

After the space of an eternity, the door swung slowly open a foot; there it remained. In the shadows of the gloomy entryway stood a plump, white-haired serving-woman dressed in traditional peasant garb: the long white double apron, front and back, over a brightly coloured dress; on the breast of the front apron rested a large gold crucifix. She regarded me with undisguised confusion and dismay.

"Vlad!" I cried. "I must see Vlad at once!"

She stuck her head out to reply, and I could see in the fading sunlight that her hair was not white, but blond streaked with silver at the temples; and that she was not as elderly as I had first thought, but suffered from the same peculiar accelerated aging that afflicted my father and sister. Her face seemed vaguely familiar, but between my past grief and my present frenzy, I had entirely forgotten until now, as I write these words, that she had attended my father's burial, and that I had seen her face amid those of other servants from time to time in my childhood. "The *voievod* sees no one."

"He will see me!" I replied indignantly. "My father—" I broke off, on the verge of weeping, unable even to speak of what had transpired.

She leaned forward to peer at me myopically, and drew in a sharp breath as she raised a hand to her lips. "Why, it is Petru's son! Good sir, forgive me. My sight is poor, else I would have recognised you at once. You so resemble him. Please, come in . . ." And she motioned me inside.

"I must see my uncle at once!" I managed in a trembling voice, to which she responded:

"Alas, young sir, that is not possible. He has not yet arisen."

"Then rouse him!" I demanded, and her pale grey eyes widened.

"Nor is that possible, sir," said she, in a tone that conveyed amazement at my ignorance. "No one may disturb his slumber now, and none but Laszlo is permitted to see or speak to him. But he shall be rising shortly, and I know he will see you. Let me take you to his drawing-room, where you can await him in comfort."

I was in such a nervous state that I did not protest, but let her escort me, with her gentle hand betimes prompting my elbow, through narrow corridors and up a winding stone staircase. For all the years I had played within the castle's shadow, I had rarely been inside it, and the novelty of it added to my agitation, leaving me quite overwhelmed.

By the time we arrived within the drawing-room, which, though windowless, was comfortably appointed and cheerfully warmed by a blazing hearth, I was so distracted that I failed to hear her invitation, and the poor woman literally had to push me down into a waiting chair near the fire.

"Arkady Tsepesh," she said, leaning over me, and I started at the sound of a strange voice repeating my name. At my look of surprise, she smiled faintly and explained, "I knew your father, young sir. He was very kind to me, and spoke of you often." Her expression grew somber. "It grieves me to see you so distraught on his behalf. I cannot remain here long—the master will be coming soon—but let me fetch you something to calm you. Tea, or perhaps something stronger . . . ?"

"Brandy."

"We have only slivovitz, sir."

"Then bring me slivovitz," I said, but as she straightened and moved to go, I reached out and touched her shoulder; she turned. "You knew my father well?"

She gave a single sad, solemn nod. The mixture of sorrow and genuine affection in her grey eyes reached through the layer of shock to touch my heart, and I asked:

"What is your name?"

"Masika, young sir."

"You speak with a Russian accent, Masika, but your name is Hungarian."

"My father was Russian, sir."

"And his name . . . ?" I said, prompting for her patronymic. As distressed as I was, I wished to be polite to her, as she was so kindly towards me.

Her round cheeks flushed rosy pink. "Ah, sir, just Masika. I dare not put on such airs with you. I am just an old serving-woman."

"You were my father's friend. Please. I would like to know."

Her cheeks deepened to a ruddy colour, but she replied dutifully, "Ivan, sir."

"Ah, Masika Ivanovna, you cannot imagine the horror I have just witnessed!" At the memory, I put a hand to my face and struggled against tears. She knelt beside me and took my hand as a mother might, while I chokingly relayed, without detail, the fact of the desecration of Father's grave.

Her expression hardened and became unreadable as her eyes grew moist. For a time, she patted my hand in silence; at last, she spoke with passionate conviction. "I know such a spectacle must tear at your heart, as it does mine. But you must never forget, young sir: your father sleeps now among the blessed dead, and no one, nothing, can disturb his slumber. He is with God."

I would have objected to the latter statement, but the former gave me a modicum of comfort, as did her sincere and maternal concern. She parted her lips as if to speak, then hesitated, as if there were something more she wished to say, but could not bring herself to voice.

"What is it?" I asked softly.

She glanced up at me with a start, and in her eyes I saw regret, mingled with unmistakable fear.

"Nothing," said she, lowering her eyelids to hide her

fright, "nothing at all. Now, let me go quickly, young sir, and fetch the slivovitz before the prince comes." She rose heavily, with a groan, then hurried out.

I wiped my eyes with my kerchief and struggled to compose myself and organise my thoughts as I stared into the fire. I do not know exactly why I fled to Uncle's to beg his help— though technically we Tsepesh still are royalty who possess some legal rights over the peasantry, the extent of those rights have become blurred in modern times. While Domnul Bibescu of Valahia might recognise V.'s authority as prince, Transylvania is under Austrian rule now, and prosecution of criminals is usually left to the authorities in Bistritz; but then, there has never been any crime to speak of in our domain, and we have never before been so personally attacked.

For Father's sake, I could not let this act go unpunished, not if I had to track down the criminal myself. It seemed to me poor Father's corpse had become a symbol of how the peasantry have reviled our family name for the past four centuries—and I swore vehemently to myself that I would put an end to their slurs forever, that I would force them to respect the name Tsepesh.

Masika Ivanovna soon returned with the slivovitz, in a fine goblet of cut crystal. She delivered it with a small curtsy, and after a swiftly muttered, "God comfort you, young sir," she turned to go.

I reached for her hand. "Please, stay a moment." Her very presence soothed me, and I wanted to question her about Father's final days at the manor, and her unspoken words.

She stiffened with panic, her eyes involuntarily going to the door opposite the one we had entered. Gently, but firmly, she pulled free of my grip. "Oh, sir! I cannot. The sun has nearly set, and I must hurry home!"

I dropped my hand. Had I not seen her anxious glance at the door, I would have suspected that she had to walk home through the forest and quite rationally feared wolves. But at the sound of footfalls approaching the far door, she crossed herself, lifted her skirts, and ran through the open door that led to the corridor. It closed behind her with an unceremonious slam.

The echoing sound reignited my anguished fury. Because Uncle is given to odd habits, and because of a misunderstanding over the family name, the peasants fear him as a monster, and have woven many myths about him, incorporating their ridiculous superstitions. These same superstitions have caused them to commit the hideous crime against my poor dead father; and for an instant, my natural affection for Masika Ivanovna was replaced by hate. Despite her kindness, she feared Uncle, and probably believed that what had occurred in the family tomb was necessary for Petru's soul to rest unmolested.

The door opened with a creak, and Uncle came forth, straight and tall, with an easy grace, but with an air of weakness and the same disturbing pallour as the past two evenings. At the sight of me—and my agitated expression—his bushy white eyebrows lifted in astonishment. (Above those eyes that so resembled Father's; and again, he spoke in Father's melodious voice, making the news I had to deliver all the more difficult.) "Arkady! Dear Nephew! I had not expected to see you this soon. But what is this? You are upset . . ."

Swiftly, I lifted the goblet to my lips and took a large gulp of the slivovitz, which stung nostrils, tongue, and throat like flame, but was not altogether disagreeable. Repressing the urge to cough, I said, (with a matter-of-factness that amazed me), "Father's crypt has been violated. They have mutilated the corpse by—"

He held up a hand, unable to hear more, and turned away towards the fire, bowed over and clutching his heart. I straightened in the chair and moved to set down the goblet and rise, thinking at first that he had suffered some sort of attack, and feeling a pang of guilt that I had so bluntly broken the news to this frail old man; but it was only grief. He remained motionless and uttered no sound for the course of at least two full minutes. I fell back into the chair and took another large swallow of slivovitz.

At last he spoke, in a voice so low it was almost a whisper; a voice I no longer recognised, for it was cold and hard as the marble tomb. "Damn them," he said slowly, still staring into the fire. "*Damn* them . . ." He whirled towards me, with such sudden vehemence that I recoiled, splashing a small amount of the liquor on my waistcoat. His hawkish features were contorted, and his eyes—no longer Father's, but those of Shepherd, bending over Stefan—burned with such maniacal, dangerous rage that I grew frightened. "I will see them pay! How *dare* they think that I—!" He seemed to note my discomfort then, for his expression relaxed somewhat, to one of mere bitterness; he turned back towards the fire and said, "I loved your father. I cannot bear to see him come to harm, not even now."

"I know," I responded. "I am sorry to bring such news, for I know it causes you grief. But I thought perhaps that you might be able to help discover who—"

Once more, he turned towards me and raised his hand. "Say no more! I shall see to it that the perpetrator of this foul deed is brought to justice. You must trouble yourself with this not one more moment."

"I cannot help but do so," I said, "for I cannot understand how someone could commit such a horrid act. It is simply beyond my comprehension." And I raised the crystal goblet to my lips and drained it.

V.'s lips twitched, as if in repressed disgust or amusement. He moved towards a centuries-old upright chair, padded with golden-threaded brocade, and sat regally, gripping the padded armrests with strong hands, looking very much like a prince ascending his throne. "What is there to understand? The peasants' ignorance drives them to insanity."

"I suppose I am shocked. I have always believed in the basic goodness of people."

His lips thinned; his tone carried a sharp irony that I

found troubling. "Then you have much to learn about human-kind, Arkady . . . and about yourself." At this, I was mildly insulted, and grew more so as he continued: "Addressing servants by their patronymics! This will never do! Royal blood flows in your veins; you are Tsepesh, the great-nephew of a prince!"

I flushed, realising that he had somehow managed to eavesdrop on my conversation with Masika Ivanovna; I wondered whether he had also heard about Father.

He must have sensed my discomfort, for his tone changed abruptly, and grew cheerful. "Come now! It is settled; leave the resolution of this matter to me, and let us speak of happier things. Is there anything else with which I may assist? Is your dear wife resting well after the fatiguing events of the past few days?"

The slivovitz suddenly went to my head; I felt a slight dizziness, and a rush of warmth surged down my spine and lingered, tingling, in my feet. I relaxed slightly, and realised that V. was simply changing subjects rapidly in order to help me over the shock, to make me think about something other than Father.

"Yes," I replied, more calmly, though the truth was that I was somewhat concerned about Mary, as the grueling trip and the shock of Father's death had left her exhausted, and that morning I had had the impression that she was troubled about something, though she denied it. "But she is still somewhat tired. It has all been quite taxing for her."

V. listened gravely. "If she is still fatigued by to-morrow, then I shall arrange for a physician to take up residence at the manor," he said. "And he shall remain there to see she is taken care of until after the child is born." When I protested that I could not allow him to incur such an enormous expense without my assistance, he waved once more the imperious hand and said, "The matter is settled. It is the least I can do for Petru's grandchild, and for his son."

His manner had grown warm again, and being reassured,

I confessed, "Before I made the terrible discovery in the cemetery this evening, I came to-night because I wished to speak about assuming Father's work."

To which he responded at once: "Ah, yes. Soon, when you have had a chance to get over the dreadful shock. But not now. It is too soon to speak of business, because you have just had another great shock."

"No," I answered firmly, "the distraction would help me; and it would bring me comfort to know I was fulfilling Father's wishes. He was quite concerned that you and your affairs be taken care of."

At this, V.'s eyes misted. "Ah, your father was aptly named: Petru, the Rock. Truly he was a rock to me, ever loyal and dependable. And you, Arkady—you must know that I love Petru's children as my very own."

He stated this with such warmth and conviction that I was seized by a welling of affection for him. To be sure, he is odd and elderly, with strange habits, but he has always been inordinately generous to our family. Despite his proud demeanor, he cuts a pathetic figure, in a way. For all his wealth, he is so lonely, so isolated, so utterly dependent upon my father . . . and now on me. I am his one real link to the outside world.

We spoke of business, then, which helped distance our thoughts from the recent horror. Uncle promised to show me Father's office to-morrow evening, where all the ledgers and bank books are kept, and bade me come earlier, so that I might acquaint myself with the servants (whom, except for Laszlo the coachman, he has never seen). It is apparently quite important that I speak with the foreman and tour the fields, for Uncle has not the slightest inkling whether spring planting has been arranged. He is indeed quite helpless.

He was also quite keen to dictate a letter, which I wrote down in Roumanian and then translated into English for a Mister Jeffries. V. seems desperate to notify the visitor to come as quickly as possible, now that the funeral has taken place; a recluse he might be, but one who is hungry for educated company beyond that of his family. I offered to take the letter to Laszlo and tell him to post it in Bistritz, as I would be passing by the servants' quarters on my way home, but V. folded up the letter without signing it, and said that he wished to give Laszlo the instruction himself.

And so I have taken my father's place. The meeting with Uncle was brief—I sensed he was restless and eager for me to leave; I think my very presence made him nervous to some degree. I mentioned, as I was leaving, my preoccupation with wolves, and asked whether they still, as I remembered from childhood, constituted a danger. V. said that this was indeed the case; and rather than have Laszlo drive me home, he arranged for me to have a caleche and two horses for my very own, so that I could be free to come and go without concern for the time of day.

And so I left, feeling much calmer than when I had arrived. But driving home in the caleche, I passed by the family tomb. Though the darkness hid the unspeakable horror there, the grief and rage and sense of violation all struck me once again.

How can I bear to live among these people, knowing the atrocities of which they are capable?

✛ ✛ ✛

The Journal of
Mary Windham Tsepesh

7 APRIL. (LATER ENTRY) This afternoon I attempted once again to engage my chamber-maid, Dunya, in conversation. Like most of the peasant women here she is small of build but strong. Like them, she wears the white double apron and beneath it a rather immodest coarse linen dress that fails to cover her ankles and is altogether revealing when the light catches it the right way. The peasants here seem to have a cavalier attitude towards the wearing of undergarments.

Dunya's colouring is fair and her dark, almost black hair has a reddish cast when the sunlight catches it. This, and her name, makes me believe she is at least partly Russian. She cannot be more than sixteen, but seems intelligent and thoughtful, although she displays the same reluctance as the other servants to meet my gaze. Even so, I perceive a certain innate boldness in her, so when I wanted to determine whether the servants' fearful attitude was a Transylvanian characteristic or whether it was inspired by something else, I chose to confront Dunya as she was tidying the bedroom. She jumped slightly as I called her name; I had to hide my amusement.

She speaks a little German, and so do I, and so I said, "Dunya, it is my custom to have a friendly relationship with my domestics. Please . . . Do not be so afraid of me." My uncertainty with German required that I be brief and direct.

To this, she curtsied and replied, "Thank you, *doamna.*" (I have learned this is Roumanian for "mistress.") "But I am not afraid of you."

"Good," I replied. "But clearly you are afraid of someone. Who?"

She blanched a little at that, and glanced over her shoulder as if afraid someone were spying on us. And then she neared—a little too near for English manners, but I have learned from watching my husband and his family that Transylvanians prefer to be physically much closer to each other when speaking than we British do—and whispered: "Vlad. The *voievod*, the prince."

I felt I knew the answer to my own question, but I asked it nevertheless, lowering my voice to the same volume. "Why?"

In reply, she crossed herself, and breathed into my ear, "He is *strigoi*."

"*Strigoi?*" It was clearly a Roumanian word, but one I had never heard. "What is this?"

She seemed surprised at my ignorance and would not answer, only pressed her lips tightly together and shook her head. When I repeated my question, she hurried from the room.

◆I◆ ◆I◆ ◆I◆

Zsuzsanna Tsepesh's Diary

8 APRIL. I am evil, evil!—a wicked woman with wicked thoughts. Sweet Papa is scarcely cold and laid to rest, and already I have had the most shameful dream.

I do not even know how to properly pray. Papa so despised the Church, he would never permit his children to learn its rituals. Perhaps he and Kasha are right that there is no God. They are both so intelligent, but I am not (sometimes I think my poor brain is as twisted as my spine) and I desperately need the comfort of the Divine.

And so this morning I knelt at the foot of my bed, as I have seen peasants do at roadside shrines, and tried to ask forgiveness. I do not know whether I was successful—the very act of kneeling made me dizzy; I have felt so weak the past few days, drained no doubt by sorrow—but I felt I could not face Kasha and good, strong Mary without first easing my conscience in some manner.

When I rose (so light-headed that I had to clutch the poster to keep from dropping again to my knees), I felt an overpowering urge to write everything down—to make confession, as it were. I have no priest; this diary shall serve as my confessor, even though my cheeks flame at the thought of recording such wickedness.

The night before last we celebrated Papa's *pomana*. It was the first time in weeks I had seen Uncle, and the experience of his kindness and loving attention doubtless triggered the dream. I have been so lonely in the years since Kasha left. Papa has been so miserable, too, and then so sick, and always too preoccupied with the dealings at the castle, that I have felt very, very alone; were it not for Kasha's letters and Uncle's occasional visits, I feel I should have gone mad.

Perhaps I have, a little. For a time after Kasha first left, I used to speak to him as if he were still there (always, out of earshot of the servants! They are too frightened of us to be trusted as confidantes; and they always find enough to gossip about). As of late, I have begun to speak to little Stefan. Sometimes I imagine he walks alongside Brutus and me through the halls, and sits beside me, Brutus curled at our feet, as I embroider. (If anyone overhears, I can always maintain I was speaking to the dog.)

Sometimes I pretend he is the child I shall never have.

Oh, it is difficult enough to have a misshapen, sickly body! But the worst pain it inflicts is the knowledge that I shall always be denied the love of a husband, and children. I am forced to lead a solitary life and depend on the platonic affections of my brother and uncle for comfort. And I am crippled by jealousy—of the happiness my brother and his new wife clearly share, even of the small attentions Uncle paid Mary at the *pomana*.

God save me from my own evil heart!

Brutus kept up the barking the night before, and last night began only minutes after I had drifted off to sleep—and so, off to the kitchen with him! I was so tired that when I returned alone to my bed, I fell at once into a dream.

And was awakened by a thrumming at my bedroom window. Or rather, in the *dream* I was awakened by such a sound —soft but insistent, as if a bird were beating its wings against the pane. The night air had grown exceptionally cold, and I had closed the window before retiring. In the dream, I rose, and went over to the source of the sound, not at all frightened by it, nor even curious, as if I knew exactly what, or who, awaited me there; as if I were irrevocably drawn.

I threw back the shutters and opened the window. And saw nothing save a shaft of moonlight, which streamed in, forming a golden-white pool of light on the floor. In that circle of light, flecks of glittering dust floated—lazily at first, then faster, faster, until they swirled, merged, and coalesced into a form.

The motion made me dizzy; I closed my eyes. When I opened them again, Uncle stood in the cone of light. I remembered at once that this was the same dream I had had the previous night, and the night before that—always seeing Uncle's face at the window. But now, with Brutus gone, he was free to enter.

He seemed somehow younger, handsomer; again, this evoked no surprise. I felt no shock, no fright, no sense of impropriety to see him standing in my boudoir in the middle of the night. No; wicked woman that I am, I stepped forward, boldly threw my arms about him, and whispered, "Uncle! I am so glad that you have come!"

He stood perfectly still and straight, as if reluctant to move. Beneath my hands, his muscles—so strong he is, for a man of any age!—tensed, rigid and firm as stone. For a moment, neither of us spoke, only gazed into each other's eyes (his eyes are beautiful enough to make a woman envious! deep, rich evergreen, large and heavy-lidded). In the moonlight, his skin glowed as though infused with radiant white fire.

And then he said, "Zsuzsa, I fear this is a grave mistake. I shall go—"

"No!" I begged, and held him more tightly, fearing he would disintegrate into glittering dust in my arms. "It is what *I* want! Don't you see? *I* have drawn you here, night after night! Only kiss me . . . !"

Beneath the fine silk of his cloak, his muscles shuddered, then relaxed, and he lifted a night-chilled hand to my cheek and stroked it. As I stared into his eyes, mesmerised, I saw his pupils redden, as if the forest therein had been abruptly consumed by flame.

"Please," I whispered, and he leaned forward and pressed his lips to my cheek. Oh, those lips were cold, but it was a cold that burned, and I fell back and let myself by supported by an arm as unyielding as steel.

"I am so hungry, Zsuzsa," he sighed. "I can no longer resist . . ."

He brushed his lips against my skin, so that I felt his breath hot upon me, and drew them down, down, across the line of my jaw, over the soft curve there to the tender flesh of my neck. I trembled in sheer ecstasy as he lingered there; then he reached with his free hand and pulled the ribbon that secured my nightgown at the collar. It came undone, and the gauzy white fabric fell down around my waist. I am fair; my skin has never seen the sun, but his was fairer and, when the moon broke through the clouds, shimmered with flecks of gold and pink and blue fire like an opal.

Beneath my white breast, he cupped his whiter hand (God forgive me! but as I write these words, I am overcome; shame wars with rapture. If he were here now, I would guide his hand myself!) and brushed his cold red lips over my skin, past the hollow of my collarbone, down between my breasts. For a moment he lingered there, and I buried my fingers in his thick hair and pressed him hard against me. He straightened suddenly, trembling as though he could bear to be denied no longer, and fastened his lips upon my neck. I felt his tongue sweep lightly, languidly against my skin, and then the pressure of his teeth.

He poised, waiting.

I am a sheltered woman. I know nothing of life and love, and so the details of my dream beyond this were vague. I know only that I felt a sharp pain, and then a flood of rapturous warmth, as if I were melting like wax in the presence of such animal heat. I felt that he and I were one, that the very essence of my being swelled like a wave and flowed out towards him as it crested and broke. I cried out and struggled altogether free of the nightgown, then twined my arms and legs about him and held on so tightly that not a millimeter of space remained between our bodies.

How long this ecstasy continued, I cannot say, but I know I lay overwhelmed in his arms, aware of nothing but a languid pleasure that pulsated to the rhythm of my beating heart. When at last he withdrew, I sensed he did so unsatiated, for my sake, choosing instead only to dim his longing rather than appease it.

My cheeks burn now like a new bride recalling her wedding night! The event had such an air of reality that even now I grow confused whether it actually happened or not; I woke shivering this morning to find myself entirely indecent and unclothed upon the bed, with the sheets thrown back and the nightgown lying in a heap on the floor near the window.

I feel closer to Uncle than ever, as if he and I truly share this wicked, marvelous secret.

Writing this, I feel bold as a harlot. Did I say I wanted forgiveness? No more! My life has been so barren and sad; whether it be the worst sort of evil or not, whether it be sickness, madness, delusion, I will not deny myself the brightest joy I have ever known. The risk of Hell is worth such happiness. Brutus shall remain in the kitchen tonight, and I shall sleep with the windows open, "perchance to dream."

If he goes to England, I shall die!

3

Letter to Matthew P. Jeffries
[dictated and translated from the Roumanian]

7 *April*

My Friend,

Welcome to the Carpathians. I was keenly disappointed to receive news of your postponed arrival, but all things work for good; there has been illness in the castle and it is just as well your visit was delayed.

However, now the timing could not be better! I received your letter from Vienna saying that you would arrive in Bistritz the evening of the eighth. This letter shall await you—as I do most anxiously. Sleep well to-night, for to-morrow morning, 9 April, the diligence for Bucovina will depart at eight. My coachman will meet you at the Borgo Pass and will bring you to me.

Your proposed Times *article sounds most intriguing. I would be happy to provide whatever useful information I can and look forward to our conversations on the subject.*

May you meet with no further travel difficulties, and may you enjoy your stay in my beautiful land.

    Your friend,
    Vlad Dracula

✠ ✠ ✠

*The Journal of
Mary Windham Tsepesh*

8 APRIL. Dear God, what shall I say to my husband?

I sense that something terrible has happened recently, something to add to his grief over his father's death. I believe he and Vlad have had an argument, or that he has made some shocking discovery at the castle.

Certainly, it can be no more shocking than the one I have made.

I had divined at once that Zsuzsanna was infatuated with her uncle, and that he did nothing to discourage her—to the contrary, he fanned the flames. But I had no idea—!

Poor Arkady was so distraught last night that he stayed reading in the drawing-room and did not come to bed until a few hours before dawn; and I am so accustomed now to the sounds of his breathing and the feel of a warm body beside me in the bed that I became restless myself. I considered lighting the lamp and writing another journal entry, but my eyes were tired after hours of reading and writing yesterday, and so in the dark I wandered over to the bay window, thinking to crack it, that fresh air might help me sleep. While there, I was taken by the sight of the near-full moon drifting through the clouds, and I sat on the velvet cushion in the little alcove window-seat. The moon was so bright that the landscape was lit up almost like the day.

Our bedroom is in the wing directly across from Zsuzsanna's; only a grassy stretch of ground separates us, and I could easily hurl a stone into her room from ours. Each bedroom features a large picture window that affords a lovely view, but we have complete privacy behind our heavy curtains, and Zsuzsanna behind her shutters.

Yet last night, I pulled the edge of the curtain aside to better see the moon—and when I did, my eye caught sight of something running across the stretch of ground towards Zsuz-sanna's room. Thinking it was one of the wolves Arkady so often warns me about, I pressed close to the glass to better see. I was not afraid, since the curtain hid me quite well and I doubted the animal could leap two floors, but I was very curi-ous, as being a city-dweller I had never before seen a wolf except in picture-books.

But before I could focus on the object of my interest, I was distracted by movement at Zsuzsanna's window. I watched as she flung the shutters back and pushed open the window, letting in the streaming moonlight.

This gave me a fright, and I almost thought to call a warning about the wolf when I noticed a figure beside her in the little alcove by the window-seat. How it arrived there, I cannot say, but I can say who it was: Vlad.

As I watched, horrified, they embraced; and then he reached for the ribbon at her throat, and when it came undone and her nightgown fell away—

To write further sickens me. I turned away, unable to bear the sight, and pulled the curtains shut.

I scarcely slept last night. I am torn. Arkady is already troubled enough by some secret sorrow, and all I would be doing would be transferring my dilemma onto his overbur-dened shoulders. Yet I cannot decide whether it is more appro-priate to confront Vlad or Zsuzsanna—or to remain silent alto-gether.

My poor darling; you have suffered so much recently. Is this what torments you? Do you already know?

The Diary of Arkady Tsepesh

9 APRIL. I am beginning to think that everyone in the castle is slightly mad.

I went there early yesterday to familiarise myself with Uncle's affairs. Most certainly I did not speak to either Zsuzsanna or Mary of the monstrosity I had witnessed in the family tomb; they could not have borne the shock. Nor did I feel that I could have borne it again, but on the way to Uncle's I found myself compelled to drive the caleche past Father's resting place, and go inside.

What I saw inside the tomb soothed my heart. The casket had been rebolted, the roses lovingly replaced, and the marble floor cleaned; the horrible saw and mallet had been removed as well, and all looked as it had before the desecration. I felt a deep gratitude towards Uncle, who had overcome his own grief to deal with this horrible matter, thus easing mine, and protecting the rest of the family.

When I arrived at the castle, my melancholy was rekindled by the sight of Father's desk, which lay just as he had left it, in a small room in the east wing with a magnificent view of the Carpathians. Everything was tidy and well organised; I easily found all of Uncle's financial information, and soon forgot my sadness as I involved myself in work.

In all honesty, I was startled by the extent of V.'s wealth. Considering the degree of it, there are fewer servants than one might expect: only three chamber-maids, one cook, one stable-hand, a gardener, and the steward—and of course, the unpleasant coachman, Laszlo. After speaking with the overseer of Uncle's fields, I made a most unsettling discovery: our family's land is worked by *rumini,* actual serfs, over whom Uncle still possesses the ancient *droits du seigneur*! Feudalism is usually an unjust system in favour of the lord, who owns the land; the serfs pay him a tithe to farm it, then another ten percent of the proceeds, in addition to paying the *bir,* a sizable personal tax for "protection." But in V.'s case, the *rumini* paid no tithe, only five percent of the proceeds from sale of harvest, and a yearly *bir* of only pennies (as though we still feared Turkish marauders and, for such a minuscule sum, would offer to all the wartime shelter of the Tsepesh castle walls). Another surprise: Uncle owns most of the village, yet receives no rent. Only one arrangement seemed to his advantage: the serfs are required to do whatever work V. bids, whenever he bids it. Today one of them was at the castle, remortaring some stone which had come loose near the entrance. He bowed politely as I neared, but as I passed by, I could hear him grumbling under his breath about ignoring his own pressing work in the fields in favour of the *voievod*'s, the prince's. He worked with a languor born of reluctance, which I resented in the light of V.'s generosity.

To think that feudalism is still alive, in this day and age . . . ! Clearly, V. collects only a fraction of that to which he is entitled. This is no way to make a profit; it would be far more businesslike to release the serfs from their obligations and rehire them as labourers at a lower, more reasonable wage, and pocket the profits made from the selling of crops himself. His extravagant kindness has, I fear, led the serfs to take advantage of him.

But that does not trouble me as much as the notion of feudalism itself, which suggests that V. "owns" the peasants and their homes outright. No man has the right to so control another. Far more just for all would be the system of a fair wage for a fair day's work.

I was surprised also by the high wages—far more than a trained domestic might receive in England—paid the domestic servants, which certainly fails to explain their cool, though polite, behaviour towards me. The undercurrent of hostility was there, again, although I still cannot decide whether they despise or fear me, or both. Masika Ivanovna alone is good-natured; this is fortunate, since she serves as chamber-maid for the east wing (where my office is located) and the west (where

Uncle dwells). The other two chamber-maids, Ana and Helga, share Laszlo's cold, sour disposition despite their youth.

Yet I begin to question Masika Ivanovna's sanity. There is a strange air of unpleasantness in this castle, no doubt due to the resentment of the servants and Uncle's odd habits, and I suspect that decades of service here would work on a peasant's superstitious mentality. After I introduced myself to the servants in the main wing and retired to Father's office to work for some time, Masika Ivanovna appeared—to perform her daily tasks, I assumed. She made a show of dusting all the furniture, then lingered uneasily, for so long that finally I interrupted my work to ask whether she had something to say.

At that, she paused and her expression became troubled, as though she was struggling to make a difficult decision. Finally she lowered her dust-rag, went over to the half-open door, and peered nervously down the gloomy corridor as if expecting to find someone hiding in the shadows. She then repeated the process by peering out the windows—! When she felt reassured, she stepped so close our faces were not a hand's width apart, and whispered: "I must talk to you, young sir! But you must swear that you will never reveal to anyone what I tell you, or it will cost me and my son our lives!"

"Your lives?" I asked, utterly taken aback by her strange behaviour. "What ever are you talking about?"

I spoke in a normal tone of voice; this alarmed her, and with a distressed expression, she raised a finger to her lips for silence. "First, swear! Swear before God!"

"I do not believe in God," I replied, somewhat coolly. "But I can give you my word as a gentleman that I will tell no one what you reveal to me."

She studied my face intently, her brow furrowed with anxiety. Whatever she found there seemed to satisfy her, for at last she nodded, then said in a low voice, "You must leave at once, young sir!"

"Leave?" I asked, indignant.

"Yes! Leave and return to England! To-day, before the sun sets!"

"Why ever should I want to do that?"

She did not answer immediately, but seemed unable to find the proper words, and so I took advantage of her silence to continue.

"At any rate, I cannot. My wife is less than three months from giving birth; I fear the recent trip has already distressed her."

The determination in my voice seemed to frighten her so that her eyes filled with tears. Distraught, she sank to her knees in front of my chair, her hands clasped in a beseeching gesture, Christ praying at Gethsemane. "Please—for love of your father, then! Go quickly!"

"Why?" I demanded, catching her by the elbow and attempting to pull her to her feet. "Why must I leave?"

"Because if you do not, it will be too late; and you and your wife and child will be in terrible danger. Because of the covenant . . ."

It made no sense; nevertheless, her words caused something in my memory to flicker. Masika Ivanovna's countenance faded. Again I saw through the eyes of a five-year-old, gazing up trustingly at my father as the knife came down in a gleaming silver arc.

At once invisible steel fingers gripped my skull, blotting out the image. I raised a hand to my temple and thought, *I am going mad . . .*

No. No. It is merely an attack of nerves, brought on by Father's death, and my terrible discovery.

A flash of movement appeared in the doorway; I glanced up quickly to see Laszlo, the coachman, removing his cap. I am not sure how long he had been standing there. He is not evil-looking—he appears a typical middle-aged Hungarian peasant, pale-haired and fair-complexioned, with round, bland features and a nose ruddy from drink—but he carries an aura of unpleasantness about him, the quintessence of whatever afflicts this castle.

Masika Ivanovna followed my gaze and turned to see our visitor. I do not think she could have been more terrified had the Devil Himself appeared. Wide-eyed and trembling, she gasped aloud guiltily and crossed herself at the sight of him, then rose and hurried out of the room, quite forgetting to take my leave.

Laszlo watched her go with a faint, condescending smirk, as though he quite understood her reaction and found it altogether amusing. And then he addressed me, saying he had come only to introduce himself formally and to offer his services whenever they were needed. I was pleased to tell him that they were not, because of Uncle's gift of the caleche.

The confrontation with Masika Ivanovna left me vaguely troubled, but I dismissed it and worked on without incident until the late evening, when I met with Uncle. I brought him up to date on the business aspects and thanked him warmly for seeing to Father's grave, but later we came close to an argument over the issue of the *rumini,* the serfs.

I urged strongly that he abolish the feudal system entirely and pay the serfs a fair wage, which would benefit both him and them. For such an intelligent man, he was surprisingly narrow-minded; he would hear nothing of it. His generosity to the family and servants was a point of pride and tradition— and there was nothing more important, said he, than the Tsepesh family tradition.

"Then look at it another way," said I, thinking to appeal to that very generosity. "Feudalism is simply immoral. You own the servants' lives; they may not leave the village without your permission, and must come to work at the castle at your whim. As human beings, they have the right to be their own lord, their own master."

"Morality is not the issue here," he replied firmly, with a trace of smugness at my ignorance. "It is our family tradition, and as such it must never be changed. Someday, when you are older and wiser, Arkady, you will understand."

I fear I lost my temper at that, and took on quite a heated tone. "Tsepesh tradition can never be as important as the rights of human beings!"

It was as if I had struck him full across the face. A cold lupine fury woke in his eyes, which for a fleeting instant gleamed red with reflected firelight from the drawing-room hearth. He made a swift, animal move towards me, one which he immediately suppressed; nonetheless, I was reduced instantly to the panicked, frightened child who cringed, helpless, while Shepherd leapt.

And then I blinked, and saw that his eyes were merely cold, but quite calm; that he sat quite still in his chair and had never moved. My mind whispered: *It is your fevered imagination . . .*

"You must not speak so about us Tsepesh," he uttered, in a low voice. "At times you take too much after your mother; she was too willful, too disrespectful of our ways. I fear you have inherited more than her eyes."

Perhaps he was right; I do not know, for I did not know Mother, but I have always been stubborn and impatient, unlike Father and Zsuzsanna. When threatened, I will fight; and so, despite Uncle's displeasure and my momentary unsettling vision, I did not concede the point.

"I mean no disrespect," said I, "and I love my family and its traditions. But feudalism is not a uniquely Tsepesh custom. It is practically slavery, and immoral."

His anger abated, but the light in his eyes remained, taking on an oddly feral quality which disturbed me even more than the imagined display of rage. He smiled, his full red lips parting to show surprisingly strong and intact teeth. "Ah, sweet Arkady! I have walked this earth so long that I have grown weary of it, but your youth and innocence make me feel young again. How refreshing it is to see someone so idealistic, so charmingly naive. Your father was thus when he came to me

—full of passion and principles!" His expression grew suddenly stern. "But you will soon come to understand the error of your thinking, as your father did, and his before him."

I tried to redirect the conversation back to the *rumini,* but he refused to discuss that subject any further as well, and instead began to speak of plans to go to England by the end of next year, when Zsuzsanna would be well, and the baby old enough to travel. I promised to do what I could to contact some solicitors about the possible purchase of property.

Impressed I may be by his generosity, but privately, I was quite put off by his condescension toward Mother, and toward my "naïveté"; I suppose the aristocracy have no better defense than to insult those with progressive egalitarian views. From now on I shall keep my opinions to myself—after all, Uncle is my elder, and a prince, no less—but when the estate falls into my hands, as it must surely do within a few years, I shall see to it that things are run differently.

And so I held my tongue, and Uncle and I quickly finished the evening's business. I arrived back home at nine o'clock to find Mary had already retired. I joined her, and spent a restless night filled with evil dreams.

The next day, 9 April (to-day), was much more agreeable. I returned in the afternoon to the castle to find Laszlo had brought a visitor: a Mister Jeffries, the young Englishman who was touring the countryside. Apparently the tavern-keeper in Bistritz is a distant relative of ours who routinely refers foreign travelers to the castle as a point of historical interest, and Uncle provides lodging and hospitality at no charge whatsoever. It was Father's role to serve as ambassador and tour-guide to these visitors, and to handle correspondence with them.

I could not help but think it odd for a man who was reluctant to be seen by his own servants or anyone else outside his family to be willing to open his home to complete strangers. At the same time, I was glad that the traveler had come, for I was already eager to hear news of England, the country I had not so long ago thought of as home.

I called on Mister Jeffries in the guest chambers in the north wing. He is a tall, spindly man, with a shock of white-blond hair, a milky complexion that flushes easily, and a cheerful, outgoing demeanour. He was quite happy and relieved to find someone in the castle who could speak English, as he had been forced to rely on his halting German to communicate with Helga; none of the other servants speak either English or German, and he had fallen into that dispirited state of *anomie* experienced by those unable to express themselves in a foreign land. (It reminded me of my early days in London.) He was disappointed to learn that Uncle does not speak English, but that I (and Father before me) had translated all of his letters, as he had intended to conduct an interview with him, and would be forced to do so in German. It cheered him greatly when I offered to serve as translator.

Although he is a journalist by trade, he comes from a family of merchants. Apparently they are quite well-off, for he sported a very fine gold pocketwatch with a silver or white-gold inlaid "J," and a gold ring with the same motif on his little finger. I could not help being secretly amused by a display of such family finery by a commoner—what is the source of such pride?

Listen to me! Only one day after my argument with Uncle, and already I am sounding like an aristocratic snob. A commoner Mister Jeffries may be, but he is nevertheless quite educated and intelligent, and he has quick, roving eyes that catch everything and an incessant curiosity—good qualities for a newspaperman.

I found his company so agreeable that I escorted him myself on a tour of the castle, though of course Uncle's private chambers were off-limits. As we climbed the spiraling stone staircase, I said, "I translated the letter which my uncle Vlad posted to you in Bistritz; so you are writing some sort of newspaper article, then, for the *London Times*? And you wish to interview Uncle? What precisely is the article about? Transylvanian history? Travel?"

Mister Jeffries brightened at this; his face is elastic, wonderfully mobile. "Not precisely. More about your country's folklore. Your uncle knows a great deal about the fascinating superstitions—"

"Yes," I replied stiffly. "We have all heard what the peasants say."

I suppose there was a hint of anger in my tone, for Jeffries caught it immediately and his own tone became mollifying. "Of course, the superstitions are all quite ridiculous. I am sure your family finds them both vexing and amusing. I am a rational man, of course, and it is my intent to show these superstitions for the foolishness that they are, to show that no truth lies behind them. Your uncle's letters reveal him to be a most kindly and gracious man."

"He is," I said, relieved. "He is most generous with his family—if a bit of a recluse."

"Well, that is only normal. Why should he want to go amongst people who believe him a monster?"

The instant Jeffries stated this, I knew at once that he had a great deal of insight. Of course he was right; it perfectly explained why V. was willing to see his family and Laszlo, yet reluctant to see the servants. The dark uncertainty aroused by Masika Ivanovna's dire warning and V.'s rigidity about the *rumini* vanished in the light of Jeffries' sunny, logical disposition.

I confided in him, then, about Uncle's desire to go to England, and the more I spoke with him about it and thought about being free of the dreary surroundings and the peasants' superstitions, the more cheering the prospect became. We discussed how backward Transylvania was compared to the rest of the changing world. He asked bluntly whether my family felt lonely here, and I admitted the town was dying and that one of my greatest concerns was our isolation.

The conversation turned to a more cheerful topic and we

chatted about England as I led him to the sitting-room in the south wing, where a large window looks out onto an awe-inspiring view: some thousand feet beneath the great precipice on which the castle sits, a vast expanse of dark green forest stretches to the horizon.

"Good lord," Jeffries breathed, taking it all in. "It must be a mile straight down." Apparently he has some apprehension of heights, for he removed a handkerchief from his waistcoat pocket and wiped his perspiring brow with it. (I confess, I repressed a condescending smile when I saw the large "J" monogrammed on the kerchief.)

I assured him it was not quite a mile, and explained how the castle had been built on a three-sided precipice (on east, south, and west) so as to be more easily defensible from invaders—most notably the Turks from the south. He listened with keen interest and even began jotting notes on a small pad, but as the vertiginous view clearly made him uncomfortable, I led him down to the main floor in the central wing, to the cavernous living-room where, in earlier centuries, my ancestors had entertained other nobility.

He was quite taken by the excellent condition of the antique furniture, and the splendour of the brocade tapestries, some of them threaded with gold. As we turned to the larger-than-life-sized portrait that dominated the vast wall above the fire-place, he drew in a breath and turned to me in surprise. "Why—it is you!"

I smiled thinly as his words echoed against the high vaulted ceiling. "Hardly. This was painted in the fifteenth century."

"But look," Jeffries insisted with enthusiasm. "He has your nose"—and here he pointed to the subject's long, aquiline feature—"your moustache, your lips"—here he indicated the drooping black moustache (in all fairness, much fuller than mine) above a generous ruby lower lip—"your dark hair . . ." Here he trailed off, for he had come to the eyes.

"As you can see," said I, still smiling, "his hair was

curled and shoulder length, whereas mine is cut quite short, in the modern style."

He laughed. "Yes, but with a proper haircut—"

"And there is the matter of the eyes. His are dark green; mine, hazel."

He glanced at me to verify this, and agreed: "Yes, you're right. The eyes are quite different; his are rather vengeful and cold, don't you think? But as to colour, yours do have quite a bit of green in them. And the resemblance is still remarkable."

"It is nothing compared to his resemblance to Uncle. Of course, Uncle's eyes are kind."

"Then I shall memorise every aspect of his face!" Jeffries exclaimed. "And when I meet your uncle, I shall recall it from memory and compare the two!" He lifted his pen above his notepad and squinted at the brass plaque beneath the portrait. "Vlad Tepes?" He pronounced it "Teh-pehs."

"Tsepesh," I corrected him. "Do you not see the little hook, the cedilla there beneath the t and the s? It changes the pronunciation."

"Tsepesh," Jeffries repeated, writing upon the notepad. "He seems an important fellow."

I straightened with pride. "Prince Vlad Tsepesh. Born December 1431, first seized power in 1456, died 1476. My uncle's namesake."

"Namesake?" The furious writing ceased; the pen froze above the paper. Jeffries blinked up at me in confusion. "Perhaps . . . perhaps there is something I misunderstand about Roumanian names."

"What is it that presents difficulty for you? The spelling—?"

"No, no, I understand that all right. But . . ." And he retrieved another piece of paper from his pocket, unfolded it, and showed it to me. "Which name shall I properly call him by?"

The note I had translated had been signed in Uncle's cautious, delicate hand; when I saw the signature, I was struck speechless. I do not know whether Jeffries noted my shock, for I recovered quickly and handed the note back to him with a forced smile. "Uncle has a propensity for practical jokes," I lied, "and so he tongue-in-cheek used this nickname given him by the peasants."

In truth, it was a nickname, though not Uncle's. It had been bestowed by fearful *rumini* upon the man in the portrait. "If this nickname pleases my generous host," said Jeffries, "then that is what I shall call him. But pray explain . . ."

"Dracula." I pronounced the hated name with distaste, then pointed. "Do you see, at the bottom right of the portrait, the dragon?"

Jeffries peered nearsightedly at Vlad's shield, whereupon rested a winged dragon, its forked tail curling about the emblem of a double cross.

"Vlad's father, Vlad the Second, was a ruler inducted by the Hungarian emperor into a secret chivalrous fraternity known as the Order of the Dragon," I continued. "He used this emblem on his shields and coins. Because of this, the *boiers* —the nobles—began to refer to him as *dracul,* the dragon, though Vlad the Second never so referred to himself, except in jest. Unfortunately, in Roumanian, the word *dracul* also has the meaning 'the Devil'; hearing that name, the superstitious peasants believed that Vlad, who was known as a fearsomely cruel tyrant, came to power because he allied himself with Satan, and that the Order of the Dragon was in fact a society devoted to mastery of the black arts. His son, Vlad the Third —whose portrait you see before you—was even more blood-thirsty, even more feared. The common folk referred to him as *Dracula,* the son of the Devil, as the suffix -*a* means 'son of.' To this day, the peasants fear our family for this reason, and persist in calling us Dracul. They mean it as an insult, not an honor."

"My deepest apologies if I have offended you," Jeffries said, his tone somberly sincere; but still he took it all down. "I can see that this attitude has caused your family no small amount of grief. Yet your uncle clearly has maintained an admirable sense of humour about it, to be able to jokingly sign this name because of the nature of the article I am writing."

His manner was so kind that I managed a small, rueful smile. "I fear I do not share Uncle's sense of humour about such matters." I did not tell him the entire truth: that the surname used for the rest of the family was Dracul, without the -*a*. By the peasants' logic, then, Uncle should have jokingly signed his name Vlad Dracul. For *only* the son of the Devil—only the man in the portrait, born four centuries before —could claim the right to the name "Dracula."

"Might I inquire as to the other symbol—there, on the bottom left, opposite the dragon's shield?" He gestured at the wolf's head atop the body of a coiled serpent.

"That is our family crest. It is very ancient. The dragon was the symbol of Vlad's reign, but the wolf represents our bloodline. The Dacians, who inhabited this country before the Romans conquered it, referred to themselves as 'wolf-men.' "

"Ah, yes . . ." His pale eyes lit up with interest as he continued scribbling. "The old Dacians. And there were legends, were there not, of their having the ability to actually transform themselves into other creatures, such as the wolf . . . ?"

"All ridiculous superstition, of course."

"Of course." Jeffries' smile was bright. "It is all superstition. But it is fascinating, is it not, to see how the legends developed from the truth . . . ?"

I had to allow the point.

"And the serpent . . . ?" he prompted. "Do you think that perhaps the peasants saw this and were provoked to think once again of the Devil?"

"Perhaps. But only an ignorant person would do so. In pre-Christian times, snakes were revered as creatures who possessed the secret of immortality, for when they shed their old skins, they 'die' and are 'born' anew. I have always taken this to symbolise the fervent desire that the family line continue unbroken forever."

The tour continued, and our conversation turned to other topics. I told him of our family's history, and of the original Vlad Tsepesh's reign and victories over the Turks, and of the many notable Tsepesh family members scattered throughout eastern Europe. He was quite impressed and took careful note of all details. I feel hopeful that the article will be both accurate and intriguing, and asked whether he would be so kind as to send me a copy of the finished product, that I might translate it into Roumanian and educate my fellow Transylvanians —though, unfortunately, those who most need to see the article are those who cannot read. He agreed to do so.

We fell then to talking about the peasants and their superstitions once again. Jeffries confessed to me that, immediately after his arrival, one of the chamber-maids—"a blond, stocky, middle-aged woman," so I knew he meant Masika Ivanovna—had taken the crucifix from around her own neck and given it to him, pleading for him to wear it. He had humoured her by putting it on, but once she had left his chambers, he removed it. "I am Church of England, and this would never do," he said, though he made it clear that he followed the practice only out of custom and deference to family, not belief. We ended the discussion about the locals by agreeing that public education was the only solution.

His company was so delightful that I insisted he return with me to the manor for an early dinner (luring him with promises of a tour of the family chapel and tomb). I left a note in Uncle's drawing-room to that effect, and promised to return his guest by nine o'clock.

And so he came with me to the manor, and Mary and I spent an enjoyable evening in his company, with the result that I did not take him back to the castle until very late.

But it is nearly dawn, and I have been writing for hours, and am exhausted. To bed now. More to follow.

+⊹+ +⊹+ +⊹+

The Journal of
Mary Windham Tsepesh

9 APRIL. I write this, having retired early while Arkady enjoys the charming company of our visitor, Mister Matthew Jeffries. I left them laughing in the dining-room to enjoy after-dinner cordials and cigars. I am glad Arkady has found some small joy in the man's companionship; he needs it, poor dear, just as I need the opportunity to privately unburden my heart by writing.

After witnessing the tryst between Zsuzsanna and Vlad yesterday night, I have been most troubled; but I have said nothing to Arkady yet, for he has seemed more troubled than I. I decided to delicately broach the subject with Zsuzsanna first, for I feared that, being an innocent, she has been led astray by her more worldly great-uncle and perhaps does not even realise that what she is doing is improper. Vlad is older and wiser and therefore to blame.

But Zsuzsanna did not present herself for breakfast or luncheon. Arkady was so distracted by some unspoken concern that he did not even remark upon it, but after what I had seen, I grew worried, and so I knocked upon her bedroom door in the early afternoon.

She called out feebly for me to enter, and I opened the door to find her still in her nightgown in bed, propped up with her long, dark hair fanned against the pillows. Her eyes are large, like Arkady's, but unlike his, very dark, and to-day they were underscored by shadow that emphasised her pallour.

Indeed, she seemed distressingly pale and drawn; her lips and cheeks had lost their former hint of rosiness.

"Zsuzsanna, dear," I said, and hurried to her side. "I missed your company to-day and came to see how you were doing. Are you unwell?"

"Sweet Mary! Only tired. I did not sleep well last night."

Her answer made me blush, but I do not think she noticed. She smiled at the sight of me, and clasped my hand; hers was cold. I assume her wanness was caused by some feminine complaint and so did not press to know its cause, but I fear it is also at least partly due to lovesickness and guilt. She looked so small and frail there against the pillows that it was impossible to think of her as a responsible adult; even her voice and expression were those of a child.

"Have you eaten?" I asked. "May I bring you anything?"

"Oh, yes! I have been ravenous. Dunya brought me two trays, and I ate everything." She nudged the dog, who lay contented across the foot of her bed and thumped his tail at the sound of his name. "It is all Brutus' fault! He has been barking at night and won't let me sleep. I had to put him in the kitchen, and he will stay there again to-night!"

"Perhaps it is wisest to let him stay." I watched her keenly for a reaction. "He only barks in order to protect you."

She laughed; her eyes were wide and innocent. "Protect me? From what? Field mice?"

"From wolves," I said darkly. "I thought I saw one near your window last night. You must take care."

There followed an awkward pause; her eyes narrowed, and she shot a swift, telling glance at me before turning away and pretending to focus her attention on the dog at her feet. She stroked him for several seconds in silence.

All of a sudden she burst into tears, and raised her contorted face to mine as she clutched my arm with both hands. "Please—you must not return to England! Tell him—please! If all of you leave me, I shall die! You must none of you leave me—!" She wept with the single-minded desperation of a child.

I was taken aback more than I can say by the unexpected and emotional reaction, but I took it as a clear admission of guilt and a confession of love. It does not matter to her so much if Arkady and I were to leave; but it would kill her should her great-uncle do so.

"But, my darling," I soothed, "we would never leave you. You must not even think such things."

"Tell *him*! Tell *him*!" she repeated in a choked voice, clutching my arm so desperately that I had to promise at once: yes, yes, I would tell him, and quite soon.

I know she did not refer to her brother. I know who "he" is, all too well.

From her reaction, I fear her guilt has driven her to nervous exhaustion. I sat with her awhile and calmed her—saying nothing more of what I had seen, lest I provoke her to another outburst. She has suffered enough, poor dear, and there is nothing I can do now except take the matter up with my husband—or Vlad himself.

But I am a newcomer to the family; it is hardly my place to take the patriarch to task. I know I must speak to Arkady, and soon. Yet, although my husband did not depart for the castle until mid-afternoon, I could not bring myself to speak to him, could not find the words.

At the same time, I cannot bear to see poor confused Zsuzsanna further taken advantage of. And so I determined that I would wait for Arkady to return home later that evening and speak to him, and I spent the afternoon hours carefully choosing the phrases that would surely break his heart.

To my dismay and relief, my husband returned home only a few hours later, with an Englishman who was visiting the castle, a Mister Jeffries. Arkady was so cheered by having a visitor—and I must admit, despite my misery, I too enjoyed his company, and found it a pleasant distraction from my worries—that I could not consider spoiling his good mood. We

THE JOURNAL OF MARY WINDHAM TSEPESH

had an early dinner with our guest. As I expected, Zsuzsanna did not come down for it and sent a message via Dunya that she was still indisposed.

Mister Jeffries, it seems, is a journalist who recently returned to the Continent after a news-gathering trip to America. Over dinner he spoke animatedly of the situation in that country; they have elected a new president, James Polk, and may soon annex a new state with the exotic name of Texas. Slavery is permitted in Texas, which has generated a good deal of controversy over there. Not only are the northern abolitionists and southern plantation owners arguing over this, but a neighbouring country disputes ownership of the territory altogether; according to Mister Jeffries, war between the United States and Mexico is imminent. The Americans are also involved in a disagreement with England as to where the northwestern Canadian border lies. All in all, they seem a very quarrelsome, bullying lot, and I was glad to be in peaceful Transylvania. Mr. Jeffries made us laugh with his nasal imitation of an American accent; after all the stress Arkady has been under, I know it did him good.

After dinner, Mister Jeffries reminded Arkady of his promise to take him on a tour of the chapel, and I said I wanted to go, too, for I had never seen it myself. The two men looked at me with concern, and Arkady mumbled something about it being late (it was no more than eight o'clock) and my needing rest in my condition. I abruptly dismissed this as nonsense, and asked only for a moment to go get my shawl; at which Mister Jeffries smiled and said slyly that I would have no trouble holding my own with Americans, and again we laughed.

In truth, I did not want to be left alone to worry over what I would say to Arkady when our guest departed; nor did I want to sit alone in the bedroom, peering through the window worrying over Zsuzsanna.

The chapel was unlike any I had ever seen in England, and more than anything else I have seen in this country revealed the Turkish influence; its interior walls were covered with paintings and mosaics of saints—literally thousands of them—in the Byzantine manner. Near the altar was a high cupola, from which hung a heavy candelabra, and at the back of the large sanctuary, against the wall, were great crypts with names engraved on gold plates.

Although the beautiful tiled walls stole my breath, Mister Jeffries seemed most taken with the crypts, which were actually compartments built into the wall like a honeycomb, then mortared off and sealed with stone, and adorned with the plaques. As we stood reading the names of Arkady's ancestors, awed to silence by the sanctuary's beauty and reverent atmosphere, Mister Jeffries took a small notebook from his waistcoat and began writing.

After a moment he turned to Arkady and said, in a hushed voice that echoed faintly off the high ceiling, "I forgot to ask . . . When we stood in front of the portrait of Vlad Dracula—"

Here I frowned, curious, at him, for I had heard a similar word, Dracul, before—on the servants' lips, and those of the old coachman in Bistritz. Mister Jeffries broke off and instantly corrected himself with an apologetic glance at my husband. "Forgive me, I meant to say, Vlad Tsepesh . . . Does the name Tsepesh have any meaning?"

Arkady stood gazing steadily at the crypts with his back to us, and I could tell from his distant tone that he was brooding over whatever has been troubling him the past few days—something I suspect is connected with the castle and his father's death. "Impaler," he said quietly, and I knew at once that he had quite forgotten my presence; in many ways he is like his sister, given to abrupt, intense daydreams which completely remove him from the present. "Hardly more noble in meaning than the name Dracul, but at least the peasants do not utter it with the same loathing, and it carries no hint of the supernatural. Impalement was a common form of execution at the time."

Mister Jeffries arched a pale, disbelieving brow as he stepped beside Arkady and followed his gaze to a gold marker on which was engraved the legend VLAD TEPES. "Indeed? History indicates it was common only among the Turks. The peasants say Vlad borrowed their methods and turned this"— and he swept his arm to indicate the entire countryside—"into a veritable forest of the impaled. The smell, they say—"

And here Mister Jeffries broke off in horror at his own words and turned to me. "Oh, my dear Mrs. Tsepesh, forgive me! How insensitive of me to alarm you, mentioning such terrible things . . ."

I laughed gaily, though in fact I had never heard these things before and was fascinated in a horrified way. At the sound, Arkady withdrew from his reverie and faced us, also distressed that such things were being discussed in my presence. "I am no delicate maiden given to swooning, sir," I said.

Arkady flushed and moved beside me to take my hand. "It's true," he said, gazing at me with affectionate concern but addressing Jeffries. "Mary is the most levelheaded person I have ever known." He glanced at Jeffries with an awkward smile. "I am constantly grateful for her trait. It is quite an invaluable attitude here, where one is surrounded by superstition and dark legends."

"My dear," I told him softly, "you mustn't try to shield me from these things. How will I be able to refute the servants' strange beliefs if I know nothing of them?" To Jeffries, I said in a firm cheerful voice, "Of whom were you speaking?"

"Of Vlad Dracul— Forgive me, madam. Vlad Tsepesh, whom the peasants call Dracula."

"The prince?" I asked.

Jeffries tilted his long face in a gesture which seemed to both confirm and deny. "His namesake." He flipped a page on his notepad and scanned it for a fact, then looked up. "Born 1431, supposedly died 1476, though the peasants would disagree."

Arkady gestured at the plaque at the foot of a crypt. "You see his marker here before you."

"But he died in that region to the south known as Wallachia, did he not? Where he reigned?"

"True," said my husband. "But the family moved northward to Transylvania soon after his death, and brought his remains with them. It was not an uncommon practice."

Mister Jeffries' tone grew skeptical. "Surely you know he is not buried here. It is a blind, so that those who would try to desecrate the body will not find it."

My husband turned towards his visitor with narrowed eyes and a faint, ironic smile on his lips. "Sir, you clearly know more about the subject than you have disclosed." He paused and gazed back at the marker. "It is true. He is buried at the monastery at Snagov, in his native Wallachia."

"The peasants would disagree with you once again, sir. They say no body lies at Snagov, either. Perhaps that is why the peasants say he is *strigoi,* and accuse your great-uncle—"

"*Strigoi,*" I repeated, unable to contain myself, as I recognised it as the word Dunya had used earlier. "Please; what is the meaning of that word?"

Arkady glanced at me sharply, clearly distressed to learn that I had been exposed to the term, but Jeffries looked me in the eye and said, "A vampire, madam. They say your kind and gracious great-uncle is in fact Vlad the Impaler, also known as Dracula, born 1431; that he has made a pact with the Devil to obtain immortality, and that the souls of innocents are the price." And he laughed as if the notion were incredibly amusing. Arkady and I did not join in.

Jeffries realised the discomfort his words had provoked, and immediately switched the conversation to a lighter topic. We departed the chapel soon after, and when I left my husband and his guest in the dining-room they were engaged in a friendly argument about America's newest literary sensation, Mister Edgar Allan Poe, and whether his poem "The Raven" was as great a work of genius as purported.

And so I retired to the bedroom, thinking that, by the time I finished this entry, Arkady would return, and I would confess everything to him; but it is almost eleven now, and still he has not come. I am tired and yearn for sleep, but I cannot keep my gaze from the heavy curtains drawn across the window; I cannot keep from worrying about what lies on the other side.

The peasants are right; Vlad *is* a monster. They simply do not realise what sort.

4

Zsuzsanna Tsepesh's Diary

10 APRIL. I am dying of love.

Another night of dreams; this morning I am so weak, I can scarcely pick up the pen. After a sentence or two, I must set it down to rest. My back aches terribly, from the top of my spine all the way to the bottom. And so strangely: sometimes it feels as if the muscles and bones are moving, stirring beneath my skin.

He came again. He came, and this time I was waiting for him at the open window. This time I unfastened the ribbon myself, though I let him gently pull the thin fabric down across my skin. I shivered at its softness; and then I shivered at the coolness of the night air against my exposed flesh, followed by the chill of his hands, and the heat of his breath.

He was just as gentle this time, and twice as bold. He pulled the nightgown until it fell about my ankles, all the while keeping his lips pressed to my skin, drawing them slowly down with the fabric over the curve of my shoulder, my breast, my ribs; parting them to taste my flesh with his tongue. I blush to write that he did not stop there, but knelt down and continued the kiss downward over the soft slope of my belly, my abdomen, and below . . .

I felt a rush of warmth and a tingling that began at the base of my spine and ascended through the top of my head, and beyond. I felt as though I had been dead all my years on earth, and for the first time, a kiss had wakened me to life. I looked down at my kneeling saviour and buried my fingers in his thick mane of silvery-white hair.

And then he drew his lips over the thigh of my withered leg. At first I flushed in embarrassment; in my adult life, I have never permitted anyone to touch, even to see my crippled limb. I began to pull away, but he drew me back, and stroked and kissed it gently, lovingly—

No. Far more than that; he kissed it with pure reverent adoration, and in that moment I loved him as a god.

The kiss continued to the very tip of my poor, twisted foot; and then he rose, and took me in his arms, and said: "Zsuzsanna. I am bound by the covenant I made with your father to take care of you while you lived. I am bound by it as well not to come to you in this way. But you are too sickly to make the journey to England—where I am determined to go. This is the only way you can accompany me. Do you understand?"

"Yes," I whispered, though in truth I knew nothing, understood nothing except that I wished to remain in his embrace always.

He smiled faintly, and said, "Of all the family in all the many years of my time on this earth, you alone have freely loved me—"

"No," I whispered. "I worship you. When I was sick, you saved my life; and no man has ever treated me so kindly, has ever given me notice, as you have. To other men, I am invisible; but you alone see me."

A look of utterly regal satisfaction crept over his face; I knew my words had pleased him. "Because of that devotion," he said, "I have broken the covenant with the family, and must pay the price; and now I make a new one in its place. I will never leave you, but will make you mine, and bind us both together forever." And when I begged for him to do so at once, he shook his head sadly. "I had hoped to to-night, but it is not to be; I am still too hungry. Soon it will be possible . . . Very soon."

And with a move swift as a serpent, he fastened his lips upon my neck.

It was as if the suddenness of the motion woke me from a trance. I felt the sharp pain of his teeth piercing my flesh and cried out, struggling in his steel embrace, full of a wild unreasoning fear. I recoiled and struck my fists against his broad, unyielding chest, tried to push him away, but with a single hand spread against my back he crushed my body against his. His grip tightened until I could not breathe. I felt pressure against my neck, and his tongue and lips working hungrily against my skin with the same soft sucking sound of a babe at its mother's breast.

I gave up fighting and fell into a swoon. At that instant, the sweet pleasure of the previous night overtook me again; and the more I surrendered, the more intense that pleasure became, until I could not repress my moans. I became aware of nothing but velvety darkness, the feel of his tongue and lips, of my blood flowing out towards him to the slow, synchronous beating of our hearts.

The ecstasy mounted until I could bear it no more and cried out. At that moment, he withdrew and let me fall back, barely conscious, into his arms. I was too weak to stand, to speak, even to see, but I heard his deep voice clearly as he said: "Enough. Perhaps too much . . . !"

He carried me over to the bed and gently covered me with the blankets. I sensed him leave, though I could not move, could not even open my eyes to watch him go. For a time I lay, feeling with each breath that I would not have strength to draw another, feeling a faint ripple of pleasure with each throb of my heart, and thinking it would be its last.

Most of all, I felt amazement that death could be such an exquisitely sensual experience.

But I did not die. I slept, and in the late morning when I woke, once again there lay the nightgown on the floor by the window. I was too weak even to retrieve it; Dunya found it this morning when she brought breakfast and handed it back to me with a scandalised expression—whilst I guiltily tried to hide my nakedness under the sheets.

Dunya suspects; and Mary, I think, knows, though it is impossible for one person to know another's dreams. I tried to convey this in my thoughts to Vlad, to warn him that others knew and might try to interfere. No doubt they must be horrified, shocked.

I do not care.

I do not understand what is happening to me; I am no longer sure what is real. I am so weak and confused; I think I am ill and dying. And I repeat: I do not care. If this be death, then death is sheer joy! For the first time in my stunted, miserable life, I am happy. I do not want God. I do not want forgiveness.

I want only for him to come again.

❖ ❖ ❖

The Journal of
Mary Windham Tsepesh

10 APRIL. Dear God, please let me be mad. Please let me be an hysterical pregnant woman who is seeing things because her head has been filled with frightening stories . . .

The horror of it is, I know I am not. I know what I have seen—and yet it is impossible!

It is now half-past one in the morning. I heard Arkady

leave with Mister Jeffries in the caleche a few moments ago; he will not be returning for at least twenty minutes, longer if he stays a bit to converse with his guest, whose company he seems to have so enjoyed this past night. I must write this down—I must do *some*thing—or lose my wits altogether. My hand is shaking so badly, I can hardly read what I have already recorded.

I could not sleep, of course, after I finished the last entry in my journal, although it was after midnight. I struggled, restless, with the sheets. Part of my discomfort was due to indigestion and the inability to find a suitable sleeping position due to my heavy belly, but most of it was mental: I was worried about whether to tell Arkady about Vlad and Zsuzsanna to-night, after Mister Jeffries had gone, or whether to wait until morning; and I was worried, too, about what precisely I should say.

Nor could I master my curiosity about what might be happening on the other side of that curtain. Surely, I decided, Zsuzsanna had taken note of my dark hint about a wolf at her window, and would at the very least warn Vlad that her bedroom was no longer a safe place to meet; I even dared hope that my oblique words had been enough to convince her to break off the secret relationship altogether.

Still, I forced my eyelids shut. Perhaps I dozed—though memory swears I remained quite conscious. Yet I fell into a strange waking dream, almost trancelike, and found myself staring into a pair of large, heavy-lidded eyes, suspended against the soft darkness.

They were set in snow-pale skin, and quite strikingly beautiful, like deep green emeralds; the pupils were large, shining, black. I recognised them at once, for they were Vlad's eyes, and they seemed to cast the same hypnotic spell I had experienced at the *pomana*—except that this time, being drowsy, I yielded to them for a moment. Doing so made my discomfort vanish and induced a very enjoyable languor which I was reluctant to disturb.

I lingered there but a moment; and then my natural stubbornness awoke and I opened my eyes and gave my head a shake to clear it.

Yet I knew I had not been asleep. This alarming realisation—and perhaps the unease provoked by the stories Mister Jeffries had told in the chapel—caused my heart to begin beating faster. With a sense of inexplicable dread, I went over to the window-seat in the alcove and timidly drew aside the curtain, just enough so that I could see Zsuzsanna's window but could not myself be seen.

The full moon shone in a cloudless sky to-night, lighting up the countryside like day. I could quite clearly see each blade of grass, each wildflower on the stretch of earth between our window and Zsuzsanna's, though the colours had all been dimmed to subtly varying values of grey.

I knew Vlad was there—knew it, though even now I cannot say how this knowledge came to me. Knew it, even before I saw that the shutters had once again been flung wide, and the window opened. The lamp in her room was unlit, so that I could not see clearly inside; but a few feet beyond the open shutters, I saw shadows wrestling in the dimness, a flash of white against black, and knew with the same impossible certainty that these were Zsuzsanna's pale skin against Vlad's cloak.

How long I remained at the window I cannot exactly say; my perception indicates hours, the clock indicates minutes. But I stood frozen, watching until the shadows retreated from my sight further into the dark room—towards the bed.

And then the darker shadow, after a time, reappeared, and climbed swiftly over the windowsill, dropping several feet down onto the grass with the easy agility of a youth.

It was Vlad. I saw him clearly, unmistakably, his white hair and skin gleaming in the bright moonlight. He looked over his shoulder, furtive as a thief making his escape, then began to run.

He passed very near my window, and I drew back, not

daring to breathe, pulling the curtains together so that only a tiny crack remained, to which I pressed one eye. As I watched, he crouched forward, and began to lope on all fours, like an animal, his dark cloak furling.

And beneath my very gaze—

It is impossible. Impossible. It is madness, yet I know I am quite sane.

It was like observing a child's growth, grossly accelerated so that the transformation of years took place in seconds. Beneath my very gaze, his legs shortened, his arms lengthened, his nose and jaw thrust forward, stretching until they formed a long, lean muzzle full of sharp canine teeth. The fabric of his cloak and trousers seemed to sink into his skin and change in colour and texture until it was no longer black silk, but silvery grey fur.

Before my eyes, he changed into a large grey wolf.

I cried out in shock. I do not think the sound I made was loud; nevertheless, Vlad—the wolf—paused and turned in the direction of my window, gazing up at it with large, pale eyes.

And—perhaps this part is imagination—I watched those canine lips pull back over pointed teeth, curving slightly in the same predatory grin that he had directed at me when he lingered in Zsuzsanna's embrace at the *pomana.*

I had never been closer to fainting in my life. I let go the curtain and reeled, staggering to the wall, and pressed against it, afraid if I let go I would not be able to stand.

When at last I gathered myself, I hurried over to the desk to write it all down, lest I convince myself by morning that it was nothing more than a nightmare.

I can hear in the distance the approach of Arkady in the caleche. I had been so worried all evening about what to tell him about Zsuzsanna and Vlad.

What shall I say to him now?

What shall I say?

The Diary of Arkady Tsepesh

10 APRIL. LATE EVENING. Jeffries has vanished. I think they have killed him.

I returned with him to the castle quite late—about one or two in the morning. I did not disturb Uncle, even though I suspected he would still be awake at such a late hour, and Jeffries said that he would be sure to convey my apologies for returning him so much later than my note to Uncle had indicated. I did not feel I had the right to take Mister Jeffries' company away from Uncle again for dinner the next day, but I did invite him for afternoon tea.

This afternoon, I left early for the castle to fetch Jeffries for tea. As I drove the caleche into the courtyard, Laszlo was just leaving in the coach with a large bundle on the seat beside him. The sight of me seemed to alarm him; he at once whipped the horses and hurried away.

I took his haste and his reluctance to speak to me as a sign of his dislike, and thought little of it, or of the bundle beside him—until afterwards, when I looked for Jeffries in the guest room. He had gone: his luggage and notepad lay undisturbed in his chambers, as did the carefully folded note from Uncle, but a search of the castle proved fruitless. He was not to be found anywhere, and none of the servants admitted to seeing him. In desperation, I called them one by one to my office and questioned them. None of them seemed to know anything about the visitor's mysterious disappearance. (Sadly, Masika Ivanovna did not report to the castle to-day, as her son has died. I shall learn more of this, for I plan to attend the funeral.)

I spoke to Laszlo last, some hours later, when he had finally returned to the castle. As I did, I noted that he had a gold watch fob and chain on his vest which I had never seen before; with an inspiration born of horror, I demanded he withdraw the watch and present it to me.

He did so, and I gasped as my eyes detected the large

silver "J" on the watch's engraved golden surface. Such brazenness! He even held it out for my inspection with the same hand that now wore Jeffries' gold ring!

I completely lost hold of my temper and shouted at him: "How dare you steal from a guest of this house! You are dismissed at once! See to it that you never set foot on this property again!"

He lifted his jowly chin, defiant, unrepentant. "Oh, I shan't be leaving, sir. The *voievod* will see to that. Besides, you have no authority to dismiss me."

His arrogance enraged me; warmth flooded my face as I cried, "I doubt that! We shall see what Vlad has to say when I tell him you are a thief!"

"I am no thief," said he. "Dead men own no property."

A horrid coldness seized my heart. I thought of the terror in Masika's eyes when she realised Laszlo had overheard; and now her son had died. "What are you saying, Laszlo? That Mister Jeffries is dead?"

"I say nothing."

"I shall speak to Uncle at once about this," I threatened —to which he simply chuckled, turned his back to me without so much as asking my leave, and walked towards the door.

And as he did—

As he did, I saw upon the back of his white sleeve a large red stain the size of an apple. A horrible chill descended over me; I know not how to explain it, but at that moment, I knew in my heart Jeffries was dead, and that I gazed upon his murderer.

"Laszlo," I said.

He paused, and swiveled his head over his shoulder to cast at me his insolent stare.

"What is this? Have you hurt yourself?" I strode over to him and between thumb and forefinger caught a bit of unstained sleeve between my fingers and held it so that I might better study the stain.

It was blood, no doubt of it—beginning to darken, but

still bright enough to suggest that it had been shed only hours before. Laszlo glanced down at it and pulled his arm away at once, but his insolence faded a bit. "Not at all. I killed a hen this morning for the cook."

And he hurried out of the room.

It seemed a reasonable explanation; yet I could not shake the sense of dread that overtook me. It was then I remembered the bundle I had seen on the seat beside him in the carriage.

I followed him out and ran down the stairs, thinking to confront him about the contents of the bundle, but he had already vanished. And so I went down to the kitchen, where I learned through roundabout questioning that the cook was stewing a lamb and had no knowledge of Laszlo's hen.

How could any murderer be so bold, so brazen, so contumelious as to proudly sport the stolen effects of his victim, then hint at the crime?

Only one who is insane.

These revelations were simply too unnerving to keep to myself. When V. rose, I called on him in his drawing-room. Ana had lit the fire and tapers so that the room emanated a cosy warmth. Hands upon the armrests, straight and regal as a king upon his throne, Uncle sat in one of the two large camel-back chairs facing the hearth. Between them on the end-table sat a small silver tray, upon which rested a crystal snifter and a decanter of slivovitz, an indulgence no doubt provided for the possibly ill-fated Mister Jeffries.

The instant I closed the door behind me, V. pushed himself from his chair with exceptional alacrity and whirled to face me, his eyes wide and full of fire. Before I could utter a word, he thundered:

"You are never to remove a guest from this castle without my express permission! Never! Do you understand?"

I was so taken aback that for a few seconds my voice failed. These were not my father's voice, my father's eyes— they were the voice of an imperious prince, the eyes of the cold-blooded Impaler in the portrait.

His face, far from possessing its usual pallour, was flushed with rage, so that his white eyebrows stood out alarmingly against his pink forehead, and an even rosier hue stole across his cheeks and the high, narrow bridge of his nose. His crimson lips were twisted, the lower one pulled down to reveal a row of jagged, glistening white teeth. He had moved so quickly and with such energy that I thought I stared at a different man. Indeed, a streak of iron grey had appeared at each of his temples.

He had grown younger. I blinked, but the hallucination did not fade. The change was slight but unmistakable—and quite impossible, as impossible as Stefan's appearance. I winced and raised a hand to my temple at the now-familiar sensation of pressure there, and heard, quite clearly, as though I whispered them into my own ear, the words:

You must be going mad.

"I am sorry," I stammered. "I shall never do it again. It was just that Mister Jeffries was such good company—"

"Swear it! Swear that you will never repeat such a mistake. Now!"

"I swear it," I whispered, truly frightened—not by V.'s temperamental outburst, but by my own impossible perceptions. "I will never do it again."

At once his anger dimmed; he straightened, and his powerful body relaxed. "Good. Good." He nodded in grim satisfaction. "I will accept the word of a Tsepesh." His tone lightened abruptly; he gestured at the chair beside his own. "Now, Nephew, sit, and tell me how I might help you."

I crossed the room and sat sideways on the edge of the chair, facing him with my hands lightly on the armrest and fixing on him my uncertain gaze, trying not to gape at his slight but obvious rejuvenation. I felt so entirely nonplussed that I was reluctant to begin; but V. smiled at me, and said:

"I must apologise for my fit of temper, Arkady, but I have only a few rules for those in my service, and I demand that they be followed. There is no quicker way to provoke my wrath." He poured a glass of the slivovitz and handed it to me, saying: "Drink."

I took it, though I did not want it, and, after a small sip, set it down.

"Now," said V., with his usual warm solicitousness, "please forgive my outburst; I can see it has unnerved you, and this was not my intent. Speak to me, Arkady. Tell me what I must do to help you."

I ventured timidly, "It is about Mister Jeffries that I have come." When this drew only an expression of polite interest, I grew bolder. "He has vanished without a single trace, leaving all his belongings behind."

"Indeed?" V. said, his eyebrows lifting with mild surprise. And then his expression grew thoughtful, and he gazed into the fire as he considered this, his ruddiness deepened by its warm glow. His anger had faded, but the blush across his cheeks had not; it seemed his show of anger had left him permanently revitalised. "Most odd," he murmured at last. "I suppose I should not be insulted by this abrupt departure. The English are full of peculiar customs."

I made a small noise of exasperation. "I lived among the English for four years. They are not in the habit of suddenly disappearing. I am afraid something dreadful has happened to him."

He stared back at me with puzzlement at the degree of my distress. "What would make you say such a thing? What could possibly happen to a guest here, in my home?"

"Perhaps . . . perhaps someone has harmed him; perhaps even killed him."

At this he laughed aloud. Embarrassment and anger brought a surge of heat to my cheeks, the back of my neck; he noted this, and immediately sobered, then in a patronising, soothing tone, said, "Dear Nephew . . . you have suffered a terrible strain over the past few days. Could it be this which has caused you to jump to this conclusion? The man has left abruptly, but how can we say harm has come to him? Perhaps he simply decided to return to Bistritz and in his haste forgot his trunk; or perhaps he has some reason for wanting to disappear into the countryside. Perhaps he foolishly went walking unattended in the forest and had his throat torn out by wolves. Who knows? Perhaps he is not the newspaperman he claims to be, but a criminal or murderer hoping to elude justice."

My voice shook (from both anger at his questioning of my mental stability and from fear that he was correct in so doing) as I replied, "Had he decided to return to Bistritz, he would have asked Laszlo to take him, and he would have taken his things. But to-day Laszlo is wearing his watch and his ring. He would not dare attempt such thievery unless he knew Jeffries would not return."

"Perhaps Mister Jeffries gave those things to Laszlo."

"I think not. I think . . . I think he may have killed him and then stole them."

"Killed him?" He was careful not to laugh, but this time only permitted his eyebrows to lift in disbelief. "Arkady, the servants would never dare harm one of my guests, I assure you. As you can see, I am most protective of them."

"Perhaps most of the servants would not. But I think Laszlo is capable of such an act. When I confronted him about the watch and ring to-day and accused him of thievery, he said that dead men owned no property. And there was blood on his sleeve, fresh blood. And this morning, when I arrived at the courtyard, he was driving the carriage away, with a very suspicious expression, and on the seat beside him was a large bundle."

V. listened keenly. At last he said, in the patient tone of one trying to reason with a madman, "Arkady, certainly carrying a bundle in the caleche can be explained, as can the blood—"

"He lied about the bloodstain," I interrupted. "He said he had slaughtered a chicken for the cook, but she knows nothing about it."

He paused, then continued, "But are you quite sure these

things belonged to Mister Jeffries? And that you did not mishear Laszlo's words? I feel certain this must all be just a misunderstanding—"

"I have no doubt what Laszlo said to me. And Jeffries' watch and ring are monogrammed with his initial. He wore them all day yesterday."

"You are quite sure of this?"

"Quite sure," I said, but I read the clear disbelief in his eyes.

"I see," V. said slowly, and turned away from me to gaze into the fire. I knew he thought me quite irrational, and struggled to keep control of my temper, lest I say something else heated that might further prove his conclusion. We sat in silence a time, and then he asked:

"What do you think should be done?"

"Go to the authorities in Bistritz," I replied, "and tell them our suspicions. Let them investigate Mister Jeffries' disappearance."

Again V. contemplated my words, and after a long pause said slowly, in a tone so soothing I thought at once I was a child snuggled in my bed, listening to Father's low, lulling voice relating a fairy tale. "Arkady . . . I ask you to restrain your impulse and trust me. I assure you nothing has happened to Mister Jeffries, and that your conclusions are . . . premature. You have been under an enormous emotional strain; perhaps sorrow is clouding your judgement. Let two days pass. By that time, I am sure the mystery of Mister Jeffries will be solved. If it is not, then you shall serve as our detective. You are bright, with a good brain; I trust you to solve the mystery, and in the end we shall see that justice is done. Only there is no need to trouble the authorities. Will you promise to trust me?"

As he spoke, I felt a wave of dizziness, and the same viselike pain in my skull—and the same conviction that I was losing my grip on sanity. Perhaps I *was* being foolish to suspect Laszlo on such little evidence; perhaps I could not trust what my own eyes had seen. After all, here was V. sitting before me, a man suddenly ten years younger.

"I promise," I said bleakly. V. refused to discuss any business, saying that I clearly needed to go home early and rest; and so I took my leave of him.

When I passed by the guest chambers again on my way out of the castle, they had been entirely emptied of Jeffries' belongings; it is as if he had never existed, had never come.

I left the castle, my heart heavy at the thought of what might have happened to poor Jeffries, my mind perplexed by all I had seen—both real and unreal.

How shall I discern the difference?

On the drive home, as the caleche rolled across the grassy knoll, I was drawn from my anxious reverie by the horses' nervous whinnies, and caught a glimpse of what had troubled them: a large grey wolf, bounding in our same direction, from the castle towards the manor. I gave the reins a snap and the horses gratefully quickened their pace; but I had come to myself enough to note my surroundings, and could not help gazing over my right shoulder at the bright nacreous beauty of the moon, sailing above the thick stand of forest.

I stared at it only a few seconds. As I did, something small and pale began to materialise against the backdrop of dark forest; I knew at once, before my eyes focused, that it was Stefan. After Father's mutilation, I could not bear to look upon my brother's face or throat, and so I fastened my gaze on his white linen shirt, and the large irregular black stain there, which radiant moonlight imbued with a satiny sheen.

Stefan raised an arm, and pointed at the forest—in the same direction as twice before.

Hesitant, intrigued, fearful, I coaxed the reluctant horses in the direction of the apparition. As I neared, Stefan vanished, only to reappear further away, almost hidden by the shadows of tall pine at the forest's edge.

I urged the horses closer. Again Stefan vanished, then

reappeared, this time inside the forest's border, and motioned me to enter.

I drew a breath and followed; the horses moved tentatively, snorting their disapproval at my foolhardiness. The passageway between the trees was narrow, and boughs brushed against the sides of the caleche, releasing the fragrance of evergreen. The instant we entered, panic and regret seized me, for the trees were so close and their foliage so dense that I found myself staring into utter blackness; by contrast, the moonlit knoll had seemed bright as day. Only the smell of pine and the brush of tree limbs revealed my location.

Blinded, I reined the horses to a stop, and tried to determine the placement of tree trunks so that I might safely direct the caleche back out. Yet in the midst of the darkness, Stefan's small form appeared once more before us, glowing with the same internal radiance as the moon, illuminating the path towards him.

Once more, I followed in the caleche. But before we arrived at the place where Stefan had stood, I detected a thrashing in the undergrowth, a low growl, a blur of movement, and pulled the horses round at once. The caleche swung about in the opposite direction, so swiftly that one wheel lifted off the ground and I very nearly lost my balance and fell—which would have proven fatal.

The forest went coal-black. I could see nothing, but felt the tension on the reins as the horses reared, heard their screams above the snarls of wolves. I slapped the reins, hard, harder, half rising out of desperation, but the horses were too panicked to obey. The wolves leapt, biting at the horses' faces; I heard the snap of their jaws, the thud of their paws against the ground, and recoiled as one jumped at the caleche, so near that I felt its warm breath against my face and heard the whistle of air as its teeth clamped shut.

This horrible scene endured only seconds, but it seemed an eternity before I found the whip and galvanised the shrieking horses into movement. We thundered out of the trees into the streaming moonlight. The wolves at first followed, nipping at the terrified animals' hooves, but soon fell away and dashed back into the forest.

The horses and I were trembling uncontrollably by the time we returned to the manor. Through some miracle, none of the animals were seriously harmed. Even so, I felt terribly guilty when I saw their bleeding muzzles, and as the stable-hand was already asleep, I tended to their wounds, speaking gently to calm them—though I think the act did more to steady my nerves than theirs. I promised them we would never again venture into the forest without Father's gun.

I could not promise that I would not go there again. Stefan awaits me. Something evil tried to prevent me from discovering what he wanted me to find to-night.

But this is irrational! My dead brother's appearances are nothing more than the result of stress and imagination. Yet the delusion is so strong, it is difficult to resist . . .

Have shock and sorrow driven me to the brink of insanity? I feel as though I teeter on the precipice. I have seen my dead brother materialise before me; I have seen V. impossibly rejuvenated. I have felt the talons of madness clutch my skull. How can I be certain if I indeed saw Laszlo wearing Jeffries' ring, or saw the bundle in the caleche, or blood on his sleeve? How can I know for certain Jeffries himself existed?

No. No. I must not doubt or I *shall* go mad. Stefan is an hallucination—compelling but unreal; but I know I saw Laszlo wearing the ring, and I know I did not misunderstand his insolent, incriminating remark.

By the time I entered the house, I had mastered my shaking and achieved some degree of calm—a good thing, as Mary was still awake. I think she is concerned about me—I have tried to hide the shocks of the past few days, but I suspect I have done too poor a job. That small crease she gets between her eyebrows when she is particularly preoccupied has reappeared. She gently broke the news to me that Zsuzsanna seems to be quite ill of some unknown malady, and though I know she was distressed by it, I could not help feeling that she was hiding something more for fear of alarming me. I worry so that she is unhappy here, or that something has occurred to upset her.

She also questioned me, asking whether there was something troubling me. I tried to reassure her that all was well, but I do not think she believed me.

We retired early, and I did not pause, as is my custom, to record the day's events in my diary; I was exhausted by the emotional strain.

To comfort me as we lay together, Mary put my hand upon her stomach so that I might feel the child moving within her; the precocious rascal kicked so hard that we both were forced to forget our troubles and laugh. My own laughter verged on tears, for I felt a resurgence of the overwhelming love and gratitude I had experienced on the wagon-lit from Vienna, when I had gazed upon my sleeping wife.

I fell asleep quickly, but woke within the hour from a dream of Shepherd, lifting his bloody head to regard me with the white eyes of a wolf. I fear returning to that dream, and so I have risen to record these words by lamplight.

Oh, Mary! Dear unborn child! To what sort of madhouse have I brought you?

The Journal of
Mary Windham Tsepesh

11 APRIL. MORNING. The night before last, I scarcely slept, though I pretended to be asleep when Arkady returned. I was too overwhelmed to make sense of what I had seen, so I spent the long hours beside him in bed, listening to his breathing and praying to God that, when I rose in the morning, I would wake to find I had been victim of nothing more than a nightmare.

I pray often in secret these days. Arkady knows of my faith in God. (How tolerantly we smile at one another, each smug in his own beliefs, when one of us makes a pronouncement concerning religion.) Not the sour, wrathful God of England's Church, Who would curse my husband to Hell for his disbelief. The God to Whom I pray is wise, loving, far too divinely shrewd to be concerned with the petty rules and jealousies and wars of humans, or to be so annoyed by my husband's rejection that He would damn him to eternal torment.

But that God seems very far from this place. Though I have privately never believed in the Devil, no stranger can fail to sense that some malignant Power holds sway here. Indeed,

God seems no longer to hear my prayers. I woke to the sorrow-ful knowledge that what I had seen had been no dream.

Far from it; the evidence for what I have witnessed grows. I pray that what I have learned today is false, but my heart and mind are divided. My mind knows that it is insanity, and utterly false; my heart, that it is true. But I cannot trouble Arkady in his time of grief with such terrible, fantastic things until I myself am certain of them.

Yesterday, when Zsuzsanna failed again to come down for breakfast, I paid another visit to her bedchamber. Before I could knock, Dunya opened the door and was hurrying out with a trayful of dishes; and this time, she did not duck her head as is her usual custom. This time she met my gaze, and her own was so plainly terrified and desperate that I remarked in German, "Dunya! Is something the matter?"

Beneath knitted reddish-black brows, her eyes betrayed such anguish that, when she gestured for silence and motioned with her head for me to step back into the corridor, I obeyed unquestioningly. She balanced the tray on one hand and with the other closed the door behind her, softly, then moved down the hall several paces before stopping and turning to be sure I followed.

At last she stopped and faced me, and leaning forward over the tray, whispered hoarsely, "He has done it! He has broken the *Schwur!*"

"I don't understand," said I; I did not recognise the word. "Who has done this?"

"Vlad," she replied, looking fearfully about. Had she not been holding the tray, she no doubt would have crossed her-self. "The *domnisoara*, the young miss, is very bad. Very bad."

"Zsuzsanna?" I glanced back at the bedroom door. "Is she ill?"

Dunya nodded vigorously. "Very bad."

At that point I was still undecided as to the explanation for what I had seen the night before; I was toying with the notion that my own mind had created a visual metaphor. After all, Vlad's seduction of his own niece and his flirtatious manner with me clearly marked him as a predatory beast. And so I blushed to think that Dunya knew about Vlad's nightly visits, and was alarmed by Zsuzsanna's resulting nervous condition— which was apparently worse this morning. Soon the news would be all over the manor, and then the village.

"I must talk to her at once," I said, and made for the door. As I did, Dunya hissed behind me: "Frau Tsepesh! *Doamna!* You must believe! He has bitten her. Your husband I know will not, but someone here must believe, and help her!"

I froze instantly, then turned back slowly to face her; she set the tray down with a clatter of dishes, crossed herself, then hurried toward me, her manner so beseeching that at first I thought she would throw herself at my feet.

"What do you mean?" I demanded, softly lest Zsuzsanna hear. "What do you mean, he has bitten her?"

She pointed at once to her neck, just above the collarbone. "Here," she said. "He has bitten her here."

It was as if I had spent my entire life in a darkened room, and for the first time, someone had entered and lit the lamp. I stiffened as I thought of Mister Jeffries' laughing words: *A vampire, madam . . . and the souls of innocents are the price . . .*

"*Strigoi,*" I whispered, without realising it until the word passed my lips. Dunya nodded, desperately grateful to have at last been understood.

"*Strigoi,* yes. Yes! We must help her!"

I am not sure what I believed at that moment. I only know that, as I turned the doorknob, my heart pounded with dread at what I would find.

Such an ominous pall hung over the room that a sense of foreboding came over me as I crossed the threshold. The air seemed heavy, chill, as stifling as the air had been inside the family tomb during Petru's funeral. I fancied I smelled a faint odour of decay. Perhaps the gloom was created by imagination and a sense of revulsion at the fact that I knew Vlad had been here only hours before.

Zsuzsanna lay with her dark hair spread on the pillow. Brutus sat on the floor with his great square head resting on the edge of the bed, near the pillow, gazing up into his mistress's face with a worried, attentive expression. As I entered, he turned his furrowed, mournful countenance towards me and whined softly, as if pleading for help.

At the sight of Zsuzsanna, I raised my hands to my lips and repressed a gasp of horror.

She resembled a living corpse—as pale as her pillows or nightgown. Her dark eyes were shadowed deep purple above and beneath; her skin, no longer supple but a lifeless grey-white, had drawn taut, accentuating the prominent cheekbones, the sharp, narrow nose, the huge dark eyes beneath slashes of jet black brows. The high, sculpted cheekbones and slight upward tilt of her eyes gave her an oddly feline appearance, and the extreme pallour a strange, consumptive beauty.

Her face had the pinched, waxen look of the dead. Only the eyes seemed alive, shining, liquid, full of a peculiar excitement. She did not so much sit as lie against three pillows, breathing in quick little gasps as she struggled to write in a diary propped on a lap tray. The effort seemed almost too great for her.

My appearance startled her. With a swiftness that clearly exhausted her she turned the little book over (though not before I chanced to see it had been written in English, presumably to render it unintelligible to prying servants). She smiled up at me with a flash of teeth; her grey gums had receded, making the teeth appear abnormally long.

I returned the smile, trying to keep the horror from it, for gazing on her I could think of nothing but a grinning skull. I was appalled to see that she had grown so ill so quickly; she had seemed slightly worn and tired the day before, but nothing like this—so close to death's door. "Zsuzsanna!" I exclaimed. "My poor dear, what has happened?"

She did not rise; she could not, but struggled to draw sufficient breath to whisper, "I don't know. I feel so weak, and my back aches so dreadfully." She gestured weakly at it with a hand, and it seemed to me—it is impossible, of course—that her shoulders were almost even, whereas before one had been a few inches higher than the other. "But it's all right, Mary. I don't mind . . ." She smiled again, her eyes aglitter with beatific madness.

"Don't talk," I ordered. "You're too weak." I turned to Dunya, who had followed me in, and was watching with an air of horrified conviction, her thin hands clasped together at her waist, as if she was secretly praying. "Dunya," I said, "send one of the servants to fetch a doctor."

"I do not need a doctor," Zsuzsanna whispered, but we gave no attention to such a ridiculous statement.

"The nearest doctor is in Bistritsa," Dunya replied. "If he will come at once, he will arrive here to-night, but he is not so good. The best is in Cluj, but that is too far away to be of help." She paused, lowered her voice, and said with utter conviction, "I know what to do to help her."

I frowned, concerned that she might say something which would upset Zsuzsanna. I did not want to speak of Vlad or superstition or the impossible thing I had seen here in front of Zsuzsanna, who was already given to fancy. "Tell one of the men to fetch the doctor from Bistritz, then."

She nodded, pausing to cast a final, mute glance at Zsuzsanna, and in her intelligent young eyes I saw rage, fear, and loathing, the look of a woman who had been violated and would never forgive.

She left, and I sat on the edge of the bed, careful not to disturb the writing tray with the pen and bottle of ink. Poor Brutus nudged me, and I stroked his great, warm solid head, but the puckered gathers of skin on his troubled brow never relaxed. Zsuzsanna still did not sit up, but moved her hand swiftly to slide the overturned diary farther away, over the blankets, as though she feared I might snatch it from her and read.

I should have liked to. I was desperately curious to know what it said.

I gently rested a hand on her arm, and laid the other on her forehead. It was not at all warm, which surprised me, as I expected her glittering eyes were due to fever. Rather, it was quite cool, and I involuntarily thought of Vlad's icy grip at the *pomana*. She shrank from my touch a little, still weakly smiling, but clearly eager to be rid of me.

"I don't need a doctor," she whispered again. "I only need to rest, and be alone."

"Nonsense," I said firmly. "Zsuzsanna, you are ill. You need care." I thought of the tray Dunya had been carrying, and realised in retrospect that the food thereon had been untouched. "Have you eaten anything?"

She shook her head, letting it loll weakly to one side. "I can't. It just seems such effort."

In reply, I shot a questioning glance at the writing implements. "I'll fetch you something from the kitchen myself. Some broth, perhaps, something that will go down easily." I began to rise.

As I did, Zsuzsanna absently raised a hand to the throat of her nightgown and tugged at the ribbon, loosening it a bit and worrying with her fingertips at the skin there. The fine white cotton fabric gaped, allowing me a glimpse of a small, red mark on her neck, just above the collarbone.

"My dear, you have scratched yourself," I said, and without thinking gently pulled away the fabric to examine the wound. My second impression, upon seeing the injury more clearly, was that she had accidentally pierced the skin with a brooch. There were two marks, not one, both of them small, dark red, and perfectly round, with tiny white centres at the exact spots the skin had been punctured. Just beneath one of the wounds, a drop of dried black blood had crusted.

My third impression consisted of a visual and an auditory memory: Vlad, standing by Zsuzsanna's bedroom window, bending low as he embraced her; and Dunya saying, *He has bitten her* . . .

It was of course ridiculous and impossible. My mind scoffed at such reasoning and dismissed the possibility at once, but I drew my hand away as swiftly as if I had uncovered a coiled serpent. While I sat staring at the wound, my heart began to pound, and a sense of unspeakable dread came over me. The child in my womb made a swift, violent movement.

An animal, I told myself. The marks had been made by an animal. Perhaps Brutus had scratched her—but no, these were puncture wounds, and I could not believe the gentle, doting creature had bitten her. Besides, these did not conform to the size and shape of a dog's mouth—nor did they conform to those of any animal with which I was familiar.

But they were the right size and distance to have come from a human—or inhuman—mouth . . .

My dismay must have been evident. Zsuzsanna lowered her heavy, coal-lashed lids and gave me a sidelong glance. Her fingers went back to the wound, her gaze straight ahead, and her expression—

Her expression, as she fingered the marks, was the most profoundly disturbing sight of all. Her colourless lips parted, and her chest began to heave as her breathing quickened; her eyes widened with a look of pure wonderment, followed by joy —then narrowed again with sly sensuality. She lowered her hand, languidly, voluptuously, letting her fingertips drag lightly over the curve of a breast, and remained absorbed in some private rapture at this revelation, as though I were not present.

I thought, *She is mad,* but surely she is not alone. Is Vlad any more sane? Am I, to consider that the old legends and superstitions are true?

She cast me another sidelong look from beneath a long, thick fringe of eyelashes, and her lips curved in a coy grin that made me think of her great-uncle at the *pomana,* of the wolf at my window. "It's only a little pin-prick, Mary. You mustn't worry so."

"Of course," I stammered, and straightened, murmuring, "Let me get you something from the kitchen, then. You need to eat," and I left, eager to be freed from the cloying, poisonous atmosphere of the room. I stepped over the threshold, shut the door behind me, and drew a deep breath of the purer air out in the hallway.

As I stood, trembling and confused, head bowed and one hand against the wall for support, I sensed movement at the far end of the corridor and glanced up to see Dunya.

"I sent Bogdan for the doctor," she said. Her eyes held a hint of fear, but that emotion was eclipsed by a more intense one: determination, which communicated itself in the firm set of her square jaw, the erectness of her posture. A tiny girl, a full head shorter than I, she nevertheless managed to project height. Her hands were curled into tight fists. At that moment, her cultural timidity was outdone by her natural willfulness, and I took comfort from the strength I saw in her expression.

I straightened, and forced myself to stop my foolish trembling. There is nothing I hate worse than weakness; had I been weak when Mother and Father died, I would not have survived. Dunya and I shared a grim look.

I said, "I saw her neck."

She nodded, understanding perfectly. "I found Brutus in the kitchen this morning again. I set him free so he could do his duty." She drew a breath, then said, in a rush, "He has broken the *Schwur*." She seemed to think these words an explanation. At first I was confused, thinking she referred to the dog —and then an eerie certainty settled over me, and I knew, by the way she lowered her eyelids and voice furtively, by the way she glanced with that same fearful expression over her shoulder, that she referred to Vlad.

"I do not know this word," I said, recognising it as one she had used earlier.

"*Schwur, Bund.*" Dunya held my gaze with her own somber, unwavering one. Clearly she felt this matter so important that it transcended all show of servility. "He has broken it, and if we do not stop him, Zsuzsanna will die."

"Then we must stop him," I said, no longer sure what to believe, but knowing only one thing: that Vlad had harmed Zsuzsanna, and that he must not be permitted to do so ever again. "But what is the *Schwur?*"

"That he will not hurt us, so long as we obey him." She released a quick, troubled breath, her gaze wandering to a distant point, as though she were scrutinising some object she could not identify. "I do not understand why this has happened. He is *strigoi,* but has always behaved with honour. He has never hurt his own. But if he has bitten her . . ." She looked up swiftly at me, and I saw the flicker of fear in her eyes again. "None of us are safe, *doamna.* Not even you and your husband."

Logically, I could not make much sense of her words, and a hundred rational questions crowded my mind all at once, but they were drowned out by one single, compelling, all-consuming phrase that seized my mind and soul and heart and would not release them: *My child. My child. My child . . .*

The thought of that monster laying a hand on my baby prickled the skin on the back of my neck, my arms, caused a cold, hot chill to course the length of my body, through its centre. I thought I would sink to my feet; somehow, I managed to stand. In that moment, I allowed myself to enter Dunya's magical, superstitious world, and I saw all too clearly, all too well.

I knew then why he had bitten his niece, why he wanted her gone. I had seen it at the *pomana,* in the flashing red fury in his eyes, when Zsuzsanna had cried out that he must not go to England. Vlad would permit no one, not even a beloved relative, to interfere with his will.

So long as we obey . . .

I began to speak my thoughts aloud.

"You are saying Zsuzsanna will die if we do not stop him."

"Die," Dunya agreed, "and herself become *strigoi.* Did you see, *doamna*? She is starting to change; already her back is beginning to straighten. But this has never been permitted; no *strigoi* but him, for the good of the people."

I raised a hand to my forehead, remembering Zsuzsanna's now-level shoulders, trying to cool feverish thoughts. "What can we do?"

"Let me help, *doamna.* Her room can be made safe so that he will not enter. She put the dog in the kitchen last night; she says he disturbs her with barking."

"Then we must see that he sleeps with her to-night."

"Yes," Dunya said. "And there are other things to keep the *strigoi* from her room."

"What?" I recovered a shred of my former sensibility; whatever Dunya did, it would have to be subtle enough that my husband would not find out and become incensed. I knew that I was terribly frightened, but I also knew that I was not certain yet what I believed, and wanted to do nothing to add to Arkady's unhappiness.

"The *knoblauch*," she said. "I will put it by the window. And the crucifix round her neck, and see that the dog sleeps with her. That is all—all that we can do now. It will be enough for now, as long as she lives. But you must know, *doamna*—if ever in the years after this she becomes ill and dies . . ."

She broke off, unwilling to state what she felt was obvious. But I did not follow, and frowned at her, puzzled. Finally, after an extended silence, I demanded, "What if she becomes ill and dies?"

"She will become *strigoi,* like him. There is something which can prevent it, and spare her life."

Again, silence, and I prompted: "And what is that?"

"To kill him, *doamna,* with the stake and the knife. It is the only way."

I do not know what to say, what to think, what to feel. At times, I laugh at myself for yielding to Dunya's ridiculous request, and think: I had an evil nightmare about Vlad because I am so distraught over discovering his affair with Zsuzsanna. It is only that, and my mind's exposure to the peasant's upsetting superstitions, and the stress of travel and Arkady's father's death. Men do not metamorphose into wolves. And Zsuzsanna has merely accidentally pricked her neck with a pin, just as she said.

At other times I think: I know what I saw outside Zsuzsanna's window; I was as awake then as now. I remember the hypnotic lure of Vlad's eyes, and the revulsion I felt. I remember the icy touch of his tongue upon my skin.

No pin, no brooch, no dog makes marks like those.

When the doctor came, I thought, *Here is an educated man.* He will explain the marks, explain Zsuzsanna's sudden weakness, reveal my concerns for the absurdities they are. I escorted him up to her bedroom and remained for the examination. He was middle-aged, middle-class, apparently intelligent and rational. But the moment I received him into the house I saw his unease; and when I led him into Zsuzsanna's bedroom and questioned him about the marks on her throat, that unease turned to fear. He gave a prescription as to her diet, and made her drink a draught to bring sleep, but when I questioned him candidly out in the corridor, he remained evasive as to the cause of her malady and would not meet my gaze.

At least he did not cross himself like the servants.

It can do no harm to let Dunya have her way, so long as Arkady does not know. After he had left for the castle and the doctor had paid his visit, Dunya and I set to work. Poor Brutus watched, his ponderous jowls resting on his paws, as we festooned Zsuzsanna's window with wreaths of garlic—the *knoblauch*—while she lay, grey and immobile as a corpse thanks to the doctor's sedative. Barking will not disturb her now.

When we finished our strange task and moved towards the bed where his mistress lay, to fasten the crucifix round her wounded throat, Brutus did not challenge us, but thumped his tail approvingly.

I asked Dunya if she wished to stay at the manor, since it was already so late. She said she could not, that her aged father would be terribly worried, so I had one of the men drive her home. She has promised to stay here to-morrow night to watch, with Brutus, over Zsuzsanna. For some reason, her presence is an enormous comfort to me. After she left, I grew frightened all over again.

But when Arkady returned home, I forgot all about myself, for he was clearly trying to hide his own terrible nervous state. I finally asked him directly what was troubling him. He said it was nothing, that when he was returning home a wolf had come very close to the horses, giving him and them a start, but reassured me lone wolves were cowardly and would not attack without the protection of the pack.

I did not entirely believe him. I think it has to do with Vlad.

At other times, I think: It is only grief. He has lost his father but recently; give him time to recover, do not press.

I cannot tell him: The legends are all true; your uncle is a vampire, and soon your sister will be one unless we kill him . . .

But yesterday evening, I located a massive German-English dictionary in the upstairs library, and sitting in an armchair two centuries my senior, with the great book spread upon my lap, found the words: *Schwur, Bund.*

Covenant.

What unholy alliance is this?

+I+ +I+ +I+

The Diary of Arkady Tsepesh

11 APRIL. A day has passed, and there is still no sign of Jeffries.

I do not sleep much. When I do, I return in my dreams to that moment of breathless panic in the forest and find myself trapped in its all-consuming blackness, doomed to experience forever the sting of pine boughs whipping against my face, the heat of wolves' breath, the snap of hungry jaws amid the screams of horses. I pull at the reins with all my strength—to no avail. The caleche wheels about in an unending circle; the branches continue to slap me; the horses never cease their shrieking, nor the wolves their snarling attack. I know I will never find my way out of the infinite forest.

Never.

In my dreams I see Jeffries, too, caught at the moment he peered out the castle's south window from a dizzying height at the great expanse of forest below. I see the flush of fear on his face, on his pink scalp where the milky-blond hair parts, on his brow as he lightly blots beads of sweat with his monogrammed handkerchief. I see the dread in his eyes . . . and then I see him fall.

Fall through the open, waiting window. I follow through that window, watching safe as a bird aloft while he hurtles downwards, arms and legs flailing, cutting through the cold mountain air with the same sharp whistle as wolves' teeth. He struggles so frantically that in mid-fall, he rolls face upward, and I can see the terror in his wide pale eyes, his contorted features, his mouth, a gaping rictus frozen in a soundless scream.

Down, down, down . . . All the while silent, save for the whistling sound of his struggling limbs, and a faint, distant snarl that comes from somewhere outside the dream.

Such a long way down.

At last he reaches the trees; and here is the joke. His fall is not broken by them, nor interrupted with bruising force and the crash of bough and brush until needle-strewn ground finds him. No; as he reaches the very tips of the tallest trees, their thin pointed branches pierce like sharpened stakes through torso, neck and arms, calves and thigh.

He lies impaled, torn, swaying with the wind that ripples through the treetops, bloody pine branches protruding from his body like the shafts of primitive arrows, a modern Saint Sebastian.

And then he smiles, the muscles in his neck straining around the branch that pierces them, rippling beneath blood, and he gazes up at me with the very same delightedly curious expression he wore when he had looked at my ancestor's portrait, and says:

"Vlad the Impaler. Vlad the Tsepesh. Born December 1431. You're an Impaler, aren't you? One of the wolf-men? Are you quite sure you prefer that to Dracul . . . ?"

I wake, heart pounding to the point of nausea, remembering the bright fear in his eyes as he peered out the south-wing window, and I think: *He was frightened not of heights, but of his fate. He saw it awaiting him there.*

The longer I analyse it, the more I realise I cannot go to the authorities in Bistritz without more evidence. *Non habemos corpum;* we do not have a body, ergo there is no crime. V. will refuse to suspect Laszlo out of blind loyalty, will continue to insist that Jeffries simply chose to disappear, unless there is proof.

And so this morning I cleaned Father's pistol—a shining steel Colt revolver, the most recent innovation in firearms and my final gift to him, sent from England—and put it in the caleche along with a lantern.

I then left for the village. I drove the horses slowly alongside the wood, purposely taking a small detour back towards the castle and returning to the spot where Stefan had last appeared, but his ghost did not reappear.

It was mid-day when I made my way to the village

churchyard, where Masika's son was being buried. I tethered the horses to a post outside the church and from a distance watched the simple peasant ceremony. There was a sad beauty to its spartanness. Six muscular *rumini* bore the pine casket on their shoulders and set it down beside the fresh-dug grave while all the women sang *Bocete* in high, wavering voices. There were no hired mourners, no elegant marble tomb crowded with ancestral shades, no plaques of gold; just villagers and family, a deep hole in the black earth, a marker made of stone which the elements would render illegible within a generation's time. Nor was there any sense of family history; Masika Ivanovna, clad in black from crown to toe, was the young man's sole relative in attendance, the only one to throw herself upon the closed coffin and wail.

After the space of some moments, the small group of women attending her gently pulled her away, so that the burial service might begin. The priest stood behind the small stone marker and recited the Fiftieth Psalm, then the liturgy in a soothing, musical tone; from time to time, the mourners chanted a response. Soon the coffin was lowered into the waiting trench and strewn with handfuls of earth and single wild roses. I thought of the beautiful spray of scarlet roses, exuding sweet perfume from their wounds, as they lay crushed upon the marble floor of Father's tomb.

When it was over, those present gave me wide berth, crossing themselves and performing the peculiar gesture to avert the evil eye—first and middle fingers forming a V and thrust towards me. One of the women who had attended Masika Ivanovna hissed at me as she passed. I was dismayed and confused by this reaction, but relieved when Masika Ivanovna, her round cheeks flushed and glistening with tears, approached and warmly clasped my hands.

We embraced like long-lost relatives. In retrospect it seems odd and inappropriate, but at the time I felt towards her a very strong and tender emotional tie, as strong a one as I might feel towards Uncle or Zsuzsanna.

Still holding my hands in hers, she drew back and gazed with fond wistfulness on my face, as a mother might. "Arkady Petrovich! How good it is of you to come! How grateful I am to set eyes on you one more time!"

She uttered the last sentence with such finality that I replied, "And you shall have many opportunities to set eyes on me again, at the castle."

Her lips pressed together tightly; she shook her head, and in her eyes shone the same grim regret and fear I had seen just before Laszlo's presence interrupted her in Father's office. "No," she said in a low voice. "I will never go back there."

"You are overcome with grief, Masika Ivanovna. In a week, perhaps two, you will feel strong enough to work again. Besides, you are my only true friend there." I released her hands and withdrew from my pocket the large gold crucifix and chain I had recovered the night before from the guest chambers. I pressed it into her palm; she looked down at it with dismay.

"Jeffries would not wear it," I explained, and after a beat added, in a low voice: "He has disappeared."

"Oh, Arkady!" she cried, so caught up in anguish that she addressed me as a familiar. "You still do not understand, do you?" At once she glanced furtively over her shoulder at the women waiting for her a short distance away. Leaning close to me, as though frightened someone might overhear, she whispered, "My own fate no longer matters to me. I have lost the two men I loved most in all the world, and I care not whether I live or die. Yet I fear so for you and your wife and child . . ."

My heart began to beat more swiftly at the thought that anyone might believe Mary in danger. "What is it you fear, Masika? That someone will harm us?" *Laszlo,* I told myself; *she knows he is a murderer.* Yet her next words served only to perplex me.

"Not physically. But there are worse sorts of injury— those inflicted on the soul." She raised her hands to her face and emitted a soft, bitter sob. "Mine has endured enough. I want only to die."

"Masika, you must not say such things—"

She continued as though I had never spoken, reaching forth to touch my cheek and gaze upon me with that gentle maternal fondness. "You are as your father was when he was young, full of goodness and kindness. But it may be too late for you already; too late."

"I do not understand," I answered, but she interrupted in a whisper hoarse and swift, as though afraid I might try to stop her:

"The covenant, Arkady Petrovich; the covenant! Come to me in the day when he sleeps. It is not safe for us to converse here in the open; there are too many ears, too many spies. To-day we cannot speak; my house will be full. But come to me quickly—in a day, two days. We must talk, and . . ." Here her voice dropped so low I could scarcely hear. ". . . there is a letter from my son you must read. He knew his time was near, and so he wrote to you. But for your sake and mine, speak of this to no one. You must swear to keep this secret. Only come—!"

Her urgency was compelling, but I could make no sense of her words. "But why, Masika?"

"Because . . ." she began, then hesitated for the space of some seconds, looking up intently at my face with grief-filled, anxious eyes, as though fearing condemnation. "Because I loved your father. Because it is your brother we bury today."

I recoiled, overcome with shock, unable to reply as she strode away quickly to join the group of waiting women, whose dark forms disappeared swift as low-flying blackbirds over the spring-wakened grass.

I waited for the last of the mourners to disappear, then I stepped forward to the burial-plot, where the gravediggers were beginning to cover the entrenched coffin with shovelfuls of dirt. The unadorned stone marker read:

RADU PETROVICH BULGAKOV
1823–1845

Bulgakov was Masika's surname, but it gave my heart no comfort to see on the marker the Russian patronymic: Petrovich, son of Petru.

I cannot describe how I feel now, or felt then. Stricken. Wounded. Betrayed. Bitterly angry, at Masika, at Father. At this young man, for dying before I met him.

When I came to myself, I asked the older gravedigger: "What did he die of?"

The man stopped shoveling to regard me with polite hostility as he lifted his rumpled cap and wiped his grimy brow with an even dirtier forearm.

"You are Dracul, sir. Surely you know." His tone was perfectly civil, yet conveyed the depth of his hatred for me—and his fear.

"Tsepesh," I corrected him, but there was no reproach, no anger in my tone, only the sincere desire to know. That name evoked a sudden image of Jeffries, lying impaled on tall, swaying branches of pine; I struggled to repress it. "Honestly, I do not. Please . . ." I paused and added, thinking of Laszlo: "Was it murder?"

He stared at me through narrowed, skeptical eyes, trying to judge my sincerity. Something he saw must have convinced him at last, for he replied, as he withdrew his scrutiny and went back to digging:

"Aye, you could say that, sir. His throat was torn out by wolves."

Zsuzsanna Tsepesh's Diary

12 APRIL. I keep dreaming of his eyes, his emerald eyes.

Yesterday, I was certain I would die; to-day I am a little stronger and can sit up and eat the soup Dunya brings. Writing is no longer a terrific effort. Oddly, this disappoints me.

Two women inhabit my body now. One is the Zsuzsanna I have always known: weak, timid, her father's good, obedient girl. That one is so grateful to Mary for all her kindness, to Dunya for caring for me in my illness. I know they love me and want me to get better, and I want to please them by doing so. That one loves sweet Brutus for his devoted presence at my bedside, and is moved to tears when he worriedly gives my hand a cold, wet nudge and gazes up at me with those adoring amber eyes. That one knows she almost died and is terrified at the prospect.

But the other—

Ah, the other. The other knows that she is changing, and embraces that change. The other is strong, passionate, and waits only for him to return, to fulfill his promise to bind us together forever.

I know he is trying to come to me. He has not forgotten. He tried last night, I think; I have the faintest dreamy recollection of Brutus lunging onto the window-seat and barking ferociously. I remember emerging from my drugged stupor enough to sense his disembodied eyes, staring at me out of the deep velvet shadows of my closed eyelids. I tried to speak, and could not; so I *thought* to him instead, and I believe he heard. I told him what they had done to the window. I warned him about the dog.

God, how the other Zsuzsanna hates Mary! hates Dunya! hates that accursed dog, for keeping him from my window. Were I not so weak and unable to rise, I would strangle the life from them for daring to separate us! They feign innocence; they will not speak of him, but they know what they are doing. They know, the sniveling liars! They freed the dog from the kitchen and put the garlic flowers in my window while I was asleep, stealing in here like thieves to do their evil work.

The fools think they can stop him.

Despite my weakness, I sense the approach of a Strength I have never known, the hint of a body free of the infirmity that has plagued me my whole life. I feel my spine moving, un-twisting, lengthening; I sit taller, straighter each day. There is a dull throb in my ankle, and when Dunya and Mary leave the room, I peer at my foot beneath the covers and see that it, too, is straightening. I smile despite the pain. At last, to be free! to be strong! I welcome this other Zsuzsanna; I am changing into something new, something wonderful. I am not sure what that might be; I only know that it is far better than any life I have ever known. At times, the weakness lifts, and I catch an ec-static glimpse of it. To be strong and free and united with *him* —*this* is Paradise.

Let the little cripple die! Let me be rid of her at last!

Father and Arkady were wrong: there *is* an afterlife. Not the simpering, harp-strumming, angel-winged, cloud-sitting eternity envisioned by the Christians, but something dark and deep and fiery, as bold and pure in its impassioned Self-devo-tion as Lucifer Himself!

They will not win. He will instruct me, and when the

time is right, I will summon him. I need only be patient, and wait . . .

+I+   +I+   +I+

The Journal of
Mary Windham Tsepesh

12 APRIL. I am so worried about my husband.

Zsuzsanna is much improved to-day. The doctor's—or Dunya's—ministrations seemed to have worked. She is still extremely weak, but she was sitting up this morning and eating breakfast when I came to see how she was doing.

The easing of my concern about Zsuzsanna has caused my fears about the *strigoi* to lessen—at least, in the cheerful sunlight of day. Then it seems I dreamed the conversation with Dunya, which now seems curiously unreal, like a distant dream. Like the nightmare image of Vlad transforming into a wolf. At times, I can convince myself that that vision was some sort of hallucination prompted by grief, travel, and pregnancy. Only one thing seems unshakably true: that Vlad is a threat to Zsuzsanna, and we must do whatever we can to keep him away.

Yet at night, I dream of Vlad's eyes, and know that it is all true. At night, I find it harder to explain the fact that Zsuzsanna's twisted spine is straightening before our very eyes.

So I will continue to indulge Dunya and let the garlic wreaths remain on the window (at night; we shrewdly removed them in the morning, and a good thing, since Arkady came to visit his sister at noon). They can do no harm (and once the sun

sets, I become convinced they do much good). Most impor-
tantly, I will see that Brutus stays in the bedroom at night.

But it is Arkady I am more worried about at the moment.
I have written about Zsuzsanna first, in hopes I would calm
down, but once again I am near tears. We quarreled to-day, for
the first time.

It was my fault. I was foolish to mention the business
about Vlad and Zsuzsanna so soon. It has only been one brief
week since Petru's death, and Arkady still grieves. It is only
natural. And yet . . .

Yet I cannot escape the fact that, since we came to Transylvania, he has become darkly moody and reclusive. He tells
me little these days, when in England he loved to have long
talks and seek my advice on subjects, because, as he said, "You
are so coolly logical about things, Mary, and I am not." He has
always been emotional, but in a positive, cheerful manner, full
of energy and passion.

Now he is silent, withdrawn, brooding. Every night he
stays up late writing in his journal after he returns from the
castle rather than come to bed to speak to me. I know that he
is unhappy there, that something has happened with Vlad to
trouble him.

When I rise in the morning, he is still asleep, his dark
head against the pillow, his handsome face, with its large eyes,
bold black brows, straight, narrow aquiline nose, growing
faintly paler each day. There are lines and shadows gathering
beneath those eyes; he has aged ten years in a week. I cannot
help thinking how he resembles his sister, and how Vlad
drains the emotional life from them both.

I feel lonely for him. The husband I knew is changing
into a distant, melancholy stranger. I worry this Arkady will
remain even after the grief for his father has lifted.

He rose this morning only shortly before luncheon, and
we shared a meal in near-total silence. He seemed exhausted,
more so emotionally than physically, and though he was absently sweet to me after his old custom, his thoughts were

clearly elsewhere. Something troubled him, and so I was reluctant to disturb him, but as the meal ended, I dared at last to speak. The fact could no longer be hidden that Zsuzsanna was seriously ill; he would discover it sooner or later (even if he was currently too preoccupied to question why she no longer presented herself at meals). As her brother, he had the right to know.

"Dear," I said, at the great dining-table that had once seen a large family and now seemed sadly vast with only us two, "please don't be alarmed, but you should know that Zsuzsanna's condition worsened and she has been seriously ill. We fetched the doctor from Bistritz last evening."

He had begun to rise. At this news, he paused in the middle of the movement and lingered there, frowning with the enormous effort of bringing his attention from the infinitely distant point it had been to the present, and the words I had just spoken. For some seconds his hazel eyes remained clouded, then cleared as at last he registered and understood my remarks. The line between his eyebrows deepened, lengthened.

"Zsuzsanna ill?"

"Yes," I allowed, careful to keep my tone bright and optimistic. "But to-day she is much better."

His gaze swept uncertainly over me, the table, the dining-hall, the small pane of sunlight filtering through the distant window. "Oh," he said. "Well, I'm glad she's better. Perhaps I should go see her."

"I think she would appreciate that." I favoured him with a small encouraging smile—conniving woman that I am, smug in the knowledge that the garlic wreaths had been carefully removed and hidden in the closet. "Let me go with you." And I rose and wound my arm around his before he could stand. I wanted to make certain that Zsuzsanna said nothing to upset him; I suppose I feared she had noticed the garlic and would say something, or that she would tearfully confess to Arkady about Vlad. I wanted any shocking news broken to him gently.

We went into Zsuzsanna's room, where she sat in bed,

once again writing in a journal and once again hurrying to shut it before we could read. The sunlight streamed in through the open shutters, illuminating the alcove where I had seen Vlad and Zsuzsanna embrace, and the sash had been thrown up to let in the pleasant, unseasonably warm air. The room seemed cheerful and pleasant, as if the bright sun had burned away the evil. Even Brutus seemed relieved, and greeted us with a peripatetic tail and a great, tongue-lolling grin. I detected a faint smell of garlic with sheepish discomfort, but Arkady seemed quite oblivious of it.

Fortunately, Zsuzsanna revealed nothing, and was sweet and considerate of her brother, reassuring him that he should not spend an instant worrying over her. The crucifix Dunya had fastened round her neck had slipped beneath her gown, and she did not mention it to Arkady.

It all went quite well—until afterwards, when we left Zsuzsanna's room together and headed down the great winding staircase, Arkady taking the inside so that I might lean heavily upon the polished wood railing.

Sotto voce, as if afraid his sister or the servants might overhear, he asked, "What did the doctor say is the matter? She seems so pale."

"Some type of anaemia, perhaps," I answered, my own voice almost a whisper. My heartbeat quickened as I struggled to find the proper words to gently approach the subject I had wanted so long to discuss with my husband. "But I fear there is an emotional component to her condition."

In lieu of asking, he fixed his wide gaze upon me and held it there until I continued, most tentatively:

"I think . . . I believe it has to do with your uncle, Vlad."

"How so?" he asked. His tone seemed neutral enough to encourage me to proceed, but in retrospect, I feel I should have caught its subtle defensiveness.

"She is distraught about the thought of Vlad going to England," I said, and despite my resolve, coloured.

The line between his eyebrows appeared again—a warning of what was to come. "But that does not make sense," he said, still in a hushed tone, mindful of the servants. "He explained very clearly to her that we would not go without her—that we would wait until she is well. Is she upset about leaving home?"

"Not exactly . . ." I hesitated, not at all certain now that the discussion should be continued. But Arkady was determined to learn the problem. A hint of impatience crept into his tone.

"Well, then, what is it?"

"It is . . . I think she is still afraid he might leave her behind." I could feel heat on my cheeks and neck, but his own impatience wakened mine, and I felt I had kept the truth to myself long enough, that it was better to say it and be done with it. "She is . . . Vlad is . . . Arkady, they are in love."

He drew back as though I had slapped him and froze two steps from the landing. His lips parted, and he stared at me with wide-eyed shock. When finally he was able to speak, his voice was so soft I could scarcely hear: "Wh-what? What do you mean?"

"I have seen him in her bedroom late at night. Twice. I think her guilt over the affair is at least partially responsible for her inexplicable illness."

Having unburdened myself of the truth, I felt suddenly weak, ill. My own cheeks burned, but it was on his that I saw sudden bright blotches of colour.

Purely dazed, he turned from me towards the stone wall and whispered, "That is impossible. Impossible."

I moved awkwardly down the last two steps and turned to stare up at him. "It breaks my heart to tell you this. You know I would not say such horrible things unless I was convinced they were true. But for Zsuzsanna's sake, I—"

As I spoke, he raised his hand to his temple in a sudden spasm of pain that made me reach towards him in concern. He recovered abruptly, and whirled on me in a sudden blaze of fury, leaning forward and teetering on the edge of the step so that I feared he would lose his balance and fall. "How dare you?" he shouted. "You are no better than the peasants, who spread vicious lies about Uncle! He has done you naught but good, given you this house and all this wealth—and you have turned on him! You are an ingrate, Mrs. Tsepesh, and he is a saint! A saint!"

"Do not raise your voice to me, Mister Tsepesh," I said, with a bit of heat myself. "I am no ingrate, nor he a saint." His words stung—and perplexed me, for I would have thought him more concerned about his sister's honour than his uncle's.

As I spoke, he stormed down the stairs, past me, waving his hand for silence and shaking his head as I tried to protest, to counter his anger.

"I have heard enough! I will listen to no more lies!" And he swept away on a tide of fury. I listened to his receding footsteps, muffled at first by carpet, then ringing loud against cold heartless stone. Had he reacted like the Arkady I had always known, I would have followed him and been certain a swift apology and reconciliation would follow—but this was someone whose behaviour I could no longer predict. I gave him his privacy until such time as he had control of his temper.

He closed himself in one of the studies and did not come out for an hour or so, when he left the manor without speaking to anyone, and took the caleche far earlier than is his custom— I suppose to go to the castle. I have no idea whether he plans to speak to Vlad about what I have said.

I regret bringing up the subject; clearly Arkady's grief is still too fresh, too raw. How can I ever speak to him, then, of what I have seen outside my window—of the wildly fantastic truth that I saw Vlad become a wolf? Of the marks on Zsuzsanna's neck, and the fact that I am half-convinced that he is *strigoi*, convinced enough to permit the crucifix and the garlic?

I am afraid. Afraid of Vlad, afraid for Zsuzsanna. Afraid for my soon-to-be-born child.

Mostly I am afraid because ever since we arrived, my husband has been slowly changing into someone I do not know. I am changing, too, from a sensible woman into a quivering, superstitious soul—especially when Dunya speaks of Zsuzsanna's slow metamorphosis into one of the *strigoi*.

Vlad became a wolf. What shall remain of Arkady and me, when our transformations are complete?

+I+ +I+ +I+

Zsuzsanna Tsepesh's Diary

13 APRIL. He knocked at the window again last night. He knocked, and I was prepared for him. I had taken the crucifix from my neck and cleared away the garlic, hiding it in the closet the way Mary and Dunya do each morning—they think they are so clever! And I had unlatched the shutters, and thrown the sash open—but it was not enough. When he came, Brutus started barking again wildly, lunging at the window as though he intended to leap through it. Nothing I could do or say would restrain him. I had to close the sash and shutters and return to bed, for fear his insane barking would wake the entire household.

I tried taking Brutus to the kitchen, and discovered Dunya there, asleep on the floor. She stirred as we entered, and I hurried back to my room with the dog.

I am stronger, but I have stopped changing. I do not like this. I do not like waiting. Something must be done.

+I+ +I+ +I+

The Diary of Arkady Tsepesh

14 APRIL. At last, I am strong enough to sit up and write. I recall nothing of yesterday save Mary's delicate features, framed by golden curls that hung down and brushed my cheeks when she leaned her face over mine. Her face, and her soft, cool touch on my brow, and her murmured words of comfort; that is all I remember. She is so good to me, so kind. I have tried several times to beg her forgiveness for raising my voice to her earlier, but she merely touches her fingertips to my lips and smiles.

Dear God, I wish I could forget the events of twelfth April, but they shall haunt me for the remainder of my life. Where will it lead? Where will it all lead? But no; I must not consider the future now. See? My hand begins to shake. No, I must simply write it down, and from the act hope to gain insight as to what I must do.

The day before yesterday, on the fateful twelfth, I learned that my sister was ill, suffering from anaemia. This was distressing enough news, but after I went to visit Z., Mary revealed that she had seen Vlad in Zsuzsa's bedroom late at night, and that the two had embraced.

I am ashamed to write that I shouted at my poor wife. I could not believe anything so horrible of my sister, of V., the generous benefactor of us all. At the same time, I knew Mary was incapable of lying, that it had to be true, yet at that moment I felt once again the grip of impending madness, and descended into mindless rage. I strode into the study and closed myself in, thinking to write it all down and lift the anger, but I was far too agitated. I left the house and took the caleche, unsure of my destination.

It was a warm spring day. Dawn had been clear, but early afternoon saw iron clouds filling the sky, and the air had the feel and smell of an approaching storm. Some inexplicable compulsion drove me towards the edge of the forest where I had last seen Stefan. As I urged the horses between the trees, a gentle rain began to fall, but the thick foliage protected us. Even so, we grew wet as the sweeping branches sprinkled us with dew.

The animals tossed their heads and whinnied their disapproval of my foolish decision to re-enter the forest. I told myself that I was not afraid, though my mouth was suddenly so parched my tongue adhered to the inside of my cheek, and I held the reins taut in slightly trembling hands. Not afraid, though I could not keep from peering up at the tops of the tallest trees, to see whether Jeffries lay swaying there with the wind.

It was day and it was warm. Wolves did not attack in daytime in warm weather, nor singly, but in packs, and then usually only on winter nights. That was the prevailing folk wisdom, yet Stefan had died on a beautiful, glistening summer's day, killed by a solitary half-wolf. I remembered Father's revolver, beside me on the seat where I had stowed it for just such an occasion. I set it on my lap.

There was no sign of Stefan. I drove the horses forward a bit, slowly, straining my eyes in the shadowy dimness for my dead brother's small form. We retraced the progress I remembered, finally coming to a stop at the place I decided was the one where the wolves had attacked.

The horses lifted their hooves and snorted, impatient, nervous. I held very still, watching the same spot in the shade of an alder tree where I believed Stefan had last been. Watching, and listening, to a distant rustling in the trees—most likely of birds and squirrels. A crow cawed, reproachful; a bird sang.

I sat watching several minutes, aware of every sound around me, of the muted patter of rain against trees, of my own breathing. At last, slowly, slowly, out of the reticulate pattern of light and sepia shadow against trembling leaves, Stefan emerged.

And gestured onward, at the deep recesses of the forest.

We followed, the wheels rolling against the damp, needle-strewn ground with the snap of breaking twigs.

Once again, my brother's spectre vanished, only to reappear once I progressed a fair distance in the direction indicated. We continued a good half hour into the forest in this manner.

At last, Stefan appeared but gestured no more; only stared intently at me a time, as might a living loved one trying to memorise the details of my face upon parting.

And then he disappeared.

Confused, I looked round, and saw nothing but the same alder and pine trees. I waited some minutes, then slipped the pistol into the waist of my trousers and crawled out of the caleche. I tethered the horses to a branch, then commenced investigating the area. There was nothing remarkable, just the same dense foliage as before, and dark soil almost entirely covered by a carpet of dead leaves and pine needles.

But when I walked over to the large tree where Stefan's ghost had stood, the ground abruptly sank, soft and spongy, beneath my feet. I pushed away the damp, vegetal detritus and discovered fresh dug earth, darker and more loosely packed compared to the surrounding soil.

My heart began to beat more swiftly. Quickly, I swept more of the dead foliage aside. As I did, I discovered something hard and white—a fragment of bone, from an animal, I thought. But before I could examine it, the horses emitted high-pitched, panicked whinnies.

I looked up to see a wolf, running swift and low between the trees, headed not towards the caleche and the captive horses, but towards me.

I straightened and in a split second's time entertained the grisly notion that Stefan had enticed me here to suffer the same fate as my two brothers; I imagined my bright blood merged with the gentle rain and bejeweling the forest with crimson dew.

The wolf lunged. I drew the pistol from beneath my coat and fired. Not four feet away, the animal emitted a shrill, canine yelp and dropped in mid-leap, at the highest point of the arc, bloodied at the juncture of leg and shoulder.

Yet it gathered itself and rose, unsteady, limping on three legs, and came at me. I was forced to shoot again; this time, the proximity permitted me to make a clean kill, and lodge a bullet just above and between its stark white eyes. The creature sank to the forest floor with a whine that terminated in a death-rattle.

I wanted nothing better than to sag weakly against the nearest tree trunk and master my trembling—but the ominous recollection of the two dead wolves lying at the open gate of our family tomb persuaded me to remain with pistol at the ready.

There came a crashing of twigs and leaves; the second wolf appeared bare seconds afterwards. I forced myself to wait until he was near enough for my aim to be certain, and when at last I prepared to fire, I had to steady my shaking right arm with my left. The wolf charged, and I squeezed the trigger, but the sparse rain that dripped down through the forest canopy left the weapon beaded with moisture; it slipped in my grasp as it discharged, sending the bullet wide of its mark.

In the fraction of a second it took to realise I had missed my target, I knew all was lost. The wolf leapt for my throat. Its body collided with mine, knocking the pistol from my hand. Huge paws struck my shoulders, slamming them against damp ground. I steeled myself for the pain of those cruel teeth upon my neck, thinking not of the irony of my fate, nor the treachery of my brother's ghost, but only of Mary and the child.

The wolf lowered its face to mine and peered at me with large, colourless, feral eyes; its panting mouth revealed a long pink tongue and yellowed fangs glistening with saliva. It snarled, and opened its mouth wide in preparation for the kill. I felt its breath, hot upon the exposed, tender skin of my throat. Gasping, I squeezed my eyes shut and braced for death.

And then the impossible occurred.

I sensed movement beyond my closed eyes, but it was not accompanied by the pain of my throat being flayed asunder. The heat on my neck was replaced by the cool damp of the forest; the pressure of paws against my shoulders disappeared.

I opened my eyes and saw that the wolf had withdrawn. He now sat on his haunches at my feet like an obedient, panting dog, tongue lolling out the side of his deadly mouth.

I pushed myself to a half-sitting position. The wolf snarled and snapped, and moved to charge again—but reluctantly held himself back at the last instant, as though an invisible, unwanted barrier held him in check.

I wasted no time questioning the reason for this remarkable phenomenon. I found the revolver nearby on the ground and moved slowly, stealthily towards it as the wolf growled his displeasure, but remained otherwise still. At last, I reached swiftly for the gun and fired it point-blank at the creature, who remained so unresisting that I felt a stab of pity. It died with a soft whine as its head sank onto its forelegs.

Afterwards, there was only silence—not even the scurrying of a squirrel, or the singing of a bird, only the soft, steady drum of rain upon foliage. The third wolf never appeared. When my trembling eased, I determined with footsteps the limits of the sinking soil. It was much smaller than I expected, perhaps only three square feet—far too small for a body. With dark mirth that verged on hysteria, I began to laugh: perhaps the tales of the *moroi* were true. Perhaps my brother had led me to a buried cache of jewels or golden coins.

Obsessed, I began to dig with nothing more than my hands.

It was sweaty work. The soil was heavy with moisture, and after an hour, perhaps two, I was soaked, covered with mud, aching. The rain was coming down hard. I was on the verge of giving up when my chilled fingers finally struck something soft and yielding beneath the inch of muddy water.

It felt like a thick layer of fabric. I frantically cleared away enough mud to determine the dimensions of the hidden prize: it was a square roughly twelve inches on each side, and when I dug deep enough to get my fingers beneath it, I could feel that it was apparently a perfectly square box of some very hard material, either metal or wood, beneath the cloth.

I knelt on the wet, yielding ground and leaned forward, wriggling first fingers, then hands, beneath the box. It took several moments before I could get a good enough grip and enough momentum to pull it from the wet earth, but at last I gave a mighty yank and it came forth with a loud sucking sound.

I fell back onto my haunches and studied my treasure: it had been wrapped in several layers of fine black silk, now soaked and filthy, but too new and in too good shape to have been more than a day in the earth. Eagerly, I unwrapped it, and discovered beneath a simple, unvarnished wooden box fashioned from the native pine, with a crude brass latch.

I set the box on the ground and unfastened the latch, cutting my thumb on its sharp, unpolished edge, but in my fearful excitement, I did not care. I flung back the latch, slipped my fingertips under the top, and attempted to pry the box open. It took a great deal of effort, as the wood was swollen from the moisture, but at last it came, and I threw back the top.

And screamed when I stared into Jeffries' wide, death-clouded eyes.

I sprang to my feet; the box fell from my hands. Jeffries' head rolled out across the soggy foliage with a damp crackling sound and came to rest face up on the very edge of the gaping grave. As it rolled, something fell from the open mouth, which was frozen in the same anguished rictus it had worn in my dream. I reached for the white object on the dark glistening ground, and picked up a head of garlic.

His neck had been sawed through in the same manner as father's, and his mouth crammed full of the pungent herb. His skin was whiter than I thought it possible for any human's to have been; it was precisely the colour of chalk, even paler than the tufts of tousled hair that stuck out wildly in all directions from his scalp.

Thunder rumbled as I stared, aghast, down at the severed head. An abrupt cloudburst beat down through the sheltering trees, spilling a violent cascade on me and my unfortunate erstwhile guest, washing mud from my trouser legs and sleeves. The rain pounded down on Jeffries' open, unseeing eyes, glued his hair to his scalp, swept away twigs and soil and the solitary alder leaf that had clung to his marble-white cheek.

For an instant I thought I would vomit; but what erupted from the depths of my terrified being was entirely unexpected.

I began to laugh.

Low at first, then rising higher in pitch until the sound became hysterical. I threw back my head and laughed harder, weeping, letting the rain mingle with my tears, letting it drum against my open eyes as it did Jeffries' sightless ones, letting it fill my grinning rictus of a mouth until I bent forward, gagging, still convulsed by hellish glee.

For I realised: Stefan had first appeared *before* Jeffries' death. Jeffries was merely coincidental, an afterthought.

There was more treasure to be found.

And I found it, little brother. Oh, I found it.

I spread my arms wide, embracing the rain, whirling in circles like a child seeing how much he could bear before becoming dizzy. I danced, crashing through the brush, unmindful of wolves, uncaring, pressing my feet into the loamy, carpeted soil, pausing when it yielded to dig in the mud like a dog hellbent on retrieving a bone.

I found bones, a graveyard full of them—and all of them skulls. Big skulls, and little ones, too. The infants were buried without any amenities; I found their heads in a mass grave. Many of the tiny skulls were irregularly shaped, and hinted at gross deformity. One child had half an extra head emerging from his cranium, as though he had endeavoured and failed to give birth to Athena.

I stopped opening the boxes after the second one—which contained the head of a man several months' decayed and slippery with moss—though I continued my mad excavation, collecting the small boxes like so many trophies. But after some two dozen—in addition to too many infants' skulls to count—I found my maniacal energy exhausted, though the ground still gave way in several places immediately surrounding me.

And how many more graveyards like this lay hidden in the endless forest?

Too many places for one man to dig. For one man to bear.

But where had the bodies gone, the larger ones of the adults, and the little twisted ones of the poor, discarded children?

Ah, Stefan, I think I learned the answer to that, too.

There were bone fragments mingled with the thatch of twigs, leaves, and pine needles carpeting the forest floor. Upon sifting through the loam carefully, I became convinced that the bodies had been left for the wolves. The fragments were all that remained after the animals had cracked the largest bones into pieces between their powerful jaws, to get at the tasty marrow.

Who can say how long I remained there, scrabbling madly in the mud? How could any human being be expected to account for the passage of time in the face of such horror?

I know only this: that when at last I collapsed, trembling, spent, unable to move another handful of heavy soaked earth, I fell back onto the ground and looked up between the branches at a tiny crevice of reddening sky, and knew the clouds had cleared, and the sun was setting.

I am uncertain what happened then; a comforting madness had entirely overtaken me, and reduced my mind to a *tabula rasa,* incapable of remembering the past, incapable of retaining the present. I do not remember if I replaced the heads and bones I discovered (I pray I did, to protect poor Jeffries and his fellow victims from any further post-mortem indignity), but I apparently managed to crawl into the caleche and drive home.

By the time I returned home, disheveled, damp, and muddy, I was in a delirium. Mary says I have been ill two days with a fever, one so dangerously high that the night of the twelfth they feared I would not live. She seems to know something terrible has happened; she is kind and loving, and does not press.

How can I ever tell her? Gods, I cannot bear to think of her living so close to such danger . . . ! I am responsible for bringing her to this chamber of horrors, and if anything happens to her or the child—

I can write no more of this, for writing makes me remember, and think, and when I begin to remember, when I begin to think, the insanity threatens again . . .

7

The Journal of
Mary Windham Tsepesh

14 APRIL. For two days, Arkady has been so terribly ill that I
have been afraid to leave his side even to write in my journal.

His daily custom is to rise late, take lunch, then read,
write, or walk until just before sundown, when he heads for
the castle. He usually does not return until after I am asleep.

But the day before yesterday, he came home shortly after
sunset. The old gardener, Ion, saw him coming. Something
about the way Arkady erratically drove the horses, he said,
alerted him, and he rushed into the house, calling: *"Doamna!
Doamna!"*

I was reading in one of the sitting rooms, but the strident
tone in the old man's voice bade me drop the book and rush
towards the foyer. Somehow, my heart knew something terrible had happened to my husband.

I arrived in time to see Ion holding open the massive
front door as Arkady staggered in, his hair and clothes disheveled, soggy, smeared with mud. His eyes were bright and wild,
his features contorted as though in pain—but he was laughing.
Laughing, such an evil sound that it froze my heart.

I lifted a hand to my throat, to the small gold cross hidden beneath the fabric of my dress, and said, almost too softly to be heard above his hysterical laughter, "Arkady."

He glanced up, startled. His eyes focused on me, and his mirth abruptly became terror, which grew until he could bear it no longer, but sank to his knees and covered his face with his hands. Beneath them, he released a long, low groan, then muttered, "The skulls! All the little skulls!"

I stepped up beside him as he knelt, and pressed a hand to his forehead; it was so hot that I glanced up at once at Ion and ordered, "Send at once for the doctor." He seemed to understand the word *doktor* well enough, for he nodded and hurried off towards the servants' quarters.

Just then, Arkady threw his arms around my legs, pressed his face to my belly, and wept, "His head! His head! Stefan was right! There was treasure in the forest!"

Dunya and another of the chamber-maids, Ilona, appeared, and the three of us managed to get Arkady to bed. That night his fever rose and the delirium worsened so that it was all Dunya and I could do to keep him from throwing himself from the bed. He shouted horrible, frightening things about bones and skulls and Mister Jeffries and Stefan, his brother, who had died in childhood—and wolves.

At the worst point that first night, he jerked bolt upright in the bed and stared at me with eyes so wide the irises were edged all round with white, and panting, exclaimed: "My God! I wrote the letter that brought him here! Father and I both—!" And he let out an anguished howl that could be heard all through the house.

I thought that night that he would die. But through the goodness of God, he lived, and by the next day he was a little better, though still lapsing into occasional mild delirium. Dunya insisted we take turns watching, though she let me sleep through most of my shift. The sweet girl is concerned about me. I feel dreadfully tired all the time, and the child drops lower each day.

To-day Arkady is better. The fever has broken, and his eyes are the clear, gentle ones I have always known.

Zsuzsanna has improved much, too. She was able to walk to the sitting room to-day, but we were reluctant to break the news of Arkady's illness, so the servants and I have entered into a conspiracy of silence. She is sweet as ever, but distantly dreamy, and at times I detect smug condescension in her smile. I cannot help thinking her recovery is more Dunya's doing than the doctor's, and so we faithfully garland the window with pungent wreaths each night, then closet them away in the daytime.

But something heartbreaking happened this noon, and I do not think we will be able to hide this truth from Zsuzsanna very long. The day was temperate and sunny, and while Arkady was peacefully napping, I went out into the little landscaped garden by the east wing, which captures the morning sunlight. I was sitting on the cast-iron loveseat there with my eyes closed, dozing in the delicious warmth of the sun when I heard footsteps nearby. I glanced up to see the gardener, Ion, carrying big brown Brutus like a pup in his arms. I smiled at first at the tender sight—until the poor dog's head lolled back with lifeless abandon, and I saw the blood on his throat and flank where he had been cruelly mauled.

I burst immediately into sobs, and cried out, "What happened?"

Ion stopped, gazed sadly down at the animal in his arms, and shook his head; whether to indicate regret at the sweet animal's passing or his own ignorance of German, I do not know.

Weeping, I pointed to myself, and said, "I will tell Zsuzsanna." And I lifted my finger to my lips in a signal for silence, hoping that he would understand not to speak of it to her or anyone else until I had done so.

He looked back up at me and nodded, seeming to understand, then slowly trudged onward, apparently intending to lay the animal to rest.

I hope he buried him somewhere near a garden or trees, where there is plenty of sunlight and growing things and small animals to chase.

I went inside and shared the sad news with Dunya. She listened solemnly, her lips pressed tightly together and her eyes downcast with sorrow. Though I said absolutely nothing of my suspicions as to the cause of poor Brutus' death, her first words were an offer to sleep in Zsuzsanna's room to-night.

I agreed at once.

Superstitious and silly it may be, but I have witnessed events which logic says are impossible, and I have a husband driven mad by some private terror. I know why that poor dog died; I have seen the reason grinning outside my bedroom window at night.

I only pray that Dunya, endowed with the same good, loyal heart but a far shrewder brain, can avoid the same fate.

✦ ✦ ✦

Zsuzsanna Tsepesh's Diary

15 APRIL, 2 A.M. It is done. I am his.

My back and leg and foot ache terribly, but I know now it is a good pain—like birth pangs, temporary and leading to a outcome so wondrous all suffering will soon be forgotten. Despite the pain, my entire body vibrates, *sings* with incredible, newfound strength; such strength, such *aliveness* that I cannot sleep, cannot return to bed, but leaned naked and bloody out the open windowsill after he left, stretching out my arms at the waning moon and inviting it to dance with me, laughing up at the stars.

Laughing at Dunya, pitiful witless creature. She lies snoring (just as Brutus did) on the floor beside the bed in deep, deep slumber. Look at her there, with her gaping ugly mouth, her stinking crucifix! She will not wake until morning, no matter how hard I laugh, no matter how loudly I taunt, singing into her ear: *Silly Dunya, silly Dunya! My ineffectual little watchdog!*

I know nothing can rouse her. I know everything *he* knows now.

I know *everything.*

Once a miserable cripple, unloved, unwanted, I am now stronger and more beautiful than you all! Immortal, because he loves me. I had no inkling of the depth of that love until to-night; I am still awed, moved, amazed to the point of uncontrollable trembling.

Oh, how I love him!

They told me about Brutus this evening—Mary and her little shadow, Dunya. A part of me, a very small part now, wept. I had to; they were watching. They expected me to be crushed and heartbroken. I obliged.

But I was so relieved. Relieved and happy, for I knew it meant he was coming that night, to-night, and I knew what I had to do. And even when Mary told me that Dunya would be spending the night in my room, "to look after me in case I was upset," I wasn't worried. I knew to trust him. (Better Dunya than Mary; for now that I know everything, I also know it is easier to influence some more than others. Mary is one of the hardest—even more so than jealously devoted Brutus was—and there is always the danger she might sway Arkady, who is already difficult enough to deal with because of the headstrong streak he inherited from Mother. But Dunya is superstitious, and like most of the local folk, readily affected, especially when asleep.)

And so as we settled down to bed to-night, I waited, heart beating rapidly with excitement, until I sensed the approach of those beautiful eyes, jewel-like, evergreen, immortal.

When Dunya fell to snoring beneath her blanket on the carpet, I knew it was time. I stole quietly from the bed, gathered up the woven heads of garlic around the window and hid them in the closet, grimacing at their repugnant smell and crinkly, papery feel.

And then I leaned over the window-seat to fling back the shutters and raise the sash; in poured the argent, energizing light of moon and stars. I stood in the center of that magnificent lustrous pool and watched as shimmering atoms of light began to swirl with rainbow colours, the way sun reflects off a soap bubble. Then the specks themselves began to vibrate, to move, to encompass me, circling faster, faster, until my overwhelmed eyes could no longer focus; and out of that prismatic diamond dance, Vlad slowly appeared—faint and ill-formed at first, like a daydream, then gradually more solid, until at last he stood, his fine skin no longer so pale, but still catching the light with fleeting iridescent glimmers of quicksilver, pink and turquoise, like mother-of-pearl, like the fieriest opal. He was younger; yes, younger, with hints of iron at each temple, making his resemblance to Father, to Arkady, all the stronger. I reached for his crystalline-cold hands, and was pulled towards him.

We kissed as relatives do—solemnly, on each cheek, hands primly clasped; and then he encircled my waist with his arms and slowly, gently, unloosed my nightgown and drew it down to my waist. I shook free of it and kicked it aside. He pressed me to him, with that strong hand firm against my bare, almost-straight back, and kissed my lips in a manner that was far from familial, with tongue and teeth and heat.

Near-faint with anticipation, I leaned away from that embrace, presenting myself to him: my head and shoulders fell back, causing my long, loose dark hair to hang mere inches above the floor; my pale torso, silvered by starlight, curved away from him like the crescent moon.

He arched his own body like a scimitar forward, against mine, and kissed me again, drawing his lips—no longer so cold—once again over my mouth, my chin, the curve of my jaw until they found my exposed, proffered neck, and the tiny, elegant wounds just above the collarbone. His tongue circled them, delicately, and I shuddered at the sensation of exquisite, feverish tenderness there. His mouth opened wide; his lips pressed against my skin; his tongue began working rapidly, eagerly over the wounds. I felt the ever-so-gentle pressure of razor-keen teeth resting against the centre of each partially healed incision—waiting to strike like a serpent, to sink deep into my flesh again.

I trembled, waiting.

He lifted his head, and whispered into my ear: "No. You are still too weak. Let me be the first to-night . . ."

To my bitter disappointment, he recoiled, as swiftly as he had struck out the time before, and released me from the embrace. I cried out softly in despair, but fell silent when I saw his hands flash phosphorescent-pale against his black cloak. It dropped to the floor, and he worked swiftly to unfasten his vest, then his shirt. He did not remove them, but let them hang undone, and reached forth with one hand to pull the fabric back, revealing a broad, powerful chest that looked hewn from marble, as muscular and unyielding firm as a young Roman god's. His other hand he raised, and drew a long, pointed nail as sharp as knife-edged steel across his heart, riving asunder his beautiful flesh and leaving a red, diagonal slash in its wake.

And then he reached deep within that wound; his gaze held mine as he found the vein and scored it. I saw the faint, transient flicker of pain in his eyes, but it was far, far overwhelmed by a growing excitement. My gaze dropped to the red ribbon on his chest, and the rich, crimson fluid welling there. I stared at it, compelled, astounded, worshipful.

He wove his fingers into the hair at the nape of my neck and grasped it, tenderly, tightly, then pressed me to him.

I drank.

I drank like a newborn babe; I drank like a lover. As icy

as his touch had been that first night, as cool as his skin, so much hotter now was that blood—hotter than any living creature's. It scalded my lips and tongue and throat, made tears course down my cheeks into my mouth, mingling brine with iron.

The taste! The dark, dark taste . . . !

I worked noisily, greedily, lapping with animal abandon; I threw my arms around him and pulled him closer to me, with a surge of strength that made him laugh, low and confident, but also with the faint surprise of one seduced, one overwhelmed to the point of sudden startling weakness. I smiled even as I feasted, hearing in that laughter a hint of the sweet, languid pleasure I had known when he drank from me. My abrupt embrace threatened his balance, and he was forced to steady himself against me, flattening his palms against my back, gradually pressing his fingers more tightly against me until, at the end, he dug them deeply into my flesh lest he fall.

As I drank, I learned. With his blood came the knowledge and perspective of centuries; I could see it all now, see why he had to leave for England. The world is changing with geometrically increasing rapidity. Our land is remote, and has been spared for four hundred years, but civilisation is nearing at last. The world and its governments encroach; he witnessed the establishment of Austrian rule with trepidation, for it marked the beginning of the end of his reign.

He has fended off their control, but eventually, they will attempt to intervene; and when they do, Transylvania will be too small. It will become difficult, if not impossible, to prevent outsiders from questioning the disappearance of stray travelers —travelers who have been all too few of late, but who bear useful news of that changing world. And with each successive generation, the villagers become fewer and more difficult to control.

The Carpathians grow less safe, less sustaining, each day. And so, with the patient, cunning foresight of an ancient predator, he had sent my brother to London, to be educated in the ways of that great city, that his own transition there might be eased.

I understood now, with dazzling clarity; and I wept, too, to know that he had loved me enough to provide the miracle through which I might accompany him to safety. To England.

Oh, more than that, it was far more than that. He has remained alone since his wife died, almost four centuries before. But now, of all women, he has chosen *me,* and as I drank, emotion flowed out from him and engulfed me like that dark red tide, and borne upon it was the knowledge that, with our exchange, he was tied to me and I to him, forever.

He had chosen me as bride because *I* had chosen *him.* I had drawn him to me, and he had seen that my loneliness was a need, a hunger, even greater than his own.

He had chosen me because I alone loved him freely—no, it is a word beyond love. I *revered* him in the manner he deserves.

I drank, and tasted his passion, and his unbending will; his hatred of the *rumini,* and his pain when they revile him as a monster.

He is no monster, no devil. He is a saint, an angel from Heaven!

No—more than that. He is a god.

I drank, and wept with sorrow for countless loved ones dead and buried, the ache of knowing that each fresh young face, each new love, would be seen to wither in turn and die. I saw the procession of a hundred faces in seconds, all of them different, all of them the same, like Arkady and Father, all of them minor variations of Vlad's own handsome visage. Again, and again and again that love, that loss, that fresh grief, creating a loneliness eternal and more horrible than the one I had tasted in my brief mortal life.

I drank, and knew we two would never be alone again.

He stirred at last, and groaned; his hands moved weakly over my back, trying feebly to push me away. With the desperate instincts of a starving animal, I pressed my face harder against his breast and furiously lapped the spurting blood, fever-hot against his cool skin.

"Zsuzsanna," he groaned. It was a prayer, a plea; I felt his incredible might ebbing. Ebbing, and in *my* possession. I sensed a power more than human coursing through my veins, and knew that, had I wanted, I could have snapped his spine like a twig.

He trusted me that much. He had held me in his arms with that much strength, and never harmed me.

I pulled back and straightened, hair falling forward, running my tongue over my lips, and caught the blood that dripped from my chin with cupped hands. I licked my palms clean like a cat, and when at last I looked up, satiated, serene, omnipotent, his eyes were ablaze with wild sensuality that verged on madness.

He seized me. Oh, he was weak and I the stronger, but I fell back and let myself be taken so my ecstasy might be complete. I swept my hair back, bared my neck for him; I held perfectly still as those sharp, sharp teeth found their two small marks, and when they pierced me again, I did not cry out, did not struggle, but released a long, low sigh.

He did not drink long this time. He left me on my feet, swaying, drunken with pleasure, and when he withdrew I clasped his hands and knelt before him, begging him to finish what he had begun. I did not want to remain behind here any longer!

But he was firm. He pushed my hands aside; he bade me stay. He is my lord now, and I will do as he bids, but I wept when he faded into the deep shadows, and I ran to the open window calling softly after him.

When the cool night air touched my skin, I was drunk again, drunk with blood and ecstasy and power.

My senses are heightened, keener. The starlight is dazzling, blindingly beautiful, and the forest sings with life; I can hear each single insect chirping, hear each solitary animal rustling in the trees, hear the distant, beautiful harmonies of wolves. The taste of his blood still in my mouth seems velvety, deeper, more heady and flavourful than any wine. I can still inhale its scent, borne on the soft breeze: bitter, sharp, metallic, but rich and full and intoxicating. From time to time, I touch a fingertip to one of the dark drops on my pearly breast, and lift it to my lips, to smell, to kiss, to savour.

I am so *strong*. I could kill Dunya as she sleeps, snap her neck with one swift twist of my hand.

But I will not. Not to-night. I will play the game just a bit longer, because it is what he wants. I will quietly fill the basin with water from the pitcher, and wash away the blood smeared on my hands and face, and the drops spattered upon my bosom. I will replace the garlic at the window, then slip into my nightgown and into bed.

Though not just yet, not yet. Dawn is still hours away, and the smell and taste of his blood against my skin is so sweet . . .

⚜ ⚜ ⚜

The Journal of
Mary Windham Tsepesh

15 APRIL. Arkady knows about Vlad. Somehow, he knows.

I did not press for details—I know too many already for my sanity—but we had a good, long talk this morning.

He was entirely recovered yesterday evening, and slept quite well through the night. Or so I believe, for I slept like one of the dead myself, exhausted from my two-day vigil, but when I woke briefly from a vague, terrifying dream about Vlad, I remember turning over and being reassured to see

Arkady, blissfully asleep and snoring softly beside me. This morning, when I rose and pulled open the curtains to let the cheerful sunshine stream in, Arkady was sitting up awake when I turned round. His expression was so penitent and concerned that I said, "Why, dear! What ever is the matter?"

As I crossed back to the bed to sit on the edge beside him, he said, "I must beg your forgiveness."

I took his hand, but I must confess that I felt a pang of fear at those words, which would freeze the heart of any wife, regardless of how much she may trust her husband. And then I remembered our argument of two days before, and laughed. "Arkady," I replied, "I have already forgotten it. Besides, you were probably already ill then and not to be blamed for losing your temper. You are incapable of doing anything so evil that it would require my forgiveness."

"It isn't that," he said, so darkly that I felt once again a chill of fear. "I want you to forgive me for bringing you and the child to—to this accursed place!"

I stiffened and said nothing, but listened and watched very carefully as he continued, lowering his eyelids and looking away from me as though ashamed, instead focusing his gaze on the bright beams of golden light that filtered through the window, and at Zsuzsanna's still-fastened bedroom shutters beyond.

"I have seen horrible things. No"—he raised a hand when I leaned forward, on the verge of speaking—"you must not ask! I cannot speak of them. I can only say this: that I promise you, I will see to it that they stop at once, and never happen again. I will make sure no harm ever comes to you, or to the baby."

"Oh, Arkady!" I cried. "For your sake as much as mine, we need to leave here! You must tell Vlad we cannot stay!" I did not speak to him of what I had seen; I was sure he had witnessed something similar, and I saw no reason to add concern for my sake to his already overburdened mind. Only one thing was important: that I could now convince him to take us both far, far from this place.

He withdrew his hand from my grasp. "But it would break his heart if I deserted him and Zsuzsanna."

"It does not matter! Tell him—tell him that the doctors have ordered a holiday, for the sake of your health. Tell him we are only going away for a short time. We could go to Vienna."

He contemplated this, and nodded thoughtfully. "Yes . . ." He met my gaze, and I smiled at the acquiescence in his posture, his eyes. "Yes. I shall meet with him to-day and tell him. I am sure he would permit me whatever necessary to regain my health. No, I am sure he would insist on it."

"Oh, Arkady," I said, with pure relief, and reached for him. He saw the tears in my eyes and caught me in an embrace so tight I gasped, but I wanted for him never to let go. Weeping, I told him I had been so worried, so worried for him all these days; I told him that he had almost died, and that I could not bear to see him bowed down another day with grief and concern. He wept too, and promised me that we would get away. He will speak to Vlad this evening, and everything will be arranged.

My heart is so light now; I have been packing my trunk and singing lullabies to myself, to the child, and studying my German phrase-book. Everything seems more cheerful at the manor: even Zsuzsanna is markedly improved, and has her colour back. Dunya and I are so encouraged that we have moved a little mattress for her into Zsuzsanna's bedroom; her presence, and the garlic at the window, should be sufficient to keep any evil at bay.

The Diary of Arkady Tsepesh

15 APRIL. It is very late, and Mary is already asleep. I have lit a fire in the western sitting-room, and as I write this, I am watching the flames. Twice I have risen and tried to throw V.'s dictated letter upon them; twice have I found myself unable to do so, seized by the now-familiar pain in my skull, followed by the feeling that, by secretly and dishonestly incinerating that document, I will have in essence cast my familial obligation onto the flames.

I am an honest man. I despise deception, yet I see no alternative, if I am to keep V. happy while seeing justice done. Nor do I know exactly what to say to Mary; she seemed so happy, so relieved at the prospect of going to Vienna. I confess, I felt the same. But now that door is closed, unless I openly defy Uncle's wishes. Unless I break with the family forever.

As much as I love Uncle, as much as I feel obligated to him, I can scarcely bear now to walk inside the castle walls. My overwrought imagination no longer perceives a vast stone ancestral home, but an ancient, grinning monster lying in wait to devour me: each time I enter, the great door's sharpened metal studs become razor-sharp fangs, the threshold a gaping maw, the dark, airless corridors a long gullet.

When I passed through those hungry jaws this evening at sundown, with Father's pistol in my waistcoat as protection, all I could think of was Jeffries. Where had he met his final fate? In the guest chambers? In the servants' quarters? Or had he been spirited outside, to be flayed alive in the dark recesses of the ominous forest?

I entered scanning the walls, the floors, the furniture, for blood. Climbing the stone stairs, I imagined Jeffries' head, tumbling down that long expanse to meet me.

You're an Impaler, aren't you? One of the wolf-men?

I slowly ascended the stairs and made my way to Father's office, fighting a resurgence of the delirium that had possessed me in the skull-strewn forest. I did no work; I could not. Nor did I allow myself to think, for that seemed a dangerous pastime. I merely sat in Father's chair and fought the cold dread that threatened to settle over me, fought to keep my wits; and when I had some uncertain degree of control, I rose and made my way to Uncle's drawing-room.

I knocked, and when V. called out, I entered.

Everything looked as before. Uncle sat in his chair in front of a blazing hearth, which made the room warm and cheery. The slivovitz was still untouched on the end-table, in the cut crystal decanter whose every facet trembled with firelight. Only V. and I had changed: he had lost twenty years off his age; I had gained them.

Impossible, impossible; I am indeed going mad.

"Arkady!" he said heartily, turning towards me with a smile; it faded abruptly and was replaced by an expression of concern. The dark grey at his temples was spreading, so that the hair on the sides was almost salt-and-pepper, and his complexion, though still quite fair because of his aversion to bright sun, glowed with robust good health. "But you are so pale! Please, sit."

He gestured at the chair beside him. I sat, trying to hide my nervousness at this latest spurt of backwards aging. He narrowed his eyes, scrutinising me carefully, then poured a glass of slivovitz, smiling once again and saying: "Your lovely wife sent a messenger to tell us you were ill. I trust you are feeling better? Here, drink. It will put roses in your cheeks."

I took the proffered glass and drank. There was no disguising the fact that my hands shook, for the slivovitz splashed from the goblet in my unsteady grasp and perfumed the air. I set it down with a clatter, in my clumsy agitation nearly upending the glass.

V. watched it all with a small smile and the same intent scrutiny. "Better?"

"Yes," I wheezed, expelling more fragrant slivovitz fumes, fighting the urge to cough at the burning sensation in my throat. "Yes, I'm quite better. The doctor said it was brain fever, but I am well now."

"He is sure? You are altogether cured?"

I averted my eyes and stared into the fire. The room seemed suddenly stuffy, overly warm. "Yes. Mostly. However, he and Mary are still quite concerned. He says I need a holiday, and Mary has suggested that we spend some time in Vienna. With your permission, of course . . ."

"No," V. said.

My mouth opened, and I emitted a small gasp. Stunned, unable to fathom what I had just heard, I stared at him. I half-expected him to laugh and say he was simply joking.

He did not. His tone was flat, hard, neutral, his expression closed. "Mary is too close to giving birth; she cannot risk further travel. Besides, the baby should be born here, in his ancestral home, not in some foreign hotel."

"But—"

"She needs you, Arkady. You cannot go without her. And I need you, too. To-day, in fact, we must write a letter to a solicitor in London about locating a suitable property for us. Time grows short. I can wait no longer."

"I—"

"There is more; guests are due to arrive soon in Bistritz. We must write another letter and have Laszlo post it to-morrow. There are many, many details to be taken care of, Arkady, and I think you were right when you earlier said the best cure for your grief is work. So let us work now. But I promise you —you will have your holiday with Mary and the baby. In England. We will all take it together."

"I cannot stay here," I said, my voice quaking as hard as the hand I lifted to my brow. "Dear God, I cannot stay—! I cannot bear this any longer! I have found—I have found Jeffries' head, buried in the forest."

And I raised my other trembling hand to my brow and lowered my face, staring down through unsteady fingers at my lap.

A long spell of silence followed, during which time I could not bring myself to raise my head. Nor did I look up when, finally, V. spoke, but I heard the somberness in his hushed tone: "Are you quite certain?"

"How could I make such a mistake about such a horrible thing, any more than I could make a mistake about Laszlo taking Jeffries' ring?" I snapped.

"I see," he said softly, but I saw he did not see at all, that he did not believe. "It is no wonder, then, that you are distraught. It is enough to drive anyone mad."

"Yes," I whispered, pressing my fingers hard against my forehead, in hopes it would ease their shaking.

"This is terrible, of course." He paused. "How is it, then, that you chanced to . . . to make this horrible discovery? Did you actually see anyone bury it . . . ?"

"No." Uncertain how to explain that I had been led into the forest by a ghost lest I further confirm V.'s suspicions of my mental instability, I lowered my hands and looked up at him.

And saw, sitting in his chair, with short, thin legs swinging six inches above the floor, hands gripping the armrests in V.'s usual manner, my dead brother, Stefan.

In the warm autumnal-orange glow of the fire, the yawning wound at his throat was quite clearly visible, and I could see that the blood which dripped therefrom onto the white linen of his torn, dirtied shirt was vermilion, fresh, bright. As I stared slack-jawed, stricken dumb, Stefan's impish grin widened in an expression of purely malevolent amusement.

I closed my eyes and covered them with my hands, unable to speak.

At the touch of a hand on my sleeve, I started in the chair and glanced up in fear—into Uncle's dark green eyes. For the most fleeting of seconds, as I opened my eyes, I fancied I saw on his lips a hint of the same evil smirk Stefan had worn. I blinked, and realised his features were composed in an expression of utter concern, utter reassurance.

"Arkady," V. said, in a lulling voice, "it was wrong of me to pursue the matter. Of course you are too distraught to answer questions on this subject at the moment. We need not discuss such things now."

I leaned forward on the edge of my chair, unable to understand his calm in the face of this gruesome revelation, unable to understand anything except that I was on the verge of insanity, and knew that it would take little more to push me over that precipice. "I cannot stay! Don't you understand, Uncle? *Some*one here at the castle—"

"Laszlo, you mean," he interrupted, in a tone that was gentle and utterly reassuring, utterly unconvinced.

"Yes!" I exclaimed, flushing with anger. "Laszlo, then!—murdered your guest. I can't remain with my wife—and baby—near a monster capable of—"

I broke off as I remembered Laszlo had lived at the castle but two years, and was unable to stifle the thought: So many skulls. So many skulls. Too many for one man to accomplish in two years' time . . .

The next thought was blotted out by a now familiar, crushing pain in my temples—the same I had felt when Masika had attempted to convey some secret to me, when Mary had confronted me on the stairs about V. and Zsuzsa. I raised my hands and rubbed them, wondering whether this agony was merely the result of nervous exhaustion, or whether it had a more sinister cause.

"Arkady," V. said, in a tone soft and somber, and as sincere as I have ever heard anyone use. "Do you love me?"

His voice contained nothing now but sheer, wistful longing. He seemed to shrink in his chair, to become a pathetically stooped old man. The imperious prince was gone. I saw only my father, worn and bowed by decades of loss and grief. He gazed beseechingly at me with eyes that were naked and beautiful, stripped of all charm and power, full of stark, simple need; the eyes that had wept over my father in his coffin.

I was taken aback and sincerely touched, despite my extreme agitation. I stammered, "Why . . . why, yes, Uncle. Of course I love you deeply. I hope you have no doubt of that."

"And do you trust me?" He straightened a bit; his voice became stronger, a little more confident, as the prince returned. There was something so hypnotically soothing in his demeanour that I calmed like a dog beneath its beloved master's hand.

I knew he thought me entirely mad—and at the moment, I believed him correct, and yearned for his help.

"Yes, of course."

"Then trust me to see that the matter is resolved," he said, his confidence now entirely returned. "Trust me to see that no harm comes to you or your family. You must believe me, Arkady—I would die myself before I would let harm come to you. I will keep you safe—I swear it upon our family name! You have been through enough with your father's death, and your own illness; and you have a baby coming soon. You are distraught and need rest; you have had two terrible shocks. You do not need any other worries. Please. Let me take this terrible burden from you." He stroked my hand; his own was cold, but I found myself relaxing further at his touch.

"Stay with me, Arkady. For your wife's sake, for the child's, for mine. Let us work now, and you will see it is the best cure for your concerns. Let us talk no more of leaving."

What could I do? What could I say? I worked with him. Together we wrote to a London solicitor with whom I had an acquaintance, inquiring whether he might represent V.'s interests in searching for some property in the London area, and possibly some resort areas as well; and I also wrote a letter for him to a newly married couple touring Europe on their honeymoon, which he directed me to give to Laszlo as I left the castle, that he might post it in Bistritz the following day.

It all seemed very reasonable while I was with Uncle, writing the letters; but as I left and headed down the long, spiraling stone staircase which led to the servants' quarters, where Laszlo alone slept, I came suddenly to myself.

What idiocy was this, asking Laszlo to post a letter which would merely bring fresh victims? Uncle might trust him, but I could not; nor, I realised, could I even bear the idea of setting eyes on his face again.

The thought came to me most clearly, for some reason in Uncle's voice, as though he had whispered it in my ear.

You must go to Bistritz yourself. For the good of us all . . .

Yes. It became blindingly clear: Grief-stricken I might be; distraught and shaken I might be—but the time had come, for the sake of my family, to collect my wits and do what was best for us all.

And so I slipped the letter into my pocket and, rather than knock on Laszlo's door, continued outside and quickly drove the caleche home.

Once safely back at the manor, I wrote a different letter to the honeymooning bride and groom, informing them of a death at the castle, and apologising for the fact that their visit must be indefinitely postponed.

The other I shall throw on the fire—if I can bring myself to do so. I will post my substituted letter and the one addressed to the solicitor when I go to Bistritz to-morrow—to tell the authorities there of the murders.

8

The Journal of
Mary Windham Tsepesh

17 APRIL. The great clock in the hall has just struck two, but I
still cannot sleep, despite the fact that Arkady insisted I take a
small sip of the laudanum. He took a great deal of it himself,
being as agitated as myself, though he tried to hide it because
he was trying to comfort me in my terror. That was shortly
before one o'clock. Now he is snoring loudly, while I struggle
against the unpleasant, helpless dreaminess induced by the
drug. It has the opposite of its intended effect: I fight to stay
awake, for I prefer to have my wits about me in critical times.

I am so frightened. Writing is the only thing that calms
me these days. My hope that we would soon leave Transylvania
was short-lived. Arkady returned very late from speaking with
Vlad yesterday evening, and this morning he would give no
details of that encounter, but only said that it would be "a
little while longer" before we are able to take our holiday.

I know what that means. In a "little while longer," I will
definitely not be able to travel. It is already risky enough as it
is. I could tell from Arkady's subdued demeanour that Vlad
has refused our request, and they have had an argument, and

my good husband could not bring himself to tell me. He spent the day traveling to and from Bistritz, then went directly to the castle, and returned home quite late, after I had retired.

He did not come to bed, but remained in his study. I knew this because I could not sleep, in part because I was bitterly disappointed about the postponement of our holiday, but also because I felt a growing uneasiness over Zsuzsanna. She seems quite improved, and her colour is better than it was when I first arrived at the manor. She was even up and about to-day. When I visited her in her bedroom, she was dressed and sitting in the window-seat, gazing out the open window to her left, at the forest in the distance. As I entered, she glanced over her shoulder at me, briefly, with a child's smile, then pointed excitedly at the distant pines.

"Look, there! Do you see it?"

I crossed the room and stood behind her to squint, and saw nothing but forest, so far away that the trees were really quite indistinguishable from each other. "What is it you see, Zsuzsanna?" I asked pleasantly, and without thinking, placed a hand upon her shoulder.

"An owl!" she exclaimed. "Can you see him? There, to the right—up in the very highest branches."

I could, of course, see nothing, and stammered a reply about her eyesight being quite remarkable, which seemed to please her, though really I knew it had to be the product of fancy. She could have made out nothing at that distance.

It was not her imaginary sighting which troubled me, but the sudden realization that my hand rested upon a shoulder which was normal—as perfect and healthy as its mate, and indeed, her entire spine, which was now quite straight.

She turned, and, trying not to ogle, I sat beside her on the window-seat and we had a brief conversation about how much better she was feeling. Her only complaint was that she did not have much appetite. I finally told her that Arkady had been sick but was entirely well now, and she seemed politely concerned, though not upset by this news. I also told her that one of the servants' dogs had recently had puppies, and hinted that the best of the litter could be reserved for her, if she wanted, but she was not at all interested. She seemed preoccupied, and kept glancing out the window as if looking for something.

At the end of our talk, she rose and saw me to the door. It was not my imagination: she was taller, and walked without a trace of her formerly pronounced limp.

This worried me. I know it did Dunya, too, for when I relayed this to her, her lips pressed together tightly, and she shook her head, saying: "I do not understand, *doamna*. It is not a good sign."

I then asked her to explain more fully the covenant, the *Schwur* of which she had spoken. She would not do so until I took her to my bedroom, and locked the door; and even then, she kept glancing nervously at the window. Her tale was so simple yet eerily elegant that I made her stop and speak slowly, that I might record it here, in her own words:

The Testament of Dunya Moroz

This is the story of the covenant with the *strigoi*, which my mother told to me, just as her mother told her, and her mother before her.

More than three hundred years ago, now almost four, the *strigoi* was a living man, Vlad the Third, known to most as Vlad Tsepesh, the Impaler, *voievod* of Valahia, to the south. He was greatly feared by all for his great ambition and his bloodthirstiness, and for his crimes he came to be known as Dracula, the Son of the Devil.

There are many stories of his terrible cruelty, especially to those guilty of betrayal or deceit. Adulteresses would have their womanly parts cut out, then were skinned like rabbits, and their skins and bodies hung from separate poles where all in the village could see. Sometimes a stake would be driven between their legs until it emerged from their mouths. Those who politically opposed Dracula died horribly as well, skinned alive or impaled. Sometimes he impaled guilty mothers through the breasts and speared their unfortunate babes onto them. He could bear no insult to his pride. There is a tale told that a group of ambassadors came from Italy, and removed their hats; beneath were skullcaps which, according to their custom, they never removed, not even before the emperor.

"Good," said Dracula, "then let me strengthen your customs," and he ordered the caps nailed to the men's skulls.

Despite his cruelty, Dracula was respected by his people, because during his reign no one dared be dishonest, or to steal, or to cheat another, because all knew recompense would be swift. It was said one could leave all one's gold in the village square and never fear it would be stolen. Dracula was admired, as well, for his fair attitude towards the peasants and his courageous fight against the Turks. He was a skilled and brave warrior.

But the day came when, in the midst of a campaign, one of his own servants, in truth a Turkish spy, betrayed and slew him.

His men believed him dead. But the truth was that Dracula saw his coming defeat, for the Hungarian and Moldavian forces had recently departed, leaving him vulnerable to the Turks. It is said that at that time he was so hungry for blood and power he made a pact with the Devil to become immortal through blood-drinking so that he might rule forever, and that he anticipated his own death, knowing that he would rise soon thereafter.

Once undead and immortal, the *strigoi* brought his family north from Valahia to the safety of Transylvania, where the Turks were not such a threat, and where he was less likely to be recognised. He claimed to be his own brother, but the truth of his identity came to be whispered on the people's lips.

He soon set himself up as *domnul* of a small village. He was fearsomely cruel to those *rumini* who disobeyed, but generous to those who served faithfully. But soon times became difficult for the villagers. Many died from the *strigoi*'s bite, and those in nearby towns were terrorised as well. Soon the population dwindled, and the survivors discovered how to keep the *strigoi* at bay. Some brave souls even tried to destroy him, and the *strigoi* became frightened his evil existence would soon come to an end. It became difficult, too, to keep secret all that was going on at the castle. He may control the mind of one man, or two, or even more, at the same time; but he cannot control the actions and thoughts of an entire village. And so he could no longer keep secrecy about what was happening at the castle. The tales spread all over Transylvania, and soon he was in danger of starving.

So he went to the village elders and made the covenant: He would not feed upon any in the village, and would support them more generously than any *domnul* in all the land, and make certain the wolves did not attack the livestock, if they in turn would protect him, help him to feed upon outsiders, strangers, and keep silent regarding the covenant.

The villagers agreed, and the town prospered; no one was killed except those few foolish souls who disobeyed. A generation ago, when the world was torn apart and starving because of Napoleon's wars, we were safe and well fed. Because of the *strigoi,* we have never gone hungry in a land that knows hunger. Cattle and horses no longer died when wolves attacked in winter, and the *rumini* lived well—so well that it became the custom to offer voluntarily those babies born too sickly or crippled to survive, of which there are many now, for few outsiders settle in the village because word of the covenant has spread throughout the countryside.

He also agreed: No *strigoi* but him, for the good of all. He pierces their bodies with stakes, then decapitates them, so they will not rise as undead.

For all the good he has brought us, we villagers fear him; for there are many stories of the terrible punishments he inflicts on those who break the pact, who try to harm him or warn those chosen as his victims. No one who ever tried to destroy the *strigoi* has survived. Many villagers grumble and wish him harm; they grumble, and grow fat off the proceeds of the *strigoi*'s fields.

They say, too, he has a similar covenant with his own

family, an agreement that he will harm none of his own, and that the rest of the members may live in happy ignorance of the truth.

At this point we were disturbed by a knock as Ilona came to change the linens. Dunya started guiltily and left at once; I had wanted to ask her more about the family covenant, but she is clearly reluctant to discuss it in the presence of the other servants—and little wonder, for by speaking of it to me, she risks a dreadful penalty—so I shall have to wait.

I thought about Dunya's strange tale to-night as I lay sleepless, worrying about Zsuzsanna, about my husband, about my child, who would soon be born into this strange and fearful house.

In the midst of my fretful wakefulness I fell into an abrupt dream-state, similar but deeper and harder to shake off than that evoked by laudanum. At first I thought sleep had come at last and welcomed it gratefully, for it was altogether pleasant.

I floated in that blissful state for an unknown period of time until I became gradually aware of a solitary, hypnotic image dominating my consciousness: Vlad's dark green eyes.

I forced myself awake at once, and sat up groggily in the bed, my heart pounding with anxiety. I knew—*knew,* though I could not explain how I had come by such a revelation—that he was with Zsuzsanna once again. I rose and stole on bare feet over to the velvet curtains. Light shone beneath the door, bearing witness that Arkady was still across the hall in the study.

I raised a hand to lift a curtain aside—and hesitated, telling myself that I was being ridiculous, that Dunya was at that very moment with Zsuzsanna in her room, that her stout little presence and the garlic ensured that no harm would come to them.

Yet I could not shake the premonition of danger. Timidly, I pulled the curtain back an inch and peered through the crack.

The moon was waning, and the night no longer so bright, but my eyes were accustomed to the darkness. I detected nothing on the grounds between our bedrooms, and was just about to let go the curtain and chide myself for being unnecessarily anxious when I realised that Zsuzsanna's shutters had been flung back.

I strained harder to see, but in the darkness, could only be sure that the shutters were open. It was impossible to judge whether the sash had been thrown up. I leaned closer, nose almost touching the window.

A dark, growling form hurled itself out of the shadows and struck the glass with such force that it cracked scarcely an inch in front of my face.

I screamed in surprise. The attacker fell back, but gathered itself and once again charged, pressing against the glass its snout and a long muzzleful of sharp yellow teeth, bared in a hideous snarl.

I dropped the curtain and ran for the door, by which time Arkady had already thrown it open. To my surprise he brandished a pistol, as though he had stood by ready and armed for just such an emergency. He threw his arm up to push me away from the danger, and, following my terrified gaze, pulled back the curtain and aimed the weapon just as the wolf lunged for the third time, again cracking the pane and rattling the window in its sash.

He fired into the darkness, staggering slightly as the weapon kicked in his hand; the pane shattered with a high, crystalline tinkle. I expected to hear a yelp, a shrill whine, but all without was silence. I was too frightened to get close enough to peer out, but Arkady's quizzical, uncertain expression said that the animal had simply vanished. He leaned forward and peered carefully out the window, and I stepped as close behind him as I could, mindful with my bare feet of the glass, and craned my neck to see over his shoulder.

There was no evidence whatsoever of the attacker, save for the shattered, saliva-smeared glass.

He turned towards me then, and I confess that my nerves gave way at that moment, and I did something I had never done before in front of my husband: I wept like an hysterical, terrified child. I know it worried him terribly to see me like that, and I wanted to stop at once, as he had been through so much himself recently—but it was some minutes before I was able to get control of myself. Sobbing, I begged him to take us away to Vienna. He promised he would, but I know he said it merely to quiet me. He could not at that moment entirely meet my gaze.

Ion and Ilona came knocking at the door, in response to the gunshot; Arkady dismissed them brusquely, then brought out the laudanum in a desperate effort to calm me, but drank more of it than I.

How can I permit myself to sleep? No normal creature could have lunged *two floors* to strike the glass. I am so frightened. Frightened to think what will become of Zsuzsanna; frightened to think what will become of my child.

I have been warned.

No, worse—I have been overtly threatened. I know this, for in that terrible instant when my face was separated from the snarling wolf's by less than an inch of glass, I saw deep into his wild, intelligent eyes.

Hungry, compelling eyes; eyes of darkest forest green.

He knows that I have found him out, that I understand about Zsuzsanna. That I am trying to persuade Arkady to take us away. Dear God, somehow he knows, and with a mother's instinct *I* know that he will never let me or my husband or child leave this place.

+•+ +•+ +•+

Zsuzsanna Tsepesh's Diary

17 April. The shutters are all open.

I was too weak to close them, too weak to replace the garlic, too weak to maintain the charade. It is just as well; now, from my bed, I watch the first rays of the sun pour through the window like melted butter, spilling across the grey, silent room, over sleeping Dunya, over the mounds of my legs beneath the quilt.

My strong, perfect legs.

The light is so radiant, so golden, so bitterly beautiful that my throat aches with tears unwept. This is the last dawn I will ever see.

Through some peculiar resolve of will, I have found the strength to write. I am determined to leave behind the record of my passage.

But for whom?

I am dying. I know that my lungs will cease to breathe, my heart to beat; yet I am assured that the end I confront is not truly death, nor the existence to which I go truly life. For I know all that he knows, and my melancholy at the thought of passing from this brief, unhappy, crippled existence is tempered by a growing awe, a growing joy: my shroud will be a chrysalis, from which I shall emerge beautiful, perfected, immortal.

Our communion is complete. Last night, I knew when Dunya would fall beneath his spell, knew the precise moment when he would arrive. I had freed myself from the restraint of my nightgown and was waiting for him by the window inside the shaft of moonglow, lifting my arms before my wondering, wide eyes, beguiled by the radiance of that silvery light on my naked skin: already I could see sparks of pink and gold, the beginnings of that glorious, opalescent fire in my own flesh.

Out of that magnificent brightness he appeared beside me. I said nothing, but lifted my long, heavy hair from my neck and presented myself to him, knowing it would be the last time he would sup there. He wound my hair tightly round his hand and pulled my head back, back, with the other hand pressing my waist to his.

His teeth found the tiny, tender wounds again; I shivered as they sank, quickly, neatly, into my flesh, shivered again as his tongue began to work, rapidly at first, to encourage the flow, then slowly, voluptuously, but drawing hard, with such pressure that I moaned at the pain.

Despite the discomfort, I did not struggle, but permitted myself to fall at once into that deep, delicious swoon, my heart racing with excitement at the knowledge (his, and now mine) that he would feed ruthlessly, beyond satiation, that he would once again take me to that uniquely sensual precipice at the threshold of death . . . and then beyond, across the great abyss.

I sensed his pleasure, too—the pleasure I had known myself two nights before, the ecstasy of utter power over another's life and death, of ultimate seduction, of pure animal hunger appeased: the fierce, bloody joy of the hunt and the kill.

And he knew my ravishment; and even, submerged, my slight, bitter remorse at leaving this life without having tasted fully of its delights.

Thus it was he stopped, having drunk but briefly (and now, I know, sufficiently). I whimpered as he withdrew, but fell silent as he lifted crimson, dripping lips to my ear and whispered, "Zsuzsa . . ."

I heard the worlds contained within that single word. I heard his question veiled therein, and in my sigh, he heard consent.

He let go my hair; it swung, soft and loose, against my bare back. The hand at my waist eased its grip and I staggered back, struggling for balance, but not yet weak, not yet drained of strength.

Yet he had drunk enough to be uncannily powerful. With the hand that had held my hair, he loosened the clothing that separated him from me—not freeing himself entirely, but revealing again the broad expanse of chest, unscarred, free of any sign of the wound which united us.

Revealing far, far more.

Oh, I have lived a sheltered life, yes, but I had read of *le petit mort,* the little death, and wondered at the term. I laughed as I reached for the instrument of my execution—albescent, as cool and smooth and hard beneath my fingertips as marble. Shuddering at my spidery touch, he joined softly in my laughter, for we saw in our shared mind's eye the same vision, evoked by my own thoughts from his ancient memory:

The forest of staked dead, four centuries ago. The adulterous and unrepentant wives he had ordered to death in his capacity as *voievod.* How they had shrieked! How they had fought when forced down on their backs against the muddy spring ground outside the castle, while the smiling, appreciative prince watched. Five burly *rumini* per woman to spread her like a star: Two to pin writhing torso and arms down, two more, one gripping each kicking calf, to part the legs wide.

And only one to thrust the pine stake (ten feet long, wider than a strong man's arm and generously oiled, sharpened to permit rapid entry, but the tip blunted just enough so death might not come too blessedly quick) up between those whoring thighs.

There are none he hates worse than the faithless; none he loves more than the loyal.

Oh, the screams, as justice penetrated the traitorous! Oh, the strangled cries as the poles were then hoisted aloft, anchored in the ground, and the weight of the body allowed to more deeply drive the punishment home! Men who dared betray the *voievod* met their fate in similarly metaphoric fashion, gored through the anus. Sometimes the offenders were suspended for days, by which time the stakes extruded from stomachs, or throats, or sometimes, most elegantly, from gaping, death-stilled mouths.

The image filled him with sudden fire, which then engulfed and consumed me. At that moment, I wanted nothing more than to be so thoroughly pierced; to open and feel him emerge like a blooming calyx between the petals of my parted lips.

His hand was still upon the small of my naked back, but gentle; I pressed against him, anxious, impatient, threw my arms around him, pleaded with him, begged him to take me, now, now, *now*.

He did not move. His lips, dark with my blood, curved slyly upwards; heavy lids lowered over those brilliant and alluring eyes. He seemed as young and handsome then as Kasha —no, even younger, and more innocently beautiful, the archangel, the light-bringer, before the Fall. He shook his head, and I understood.

He would not take me. I had been the seductress all along; I had summoned him to me. He had broken the covenant only at my insistence, because of my need, and if he were to break mortal, familial taboos to consummate our marriage in the flesh, it would have to be my doing, as well. *I would have to take him.*

He remained motionless, a marble statue as I locked my fingers behind his muscular neck and hoisted myself aloft like one of the doomed adulteresses, pulling my torso at first too high, then slowly easing downward until I discovered the effective angle.

I locked my legs around him, and with a swift, violent motion, impaled myself. Impaled myself. Again. Again.

He gripped my hips, his knifelike fingernails cutting into my flesh, and thrust forward till he could fill me no farther. With a savagery that terrified and tormented and delighted me, he tore at my neck with his teeth, transforming the pinpricks there into gushing wounds. The warm river of blood overflowed his hungry mouth and cascaded over my breast, my stomach, trickling down to where we two were joined.

I writhed against him as he drank until my skin was sticky with blood; until I was spent and throbbing with pleasure; until I was dizzy and faint and once again overwhelmed by the peculiarly languid, ecstatic sense of death's approach. My arms fell back, too weak to cling to his neck. He alone supported me, one hand spread at my hips, the other between my shoulder blades.

At last, he withdrew from my neck, from between my legs, and lay me back on the floor near the open window. I stared up at the sky, at the waning moon, and the sheer blinding brightness of it pained my eyes, yet I could not tear my gaze from its brilliant flashing-colour beauty. I saw colour everywhere: in the shimmering, mother-of-pearl moon, in the stars, in the stand of evergreens far beyond, which had never before been even visible to my naked gaze from this distance. I could see the bright blues and reds in my quilt, see the green in Vlad's eyes as he knelt to clean the congealing blood from my body with his pink tongue. My vision in the darkness was keener, more remarkable than a raptor's.

And I heard everything: every stirring in the forest outside, even Arkady's snoring in the bedroom across the grounds from mine. I heard the soft movement of sheets as Mary tossed in the bed, and knew she was awake. I heard the beating of my own heart, as deafening as it was achingly pleasurable, and nearby, Dunya's steady heartbeat and stertorous breathing. I could smell the warmth of her flesh, smell the scent of living blood mingled with my own—the cooling blood of the dying, the blood of the near-Changed.

And then Uncle—

No, not my uncle. My husband drew back from my now-unstained body, and ran his tongue over his bloodied lips. Looking deep into my eyes, he said, "It is not yet finished."

I understood; and with agonising effort, lifted an arm to his head and guided it to my neck.

Astoundingly, the deep gashes there had already entirely healed. I felt no pain, no tenderness, just the feel of his tongue against smooth, undamaged flesh; and then I felt his lips move against my skin as he smiled. I smiled, too, weakly, for I knew it meant the Change was nearly complete.

Yet he hesitated; then brushed his lips against me as he moved his head down, over the ridge of my collarbone, down onto my breast. He encircled the nipple with his tongue, then paused, delicately settling his teeth there, until I felt the sharpest of them dent the very center of that pink-brown flesh.

Despite my weakness, I felt a sudden thrill at the realisation of what he was about to do. I laced my fingers tightly into the hair at the nape of his neck and forced him against me.

He pierced me once more, for the final time, and I gasped as I felt his teeth sink sharp into that tender, dark skin so near my heart. He sucked like a babe at my breast, with each pull of his mouth and tongue causing a renewed throb of pleasure between my legs. I cradled his head in my arms, a loving madonna surrendering my lifeblood to this infinitely old and wise saviour-child, my progenitor. He drank until my arms dropped and I could cradle him no more, until I descended into veiled, shadowy rapture, into dark, mindless ecstasy.

For hours I knew nothing. I remember the distant sound of an explosion, but it was merely a faint silver ripple against the deep velvet background of darkness.

Then, just before dawn, I emerged from my trance to discover he had gone, and left me in my nightgown in the bed. I was consumed by an urgent need to write this, my final entry, and so reached for the diary hidden beneath my pillow, and the pen and ink at my night-table.

At times I feel a stirring of fear at the realisation that death is so close at hand; but then I shut my eyes and allow myself to drink of his constant presence, his depthless intelligence, and I know I am not alone. The knowledge of what I am soon to become comforts me. I go to the tomb victorious, certain of my resurrection.

To whomever reads these words: Do not weep for me, and do not judge. The life to which I go is far sweeter than the one that I have known.

The Diary of Arkady Tsepesh

17 APRIL. It is late morning, almost ten o'clock. Mary has risen and gone downstairs. I write these words in bed, staring out at the bright sunshine filtering through the open window.

Hoping to dispel gloom, I have pulled the curtains back, but from my comfortable vantage point against the pillows, I can see the light glint off the cracked, pockmarked pane. Last night's horrors—indeed, the whole, jumbled confusion of yesterday's puzzling revelations—seem distant, veiled by the lingering mental fog induced by laudanum.

To think that this bit of broken glass was all that stood between my wife, my child, and Death—!

Mary was quite beside herself with terror last night—and so was I, though to comfort her, I hid it. While I was reading in the study, a wolf leapt directly at the window while she was gazing through the pane. Had it burst through the glass—

I cannot even write the words, cannot bear to think of the mildest harm coming to her or the child. Last night she wept as she begged me again to take her from here, and the sight of her thus tore at my heart. I promised I would.

But I cannot see my way clear to accomplishing it. Even so, I must try. I have never seen Mary hysterical—but then, never in my life have I heard of a solitary wolf attacking a human so boldly. In those precious moments when rationality returns, I can dismiss it as a strange, random event, as meaningless as it was distressing.

But Mary kept repeating, in her frenzied state, that it was an omen, saying that the creature could easily have killed her had it wanted, that it spared her to drive home the threat. She would not tell me who, or what, she believes has warned her, other than pure Evil itself.

Her words made me think of the wolf's paws against my shoulders, its breath hot against my throat. The wolves seem but a symbol, a reminder of the madness which lies in wait, eager to devour me.

If I believed in God, I would petition Him to take me and spare my family. I can see why the peasants feel the need for an omnipotent parent, a divine watchdog—what hell it is, to know there is no greater power than myself to protect my wife and child—I, who am weak and utterly unreliable, on the verge of mental collapse! Earlier this morning, in the grey light of sunrise, I opened my sleepy eyes briefly—and saw, impaled on the bedpost at my feet, Jeffries' head. He was looking down, laughing, wearing the same malignant, mocking grin Stefan had worn when he appeared in Uncle's chair.

I think I and Uncle and Zsuzsanna and all the Tsepesh carry madness in our blood. After yesterday's events, I am convinced.

The night before last, I finally brought myself to cast V.'s letter into the fire. I left the manor yesterday dawn in the caleche and headed directly for Bistritz full of agitation and hopefulness. When I reached the city shortly before two o'clock, my agitation lessened as my hopefulness grew, for I felt an exceptional degree of relief when I handed the inn-keeper the sealed letter I had written, informing the visitors that they should not come.

The innkeeper is a pleasant, round-faced man, heavy, but with hawkish features that indicated our distant blood ties; he recognised me at once, since Mary and I had spent a night gratis in his establishment, and welcomed me warmly, though he was curious as to why I, and not Laszlo, had come. I mur-mured a vague reply about having other business in town as I gave him the letter. He thanked me as he received it, saying that the timing could not be better, as the guests were due to arrive sometime later that afternoon. I merely smiled, knowing that he thought it contained instructions on meeting Laszlo's coach.

The innkeeper insisted on serving me luncheon "on the house," and afterward, I took the solicitor's letter to the postal office. Everything had gone smoothly, and I took enormous comfort from knowing that the newlywed guests would be protected from harm. Only one task remained.

Yet as I entered the constabulary and stepped up to the tall, uniformed lad behind the first long wooden desk, I began to feel some trepidation, for there was no concrete evidence tying Laszlo to the crimes other than the fact that he had nicked some of Jeffries' things and lied about a hen. It was my word against his. And how could I prove Uncle's blamelessness in this? How could I prove that *I* was not mad and the killer? After all, I knew the location of the skulls . . .

Suddenly lost, I stared up at the posters on the wall beside him, artistic renderings of the escaped, the criminal, the insane. I searched those hard, scowling faces for similarities, some quirk of lip or glint of eye that marked a murderer, a crazed man—some clear tendency that I had seen before, in Laszlo's visage.

"Yes, sir?" the young *jandarm* asked. He was fair-haired and peered at me through round spectacles with eyes of astonishing blue. His tone was frosty, openly condescending, despite the fact that my dress and demeanour marked me as nobility, educated, rich. He may have been of a lower class, shabbily groomed and poor, with inferior education and an inborn resentment of my influence and wealth, but he was Saxon—which made him the former conqueror, and me the formerly conquered. It was his one advantage, and he was not about to let it escape my notice. There was boredom in his tone, too, the *ennui* of one who has seen so much there are no surprises left.

As I turned from the posters, two uniformed officers passed, one on either side of a very drunken, barefoot Tzigani woman who would have fallen had they not firmly gripped her upper arms. I blushed and averted my eyes as they passed, for the woman's blouse had been torn at the collar and gaped open to the waist, revealing beneath several strands of cheap beads but no undergarment. Her dark hair had tumbled free from her scarf, which had slipped down and hung, in danger of falling. There was blood and dirt on her face, as though she had been struggling in the mud, and though she could scarcely walk, she kept growling and lunging viciously at the men who restrained her, as though she intended to bite them.

The officers drew back their faces quickly enough, but laughed derisively to show they were not frightened. As they passed me and their seated colleague, one said, smiling: "She says she is possessed by the spirit of a wolf. It's a spirit, all right: cheap wine."

The three men laughed. But the woman balked, unwilling to go further, and raised an arm, which, swaying, she pointed directly at me. *"He* does not scoff; he understands," she hissed. *"He* is one of us!"

I froze, discovered.

Laughing, the two officers dragged her off; the young Saxon behind the desk gazed up at me with a condescending little smile, but used the most polite tone and form of address possible as he gestured at the dirty wooden chair across from his desk. "Please, sit, *Dumneavoastra . . . ?"*

"Tsepesh," I replied stiffly, and gave the filthy seat an uncertain glance. It looked as though someone had recently spit on it, and when at last I settled into it, I felt a sensation of slight moisture.

"And what do you wish to report, *Domnule* Tsepesh?" He pronounced the name "Tzepezh."

Murders, I almost said. *How many? I don't know. Too many for me to count . . .* But I told him instead, "I wish to speak to the head constable, please."

His tight smile widened a bit, but a slight hardness crept into his gaze. "Ah. I am sure the constable would like to speak to you, my good sir, but he is engaged at the moment in some very pressing business. I assure you, I can assist you in whatever you—"

"I must see him, if it is at all possible—"

"And I assure you, it is not."

"I see." I rose, adjusted my clothing, then extended my hand. "Well, good day, then."

Apparently mildly surprised by my abruptness, he rose and took my hand—then palmed the gold crown therein, and with the smoothest, most practiced movement I have ever witnessed, slipped it into his pocket.

I turned and feigned movement toward the door.

"One moment, sir," he said, still standing behind the desk. "There is a slight chance the constable has finished his business and is free. I will go check, if you like."

I faced him. "Please."

Within a minute, he returned and said, with an attitude considerably warmer, "The chief constable will see you now."

I followed him down a narrow corridor of closed doors to a room at the far end, and stepped forward when he held the door open for me, with that stiff Teutonic formality that we Transylvanians so enjoy parodying in our jokes. Once I crossed the threshold, the door closed quietly behind me.

The man behind the desk was a native countryman, shorter and heavier than his young counterpart.

"*Domnule* Tsepesh," he said softly. His voice and posture were less formal, far warmer than the young Saxon's. Indeed, there was an odd familiarity in his tone, and I thought I detected a gleam of recognition in his eyes; he nodded faintly to himself as he looked me up and down. Yet I was sure I had never seen him before. He must have been Father's age—he had a head of waving silver hair, but his eyebrows and curling moustache were still almost entirely black, which gave his face a stern, dramatic appearance. "I am Chief Constable Florescu. Come in. I have been expecting you."

The incongruous statement temporarily stymied me—his

anticipation could have endured no more than a few seconds—but I stepped forward and took his hand. His grip was warm and firm, and he studied me with an emotion in his dark eyes that I detected from time to time during our conversation in his expression, his voice, his posture. While I was with him, I tried to name it, and could not—its identity remained elusive to me until now, as I write these words.

Pity. He looked on me with pity.

Florescu gestured for me to sit (this time in a chair padded and much cleaner than the one in the outer office), which I did. He took his own seat, folded his hands upon his desk and leaned forward, fixing upon me a gaze that was most oddly unbusinesslike: kindly, almost paternal, but also pensive, thoughtful, guarded. "So," he said, with unmistakable reluctance, tempered with resignation. "Perhaps I should let you tell me why you have come."

Though I had rehearsed my little speech several times on the ride over, my chosen words deserted me at that instant. I stammered, "It—it is a very delicate matter. I should explain myself. My great-uncle is Vlad Tsepesh—"

Florescu gave a single, solemn nod. "The prince. Yes, I know of him."

"I have come here not so much to make accusations as to . . . discreetly aid in an investigation. The prince would be angry if he knew I had come here; I do not want this to reflect on him in any way. But I believe that one of his servants is guilty of a crime. Several, in fact—"

"Which crime would that be?" he interrupted, but his tone was calm.

"Murder," I said, and released a long breath.

His response was measured, even, not at all hasty—the response, I decided, of a man who has heard so many horrible confessions that none can shock him anymore. He did not recoil, did not flinch, but stayed perfectly still, hands folded, asking the question and eyeing me with the composure of a professor giving an oral examination. "And who do you believe has committed these murders?"

I got the odd impression he was an actor, playing a rehearsed role. And beneath his words, a puzzling undercurrent of the real emotions: pity, regret. A desire to help.

"My uncle's coachman," I replied. "Laszlo Szegely. Though he likely had someone assisting."

"Why do you make such an accusation?" Again, calm, measured. "Have you actually seen him commit these crimes? Do you have evidence?"

"I saw him with articles stolen from the dead man, and with fresh blood on his sleeve not his own, hours after the man's disappearance. Earlier that morning, I saw him leaving the castle with a bundle large enough to have held a body." I paused, shuddering to think of the bundle's square shape; had it been poor Jeffries, he had already been dismembered. "Perhaps it is not enough to hang him. But my hope was that if you carried out a discreet investigation, you would find enough proof to convict the killer. I have nothing else, except my own instincts concerning the man's character. There is something . . . criminal about him. At the very least, if you could investigate him—"

"There is no need to do that," the constable said abruptly. He hunched forward, his tone and gaze compellingly earnest. "I can tell you about Laszlo Szegely. If you are certain you want to know the truth of the matter."

Surprise lowered my voice to almost a whisper. "Of course . . ." I leaned forward, eyes wide, ready to hear.

"Szegely," Florescu said, and gave a small, sickly smile that vanished as quickly as it had appeared. "A butcher by trade. Never married, no children. He came to us by way of Buda-Pesth, because he was hoping to evade the authorities there."

"For murder?" I asked swiftly.

He shook his silver head. "Grave robbery."

"He did this here, in Bistritz, as well? You caught him?"

The constable nodded.

"You should have put him behind bars and kept him there," I said, in a low, ugly voice that shook. "Perhaps there are not enough corpses in the mountain villages for him, because he has taken to creating his own dead. I found them myself. The forest is full of buried heads." Unable to continue, I stared, horrified, down at my hands, thinking of Jeffries, of all the tiny, tiny skulls.

Florescu and I sat in silence a full minute; I could feel his gaze on me, pitying me. Sizing me up. Thinking. I heard him fumble in his desk, draw something out; I heard the flare of a match, heard several strong intakes of breath, then smelled smoke, and the scent of fragrant pipe tobacco.

At last the constable said, very softly, very kindly: "*Domnule* Tsepesh. You resemble your father so very much."

I raised my head, startled.

Florescu's eyes softened, but he could not bring himself to smile. "He came here, just as you did, more than twenty-five years ago; I dare say before you were born. I was not chief *jandarm* then, naturally. But I remember him because he was so distraught. And, of course, because I was one of two chosen to return with him to look for the bodies in the forest."

I stared, struck dumb, astounded, unable to comprehend. Laszlo had worked at the castle for only two years. How was it possible . . . ?

The constable was silent a time to let his words sink in; and then he added, "But I was the only man who returned to Bistritz. It would be better for you, *domnule,* if you forget ever having seen such things. It would be better for both of us."

I half rose in outrage. "How can you say such a thing, when my wife, my family, are living with a murderer nearby?"

Florescu merely looked at me and drew on his pipe, his face suddenly a narrow-eyed mask, unreadable.

"What do you want?!" I demanded angrily. "Money? I am wealthy! I can pay more than whoever else has bribed you!"

"No one has paid me," he replied evenly, without a hint

of offense. "At least, not with anything as worthless as money. Though it is true; I arranged Szegely's freedom only two years ago, at the request of another."

"Who?"

"Your father."

I let go a breath and sank back into the chair, too stunned and outraged to speak, to protest. Florescu continued calmly from behind a veil of pipe smoke. "Just as someday you will come, *domnule* Tsepesh, most likely to my successor, when Laszlo is dead and you must make your own arrangements." His tone grew familiar, confidential. "You are young now, and there are things you do not yet understand. But you will. There are times when it does no good to struggle against the inevitable. The more you fight, the harder it will be for you. For your family.

"Perhaps someday your son will come to visit my successor, who will go to that same forest. And he will take men, and guns, but the outcome will be the same: only one man will emerge, and that man will find his promotion to this office comes very easily.

"I have spent my life devoted to the dispensation of justice; but there are some situations far beyond the pale of law— man's or God's. I will not go again to that forest. I am not a brilliant man, but I learn quickly where my life is concerned."

He paused, and in that instant I tried to speak, but he began talking swiftly once more.

"There is nothing you can do, understand? Nothing either of us can do." He rose and crossed from behind his desk to the door; his tone grew insincere and loud, as though he spoke for the benefit of those who might be listening. "I ask you to leave now. These are only silly rumours, this business of a murderer in the forest. The peasants have been telling these foolish legends for hundreds of years. Everyone at the constabulary knows this, and if you speak to anyone else, they will laugh if you tell them why you have come.

"Do you understand, *domnule* Tsepesh? It has all been

arranged, long before you were born. There is nothing you can do. Go home and take care of your family." He turned the knob and flung open the door.

I rose, red-faced, choking, not permitting myself at the time to understand. "No. No, I do *not* understand. And I will go all the way to Vienna, if I must—!"

His voice grew low, quiet, full of regret without a trace of anger. Full of that damnable pity. "And I would inform my superiors there that you are a madman. I assure you, *domnule,* nothing would be done. Just as I assure you that it is not I who threaten you when I say: For love of your family, do not do so."

I left, trembling with fury, and headed back into the Carpathians. At first, in my shock and rage, I told myself that Laszlo had sinister friends at the *jandarm's* office—a group of criminals with influence so broad the chief constable himself feared them, and made veiled hints about them. Florescu was a liar, a damned liar who was party to every one of the murders by his refusal to investigate. I could believe nothing he said— certainly not his vile insinuation that Father had known any- thing of Laszlo's background!

I decided that the only logical course of action was to inform V. about Laszlo's past and the constable's strange reac- tion to news of the bodies in the forest; this, I felt, would convince him that we should all seek refuge from danger in Vienna, whilst I informed the authorities there. I could not believe Florescu's influence reached that far.

And then, as the hours passed on the long drive home, I calmed and began to think.

There had been too many skulls in the forest to have been the work of one man over the course of two years. I had uncov- ered at least fifty, most of them children, and stopped only because I had not the strength, physical or mental, to continue. How many had I failed to find, littered through the infinite forest?

I burst into angry sobs, grateful for the privacy afforded by the lonely mountain road, as I recalled Florescu's contention that my father had arranged for Laszlo's release. For a moment, I dared allow myself to consider that the chief *jandarm* had been telling the truth. But why would Father have knowingly arranged for such a man's release—a man skilled in dealing with the disposal of corpses? Why, if he did not share complicity in the murders?

I drove the horses hard over the mountain pass, rendered thoughtless by cold, unnamed dread. Afternoon gave way to dusk. Sunset must have been breathtaking, with the pink glow reflecting off the snow-covered peaks and limning the entire blooming landscape with unearthly radiance, but I saw none of it. Masika's voice spoke in my head: *Come to me, Arkady Petrovich, in the day when he sleeps. It is not safe for us to speak here in the open. Come to me quickly . . .*

It was no longer day, but I felt compelled to speak with her at once, to learn the truth I could not at that moment bring myself even to think, yet which my tormented heart knew was true.

By the time I reached the village, all was shrouded in night; the streets were empty, and the rows of small huts dark. I had no idea where I might find Masika Ivanovna, yet my desperate compulsion to speak to her was too overwhelming to surrender and return home. I lit the lantern in the caleche and, taking shameless advantage of my position as nephew of the prince, knocked on the first door I came to with the intention of asking Masika's location.

No reply came; I took this to mean the hut's inhabitants were asleep, and so called out. When still no answer came, I pushed open the door with the lantern held high, and stepped inside—only to see that the hovel had been entirely deserted, and its contents removed.

I proceeded to the next home, only to find the same eerie circumstance there—and at the next hut, and the next. On the fourth try, however, I met with success. The sleepy peasant inside would not welcome me in, but instead called out directions from the other side of the latched wooden door.

I hastened to Masika's home—a small cottage with a thatched roof acrawl with rodents, their tiny eyes gleaming in the light cast by my lantern. In the solitary window, a feeble light flickered, but when I knocked stridently upon the door, there came no answer, no sounds of stirring within. I grew bolder, calling Masika's name as I pounded, but received in reply only silence.

At last I pushed against the door. Unlatched, it swung open; I stepped inside, and there saw Masika Ivanovna, still dressed in her mourning clothes, sitting at her crude-hewn dining-table. She had slumped forward in her chair so that her forehead and one arm rested upon the table; two inches from the top of her scarf-wrapped head stood a candle, melted to the base of its holder so that wax had poured out onto the wood and the remaining bit of wick sputtered with dying blue flame. Beneath her hand rested a folded piece of paper; nearby sat a small icon of Saint George, and on the dirt and straw floor surrounding her was an almost perfect circle of poured rock salt. Clearly, she had fallen asleep waiting for someone who had not yet come.

Shivering slightly at the crunch of salt beneath my boot, I moved to her side, touched her shoulder and said softly, "Masika Ivanovna. It is Arkady Tsepesh; do not be afraid."

She did not stir. I shook her shoulder, gently at first, then more insistent, raising my voice until it became a shout; until I realised she would never wake.

I lifted her beneath both shoulders then, and set her back gently in the chair. The crucifix I had returned to her at Radu's funeral now hung around her neck, and swung briefly in the air.

Words cannot describe the horror I saw frozen upon that sweet, worn face, in those wide, bulging eyes; it was the same anguished terror I saw on Jeffries' severed head. Yet Masika bore no visible mark upon her person.

I reached for the now-cold hand upon the table, clasped it, sinking down onto my knees beside her, and wept, feeling as though I had once again lost a mother whose loving company I had never known.

When I rose, drying my eyes, I spied upon the table the folded paper that had lain beneath Masika's hand, and read my own name written there, in script I did not recognise. Compelled, I lifted the letter and unfolded it to read:

To the brother I will never know:

I write this on behalf of our father, Petru, who was unable to tell you the truth himself before his death. He said that your innocence has protected your life, and those of your sister and wife; he feared telling you because, he said, Vlad was too close to you, and would realise at once that you had been warned and would retaliate. But I risk telling you in secret now in hopes that the knowledge may spare you life in the hell where our father dwelt.

My mother says Vlad has not spoken to you yet of the family covenant; but the time will soon come. When it does, remember: Believe nothing he tells you, for he will lie if it is to his advantage. He will tell you he abides by the covenant out of a sense of honour, or love for the family, but this is false. What the peasants say is true. He is strigoi, *a soulless monster, a murderer, and the covenant is no more than a game to him; he will adhere to it only so long as there is profit for him. Your father too long believed that Vlad possessed some good in his heart, but in truth, the prince knows only evil. He is like an old wolf who has made so many kills he grows bored, and must find new pleasures; destroying innocence is one of them. He toys with you now, as he toyed with our father when he was young, and his father before him. This entertainment remains fresh for him, for he can only enjoy it once a generation. He will say that he loves you, but in fact he desires only to corrupt you, to break you as he did Father.*

With my whole heart, I beg you: Flee from him. Escape before he destroys your soul.

But plan carefully, and wisely, and know that failure may cost you your loved ones. Father tried to flee, and in retribution your mother, and our brother, Stefan, were taken from him. Yet I believe there is still time for you, if you are shrewd and cautious and realise that Vlad cannot be trusted; and I believe to my dying day and beyond that love can overcome all manner of evil.

I must end swiftly now, though there is much more that needs saying. But I cannot remain in my mother's house once the sun has set, for her safety's sake. I must go.

I pray for you, Brother. Do not be so shrewd that you cannot pray for yourself.

Radu

I sank once again onto the floor, sitting back on the cold, packed earth, letting the letter flutter down onto my lap. The shock of both Masika's death and the letter's contents gave me a lunatic's clarity of perspective; for the first time, I saw how tightly the pieces fit: All those skulls. Laszlo's insolence. The peasants' stories that V. was a bloodthirsty monster (there was no such thing as a vampire, of course, and I did not take Radu's use of the word *strigoi* literally, but it would explain the origin of the legend). V.'s fury that I should interfere with his guests, his insistence that I not tell the authorities . . .

There could only be one conclusion. V. was a killer, and my father his accomplice, both of them suffering from the family madness that had begun to infect me. I cried out to think that I, too, was fated to descend into this insanity, that my hands should one day be stained with blood.

Are you an Impaler? One of the wolf-men?

"No," I whispered. "No . . ."

I scrambled to my feet, stuffing the letter into my waistcoat, and climbed back into the caleche, eager to be far away from the eerily deserted village. I arrived at the castle in good time, though it was now shortly after midnight. Nervous, perspiring despite the cool of night, I headed directly for the door to V.'s drawing-room, pistol hidden beneath my waistcoat. I knocked; V. called out his customary inquiry, and I gave my customary reply.

"Arkady!" he exclaimed jovially, from the other side of the heavy wood. "Nephew, come!"

I put my hand upon the polished brass of the knob, and turned.

A flash of silver. My father bringing down the knife, cutting my tender flesh. And behind him, a throne—

Pain blotted out the image. I squeezed my eyes shut until it was gone . . .

Then opened them to the familiar sight of V. in his drawing-room—a sight which would never, could never, look quite the same. As always, there was a blazing fire in the fire-place, and the room seemed stuffy and uncomfortably warm. I ran a hand across my forehead and drew it away wet, then closed the door behind me.

V. sat in his chair, with his hands on the armrests, but this time he did not greet me; in fact, he did not even so much as glance up, but kept his attention focused on the crackling blaze. At his elbow, the end-table still bore the shimmering decanter of slivovitz. Reluctantly, I forced my gaze from it to V., who stared straight ahead into the crackling flames, his expression immobile and unreadable as stone.

He was still as young as the last time I had seen him—a man now of fifty, rather than eighty, years. Yet I could not permit myself to react, to be distracted or frightened by this clear sign of my own incipient madness; the issue at hand was far too urgent.

"Uncle," I said quietly. The matter called for a strident, agitated tone, but the overwhelming silence in the room filled me with a sudden unwillingness to break it. "I am sorry to disturb you, but there is a matter of the most extreme urgency we must discuss."

V. gave no sign of hearing; his eyes never strayed from the object of their focus. This behaviour was so unlike him as to be unnerving, but I made myself continue:

"It has to do with the terrible discovery I made in the forest."

He spoke, still staring into the flames. His voice was low and soft, but it was an ominous softness, of the sort heard in the deep, deadly growl of a dog just before the attack. "You would betray me."

"What?" I whispered, my pulse quickening at what I took for an admission of guilt.

He whipped like a serpent in his chair to face me with eyes ablaze with reflected firelight; the stony expression was now one of murderous rage. "You would betray me! Where are the letters?!"

I gaped at him, stunned to silence by his explosive fury, stunned that he should know.

"Liar!" he shouted, with such force that I knew it carried throughout the castle. The words seemed torn from him, from a wellspring of hatred that ran so deep he shuddered as he screamed, "Deceiver! I know you did not give them to Laszlo as I asked!" The firelight sparkled, reflecting off the spray of saliva that accompanied his words like venom.

His anger was a terrifying thing, but for his sake, for Mary's sake, for all of our sakes, I could no longer permit myself to tremble like a child in his presence. The dead in the forest could no longer be ignored. If he had killed them, dear uncle or no, insane or no, he must be stopped.

I straightened, lifted my chin, did not permit my voice to shake as I said calmly, "I took the letters to Bistritz myself."

"And posted them both? Do not lie to me, Arkady! I warn you—I do not deal kindly with liars!"

For a moment I considered whether it might be simpler just to lie, and persuade him through deceit; but he would learn the truth soon enough, when his guests failed to appear. "I posted the letter to the solicitor," I admitted. "But the letter to the guests—"

"You destroyed it!"

Unwavering, I met his gaze. "Yes."

He turned away with a long hiss, fury simmering in his eyes as he stared once more into the fire.

"Uncle," I said, with gentle firmness, "I did so because I am enormously worried for your sake. For Mary's and Zsuzsa's.

For the baby's. I will not have my family living with . . . with such horrors surrounding them."

He swiveled towards me again, half rising from his chair as he thundered: "And did I not swear to you that no harm would come to you? Did I not swear it, upon our family name?"

Dracul, I thought, *or Tsepesh?* But I did not say it, for it would only prolong the argument; and I understood now why he could, with such certainty, guarantee our safety.

I saw madness in his eye, and it tore my heart; I knew then he was at the very least aware of the murders, if not the perpetrator of them.

"Did I not swear it?" V. demanded. "Answer!"

"You did. But, Uncle—"

"How could you fail to believe me? How could you think that I would lie to you, or be disloyal? I told you not to go to Bistritz, yet you insisted on disobeying! I told you never to interfere with my guests! This *one* rule—and you have broken it again!" He rose and reached for the decanter sitting on the end-table, and as I watched in horror, moved as if to cast it on the flames, then turned and hurled it so that it flew over my head and struck the closed door behind me, shattering with a glittering spray of crystal and plum-scented slivovitz.

I ducked and shielded myself with an arm, narrowly escaping injury; had he aimed any lower, it would have struck me. And then, very deliberately, I raised my head and brushed crystalline shards and brandy from my shoulders, and looked at him through enlightened eyes.

My heart pounding with horror that I should ask him whom I loved such a question, I slowly said, "The dead in the forest, Uncle. How did they come to be there? How did they die?"

His rage had abated somewhat, but his chest still heaved slightly, and his face was flushed. His eyes narrowed as he scrutinised me intently, saying, with terrifying softness, "Sometimes you take too much after your mother, Arkady.

You must learn not to be so willful. You must learn to withdraw yourself from other people's affairs."

My knees went weak, as though the very ground on which I stood collapsed beneath my feet; somehow I managed to remain standing, but I could manage no more than a stricken whisper. "What are you saying?"

"That it is pointless to worry about what lies in the forest. It would be wiser to direct your attention to your own affairs. Now go! Go and think carefully about your mistake, so that you avoid such idiocy in the future."

I left, stunned and horrified, feeling as though the world itself had been suddenly turned upside-down, as though I were surrounded by dark swirling evil, by a whirlpool of madness that would soon pull me under to drown . . .

But that is not the extent of my current horror and misery. I have just risen, prompted by an inexplicable impulse, and discovered in the pocket of my waistcoat Radu's letter— *and* the letter *I* had written instructing the visitors not to come to the castle. Dear God, is my memory no longer my own? Did I only dream that I succeeded in burning V.'s letter in the fire? And if so, *which letter did I leave with the innkeeper in Bistritz?* If the visitors come—

I am going mad. As mad as my dear father must have gone to discover such evil, as mad as my uncle, my kind, generous, loving uncle. I wish could blot out my reason, force my mind to stop its relentless working, its unavoidable conclusion that the murders were the work of, at the very least, decades, so Laszlo cannot have been solely responsible. Nor could my father have been, for he died before Jeffries ever appeared.

Oh, gods! V. is a murderer, not the immortal monster of legend the peasants claim, but a monster nonetheless, and I have played his unwitting accomplice in bringing Jeffries here.

What can I do? Despite Radu's claims (including the preposterous one about Stefan; my brother was killed not by V. but a *dog,* a tragedy I witnessed with my own eyes) it is diffi-

cult to believe that V. would harm any of his family; the object
of his madness seems to be outsiders . . .

. . . and the poor crippled and unwanted babies sacri-
ficed to him by the peasants (in return for their safety?). I am
torn between protecting him and turning him over to the
authorities in Vienna; how can I betray my dear benefactor? At
the very least, I must try to procure him a doctor, a specialist
who might help. But I cannot permit—

No time to finish! I have just glanced up and seen
through the open window Laszlo, driving the coach toward the
castle. And within, the two visitors—! For their safety's sake, I
shall follow at once . . .

❧ **9** ❧

The Journal of
Mary Windham Tsepesh

17 APRIL, LATE AFTERNOON. Zsuzsanna sleeps. So grey and waxen is her skin that were it not for the slight, rapid rise and fall of her bosom beneath her nightgown, I would deem her days dead. I sit at her bedside, fighting tears, fighting to be strong for the sake of Arkady, who will soon come to take his place in this heartrending tableau. I long for and dread his arrival.

I understand now why he took to keeping a diary after his father's death. I cannot bear merely sitting by Zsuzsanna's side, awaiting the approach of the inevitable. Dunya was kind enough to fetch my pen and journal, and so I write. It dulls the ache, and the fear, though nothing could now erase them.

As soon as my sweet husband is recovered from this fresh grief, I shall convince him to leave. I do not care if my time comes on a carriage, or a train; my child will not be born in this accursed house, will not come to know whatever hell his poor father has endured because of that monster's love.

The legends are all true. I knew it in my heart the instant

Vlad pressed his lips to my hand; knew it, though schooling and reason would not permit me, until to-day, to fully believe.

But those things have no power here. In this damned and magical place, only Evil holds sway. I will fight it with all I know to be the highest Good: the love between myself and my husband, our love for our child.

He *shall not have them.*

But Zsuzsanna is lost to us.

Oh, if only I could forget the way he looked at my belly at the *pomana* . . .

I can write no more of this; the pain is too great. Let me try to find peace in the orderly recounting of the day's events.

Despite the laudanum, I woke early this morning, unable because of last night's terror to sleep long, though I held a faint hope that perhaps it had been only a vivid nightmare. Arkady was still sleeping soundly, with his pistol beside him on the night-table—the first unhappy sign that last night had been no dream. I rose, went over to the window, and pulled back the curtain to reveal sunlight glinting off the cracked, pockmarked pane.

It is an omen. I try to convince myself otherwise, but I can no longer deny what I know.

At the sight, I felt a sudden pain in my belly—not as sharp as I imagine a birth-pang would be, but more of a rippling ache. I attributed it to indigestion and distress, and held my side until it passed. It did, swiftly, and I closed the curtain and dressed, leaving Arkady to sleep.

On my way toward the staircase, I paused at the open door to the next bedroom, then went inside to stand before the cradle there. Earlier in the week, Dunya brought it out to clean it. It is solid, polished cherry, a beautiful thing; Arkady and his father—and who knows how many generations of Tsepesh children—have lain in it.

The sight of the little cradle, its edges burnished to a dull gloss from the touch of so many mothers' hands, brought me to tears. I was bitterly disappointed because I realised (then—

but I will not stay now) that I could probably no longer travel, and that the child would be born here at the manor. Movement grows more difficult each day. The baby has dropped lower, and with a mother's instinct I know my confinement is near its end.

Sadly, I made my waddling way down the stairs to breakfast. I was ravenous and ate everything Cook put in front of me, but eating provoked more indigestion. Cook kindly made me a tisane of mint, and I drank it out in the little garden, where it was sunny and warm. I asked after Dunya, thinking to instruct her to launder the linens and blankets for the little cradle, but none of the other servants had yet seen her.

Feeling the warmth of the sun and the cool breeze on my face, listening to the singing of birds, I felt strengthened enough to give myself a silent talking-to, for the baby's sake. I knew the poor child sensed his mother's anxiety; it would not be good for him, or me, to approach the moment of birth with a mind tormented by visions of wolves and vampires. And so I made a pact with myself to banish dark thoughts. From that moment on, I was resolved to be cheerful, to spend my days thinking not about Zsuzsanna or Vlad—that I would entrust to Dunya—but about the baby's arrival. All this talk of *strigoi* —it had to be nonsense, and all the strange things I had seen were the result of pregnancy, grief, and worry over my husband. The wolf who had attacked at my window had no doubt been rabid, and his green eyes the product of my imagination, which was sorely troubled by the knowledge of Vlad and Zsuzsanna's illicit romance.

I simply could no longer allow myself to believe Dunya's silly stories. For the sake of my child.

And if we could not go to Vienna, so be it; I would find a way to feel happy and comfortable here, at least until the baby was old enough to travel. There was no point in pressuring Arkady into an unpleasant argument with Vlad.

Once I decided, I felt much relief. I went back upstairs, thinking to wake Arkady and apologise to him for my earlier attack of nerves, and reassure him that, if Vlad found it inconvenient for us to leave now, we should not fret, but instead focus on the upcoming joy. We deserved to permit ourselves some happiness.

But Arkady had already gone, apparently in a hurry, for he had left his cabinet open, and his diary lay open, as though hastily abandoned, near his pillow.

I carefully shut it, set it on his night-table, and stoppered the open bottle of ink I found there. I would have gone back down to the kitchen to search for him, but the thought of navigating the stairs again held me back. Instead I made my way to the east wing and Zsuzsanna's bedroom, holding in my mind the cheerful notion that I could spend the day with Dunya and my child's aunt sorting through heirloom baby clothes and linens, and readying the nursery. I remembered how radiantly Zsuzsanna had smiled, when she spoke of how good it would be to hear the laughter of children in this house again.

It was quite late by this time, almost noon, but her door was still closed. I knocked; no answer came. I called; hearing no response, I timidly opened the door a crack and peered inside.

Sunlight streamed in through open, unshuttered windows. My eyes caught sight of the far window-seat first, and I noticed that Dunya had already taken down the garlic flowers.

And then my heart froze when I heard the sound of gentle snoring, and realised both women were still asleep. I stepped inside, and as my gaze fell upon Zsuzsanna, I raised a hand to my lips and cried aloud:

"Dear God!"

She had been writing as she lay on her bed, but weakness had caused her to drop the pen and overturn the ink bottle; the indelible black liquid now stained quilt and sheets. Her little diary lay face-up, the leaves opened like a fan.

But it was not the large, black splotches on the bed that had made me cry out. Zsuzsanna was paler than the linens, paler than the pillow on which her head lay. She gasped, chest heaving as she fought for breath, her contorted white face lined with soft, dove-grey furrows that looked rendered by a watercolour artist's brush. Her open lips revealed colourless gums which had so receded that her teeth appeared ghoulishly long.

"Zsuzsanna," I said at last, and hurried to her side. I took her hand; it was icy and limp as that of one dead.

She was fully awake. Her dark eyes, encircled by aubergine shadow and wide with childlike innocence, stared up at me with frighteningly intense lucidity; she struggled to draw enough air to speak, and failed.

"Don't move," I whispered. "Don't talk . . ." I moved the diary and the ink to the night-table, noticing as I did the crucifix there, set atop the coiled, broken chain, as if she (or someone else) had impatiently torn it from her neck. I settled beside her, avoiding the large damp spot on the quilt, and gently brushed the hair back from her cool forehead.

The safe, happy world I had endeavoured to create for myself that morning collapsed utterly around me. I knew Vlad had come again last night, to visit Zsuzsanna—and to threaten me.

I will kill him before I let him harm my husband or my child.

I went over to Dunya, lying on the floor beneath a blanket, seized her shoulders, and shook her. Her stupor was greater than any produced by laudanum; I could only think of my waking nightmare of Vlad's green eyes as Dunya's head lolled sleepily on her shoulders. She did not even open her eyes until I shouted in her ear:

"He returned! He returned, and Zsuzsanna is on the verge of death!"

This seemed to draw her back. She blinked, and rubbed her eyes; and then she saw Zsuzsanna, and covered her face with her hands as she let go a horrified wail that broke my heart.

But there was no time for pity. I gave her another shake, and said, "Go at once downstairs and have one of the men fetch the doctor!"

She lowered her hands, threw back the blanket, struggled to her feet. Tears glistened in her eyes as she leaned over Zsuzsanna—who watched us with that oddly intense gaze—and gently loosened the nightgown at her throat. She pulled the fabric down an inch or two, and drew back with a gasp.

I moved beside her and followed her gaze, to the place on Zsuzsanna's milk-white neck, just above the collarbone, where those terrible red marks had been. Impossibly, they had altogether disappeared, leaving no trace, not even tiny scars— nothing but pearlescent, unblemished skin.

Dunya drew her trembling hand away, and straightened, then motioned for us to go into the corridor, lest Zsuzsanna should overhear.

I followed her out into the hall with a sense of dread.

"It is too late for the doctor," she whispered sadly. "You saw that the marks have healed. The change is complete; she will be dead before to-morrow comes."

I felt a surge of anger at hearing those words: It was unfair that Zsuzsanna should be so cruelly stricken, unfair that Vlad should triumph. The poor woman had endured a difficult enough life, and now she would die at a time when she should be joyously awaiting her nephew's birth with her family. My resolve to be cheerful for the child's sake crumbled; Vlad had won again.

I vented my rage on Dunya, shouting: "I don't care what superstition says! Go get the doctor! We must do *something* to help her!"

The poor girl recoiled, trembling, then curtsied and flew down the stairs. I returned to Zsuzsanna's bedside and took her cold, lifeless hand; she looked up at me with those great, strangely euphoric eyes.

"It will be all right," I soothed. "We have sent for the doctor. We'll make you well . . ."

She drew a hitching breath and released a soft sigh on which was carried the barely audible word: "No . . ."

"Don't speak like that," I said firmly, still feeling the undercurrent of my fury at Vlad, at fate, at God, that such a cruel thing should be happening to such a helpless innocent. "Of course you'll get better."

Her eyes were glittering, bright with excitement and a vibrant, radiant joy in sharp contrast to her cadaverous appearance. She fought to take another breath, and with an effort that was painful to watch, whispered, "No . . . I *want* . . . death . . ."

I fell silent, pierced through the heart. There was nothing I could do but remain beside her and hold her hand, and when Dunya reappeared, breathless from running on the stairs, I sent her away again to fetch Arkady.

She was gone some time. During her absence, Zsuzsanna closed her eyes, and appeared to sleep; and I—God forgive me —could no longer resist the lure of the little diary on the night-table. I know it is a sin to invade another's privacy, but I had to know the truth, had to know whether my real enemy was Incarnate Evil, Madness, or Superstition.

And so I stealthily slipped my hand free from hers, took the diary from the table, and opened it to the final entries.

There are no words. No words to describe the revulsion, the horror, the lurid fascination those pages held for me. I cannot—I cannot write here of what I read. Decency forbids it.

Zsuzsanna had taken the vampire as lover.

My first thought was that this was the most grotesque, obscene sort of fantasy; but can fantasy kill a woman? If she is mad, then we are all mad with her, and living in a world in which the magical, the impossible, the fantastically evil, are resoundingly real . . . and deadly.

I devoured the last four entries with a swiftness born of titillation and terror, then set the vile little book aside and raised shaking hands to my face.

I thought: *We must flee at once.*

I thought: *He is free to go to England now.*

I thought: *We must kill him quickly.*

I stared at sleeping, dying Zsuzsanna, and in my mind heard Dunya's solemn voice: . . . *kill him,* doamna, *with the stake and the knife. It is the only way* . . .

Zsuzsanna stirred, languidly lifted her eyelids, and gazed up at me.

I retook her hand, and tried to compose my expression into one of comfort, tried to smile.

How large those eyes were, how infinitely dark and deep and loving. They shone with the gently mad, beatific radiance of a saint, shone like a midnight sea rippling with moonbeams. They caressed me, pulling like an ocean current.

Without realising it, I leaned closer to the dying woman until her soft, gasping breath warmed my cheeks, until our two faces were scarcely a hand's width apart. At that moment I was suddenly struck by the fact that in death, Zsuzsanna's heretofore plain face had taken on the classic beauty of an alabaster Venus, sculpted by the most brilliant of Roman artists. Her mouth seemed softer, fuller, touched by the same newly unleashed sensuality that emanated from her fathomless eyes, eyes that grew larger as I approached, until they filled the entire world.

"Mary," she mouthed silently—or perhaps she did not speak at all, perhaps teeth and tongue and lips never moved. Perhaps I merely imagined that she struggled to speak my name. "Sweet sister. Kiss me before I die."

I surrendered, sinking deep into the dark ocean of those eyes with the euphoric peace of a drowning swimmer who at last yields to death. I brought my own lips closer to those pale parted ones until I hovered two inches above her. She smiled with the same dreamy pleasure that now engulfed me, and her tongue flicked in anticipation over white, gleaming teeth.

The door swung open with a resounding slam. I straightened, startled back into ordinary consciousness.

"*Doamna!*" Dunya exclaimed breathlessly. She stood in

the doorway, one hand against the lintel, sturdy little body taut, frozen with alarm. I knew at once that she had purposely made a loud noise. Zsuzsanna did not stir, but the tenderness in her eyes had entirely vanished, replaced by an unmistakable glint of hunger—and livid hatred.

"*Doamna,*" Dunya repeated, her manner oddly formal, "if I could speak to you in the corridor . . ."

I rose stiffly, as though I had been sitting in the chair for eternity instead of half an hour, and followed the girl into the hallway.

When we were both outside the room, Dunya reached for the door and closed it, so that there would be no chance of Zsuzsanna overhearing. The instant it clicked shut, she became galvanised, and whispered, all in a rush, with the air of a panicked conspirator: "You must not kiss her, *doamna,* nor permit anyone else to! She is hungry, and there is a chance now that her kiss could create new *strigoi.*"

I leaned against the wall, suddenly weary, and rested my hands on my stomach, wishing that I could cover my poor child's ears, to protect him from all this insanity. "It is true," I said softly, more to myself than Dunya. "Everything about Vlad. I have read Zsuzsanna's diary."

Dunya's full lower lip began to tremble. In a high, unsteady voice, she said, "It is my fault, *doamna.* She will die because it is all my fault." And she covered her eyes with her hands and began to weep, with bitter, rasping sobs that shook her small frame.

I put my arms around her and patted her back, softly and regularly, as a mother would a colicky infant; she clung to me desperately, like a child, and gasped, "He made me sleep . . . If I hadn't been so weak . . . But I do not understand why she became so strong . . ."

"He deceived us both," I said soothingly. "She wrote in her diary. He made her drink from him, to deceive us, and to bind her to him. We must be careful now; he knows everything she sees and hears."

Dunya got control of herself at last. She straightened, then crossed herself, and with her index finger caught a single tear that slid down her cheek. I released her from the embrace with a reassuring pat on her shoulder.

"What can we do to help her now?" I asked.

She shook her head. "There is nothing now that will prevent her death. All we can do is prevent her from becoming *strigoi*."

"By killing Vlad," I whispered.

She hesitated. "He is so old and cunning . . . Many have tried. All have failed. There is another, safer way."

I felt a glimmer of hope. "What must we do?"

She looked down at the carpet, unable to meet my gaze, her lips twitching with the effort to repress further tears. "After the *domnisoara* is dead, but before she can rise as *strigoi*—which she will do in two days, perhaps three—drive the stake through her heart. Then the head must be severed, and garlic put in her mouth, and this buried separately from the body."

Aghast, sickened, I put a hand to my gaping mouth and leaned once more against the wall, fearing my legs would fail me. In my mind's eye, I saw the glint of a large steel blade as it hacked through the skin of that small, tender neck. I saw the thick wooden stake positioned between her breasts, heard the ring of the hammer as it came down, driving that stake home, heard her anguished shriek as her eyes flew open, wide with startled agony . . .

Arkady would never permit such an atrocity to be committed against his sister. If it was to be done, it would have to be done in secret; but such a heinous act seemed impossible to accomplish without discovery.

"Why?" I asked, when I once again could speak. "Why such a horrible thing? Why . . . must the head be buried apart from the body?"

She finally looked up, and straightened her small shoulders, trying to summon resolve. "Because the regenerative powers of the *strigoi* are so great that, unless the head is buried in a different place, even such terrible wounds might heal, and the undead rise again." She glanced back over her shoulder at the closed door. "You saw her, *doamna.* Her body is perfect now."

It was true. I had been too shocked to pay much notice, but now I recalled the body of the woman lying on the other side of the door. Zsuzsanna reclined straight on her back, both shoulders perfectly formed, with no sign of curvature in her spine. And beneath the quilt, the shape of her legs was clearly visible—a matched, healthy pair.

I raised my hands to my face and wept bitter tears to think she would die, and far bitterer tears to think what we would do to her once she was dead. I doubted myself physically capable of the deed, because of the pregnancy, and Dunya was too small to accomplish the gruesome act herself. So I collected myself, thinking all the while that we were quite insane to be having such a conversation, and asked, "Dunya . . . is there a man whom we could pay to do this, after she has died?"

Tears streamed down my cheeks, but I was quite composed as I said this. Yet my voice or expression must have evoked pity, for Dunya awkwardly touched my shoulder—timidly, at first, knowing it the utmost forwardness for a servant to touch the mistress uninvited, yet so overwhelmed by compassion that she could not resist. "Of course, *doamna;* there is someone who will do so, but he will refuse payment. But please do not worry about such things. I will take care of them for you."

She said it so sweetly, in such a soothing tone that I began to cry again, and could not speak for a time. She put her arms around me then, and we two wept like sisters.

I said, "Dunya, I am so terrified. I am about to have a child, but I do not want to do so here. I am afraid it is not safe. A wolf attacked at the window last night. It leapt at me, and shattered the pane. It was so close, I saw it clearly. It had Vlad's eyes. It was him. I know; I have seen him change."

She seemed not at all shocked by this, but nodded, pat-
ting my shoulder in an effort to reassure me. "I will keep you
safe, *doamna,* with the cross and the garlic. We will let no harm
come to you."

"Am I going mad? I saw him change into a wolf, before
my eyes . . ."

"You are not mad," she said, with such authority I felt a
measure of comfort—an unhappy comfort, to know that such
evil indeed existed. "It is true, he can become a wolf. And if he
kills another while in this guise, that soul shall become *strigoi,*
unless prevented. But he also commands the wolves. We who
live near the forest know that the creatures by nature are shy;
they do not threaten the villagers—only livestock, and only in
winter, if they are starving, and then only in packs. A single
wolf is no threat, and we do not fear it—unless *he* commands
it. For he knows how to make them kill whomever he wishes
—though this death is a natural one, and the victim's soul
returns to God."

Out in the hallway, I made her swear that she would
arrange in secret for Zsuzsanna to be freed from the curse of
the *strigoi,* and would say nothing of any of these things to
Arkady, or to anyone else. She promised, but warned darkly
that the servants were growing suspicious of Zsuzsanna's pale-
ness, and that rumours were already circulating in the village
as to its cause.

As for Arkady, it seems he took the caleche in a great
hurry this morning, and apparently headed for the castle. One
of the servants has gone to fetch him, but I do not understand
what is taking him such a long time to return. I fear Zsuzsanna
will die before he comes.

I have sat with her this past hour, and she wakes occasionally to feebly ask for Vlad.

I do not know what to tell her. I have no desire to invite
the return of such evil to my home. Yet she asks so pitifully, I
do not know how much longer I can refuse.

Dunya remains with me, and has been a great comfort. I

asked her to explain more fully, once Zsuzsanna was asleep, the covenant between Vlad and the family.

"It is as I told you, *doamna,*" she said. "An agreement similar to the one with the villagers. He will harm none of his own."

"Yes, I remember. But in exchange for . . . ?"

She lowered her eyes and released a little sigh of reluctance before returning to the same high-pitched tone of rote memory she had used earlier when telling the tale of Vlad's pact with the town. "He will harm none of his own, and the rest of the family members may live in happy ignorance of the truth, and be free to leave the castle forever—in return for the assistance of the eldest surviving son of each generation."

I stared at her in horror, knowing in my heart what she would reply even as I demanded, "What do you mean, *assistance* of the eldest son?"

She turned her face away, unable to meet my stricken gaze. "His help, *doamna.* To see that the *strigoi* is fed. For the good of the family, the village, the country."

My poor darling . . . !

✠ ✠ ✠

The Diary of Arkady Tsepesh

17 APRIL. ADDENDUM WRITTEN ON SEPARATE PARCHMENT. I have closed myself in Father's office; his revolver lies on the desk, near my right hand. In half an hour, I shall go back downstairs and escort Herr Mueller and his wife to the safety of the manor. Until then, I must do something to ease my nerves and keep my mind free from images of Jeffries' severed head, and the manner in which he met his doom . . . at Laszlo's hands, or V.'s?

And so I write, using Uncle's stationery.

When I saw Laszlo and the guests ride past the manor, I threw on my clothes, grabbed the pistol, and went at once to the stables, where I harnessed the horses to the caleche. We made top speed to the castle, and as we made it to the crest of the slope, some fifty feet distant, I could see that the carriage had already been unloaded, and the stablehand had led the horses back to the stable.

I pulled up into the front courtyard and tethered the horses to the front post. There was no point in unharnessing them; I would not remain here long.

The door had been bolted, and so I rang and waited, pacing impatiently until Ana answered.

"Where are the guests?" I demanded.

Her eyebrows lifted, and her eyes widened in the face of my heated intensity. "Why, upstairs, of course, sir. Helga has drawn them a bath; they're rather tired and dusty."

I pushed past her and headed up the stairs directly for the guest chamber in which poor Jeffries had stayed. The door was already closed, and when I knocked, an answer was so long in coming that I at first feared Helga had taken the guests elsewhere.

And then I heard a splash of water, and very muffled and faint, a feminine giggle; then a young man's voice, somewhat nearer, calling out in German.

"Go away."

"I am a member of the Tsepesh family," I called, in the same language, "and I must speak to you at once."

"Who?" His rising, indignant tone revealed that he had heard the name, but did not recognise it.

I flushed, remembering how V. so facetiously signed his correspondence with guests. "One of the family Dracul," I called, and when expectant silence followed, added, "I am sorry to disturb you, but the matter is urgent."

"One moment," the young man replied.

I waited patiently for the requested moment—actually several moments—while beyond the closed door came faint, muffled sounds of conversation, movement accompanied by more splashing, then the closing of the inner door to the bed chamber. Footsteps came at last, and the door swung partway open to reveal a clean-shaven, bespectacled young man with curling, golden-brown hair that was decidedly damp and tousled. He could have been no more than eighteen, with a well-formed, handsome face that sported a small, turned-up nose which accentuated his youthfulness. I did my best to appear not to notice that he leaned out so as to hide the lower half of his body; the upper half was covered with a damp silk smoking-jacket which stuck to his skin.

"Herr Mueller?" I asked politely, retrieving from memory the name on the letter V. had dictated.

"*Ja?*" He struggled to maintain civility, but did not entirely succeed in hiding the fact that he was eager to be rid of me; he kept a hand on the doorknob in hopes of dismissing me quickly.

"I am Arkady . . ." I hesitated. ". . . Dracul, nephew of Prince Vlad. I am sorry to disturb you and your wife's privacy"—at this, the young man blushed violently—"but there has been a mistake. Our coachman should not have brought you to the castle, but to the manor, where a room is prepared for you. I shall take you there now." I had no desire to frighten these good people; if I could whisk them from the castle unaware of the danger, so much the better.

"But the room here is perfect!" Herr Mueller exclaimed. "Lovely! And besides . . ." He peered at me with a trace of suspicion. "Your uncle left a note in the room welcoming us here. Why must we leave?"

I struggled to think of a compelling reason other than the truth. "Yes, well . . . Did you ever get *my* letter in Bistritz? The one warning of illness in the castle?"

His eyes widened slightly; he took a step back from me,

from the door. "Why, no . . . Just the letter from your uncle, explaining when to meet the coach."

The letter I thought I had cast upon the fire. I struggled not to blanch at this revelation.

"Ah," said I, gravely, "it must have missed you. It's nothing *too* serious, of course"—and at this, his eyes narrowed and he took another half step back from the door—"but we felt it would be safer to put you up at the manor until the disease has left the castle."

"What disease is this?" Herr Mueller insisted, but I countered that such details were better discussed once we arrived at the manor.

Herr Mueller became eminently reasonable then, but begged for some time—"Thirty minutes, no more"—for the sake of his wife, who was "tired and indisposed, and was in the midst of bathing." I told him sternly I could allow no longer, and instructed him to keep the door locked and open it only when I—and no other—returned for him.

I went directly up to my office, and wrote a very short note to V., saying that I knew I was breaking his rule about interfering with visitors, but that it was utterly necessary and for his own good, as well as that of the guests. I thought at first to leave it in his drawing-room, on the table where he would be sure to find it—but now I grow nervous that one of the servants might remove it. And so I have decided to slip it beneath the door of his private chambers.

Thinking of doing so evoked again the strange, elusive image buried in my childhood memory:

The silver flash of the knife; the pain as it cut the delicate flesh at my wrist. My father, holding my arm over . . . something dully gleaming gold. I cannot see it now. But I remembered once again the ancient throne, and this time, the words JUSTUS ET PIUS, just and faithful . . .

Invisible claws dug into my brain with such vehemence that the pain overwhelmed me. I cried out and sank forward, elbows and face resting on the inkblot, hands clutching the back of my skull, and surrendered for a time to blackness.

I have recovered now to find myself staring at the letter in my hands. Time to slip it beneath V.'s door, then quickly collect the guests.

Footsteps on the stairs! Someone is coming; the revolver—!

❉ *❉* *❉*

The Journal of Mary Windham Tsepesh

18 APRIL. It is the wee hours of the morning, and I cannot sleep. This house is so full of misery and despair, how can any of us ever slumber peacefully again?

My husband was so undone by the news about Zsuzsanna that at first he waved a gun at poor Mihai, who had to coax him down the castle stairs into the carriage and drive him home; another servant later retrieved the caleche. Arkady is with his dead sister now, and cannot be persuaded to leave her side. I fear for him, despite the fact that Dunya says she doubts Vlad will harm him, especially as he is the eldest son, and such a thing has never occurred in all the centuries the covenant has been in effect.

Nor has he ever bitten one of his own family, I almost retorted, but held my tongue; I know she means only to comfort me. Yet there can be no comfort. The truth is none of us are safe.

Until her brother arrived, I sat with Zsuzsanna and held her hand. She grew somewhat restless and incoherent, and began to ask for Vlad. At first I had not the faintest intention of yielding to her request, but she grew so tearfully, heartbreakingly desperate for him that despite my resolve, I began to relent, and took Dunya aside to ask whether this was safe.

"He can do her no further harm," Dunya whispered solemnly. "As for us—he cannot harm us unless we allow him; so long as we wear our crucifixes and avoid his charms, we will be safe. But he must know that it is Zsuzsanna, and Zsuzsanna alone who invites him here."

Thus I sent a second servant to the castle, to give V. the message that Zsuzsanna was dying and asked for him.

Soon after, poor Arkady arrived. Though I had succeeded in composing myself as I sat at Zsuzsanna's side, wishing to be strong for my husband's sake, at the sight of his grief-stricken face in the bedroom doorway, I dissolved in tears.

He strode quickly to her side. I withdrew, and he sat on the bed and gathered her to his bosom, lifting her head and shoulders so that her dark hair streamed down over his arm and onto the pillow.

"Zsuzsa . . ." he sighed, tears spilling down his cheeks, and tenderly stroked her face. "Zsuzsa, how can this be?"

His presence brought her to herself again, and endowed her with strength. She smiled up at him with the sweetness of a saint, her eyes once again radiating that uncanny serenity despite the fact that her breath came in sharp gasps. "You mustn't cry, Kasha. I'm happy now . . ."

He released a bitter sob, and said, "You can't leave, Zsuzsa. I'm so lonely, now, with Stefan and Father gone. Don't you go, too."

Her smile widened, showing a flash of long teeth as she whispered, "But I'm not leaving you, Kasha. You'll see me again. We'll all go to England together."

I stiffened and repressed a shudder at this, but sweet Arkady's face contorted in a spasm of grief, which he quickly stifled and replaced with a mask of courage. "Yes, of course," he said, in a placating tone. "You must get better, so we can all go to England together. You, me, Mary, Uncle, and the baby . . ."

"Yes, the baby," Zsuzsanna hissed dreamily, and fixed on me a gaze full of such hunger and longing that I thought I should faint. "We will all be so happy when the baby comes. We will love him so much . . ."

Arkady bowed his head in grief.

She fell silent a time, and nothing could be heard in that sad, sunlit room except her laboured breathing. I looked away, unable to bear more of the heartrending tableau until I heard her gasp, "Arkady . . . Kiss me. Kiss me one last time . . ."

I glanced up to see her looking at her brother with those huge, sensual eyes, eyes as compelling, as alluring as the dark green ones that haunted me on the verge of sleep. At once I put an arm on my husband's shoulder, to restrain him—and Dunya, alerted, had stepped over towards him, swooping like a mother hen protecting her brood.

Yet we were too late; Arkady bent to kiss her. She parted her lips, ready to meet his, but at the last instant, he turned his face and gave her a chaste, brotherly kiss on the cheek. She raised a feeble hand to his jaw as though to direct him into the embrace she desired, but she was too weak, and as my husband raised his head, I saw the keen disappointment in her eyes.

Lucidity deserted her then, and she lapsed into begging for Vlad, who I knew would not come, for the sun was still high in the sky. She alternated between restlessness and sleep, and in the late afternoon, the doctor arrived, but could do nothing except leave behind a foul-tasting medicine which she refused to drink.

As sunset approached, she woke and became extremely restive, crying pitifully for Vlad by name—no longer did she refer to him as "Uncle." By then she was terribly weak. We were all amazed that she was still alive when darkness finally came.

Vlad arrived shortly thereafter. I dreaded setting eyes on

him again; but when he entered the room, I felt no thrill of fear or hate, for his demeanour was not at all what I expected.

Oh, yes, he was a man twenty, thirty years younger than the one I had met at the *pomana*—as handsome as my own husband, with the same striking, heavy black brows, and now black hair streaked with silver.

I expected a trace of the wolfish, gloating grin on his lips, a glint of mocking triumph in his eyes. But no—there was only sincere, somber concern reflected in his posture, his step, his expression. He ignored us all and went straight to Zsuzsanna, who still lay in her brother's arms, and took her hand with a grip so strong cords stood out on his pale wrist. Arkady's grief-dazed eyes flickered with fear, which soon was washed away by tears.

"Zsuzsa," Vlad said, and I marveled to hear emerge from that monster's lips a voice undeniably gentle, full of love and compassionate sorrow; marveled to know that Devil Himself still possessed the remnants of a human heart. He spoke to her in Roumanian, and I did not comprehend every word; but I understood perfectly from his tone what he said to her. I know he told her he loved her, and not to be frightened; I know he told her he would never leave her side.

His voice was so charming, so compelling that, hearing it, I believed he meant every word with all of his wretched soul.

And he bent low and kissed her on the lips.

Arkady was sobbing by then, and had covered his eyes with one hand, leaving the other around his sister's shoulder. But I watched, and saw, with the same fascinated revulsion with which I had read Zsuzsanna's diary, the deep sensuality, the barely contained passion, hidden in that brief embrace.

Vlad reluctantly lifted his mouth from Zsuzsanna's, and I saw the sudden blaze in his eyes, and the utter worshipful devotion in hers. She seemed at that instant to bloom; the barest flush of colour entered her cheeks, and her eyes shone with a joy so intense it verged on lunacy.

She relaxed utterly then, and gave up all struggle as she lay in her brother's arms while Vlad sat beside them, clasping her small, frail hand between his two large ones. She died with her eyes open wide, staring raptly into her killer's; and it was only after Dunya remarked that Zsuzsanna had not drawn a breath in some time that we realised she had gone.

Arkady broke down, overwhelmed by grief, hugging Zsuzsanna's body tightly and crying out in Roumanian. Vlad wept—wept, actual tears!—with him, then put a hand on his shoulder and tried to comfort him, but there was nothing that could be done to ease Arkady's pain; he pushed his uncle's hand away, angrily, and then turned to me and ordered: "Leave! Leave me alone with her!"

Heartbroken, I obeyed, and went with the others into the hall. Dunya excused herself, saying that she had to prepare for the body to be washed—and she shot me a glance warning me to be careful of Vlad.

She left, and I was alone in the corridor with the vampire.

His grief and distress in Zsuzsanna's bedroom had been so genuine that I had actually felt sympathy towards him; but now, it vanished, for as he turned to watch Dunya leave, I caught sight of his expression, and the gleam of victory in his eye. And more: an intelligence so utterly cold, so utterly calculating, that I felt no fear, only such hatred that for a moment I could not speak.

Despite his display of devotion towards Zsuzsanna he was no less a monster, no less her murderer.

As he faced me, his expression once more became that of the concerned relative, and he said to me in German: "Your husband has been through too much. You must try to comfort him now."

In response, I slipped a finger beneath the collar of my dress, caught the gold chain there . . . and drew out the cross, so that he might see it.

His eyes gleamed red, like an animal's catching the lamplight at night. He took a step back from me, but I caught the fleeting expression of fury that crossed his features. Most inappropriately at this time of great sorrow, his lips resolved themselves into a slight, bitter smile that revealed teeth.

"So," he said. "You are becoming superstitious, like the peasants?"

"Only because I have read her diary," I replied, my own lips twisted with loathing. "Only because I know what—who —killed her. Only because I know you have broken the covenant."

As I spoke, his smile faded, but the deadly teeth were still revealed. For a moment, he regarded me with such infinite rage that I felt a wave of dizzying terror. "You have learned more than Zsuzsanna's pages could have revealed," he said slowly, fixing his magnetic gaze upon me. "Who has spoken to you? *Who?*"

Suddenly fearful for Dunya's sake, I replied with silence.

He spoke again, with the lethal languor of a serpent coiling for the strike. "Only the ignorant," he said, his gaze still on me, "believe they know everything. You are not capable of understanding. How dare you speak to me of the covenant, of something I revere, something you know nothing of? I *love* Zsuzsanna . . . !"

Conscious of Arkady weeping beyond the open door, I dropped my voice to an impassioned whisper. "That is not love. That is vileness. Pride. Monstrous evil . . ."

He lowered his own voice to a hiss that sounded like an angry viper. "It is not yours to judge, to understand!" Suddenly his fury cooled, and his eyes took on that compelling loveliness, and he smiled—sweetly, as sweetly as Zsuzsanna had when she had begged me to kiss her.

"In the past, I would have decreed only one sort of fate for such a woman who dared insult me," he said softly, studying me from head to toe with that intent, sweeping gaze. "But you are a beautiful woman. Such eyes—like sapphires set in gold. Perhaps someday you *can* be made to understand. I have been alone, I have denied myself companionship too long. Too long . . ."

And he reached for me—gently, with the back of his curled fingers, as if to touch tenderly my cheek, but the cross at my throat held him back. Instinctively, I recoiled, and moved away until my back was pressed against the wall. He followed, until his hand hovered two inches from my face, and caressed the air above my skin. I trembled as he lowered it lovingly, lingeringly, as if stroking my cheek, the curve of my jaw, the sweep of my neck.

For a horrible instant, I found myself staring into his eyes, all grief, all disgust forgotten, thinking of nothing but their exquisite deep green beauty, of the titillation—God forgive me—I had felt while reading Zsuzsanna's diary, of the intense pleasure she had experienced, of how I might experience that pleasure, and more, should I simply tear the cross from my neck and pull him to me in that dark hallway, and feel his teeth sink deep into my flesh . . .

I raised my hand to my throat and closed it over the cross.

As I did so, the child within me stirred. I came to myself and felt a wave of revulsion greater than any I have ever known, and cried, "I would never allow it! I would rather die!"

He smiled evilly, and opened his mouth to speak, but I would not permit him. I trembled as I spoke—but with rage, not fear. Hatred and love gave me the courage to speak the truth.

"I will not stay," I said, lowering my shaking voice, once again mindful of my grieving husband in the nearby bedroom. "Nor will I permit Arkady to remain and be abused. You have mesmerised him somehow to make him stay here, to make him love you, but you have no power over me!"

"Do not be so sure, my beautiful Mary," he said—but this was entirely my imagination, for his lips never moved. He lowered his hand, but rather than step back, he leaned forward, threateningly, until those green eyes loomed large in my field of vision as he whispered, with the same hideous leer I had first seen at the *pomana:*

"Then for your own sake, and your child's, I would advise you to be mindful of wolves."

He left. I could say nothing, do nothing, but sag trembling against the wall in the corridor and listen to Arkady's tortured weeping.

My husband refuses to leave his sister's body. To-night he is safe, Dunya says; Zsuzsanna will not rise until after she is buried. And so I instructed the servants to leave him, as he requests.

Dunya and I are sleeping to-night in the little nursery, and have garlanded the windows with garlic wreaths. I cannot bear to be alone, or to spend the night in my bedroom, thinking of the shattered pane hidden behind the curtain. I hold the faint hope that perhaps *he* will not be able to find me here, and so I have brought my pillow and blanket, journal and pen. Dunya's presence is a sincere comfort.

As terrified as I am, there is a very strange relief in no longer doubting the peasants' tale of the covenant and the *strigoi.* The truth may be horrible, but at least I know for certain the Evil that I fight; and I know it cannot be stronger than the love I bear for my husband and child.

Zsuzsanna's death is but a temporary triumph for him. He will not win. He *will not.*

10

The Journal of
Mary Windham Tsepesh

19 APRIL. Arkady has gone mad. He refuses food or sleep and will not leave his sister's side, despite the fact that we buried her this noon.

The night Zsuzsanna died, he remained with her body. I did not try to dissuade him, as Dunya assured me he was in no danger, and I believed he was doing so out of Transylvanian custom; after all, he had sat vigil with his father's body the night we arrived at the manor.

But yesterday morning, he was still with her. Dunya came to the nursery to report that Arkady refused to leave Zsuzsanna alone with the servants, even when the women came to wash her; and when the men laid her in the coffin and carried her to the main drawing-room, he never left her side. This worried Dunya, for she has told me that it has been arranged for Zsuzsanna to be freed from the *strigoi*'s curse once she is buried and everyone has left the tomb.

After speaking with Dunya, I went to the drawing-room, but the door was locked and bolted, and Arkady appeared not to recognise my voice. He would not so much as come to the door—only shouted threats that he would use the pistol were he not left alone. Disheartened, I returned to the nursery—and though I was not raised a Catholic, found myself praying at the little shrine to Saint George Dunya has erected there. Grief and misery left me unusually exhausted, and so at last I fell into an unpleasant sleep.

In late afternoon, I was wakened by the distant sounds of a commotion. Later I learned from Dunya that my husband had brandished the pistol at two women hired by Vlad to sing the customary songs of mourning to Zsuzsanna's corpse, and had chased them from the room. The child began to kick so forcefully that afternoon, that I could not return to sleep, could find no rest.

By the time the sun set yesterday, Arkady still had not emerged from his vigil. The onset of evening reawakened my fears and my sense of urgency; I could not bear to think of my husband alone beside his undead sister in the darkness. And so, with a final silent plea to Saint George, I went to try to persuade Arkady to return with me to the safe haven of the nursery.

Chin lifted, shoulders squared with determination, I knocked on the door of the drawing-room. In reply, I received a harsh shout:

"Go away!"

"Arkady," I answered at once, and drew a breath, preparing to launch into a rational discourse as to why he should open the door. But at the sound of his voice, so strange and bitter and broken, I released instead a sob, and slowly leaned against the door, overwhelmed by the horror of our circumstances.

I could not find my voice; could only weep. For a few seconds there came silence—but then beyond the door came the muffled sound of footsteps, and the creaking of the bolt as it was pulled back. Slowly, the door opened, and in the wavering shadows stood my husband, with the pistol held in his right hand.

The sight of him pained my heart. He was rumpled, unshaven, with deep shadows beneath his tormented eyes, and at his right temple an unmistakable thin ribbon of silver had appeared in his thick coal-black hair in the hours since I had last seen him—put there by Vlad, who each day seemed to grow younger.

"Mary?" he asked tremulously, in a voice so childlike, so helpless and broken, it evoked more tears. He lowered the pistol ever so slightly, and frowned as he peered at me with red, swollen eyes encircled by dark shadows. His eyes have always been, I felt, his most handsome feature—in fact, the word "beautiful" is more appropriate. Like his "uncle" and sister, he has striking, breathtaking eyes: light hazel, flecked with much green, and encircled by a ring of dark brown.

Those pitiful, lovely eyes were utterly lost, as bewildered as those of a little boy wandering dazed through endless forest. He fixed them on me, and I saw them narrow, saw them flicker with uncertainty as he reached deep into his memory and tried to recall whether he truly knew me, whether I could be trusted.

"Yes, dear, it's Mary," I said gently, and took another step closer to the threshold. He tensed, but did not raise the pistol further; and when I held still, waiting, he lowered it at last until the barrel pointed at the floor, but did not ease his grip.

I entered and moved slowly, deliberately beside him as he turned and walked back towards the casket in the room's centre. Inside, no lamps had been lit, and the corners were shrouded in blackness. The only light came from great solitary candelabra, twenty-armed and almost my height, that stood at the head of the open coffin.

All twenty tapers were lit, and they cast onto Zsuzsanna a wavering golden glow that imbued her with such stunning loveliness that she seemed unreal as a statue, a magnificent work of art intended to represent the ultimate quintessence of Beauty. No living human could ever possess such allure. The sight of her stole my breath, caused me to raise fingers to my lips. Yet as I gazed at her, I realised that the effect was due to more than the candlelight; her very being seemed to radiate with an internal light, and her skin possessed the same peculiar phosphorescent quality I had first noticed in Vlad's skin, at the *pomana.* Indeed, it seemed, as I continued to look, to gleam with subtle flashes of pale silvery blue.

So enchanting was the sight of her that I had to close my eyes and force myself instead to look upon my husband, who settled into a chair pulled alongside the casket, the place where he had apparently spent the last several hours. Arkady, too, gazed upon Zsuzsanna so steadily he appeared entranced; and when I called his name at first gently, and then more loudly, he never heard, but continued staring at his sister with the distant, slack expression of one mesmerised.

I reached down to touch his arm. He whirled, and raised the pistol still clutched in his right hand, as though he had already forgotten that he had invited me in. I recoiled, and watched as the fear in his eyes eased, and was replaced once again by recognition.

"Arkady," I said softly, and when his expression faintly warmed, I grew bold and reached again to stroke his shoulder. I was not at all certain, when I entered the room, what I should say; I knew only that we had both come to a point of utter desperation, and so I spoke to him from my heart. "Arkady, I need my husband back. I need your help."

My words pierced his veil of despair and touched him. Slowly, he set the pistol down beside him on the chair cushion, and turned to gaze up at me with eyes that spoke of his fierce struggle to emerge from his interior darkness.

But I saw in that gaze a glimmer of the man I had known, and was heartened. "Come to bed, darling," I whispered. "Come to bed. It's time for both of you to rest."

He laced his fingers into his newly silvered hair and clutched it, shaking his head; his voice carried a hint of the anguish which had driven him to madness. "I can't . . . I dare not leave her . . ."

"There's nothing to be afraid of," I soothed. "We can have one of the servants sit with her."

"No!" He whipped round like a serpent to face me. "We can trust them least of all!" He lowered his voice to a conspiratorial whisper, as though afraid one of them might overhear, but his eyes were oddly lucid. "I trusted them once . . . with Father's corpse. If I told you what they did to him . . ." He shuddered, and again shook his head. "No. I will trust none of them with her."

"Arkady," I said firmly, "You said you have seen terrible things at the castle. Well, I have seen horrible things here. This house is no longer safe, and I need you. And not just I . . . Your child needs you as well." And I placed his hand upon my stomach and let him feel the restless child. His expression softened at that, and for a moment I thought he would weep. But instead, he rose from the chair and embraced me, clasping me so tightly I could scarcely draw a breath.

Yet I was grateful for that embrace; hot tears spilled onto my cheeks, and I held him with a desperation to match his own, terrified that if I dared let go, our little family might never be together again.

"I am so frightened," he whispered into my ear, our wet cheeks pressed together; tears streamed down our faces, but I could not tell which were his and which mine. "So frightened that anything should happen to you or the baby."

"And I am frightened for your sake," I said, "because of what has already happened to you. Arkady, you are not yourself; you are sick with grief. Do you remember we had agreed to go to Vienna, because the strain was too great? We must do so at once, before any further evil befalls us."

"Yes . . ." he murmured absently. "We should go." And then I felt his body tense against mine, and a muscle in his jaw begin to twitch. "But I cannot leave her. Not yet . . ."

I stiffened myself, and pulled back from the embrace,

though our arms were still about each other's waist. I decided to try to lead him gently to the truth of what Vlad really was.

"Arkady . . . you do see how beautiful Zsuzsanna is?"

He sighed, and, releasing me from the embrace, turned towards the casket to look on her once more with sorrowful appreciation. "Yes . . . Yes, she is beautiful . . ." He choked, fighting back tears.

I stood beside him, and put a hand on his shoulder to comfort him. "More beautiful than she ever was in life. But . . . have you forgotten her spine was curved, and her leg withered?"

He looked suddenly up at the shadows dancing on the high ceiling, as though unwilling to confront the memory, as though afraid what contemplation of it might reveal. His breath began to come quickly, and his shoulders to rise and fall, as though he were struggling to repress the conclusion reason might bring.

"No," he said bitterly. "No, I haven't forgotten."

I gestured at the body in the coffin. "Look at her, Arkady. Look at her! You can see she does not look as the dead ought to look after a day's time. Her back is perfectly straight; she is taller. And look at her legs!"

And despite himself, he looked down at his sister's corpse, and the two perfect, well-formed legs beneath her gown.

"They are both perfect now," I continued. "What could cause such a miracle?"

He clutched his forehead. "Insanity! The same insanity that caused me to see Stefan, to see the wolves spare my life; that causes Uncle every day to grow younger! And I have done this to you, Mary, to the person I love most in all the world . . ." His voice cracked. "I cannot bear to see it happen to you . . ."

I heard the wildness in his voice, but also the stirrings of unwanted revelation; I felt I could not afford to desist. Gently, but firmly, I said: "Arkady, I am perfectly sane; I am the same

Mary you have always known, and I tell you now, you are not mad to have seen these things. Zsuzsanna is perfect now because she is *strigoi,* one of the undead." I hesitated. "Did you not see Vlad, when he came to be with her? His hair is black, where once it was silver; he appears thirty years younger. How do you explain it?"

His gaze went directly to the small gold cross, which I had thoughtlessly failed to slip inside my dress before coming to speak to him. His eyes narrowed at the sight of it, and he lifted his gaze to mine and with horrified revelation whispered, "Good Lord, you are just like them now, aren't you? You are as misguided as they! You would like nothing better than for me to go to sleep, so you can help them violate her body, just as they did Father's—!"

The look of hurt betrayal on his face broke my heart. I wound the fingers of my left hand tightly round the crucifix until it cut into my flesh, and cried out to think my husband so under the vampire's spell that he was lost to me forever; to think that the blood which flowed in his veins—and the veins of our child—tied us irrevocably, eternally to the monster.

To think those bonds of blood could never be loosed, and that my child was doomed to trod the path of his unhappy ancestors.

Silently, I called upon Saint George, to wield his shining sword, and with one sweeping deadly blow, sever those crimson ties.

My despair must have shown clearly, for at the sight of it, Arkady choked, and all the anger seemed to leave him abruptly. He sagged with exhaustion, and in a low voice full of misery, asked, "Do you have any idea what you imply, by saying these things are true?" His voice dropped to a whisper. "Poor Mary. My sweet darling, I have tainted you, the one I love most, with the evil here. I have brought you and our child into a viper's pit. It is all true . . . Uncle is mad and a murderer, just like my father, his accomplice, and I am destined to become like them . . ." He buried his face in his hands, overwhelmed by the same vision of bloodstained generations that had visited me, and said, "My child! My poor child!"

His torment was so keen I felt it, too, and could only stare sorrowfully at him as we were both stricken to silence by the utter cruelty of the truth. I waited, hopeful that he would come to his senses, that I could convince him to flee this place with me.

"You are no murderer," I said, with trembling voice. "But Vlad is *strigoi,* and he controls you. Let me bring you Zsuzsanna's diary. She has written of how he drank her blood . . ."

But I had not spent my childhood being taught to love and revere Vlad, and the vampire's blood did not flow in my veins. It was easier for me, a strong-willed outsider, to resist Vlad's mesmerism, to accept the truth, than it was for my poor husband. He raised his face and said hoarsely: "Oh, Mary . . . Mary . . . It only proves that she is as mad as I. Go. Go now! I can bear no more!"

When I hesitated and opened my mouth to contradict him, he raised his voice: *"Go!"* And he went back to the chair beside the coffin, retrieved the pistol, and retook his place as guardian of Zsuzsanna's corpse—unaware that by so doing, he served neither reason nor loyalty nor love, but the most malignant of purposes.

I think his "uncle"—or more likely, his grandfather, removed by two dozen "greats"—has more influence over him than we shall ever know. At that moment, I saw Vlad's eyes in the flickering gloom, heard in my mind his mocking laughter: So we thought he could be so easily outwitted, did we? So we thought Zsuzsanna was ours to do with as we wished?

Arkady's expression was hard, unreachable, as he turned his profile towards me and sat gazing down, grief-stricken, at his sister's voluptuous corpse, radiant in the wavering candle-light. I knew it would do no good to argue with him then, and so I left, downcast, defeated, but telling myself that exhaustion would most certainly claim him later that night.

It did not. He sat with her through the night of the eighteenth, and when, this morning, I learned from Dunya that he still remained by her side, wild-eyed, near delirium from refusing food and drink, my heart sank.

The funeral took place at noon. It was the most pitiful of affairs. Only four of the servants came, as tales of Zsuzsanna having died as a result of the bite of the *strigoi* had caused the rest to stay away. They came first to the drawing-room, and stood before the open coffin to pay their dead mistress a respectful moment's silence, with caps removed. Ion wept, and I thought I detected in his sorrow a hint of the indignant anger I had seen in Dunya, when she had first learned of the broken covenant. He tried to slip his own crucifix into his dead mistress's hands, but Arkady, watching jealously, snatched it from him. For a moment, I thought my husband would fling it; instead, he thrust it in his pocket so that it might not be retrieved and shouted at the old gardener in Roumanian. I felt terribly sorry for the old man, and wished I could speak his language so that I could comfort him, for he regarded my husband with tearful bewilderment but replied not a word.

Ilona and Dunya came too, and stood gazing at the corpse with uneasy reverence, and more dread than sorrow—for they knew better than any the startling changes which the *domnisoara*'s body had undergone. The bright fear in Ilona's large eyes said that she, too, understood her mistress would rest neither peacefully nor long, that the casket was a wooden womb which would birth a child perfect, beautiful, and monstrous.

Mihai and frail, dear Ion helped Arkady carry the casket into the tomb, which was a great struggle for the three of them; and because the others had left, no one had prepared the tomb for the ceremony. Zsuzsanna was laid to rest—no, not to rest! Not unless I can coax Arkady to leave her to-night—without flowers or candlelight or song in a tomb grimly festooned with spiderwebs and dust.

Rumpled and wild-eyed and unshaven, Arkady spoke. I

do not remember what he said; I felt through the whole ceremony unwell, on the verge of fainting, and was relieved when
it lasted no more than a few minutes. And then our somber
little group trudged out—all except Arkady, who sat on the
cold stone floor in front of his sister's coffin and drew out the
pistol, clearly intending to sit vigil.

I was too distraught to try to plead with him anymore,
and wanted only to hurry outside and be free of the still,
oppressive air in the tomb, but Dunya paused to speak to him
in Roumanian. In response, he took aim at her with the pistol.

We left him there. What else could we do? All the words
in the world cannot help him or his sister at this point.

I had Mihai take a message this afternoon to the castle,
saying there would be no *pomana* this evening, as Arkady was
indisposed.

Like the servants, I am prepared to flee. I have packed the
trunks, and now need only to retrieve my poor husband. I am
determined to make good on my promise to Vlad: We will not
stay.

Dunya says the vampire cannot cross running water, except in his coffin of earth. Very well; Arkady and I shall make
our escape at morning, and will not stop until we cross the
Muresh River, which we should make by dusk if we drive the
horses hard. Until then, we will remain ensconced in the nursery, which Dunya has made a safe haven, with garlic wreaths at
the window and door, and everywhere else, the portraits of
saints. She keeps a candle burning in front of an icon of Saint
George, who wields a sword, ready to lop off the head of *dracul*
—the dragon.

The Devil.

I remembered it was the word by which Mister Jeffries
referred to Vlad; Dunya has explained to me that the villagers
call Arkady's family by this name.

I have been praying to Saint George, too—praying that
he will protect my husband and child. I would kill the dragon
with my own hand, if that were possible, but Dunya says it is

too dangerous to attempt and that, during the day when it is safest to destroy him, the door to his resting place remains locked and bolted, and is too heavy for any single soul to break down. Those who have tried have all met violent deaths.

How many centuries must we wait for the holy dragon-slayer to incarnate on this earth and deliver us from this monster?

Dunya and I have discussed what must be done to bring Arkady out of the tomb, to prevent Zsuzsanna from rising as *strigoi* to-night. It seems impossible that he could stay awake much longer; but if he does, it is my plan to go to him, like Delilah, offering to ease his thirst . . . with a draught containing laudanum. If sweet words will not coax him, then the poppy will.

The sun is lower in the sky; it is time.

Saint George, deliver us.

❧11❧

The Journal of
Mary Windham Tsepesh

19 APRIL, ADDENDUM. Dear God, he has infiltrated our little haven of safety! He sleeps among us—and I cannot go warn my husband, who is at the mercy of another, more monstrous, child about to be born. Vlad knows everything we planned.

While Dunya, poor innocent pawn, knows nothing. She smiles sweetly at me even now as she pours me a cup of pain-relieving tea, unable to decipher the mysterious legends I scrawl across the page—quickly, before the next wave of agony comes. I fear this will be the last diary entry I shall ever make. I will leave it where my dear husband can find it, should he survive this night.

The pains started shortly after I returned from speaking to Arkady in Zsuzsanna's tomb and was walking with Dunya back to the manor. In the middle of the grassy lawn, I sank to my knees, reaching out, and in my flailing distress caught hold of Dunya's dress just beneath the collar.

The fabric at her neck gaped to reveal the tender skin just above the collarbone, and the two small red marks there—round, with white centres.

Grief pierced me like a sword, filling me with the same icy agony as the instant I learned, so many years ago, that my mother and father were dead. True, Dunya is still alive—she breathes, she speaks, she moves—but she is as lost to me as my parents, long buried in the cold earth.

I released a horrified wail at the sight; Dunya thought I cried out in the anguish of childbirth. I wanted to flee, to run away into the forest. At first I struggled, and would not let her lay a hand on me; but I was soon forced to let her help me back to the nursery.

Once there, I fought not to shudder at her touch, too disabled by my condition to do anything but let her tend me. But she has been as gentle, as devoted as a sister. I look now at her loving, guileless face and can only weep.

Monster! Monster! Someday I shall make you pay for what you have done to her, to Arkady's sister!

I can see in Dunya's eyes that she, unlike Zsuzsanna, is entirely unaware of what is happening to her; my dearest friend has become my most dangerous foe, and she does not even know it. How long has he used the poor innocent girl? Did it happen recently, or has she been his since the night she slept in Zsuzsanna's room? Does she slip out to him at night, when we are asleep? Has she always been his spy?

Or did I betray her by telling V. I know of the covenant? Is this how her faithfulness to me is rewarded?

I cannot bring myself to tell her, to rend her heart. Dunya, my loyal Dunya! The *strigoi* has won. You and I both are lost . . .

Pain again. I can write no more. God help us.

12

The Diary of Arkady Tsepesh

21 APRIL, ADDENDUM ON SEPARATE PARCHMENT. 1 A.M. I sit listening to my wife's screams as I write a warning to the child who is now being born. Days have passed since last I wrote in this journal, and in the interim I have experienced more grief and horror than words can convey. Zsuzsanna died and was laid to rest in the family tomb. Of that period I remember only the instant she died in my arms, her beautiful dark eyes fixed on her uncle's.

The whole event is a blur; my will was broken slowly, inexorably, by first my father's, then Jeffries', then my sister's deaths. And when the talons of control crushed my mind as I sat three days earlier in this same room, this time they would not release their grip.

Oh, but what I have seen this night transcends any previous terrors. What I have seen so shocked me to my very essence that I emerged out the other side of madness, and am sane.

Sane—and for the first time in my life, no longer a puppet.

Let me record, then, what I can remember clearly. I have stated here all I can remember of my sister's death; I was apparently awake three days and would not eat, and remained with Zsuzsa in the tomb, but of this I have only fleeting recollection.

My wife came to me less than an hour before dusk the day Zsuzsanna had been buried. This I remember well because of the emotions it provoked, and because of what followed.

I remember sitting in the tomb on the cold marble floor beside my sister's sealed casket, my back propped against the cool wall, elbows on my knees, both hands grasping the revolver. I was in an odd state of consciousness, neither waking nor dreaming, but somewhere between the two, where dreams seemed free to intrude upon and merge with reality.

I had been inside the windowless building since mid-day, and had left the great stone door open that I might better hear and see an intruder's approach. The door opened on an antechamber, which contained dozens of older coffins, and a narrow corridor led back to a second wider chamber, full of even more deceased, to which had been added the alcove where my immediate family was buried. Only a small shaft of sunlight penetrated the outer chamber into the alcove, leaving it dim and shadowy, but my eyes had grown accustomed to the lack of bright light, and I was able to tell by the increasing gloom that the day was waning.

I fell into a strange waking dream wherein I imagined that my father, mother, and Stefan lay perfectly preserved atop their coffins. As I watched, they rose with the slow, silent dignity of the dead to sitting positions, opened their eyes, and gazed down on me with expressions of benevolent concern.

I was most of all surprised to see my mother—and quite clearly—for I had no memory of her whatsoever, only a vague mental image based upon a small oil portrait of her my father had, which was painted some years before they were married. I knew from the painting that her hair had been pale, but when I saw her sitting upright atop her casket, I was most amazed to see how much she favoured my wife. Oh, she was larger of bone and build and bosom, with a square jaw and wider face, but the resemblance was undeniably there, especially in the eyes. She wore a low-cut white silk gown with short puffed sleeves and a wide blue ribbon beneath her breasts, in the form-revealing, immodest *empire* style that had been popular more than twenty years ago, when women dampened their dresses to make them better cling. Her long curling golden hair was tied back with more blue ribbon, but otherwise allowed to fall free like a young girl's.

She seemed so young, even younger than Mary, and looking down on me with confident, tender brown eyes, gave me a smile that made all grief and madness and heartache fall away.

Beside her, Father sat, and my throat constricted to see him young and strong and unbowed by grief.

And then Stefan rose beside them, a thin, knob-kneed, smiling-eyed child, and in those shining orbs I saw a love, a tenderness that had been absent from the eyes of the *moroi* who had led me into the forest, the *moroi* who had no doubt been a malevolent imposter.

At the sight of them, the familiar skull-crushing pain seized me. I cried out and held my head between my hands, pressing hard as though to blot out my consciousness.

Yet, surprisingly, the pain could not cause these images to disappear. My family remained, and directed affectionate smiles at me. I panted, disabled by the agony, but my fear began to ease in their presence; and as the fear eased, so did the pain, only slightly, but enough to permit me to open my eyes and look upon them.

Their appearance evoked no trepidation in me, as Stefan's materialisation once had, for they emanated such intense concern and love—all for me—that I began to sob out of sheer wonder and gratitude.

In the past weeks, I had seen little of good and far too much of evil, but when my family appeared round me, I felt it was a sign that good would triumph after all—that the evil which had littered the forest with skulls would be defeated, and justice done. I felt—I felt (even now it is difficult to speak of it without a welling of emotion; the sense was so strong) that though they were dead, my family put their arms around me, tried to give me strength. Most of all, I felt my mother wished me to know that love would conquer all despair, that all my grief and confusion would vanish if I would merely listen to my heart.

I believe this even now, with all my being. If there is absolute Evil in the world, then certainly there must also be absolute Good, which revealed itself to me through the love of my dear, dead family; a Good powerful enough to break through the mental bonds which held me enslaved.

Tears of joy streamed down my face—and in the midst of this amazing revelation, I heard footsteps at the entrance to the tomb. Yet I was too overwhelmed by emotion—by love—to be frightened or to raise the revolver.

And when I heard my wife's voice, at the same time frightened and determined, softly call my name, I knew it was a sign. I understood my family's message then: that I was lost, enslaved by misery and confusion, but Mary's love for me—and mine for her—could dissolve the vampire's hold over our family and save our child.

Hopeful, I set the gun on the floor by Zsuzsanna's casket and struggled to my feet toward the source of that lovely sound.

Yet I was too dizzy and weak to remain standing. I sank back to the floor just as my beautiful wife's silhouette entered the alcove. A stray beam of sunlight glinted off her face, revealing eyes glistening with tears.

"Arkady?" she said, her voice high and uncertain; eyes unaccustomed to the dark, she hesitated, unseeing, only feet from me, then took a halting step forward. A second ribbon of fading sunlight fell lower, across her bosom, and gleamed blindingly off the little gold cross and the faceted crystal decanter in her hands.

"Here," I replied, and watched as she peered into the shadows and caught sight of me.

I suppose I sounded weak and pathetic, for she said, "Oh,

Arkady," with such pity and anguish, I was stricken with love for her. With great difficulty because of her swollen stomach, she set the decanter on the floor beside us, then struggled to sit. I tried again to rise, and managed to meet her partway and awkwardly help her the rest of the way down.

My dead family had vanished by that time (though the terrible pain in my head remained) so that we were surrounded only by silent caskets, but I felt their love encircling me still. And so I encircled my wife with my arms, and pressed against her and the child.

She wept quietly a time, without making a sound, but I felt her tears warm against my neck. After a time she lifted her face, and said in a voice calm but weary as my own, "I have been so worried about you. If you continue this way, you will make yourself ill. Please . . . come home with me."

The pain gripped me again so hard I moaned, to her dismay and concern. But as much as I loved her at that moment, as much as I would have given my life to make her happy—I could not honour her request. Why? I told myself at the time it was grief; I thought I did not trust V. or anyone else to protect Zsuzsa's body. I thought that if anything happened to it, I would not be able to live with myself. And yet . . . The truth was I remained because some external force *demanded,* compelled that I remain; because the invisible claws still gripped my poor, confused brain.

Now I understand.

But at the time, I did not question my reasons. I merely stroked Mary's golden hair and murmured, "My darling, I cannot leave. But if you wish, you may stay here with me. I will keep us both safe."

She tensed in my arms. "But you haven't eaten or drunk in two days."

"Ilona brought me some tea in the drawing-room," I said, but that had been—a day ago? Two? I could no longer judge time. I had no sense of hunger, but my thirst was great, and I looked longingly down at the decanter on the floor.

Mary seemed to read my thoughts. She reached for the decanter, removed the glass which had rested inverted over the stopper, and poured some of the contents into it. "I knew you must be terribly thirsty," she said, in a caressing, coaxing tone. "I brought you tea with a little plum brandy in it; still warm, to keep the evening chill away."

The floral, fiery fragrance of the tea and slivovitz was heavenly, tempting, as was the high-pitched melody of the liquid filling the glass. I realised then how my parched throat ached, how my dry tongue adhered painfully to the cottony inside of my cheek. I seized the glass from my wife's hand and drank it down greedily, draining it in three swallows, unmindful of the tea that dribbled down my chin.

"More?" she asked, and filled the glass again before I could reply. I began to drink again, eagerly—then hesitated after the second swallow, alerted by instinct. I drew the glass away, stared at it, then stared at Mary.

My conniving wife. My loving Judas.

I swallowed, then flexed my tongue against the roof of my closed mouth, savouring critically: yes, there was the flowers-and-earth taste of the tea, and the sting of the brandy . . . but there was another component as well, faint but altogether familiar.

The bitter taste of opium.

The compulsion said to be angry; to scream at her, berate her; to hurl the glass against the marble wall and see it shattered into a thousand pieces. But the memory of my love for my family gone and my family yet to be stayed my hand. I set the glass down and said, sadly, "You have betrayed me."

A shaft of red, dying sunlight shone behind her, leaving her features in shadow, but even in the gloom I saw her determination in the squareness of her shoulders, the lift of her chin. "For love's sake," she said. "To save you and the child. Arkady, come with me."

"I *can't*," I replied, and released a sob. "Don't you understand?"

As I spoke, she rose to her feet, then gazed down at me. Her voice was utterly weary, utterly determined. "Yes. Yes, I understand. He controls you—but he will not for long."

And she left without another word, moving out into the feeble sunlight with the fixed expression of one resolved to be victorious. I knew she would merely wait a brief time for the laudanum to do its work, then return.

Yet the instant she was gone, I gave way to the unreasoning fury. How dare she be so blatant about her plan? For I knew that she intended for me to fall prey to the laudanum in my weakened state, then with the aid of accomplices would fetch me. And what would they do to poor Zsuzsa, once I was conveniently removed?

I stood, snatched the decanter and glass and threw them blindly, then turned from the tinkling shower of shards to sink to my knees, pitching forward until my forehead rested against cool marble. Thus I remained, in a state of utter despair and confusion, both in love with my wife and full of unreasoning rage towards her.

As I huddled there, the sun set and the shadows lengthened, then faded altogether into gloom. Soon the opium began to lower its soft grey curtain over my faculties, and sleep threatened. I struggled against it, tried to force my wandering attention on the sounds outside the tomb, to listen for intruders who would certainly soon come. But I fell into another half-waking, half-dream state, my face still pressed against the floor, my hands against my closed eyes. I felt the talons sink into my brain once more, but this time I yielded peacefully and did not struggle.

The darkness around me filled with a preternatural brilliance and I lowered my hands to see Uncle's green eyes, ablaze with an interior incandescence. Yet the dark outline of his form remained invisible—only his eyes appeared, though I clearly heard him speak.

Be strong, Arkady. Stay awake but a little while longer, and all will be well.

His voice was musical, soothing, pleasing to the ear, and soon I calmed. Despite his urging, I fell after several moments into a sound slumber. How long I slept I do not know; but I was awakened some time later when the corridor lit up with the distant, yellow glow of a lantern, and footsteps echoed in the tomb's entrance—followed by a lupine snarl, and a man's horrified screams.

I clambered groggily to my feet, and groped in the shadows for the revolver, found it on the cold floor, then ran towards the commotion.

Just inside the open entrance to the antechamber, the lantern lay on its side, and the oil had spilled out in a puddle on the marble and ignited. I watched by the light of that small blaze as a large grey wolf pushed its muzzle past flailing arms, sank its teeth into the throat of a man, and shook him as a terrier might a rat.

I raised the gun, ready to fire—but the rapid movement, combined with my exhaustion and the laudanum's effects, blurred the distinction between victim and attacker. I cried out in frustration, unable to aim, afraid to fire, lest I instead kill the human.

The victim let go a gurgling, gagging cough; his arms fell back limp against the marble as the wolf bent lower, sinking its teeth more deeply into flesh and muscle and bone before giving another, more thorough shake, then lifting its prey more than a foot off the ground.

The wolf let go, satisfied its job was done, and observed its handiwork. The man fell back, his skull striking the marble with an ugly crack, the impact spattering fat drops of blood on the white walls and floor.

I gasped as I recognised the old gardener, Ion. His white moustache was soaked with blood, his dark eyes wide with terror, his mouth slack and bubbling with the same crimson foam that welled up from his exposed windpipe.

With bright, deadly golden eyes, the animal looked up at me and emitted a low growl.

I raised the revolver to shoot. To my surprise, the animal turned, and, rather than attack, bounded out of the tomb and into the night. I did not pursue, but instead knelt beside poor Ion, who was already dead. Only then did I notice on the floor beside him a cloth bag, stained with blood.

I opened it, and found within the mallet, the saw, the stake, the garlic. The sight filled me with wild, mindless hatred; I could not forgive Ion for the act. Driven by overwhelming compulsion, I took the bag and its contents over to the place on the floor where the oil had spilled, and fed it to the flames, slowly, coaxing them to consume as much as possible. The metal saw remained intact, and the mallet's handle was only slightly blackened, but the garlic ascended to heaven like the most pungent incense, with copious, eye-stinging smoke. I took pleasure in seeing the stake charred and broken into small pieces.

By then all the oil was consumed and the fire went out, leaving me in hazy darkness. I slipped the revolver into my waistband and rose, dizzied by smoke and opium, and stumbled back towards the inner chamber.

As I entered the narrow corridor, I spied at its other end a fleeting flash of white, and hesitated, at first fearful; but the flash had been gently radiant, like feeble candleglow, before disappearing. This was no wolf, but a person carrying a failing lamp—Mary, I decided, who had returned and somehow slipped into the inner chamber without my notice.

I called her name.

And heard, echoing within the second chamber, a soft sigh, almost a groan, a sound that was at once human, feminine, yet strangely feral. And with that sound—I do not understand how or why, but with that sound . . .

All confusion, all doubt fell away. There was still fear, yes, deeper and greater than ever before, and grief. I can only compare my mental experience to that of a man who, ignorant of the fact he has been blind for decades, suddenly regains his sight. The shackles of control fell away, the invisible claws that clutched my skull withdrew. For the first time since child-hood, my mind was truly my own.

The light grew as Zsuzsa stepped into the outer chamber.

Gods! she was lovely, as radiant as an angel. It was her pale, shining skin that had glimmered in the corridor, and I saw it in the darkness as clearly as if she had been surrounded by a thousand burning candles—nay, that seemed to blaze bright within her! Impossible for any man not to be drawn like a moth to that inner flame, to those full, red satin lips, to those gleaming teeth. To those eyes, whose gentle dark brown colour had not changed, but which now seemed burnished with gold; blank, wild eyes which looked upon me and did not know me. Her hair had become lustrous and black, asparkle with glints of electric blue. That hair fell unfettered and soft to her waist, over a body whose shape showed clearly beneath the diapha-nous grave cerements: a body newly perfect and full and wom-anly.

All this I perceived in the space of a second, no more. For that brief time, I felt an urge to step forward, to embrace her, to kiss those crimson lips, to weep with joy at her resurrection; but my mind was free, and my thoughts clear. My elation turned quickly to horror as I understood with blinding convic-tion the truth about V., about my poor dead sister.

Dear God, I only thought I knew fear. But what I have experienced of it in my past is like a tiny crystalline pond compared to the storm-dark, turbulent ocean that surrounds me now.

I turned and ran; ran as though the Devil Himself pur-sued, across the uneven slope towards the manor, my mind swirling with revelations:

That my uncle was indeed the *strigoi* of legend. That I had been controlled, led step by step by V., masquerading as my brother's ghost; that he had controlled the behaviour of the wolves, who were meant to kill other prying souls who went into forbidden areas of the forest—but *not* to harm me. That he had stopped the wolves in time . . . in order to lead me to the conclusion of my own madness.

He toys with you . . . It is all a game.

All a sadistic game to lead me to the forest, then to Bistritz, then to the verge of insanity . . . but for what purpose? For this one night, when I was but a pawn to protect Zsuzsa? To break my will, that I might co-operate in murder? In the procurement of victims?

But V. needs no one's help; could it be that he torments me for the sheer simple pleasure of it? No. It must be something more; he is too shrewd, too calculating. But if so—why now has control of my own mind, my thoughts and emotion and volition, been returned to me?

I ran straight to the stables and there harnessed the horses to the caleche, intending to fetch Mary immediately and flee with her into the night. Yet before I could climb into the carriage and drive it round to the front of the manor, I heard a sudden shriek:

"Domnule! Domnule!"

The little chamber-maid, Dunya, dashed towards me out of the darkness, gesticulating wildly; her scarf had come loose and slipped down upon her hair, and her face was red and shining with tears. *"Domnule, hurry!"* she cried, sobbing and gasping for breath such that she could scarcely get the words out. "The child is about to be born, and he has taken her! He has taken her!"

My heart froze; I knew at once of whom she spoke, yet I grabbed her shoulders and shook them. "Who? Mary? Has someone taken Mary?"

"Vlad!" she replied.

"Where?"

"The castle . . ."

I swung up into the caleche and took the reins; beside me, Dunya wrung her hands, crying out pitifully, "Do not leave me! Please, let me come!"

"It is safer for you here," I said, and urged the horses on;

but she managed to catch hold of the moving carriage and climbed up, saying, with a determination that touched me:

"She is my mistress; I cannot desert her! The baby is coming and she will need me."

So I headed for the castle equipped with nothing more than a lantern, Father's revolver, and the chamber-maid.

As we drew near to those grey stone walls, they appeared especially forbidding and forlorn; at first I assumed it was my state of mind that made them so. Then I realised, as I stared at the great ancient battlements rising dark against the darker sky, that not a single window shone with light.

I pulled the caleche into the courtyard and handed the reins to Dunya. "Remain here. If I do not return with Mary within a quarter-hour, take yourself to safety."

Fright had made her eyes great as saucers, yet she replied stoutly: "I will stay here until you return with the *doamna*." I tried to leave the lantern with her as well, but she insisted I carry it; and so, with lamp in hand, I tried to push open the great front door, which had been bolted shut. I therefore went round to the small entrance on the castle's eastern side, which I knew of only because I had seen the servants make use of it. With my free hand I drew the revolver, and made my way through the narrow corridors and up the winding front stair-case toward the guest wing.

I strained to hear the sounds of a woman groaning in childbirth but the castle was bereft of light or sound as a tomb, save for the wavering yellow glow cast by the lamp and the ring of my hurried footsteps. Yet I could not shake the notion that in the shadows lurked an evil, watchful intelligence, cog-nizant of my every move. I dashed from room to room, floor to floor, faster, faster, calling out softly at first and then, in des-peration, shouting Mary's name.

Silence; only silence, and gloomy bedchambers centuries unused and veiled in dust.

My pace and agitation increased until at last only two rooms remained unsearched: the guest quarters, and V.'s private chambers. The direction of my search caused me to arrive at the guest quarters, my best hope, first. The door where earlier a tousled, damp Herr Mueller and I had spoken stood wide open, and the rooms beyond were as dark as the rest of the building.

My sister's death and my terror for Mary's sake had caused me to totally forget the poor visitors for three days; I remembered them now with a thrill of dread. Raising the lantern, I moved through the outer salon into the bedroom, this time calling both Mary's name and the Muellers'.

To my bitter disappointment, this chamber also was deserted, though the signs of the most recent inhabitants were all too evident: a woman's fine white lace-and-silk nightgown, of the elaborate sort worn by brides on their wedding night, dangled from the edge of a nearby chair, where it had been tossed with joyful abandon; and upon the great canopied bed, in the centre of which I spied a tiny flower of dried blood, sheets and pillows and coverlet had been flung back and twisted into careless, rumpled piles.

Only one of the half-dozen pillows remained in its place, at the far left corner against the headboard. Propped against the solitary pillow, as though she had been placed there with utmost care to watch the proceedings, sat a child's doll in a lace christening gown, with hands and face of china and a body of rag. She had slumped forward from the waist, her face pressed against the sheets, her limp, lace-ruffled arms flung forward so that her intricately posed little hands rested beside lacquered brunette curls.

In the far corner of the room was a bath-tub filled with grey water. Near the bed a trunk sat opened and riffled through, as though the owners had retrieved items of clothing; but there were so many belongings scattered around the room that they more than accounted for the entire volume of luggage which might have been crammed into the trunk. It seemed that for once, at least, the servants had not made off with whatever booty was to be had.

The lamp revealed no clues as to what had become of the young couple, and so I left the guest quarters with a sense of foreboding and fatalism. I could think only of V.'s secret chambers; I knew the answer to my wife's fate, and that of the travelers', waited there.

I made my way through night-shrouded corridors to Uncle's rooms, and the nearer I drew, the more my dread increased.

I arrived to discover the door to V.'s sitting-room open and the hearth and tapers unlit. I stepped inside and faced away from the fireplace and saw, gilding the slightly ajar door that led to Uncle's private chambers, a ribbon of light.

That strip of light pulled like a magnet. I set the lamp upon the end-table, and crossed the sitting-room to stand before that door.

Reality faltered. I knew that I, an adult, married and soon to be a father, put my hand forth and grasped the doorknob. At the same time I was Arkady the child of twenty years before, who clung fearfully to his father as Petru reached for the door.

The adult Arkady's hand turned the knob and pushed; my father's ghostly hand did the same.

And at the sound of the hinge creaking, the door to memory opened to allow me my past. The grown Arkady vanished, leaving only my child-self and my father in the long-repressed reality of twenty years ago, in the grim days after Stefan's death.

In the second it took for the door to swing inward, groaning, I remembered:

Crossing the threshold with my father, his hand tight upon mine, his voice soft and soothing as he said, No harm will come to you, Kasha. Only trust me, and trust Uncle . . .

The light of a hundred candles glittered in his tear-filled eyes.

We walked through the narrow entryway, then emerged into a grand hall. The side on which I stood, the left, was hidden from view by a ceiling-to-floor black velvet curtain, large enough to conceal a small stage.

In front of us, on the back wall, was yet another closed door leading to yet another secret chamber.

To our right, across from that mysterious theatre, sat a platform of dark, polished wood, with three steps leading up to a throne. The platform's base was inlaid with gold, which spelled out the phrase *JUSTUS ET PIUS.*

Just and faithful.

On either side of the throne were tall candelabra, laden with blazing tapers, and upon it was seated Uncle, who gripped the armrests in his customary regal posture.

He emanated such confident power, such virile strength that I looked on him with the same fear and admiration I would have a beautiful lion: terrified of his wrath, breathless at his magnificence. His robes were scarlet, and atop his head rested an ancient gold diadem studded with rubies. Behind him, hung upon the wall was a crumbling warrior's shield of incalculable age; I could just make out the fading winged dragon thereon, and realised that this was the shield represented in the portrait of the Impaler.

At V.'s right hand was a golden goblet, set with a large single ruby, and resting in a special hollow carved into the throne's arm so the contents should not spill.

But the jewels that outshone all others were his eyes, which, standing out against the white of his skin and the silver of the hair that flowed onto his shoulders, pierced me with their pitiless emerald brilliance, their frightening intelligence. His beauty was as Zsuzsanna's had been when she had risen from the tomb: like the sun, too radiant to bear.

Stunned into reverent silence, we approached the prince upon the throne. At last my father genuflected, then crouched down to put his arms around me and say, in a tone of unutterably sorrowful resignation: "Here is the boy."

"You are sad, Petru," the prince said thoughtfully, in a deep, handsome voice; I emitted a gasp of surprise, for he had seemed too *unreal, too lovely, too much a work of art to speak.* "But there is no cause. I love the boy, and will treat him well."

"As you have treated me?"

A rebuke; but the prince remained distant, unmoved. "No harm need come to his loved ones unless he betrays me. He would have been spared this; his brother Stefan would have served as eldest, and Arkady would have lived a life free from this charge, but your actions have brought him here. You alone are responsible for the grief that has visited your family, Petru. I am harsh, but just. Remain faithful to me, and I shall remain faithful to you. It is all I ask."

He lifted an object; silver flashed as he drew the knife across his own wrist, and held it over the golden chalice over the arm of the throne. He bled little, but a few drops which came only when encouraged; and then he held the dagger towards my father. "It is time."

My father hesitated, then stepped up to the throne and reluctantly took the knife from the prince. He held it aloft for a moment, and I saw again the glint of candlelight on sharpened metal. "I can't," my father cried, anguished; his voice shook.

"You must," the prince replied, in a voice stern and unyielding, but I heard the odd undercurrent of tenderness there. "You must. I dare not trust myself. He is your son; you will be gentle."

My father's fingers tightened on the dagger. He lowered it, slowly, then with his other hand took the chalice proffered by the prince.

I watched him return to my side, feeling nothing but a child's curiosity. I trusted my father, even when he lifted the chalice to my lips and forced me to take a tiny sip. Gagging, I tasted salt and metal and decay; but the effect of that small taste of blood was overwhelmingly intoxicating. I grew unsteady on my feet, for the effect was warming as wine and altogether pleasurable. I felt a sudden wild, inexplicable burst of love and gratitude toward Uncle as I sank down to a sitting position; my father knelt beside me. When he set down the chalice to take hold of my arm and turn the inside toward him as he raised the dagger, I felt no alarm, only mild apprehension as to whether the cut might briefly hurt.

Certainly I felt no fear for my life as he brought the keen edge of *the dagger's blade down against the tender inside of my wrist, and nicked a vein there, whispering: "I'm sorry. Someday you will understand . . . it is all for everyone's good . . . For the good of the family, the village, the country . . ."*

The pain drew me from my cosy stupor. I cried out in indignance, and continued to do so as he held my small but copiously bleeding wound over the chalice and milked it.

I struggled feebly, but Father held my arm steady until the bottom of the golden cup was covered with my young, dark blood. And then he produced from his pocket a clean handkerchief and secured it firmly about the cut, holding it a time to stanch the flow.

Finally, he rose, and gave the cup to Uncle, and returned to me. I lay, faintly dizzy, with my head in his lap as he stroked my hair, making soft sounds of apology and comfort while Uncle cradled the chalice in cupped hands and lowered his face to it, eyes closed in pure bliss, breathing in its scent like a connoisseur inhaling the fragrance of the finest century-old cognac.

Then he opened his eyes, bright with anticipation, and said: "Arkady. Thus I tie you to me. Leave home you may—for a while, but this shall ensure your return to me, at the proper time; and, at the proper time, your will shall be returned to you, and all be made known. This I swear: you and yours I shall never harm, and shall generously support, so long as you support and obey me. Your blood for mine. These are the terms of the covenant."

Smitten with love, I watched from Father's lap the flash of candlelight upon gold as V. upended the goblet and drank.

I cried out and clutched my head as iron claws sank deep into my brain.

Of a sudden, I came to myself, to the adult Arkady of the present. The entire memory had returned, full-blown and complete, in the split second it had taken to unlock the door and push it open.

Now I crossed that threshold alone.

I passed through the small entryway into the great room. There, to the right, sat the prince's throne—empty now, though one of the flanking candelabra, tall as I, had been lit.

There, too, was the aged shield, though missing was the chalice which once held my blood. In the centre of the far wall stood the door which lead to even deeper mysteries, and to the left . . .

To the left, the black velvet veil had been pulled aside to reveal what had once been hidden:

Bolted to the wall, a set of black iron manacles; propped nearby, four oiled, glistening wooden stakes, twice a man's height and worn at one end to blunt points; a rack; and, dangling from the ceiling, the thick metal chains of a strappado, used to hoist victims by their arms into the air. Beneath manacles and strappado were strategically placed wooden tubs, the interiors clean but stained by countless years of use a permanent reddish-brown.

To one side of this chamber of horrors stood a carving-block which contained an assortment of cleavers and knives, and beside it a sturdy waist-high table, the length and shape of a coffin.

Upon this table Herr Mueller lay naked and prone, the bare flesh of his back the shocking white of an alabaster statue. Only his upper body rested upon the table; his legs dangled to the floor, bent slightly at the knees because of their length, so that his body formed an equal-armed if not altogether straight "L." Above his tangled mane of curling, sand-coloured hair, his arms were extended like a diver's, and at first, I thought he gripped the table's edge—

But no, his hands were utterly relaxed. I thought immediately of the little cloth and porcelain doll, slumped forward upon his wedding bed.

He was as limp and lifeless as she; dead. Quite dead.

And *moving*.

Moving, dead torso jiggling back-and-forth, stray golden-brown curls bouncing, head lolling ever so slightly, dead arms sliding up-and-down against the table, unfeeling fingers polishing the dull-gleaming wood limply, horribly, to the rhythmic slap of another's flesh against his.

I lifted my gaze and saw Laszlo, eyes closed, lips parted in dreamlike ecstasy, gripping the corpse at its hipbones as he stood directly behind it at the table's edge. His trousers were unfastened, pulled down to his thighs, and the hem of his long peasant's shirt swept over the small of the dead man's back as he thrusted.

I looked again at the body, and knew that the face hidden from me was frozen in the same rictus of horrified anguish Jeffries had worn.

I did not think, reflect, recoil. I raised my father's gun, aimed point-blank at the centre of the living man's skull, and opened my mouth to shout: *Stop! In the name of God, stop, or I will fire!*

Quickly, so quickly that I had no time to utter the words, Laszlo disengaged himself from the corpse, pulled a cleaver from the block, and hurled it at me.

The handle of the cleaver knocked the revolver from my hand; it went skittering into the shadows as Laszlo propelled himself over the table.

Even by wavering candlelight, I could see his face was transformed. No longer was he the dull, gloating coachman, but a wild-eyed fury. He lunged like the wolf who had attacked in the forest the day I had discovered the hidden graves. I threw up my arms in defense, half believing that he would not harm me—that, like the wolf, he was simply there to threaten, to discourage, to test.

We staggered backward like hell-bound dancers, his right hand clutching my left wrist, my left hand clutching the wrist of the hand which reached for my throat. We stood as close as lovers, so that I could smell his scent: sour sweat, mixed with the faint odor of faeces and decay.

So we proceeded, our arms trembling mightily in deadlock, his madman's strength forcing me back, away from the grisly site where Mueller and Jeffries had met their deaths— until the mortared stones beneath my feet grew uneven, and I lost my balance and fell.

My back struck the cold stone floor, forcing air from my lungs. I struggled to rise at once, seeking my attacker's throat and trying in vain to clutch it, but my left shoulder was pinned fast, evoking the image of the wolf in the forest, paws upon my shoulders, holding me down but resisting the temptation to kill.

But this human wolf had no such compunctions. My attempt to rise distracted my strength less than a second—but it was enough. Face contorted in an agony of effort, teeth bared, he broke my grip and seized my throat.

I cried out—a short, indignant yelp—and grabbed his wrists, fighting for air that would not come. I feared my battle was lost, that I, too, would suffer Jeffries' and Herr Mueller's post-mortem indignity upon that table.

Yet my cry was followed within two seconds—no more— by an abrupt, ringing explosion to my right. In my confusion, I thought the revolver had spontaneously discharged, but when my gaze darted in the direction of the noise, I saw that the inner chamber door, which now we lay several feet from, had been flung open with force.

V. stood in the doorway, blazing—not with glory but wrath. His dark brows were knitted together, and his features twisted by a rage terrible to behold. At the same time he was beautiful, too, in the pitiless, blinding manner of the sun, of an avenging angel. His hair was entirely jet, save for a few strands gilt with vermeil, and his skin radiated the blush of eternal, virile youth. I thought I looked upon myself perfected, redeemed. Our gazes locked, and the fury in his eyes merged with unspeakable astonishment.

"What impudent magic is this?" he whispered passionately. "Too soon—you are freed too soon! Do you think to ruin my plans?"

I stared at him with blank incomprehension. He narrowed his eyes, seemed to judge my reaction sincere. As I watched, he came towards us with impossible swiftness; or rather, he simply *loomed* large within my field of vision, and without seeming to have moved at all, was suddenly standing beside us.

At the sight of him, my attacker recoiled and knelt like a penitent as I fell back, gasping, against the floor. I fingered my throbbing neck and finally managed to sit while Laszlo wept:

"Do not be angry, *Domnia ta!* He tried to kill me—"

V. spoke again, and his voice, though soft, sounded in the silent chamber like thunder, like the wind and crashing cymbals, like the voice of God.

"Then you should have let him."

The prince parted thumb and forefinger of one hand to form a vee and swooped down to catch the soft part of Laszlo's neck therewith. With a muscular arm, he lifted the quivering coachman—high, higher, until Laszlo's feet dangled inches above the floor and his purple, gasping face hovered a foot above Vlad's own.

"Death is all you deserve!" V. hissed, with eyes that shone like dazzling green stars. "When you first came to me, did I not make you swear above all else that you were never to harm him? Never to cast so much as an untoward glance at my family, and least of all, *him*? Did I not? Did I *not*?

"I have allowed you everything you desire, and still you disobey! This I will never forgive!" He shook the gagging man like a puppet; Laszlo kicked the air, struggling vainly to breathe, to protest as V. closed his hand around his throat.

In the echoing stillness of the great chamber, I heard the wheezing sound of air being forced from a windpipe, of bone and cartilage grinding together.

"No!" I shouted hoarsely. "Stop!"

I lunged. He glanced at me and raised his free hand—merely raised it, and flicked it as though he were dismissing a housefly—to send me hurtling backwards across the room.

My shoulders and back struck the table where Herr Mueller's corpse lay, knocking the wind from my lungs. For seconds I lay stunned, unable to draw a breath; in the silence, I heard the dying man gag, then begin to gurgle, drowning as the pressure broke blood vessels in his throat.

I came to myself and scrabbled across the floor, searching vainly in the darkness for the lost gun, knowing the weapon would be useless against V.; yet I could not sit idly by and watch a man, however twisted and evil, be murdered.

At last came a sound of abrupt, strangled finality which sounded more catlike than human. I glanced up to see Laszlo swaying as he dangled from V.'s hand with the same eerily lifeless movement I had witnessed in Herr Mueller; his pale eyes bulged from an apoplectically red face, and his tongue thrust forth from an opened mouth. At his neck, V.'s fingers dug so deeply into the flesh I was surprised it had not torn.

I crawled away from this vision on my hands and knees, and did not turn to look behind me at the sound of the body being dropped against the stone. I wanted only to flee myself, to find shelter from awareness; to join Laszlo in the mindless dark. I continued until I collapsed in the open doorway to the inner chamber and lay my cheek against the cold stone, exhausted by the struggle, drawn to the dark. Yet as I turned my head to lay it down, I glimpsed more radiant white within, partially eclipsed by a foyer. Curiosity made me straighten, and crane forward, struggling to see beyond the corner of the entryway.

Another flash of white, accompanied by a woman's soft moans. I thought at once of my poor Mary, and my heart began beating rapidly. I grasped the lintel, pulled myself onto unsteady legs, and entered, my heart full of dread. The room opened to my left, on which side the wall jutted out a few feet, to prevent those outside the door from seeing in when it was opened. I moved forward only far enough to take in the entire room, and there I remained.

It was perhaps a third as large as the outer chamber, windowless and airless, with the same faint smell of stone, earth, and decay as the family tomb. It was darker than the outer room, so I could just distinguish the shapes of two coffins, side by side, in front of me. Both were black, and the larger one was draped with a banner bearing the same dragon emblem as the Impaler's shield. Nearby, at the smaller coffin's head, awaited yet another startling combination of flesh for my eyes to decipher.

In the foreground stood a creature with a schoolgirl's face and a woman's blooming body whom I knew was Herr Mueller's child-bride. She was half-naked, her dress unbuttoned and rolled down to her waist, her head tilted to one side so that long, brunette curls—much like the curls of the china doll—cascaded down over one seashell-pink shoulder and breast. But even her perfect porcelain skin seemed dull in comparison to the radiant white flesh of the woman who stood behind her.

My sister, brilliantly lovely in her grave cerements, just as she had appeared to me earlier in the family tomb. Zsuzsanna had fastened her lips upon that incarnadine neck to suck gently there, steadying herself by one hand clasped about the bride's waist, the other cupped beneath her full breast. A strand of Zsuzsa's hair, black with a dull blue sheen, had slipped forward and fallen from the place she drank down the woman's torso to her waist, like a trail of darkened blood.

And behind my sister, against the wall, stood a waist-high altar, draped in black, upon which burned a single black candle which illumined the items thereon: the golden chalice, the silver dagger with the inscribed black hilt, and a stone pentacle, ill-dignified.

Frau Mueller's expression was slack, and her primrose lips parted with a dreamer's sensuality; she arched her back against Zsuzsa and released small sighs that seemed inspired as much by ecstasy as pain.

I released a sound, too; a loud gasp, at which my sister's eyes flew open at once. The girl cried out and struggled, this time in unmistakable fear and pain—but feebly, still entranced, eyes still closed. Zsuzsanna fanned her hand over the girl's breast and pressed her tightly to her, as though anticipating a struggle, and looked up in my direction.

Crimson dripped from my sister's lips, stained her teeth and tongue. Blood welled from the two small wounds on the girl's neck. One tiny red river trickled down onto her breast, onto her seducer's hand; the other braided itself into the stray lock of Zsuzsanna's hair.

My sister blinked at me with burnished brown-gold eyes, eyes that were blank and feral, the eyes of a lioness interrupted while feeding on the kill. She did not know me, for there was no sign of emotion or recognition in them; but she must have judged me harmless, for she went back to her prey almost at once. I watched as she bared inhumanly sharp teeth; watched as they sank into tender flesh and widened the wounds. The girl cried out sharply and struggled, at which Zsuzsanna swiftly fastened her lips upon the wounds and began to suck.

The girl at once fell still.

I would have thrown myself upon them and tried to free the girl, but I had already felt the vampire's strength. I turned, thinking to fetch a weapon from the outer room, but a hand upon my shoulder stopped me.

"Arkady."

I looked up. V. stood before me, no longer the radiant avenging angel, but an utterly human creature that spoke to me with my father's voice, gazed at me with my father's eyes, held my father's Colt in his right hand.

Without thought, I snatched it from him and hurried towards my sister, whose lips were still pressed to the neck of the girl in her arms. I stepped beside them, pressed the cold metal barrel of the revolver against my sister's neck, careful to angle it so that the girl was not threatened, and begged, "Zsuzsa—stop!"

Zsuzsa's eyes had been closed in focused ecstasy as she drank; now she did not cease her drinking, but growled deep in her throat and lifted her lids enough to look at me from the corner of her eyes. And in her satiated, slightly drunken gaze, I saw no fear.

"Stop! For the love of God, stop!" I shouted, but I knew

she would not, just as I suspected that what I was about to do was useless, yet I did it nevertheless.

I squeezed the trigger. The weapon discharged; I stumbled backwards at its report and coughed as a puff of sulfur smoke stung my throat, nose, eyes.

Zsuzsa staggered, her blood-smeared face raised, her lovely features contorted, her sharp pearl teeth champing with rage. Still she held on to her victim. As the smoke cleared, a blackened, gaping tear in her neck became visible, and began to spurt bright, fresh blood which I knew was not her own.

Then she steadied; and as I watched, astounded, the wound ceased its bleeding, and began *to close itself.* Within seconds, it was entirely healed, and only the shadow of gunpowder remained as evidence of the insult. Zsuzsa bowed her head once again, entirely unafraid of me, and pressed her lips again to the girl's throat.

I threw myself upon her and tried to pull the girl away, knowing it was hopeless. And my sister—my small, frail sister, once crippled and so feeble she could scarcely walk down the manor steps to greet me—balanced her victim in one arm and with the other struck me.

The strength of that blow propelled me across the room and into the wall; the gun clattered to the floor. Somehow I managed to stay on my feet, and sagged, with a low cry of defeat, against the cold stone.

There was nothing I could do to save the poor girl's life; nothing I could do except watch, sobbing silently, as Zsuzsa drank. Frau Mueller's approaching death seemed to fill my sister with increasing excitement and abandon, and she began to drink more greedily, in loud, frenzied gulps, until at last the girl gave a long, weak groan, and fell. Zsuzsa caught her, wrapping her arms about the girl's waist, and lifting her as easily as a mother might an infant, held her in her arms and continued to drink until Frau Mueller released a long, rattling sigh.

V., who had been watching with solemn approval,

stepped forward, and, taking the girl from Zsuzsa's grasp, said: "Enough! It is over. More is not good, not when she is dead."

And panting Zsuzsa, her lips dripping blood, seemed to accept this. Lazily, like an animal who has fed well and then goes to lie in the sun, she closed her eyes with contentment and sank down onto the stone floor in front of the altar to rest.

Carrying the girl's milk-white body in his arms, V. turned to me and said, "Come."

"My wife!" I demanded, sick at heart to think that she might have suffered a fate similar to Frau Mueller's. "What have you done to my wife?"

"Come," V. commanded, in a tone that said if I wished ever to see Mary again, I must obey at once.

He moved through the doorway. I picked up Father's revolver and followed, past the motionless heap that remained of Laszlo, to the theatre of death and the butcher's table, where V. laid Frau Mueller's corpse beside that of her husband.

He looked up at me and paused; at once I repeated, "My wife! Where is Mary? Tell me at once!" Uselessly, I brandished the revolver.

A small smile played upon his lips; with a strength that dwarfed mine, he reached forward and easily pulled the gun from my grasp, but did not point it at me. "So," he said. "You have come to yourself, then."

"My wife—!"

"It merely seemed fitting that the child should be born here. She is in labour, but quite well. Dunya attends her."

"Dunya . . ." I broke off, having intended to say, *Dunya waits for me outside in the carriage; it is impossible!* Then I saw the amusement in his gaze, and closed my gaping mouth in horror at the realisation that both I and the little chamber-maid had been his pawns.

The merriment in his eyes died abruptly; his tone became hushed, that of one explaining the most sacred of mysteries. "We shall discuss your wife shortly. But first . . . You have learned the truth tonight, Arkady. This is what I am; accept it, and do not fear us."

"I can never accept such brutality," I whispered, inclining my head at the victims lying upon the table but closing my eyes, unable to look.

"The brutality of Nature Herself," said he. "We are predators; who can fault us for struggling to survive? Who can tell the hawk he must not hunt, the lion he must not kill? Who dares call that sin?"

"Hawks do not coldly plan to torment and kill other hawks," I countered, my voice trembling, my features contorted with disgust. "Nor lions other lions. But it is murder when humans set forth to do so."

"Arkady," he replied softly, "we are not human."

To this I had no reply, but averted my face, wanting to flee the grisly sight upon the table.

V. spoke again, in the same reverently somber tone. "Do you remember the ceremony, and what was spoken of the covenant?"

"I remember." Bitter, I stared down at the floor, recalling the numbed, hopeless grief in my father's eyes.

"The ritual is complete. I took your will from you then, to ensure that you would return to me now. These are the terms of the covenant: That you will assist us in attaining nourishment; that, for the good of the town, you will prevent the creation of new *strigoi*. In return, I will never harm you or yours, but will see you and they want nothing—"

"But you have broken the covenant! You have harmed Zsuzsa!"

V. lifted his chin regally. "I have given her life; she had none before. For love, I have made her *strigoi,* that she might know happiness with me. I accept the responsibility of caring for her always. Will you help us?"

And he raised the gun in his hand. For a confusing instant, I thought he might aim it at me; instead, he turned the barrel towards himself and pressed the butt into my palm. I closed my fingers around the weapon and stared at him.

"I give you back your will, Arkady. You must freely decide whether to return my love or to reject me, knowing what I am and what I require." V. paused, then gazed down at the corpses and asked, "You have heard, I am sure, of the peasant superstition concerning the prevention of new *strigoi?*"

I looked down at the two dead innocents lying before me and whispered, "I know it is what they did to Father's body."

"Yes," V. said, then turned to gaze at the instruments arranged beside the table; and I followed that look and saw the mallet, the shortened stakes, the knives.

I understood immediately what he wished, and cried: "No, I cannot!"

Had I believed I had any chance at all of overpowering him, I would have destroyed him in that instant with the implements surrounding us—but there was nothing I could do.

V.'s expression was perfectly hard, perfectly cool, perfectly matter-of-fact, as though we discussed some business matter concerning the estate over which we minorly disagreed. "Your father despised this task, also; and so he procured Laszlo. If you wish, you may make similar arrangements. I do not care how it is done. But this once, it must be done now—and quickly! You must, Arkady. I cannot. You *must.*"

"No!" I turned and headed to leave. Immediately, a gust of wind swept through the room. The door to the outer chamber slammed shut in front of me, and the bolt slid into the lock.

Behind me, V.'s voice said, "If you do not, they will rise as *strigoi* . . . and they are not bound by the covenant, as I and your sister are. They will be free to harm anyone: your wife. Your soon-to-be-born child."

I faced him. "But if I refuse to fulfill my role in the covenant? You say I have free will, that I can decide, but I am hardly acting of my own volition if you resort to blackmail—"

V.'s face was an impassive mask. "You are free. And I, like any predator, am free to act in a manner that ensures my survival. I am *voievod*. I do not deal lightly with those who would betray me."

"You killed Stefan," I said softly, hatred suddenly eclipsing fear. "You killed my mother . . ." I thought of the wolf-dog who had killed both my brothers, of the wolf at the window who had come so close to killing my wife, and my knees began to fail. I grasped the table's edge to steady myself.

His expression, his voice, were utterly without emotion. "It broke my heart, of course. But your father could at times be enormously stubborn. It was his choice to disobey and cause such tragedy." He lifted a stake and the mallet from the tools beside the table and proffered them to me. "Just as it is your choice now. Can you be strong, Arkady? Can you set aside your own self-interest in order to do what is best for your family? For the village?"

"Are you threatening my wife and child?" I whispered.

And the Impaler smiled, ever so faintly, and said, "It would do no good to threaten *you*, Arkady. You are too full of romantic notions of heroism and self-sacrifice."

I looked into those jade eyes, knowing that I was truly free from their hypnotic allure, that the Impaler told the truth that my mind was my own. The return of my will I could not fathom, except to think he allowed it out of some twisted notion of honour. "If I agree . . . will you take me to Mary? Will you swear not to harm her, or the baby?"

V. gave a solemn nod. "As long as you abide by the covenant . . . so shall I."

Very well, then; for Mary's sake, I decided I could bear to play his game long enough to set the Muellers free from the *strigoi*'s curse. Indeed, if V. would not free them, I was obligated to see that they did not rise.

I took the stake and mallet from him. V. turned Herr Mueller's body over so that the slack face gazed sightlessly up at the dark ceiling; and then the monster fastened his keen gaze upon me, his eyes ablaze with unholy light.

With shaking hands, I set the stake so that it dented the greyish white flesh of the dead man's chest, just above his heart; and then I lifted the mallet above my head, and with one strong, ringing blow, brought it down.

Mueller's body jerked limply, lifelessly—then writhed, come suddenly to life in a burst of hideous energy. At the same instant, his grey lips parted to emit such an ear-piercing shriek that I recoiled and dropped the mallet, utterly unnerved.

"He is alive!" I cried with horror.

"He shall not be for long!" V. retrieved the mallet and gestured with it at the miserable creature on the table. My first blow had plunged the stake some two inches deep into his heart; impossible, indeed, for anyone to survive such a mortal wound for more than seconds. "See how he suffers! Hurry—release him from such pain!"

I emitted a sob and stood frozen, unable to bear the sight of such agony; unable to kill.

And then Mueller let go a moan too piteous for any mortal heart to bear.

"Again!" V. urged, thrusting the mallet at me. "Harder! Quickly!"

I seized the mallet and struck again. Mueller thrashed like a great dying fish and howled.

I struck again and again, grimacing, tears streaming down my cheeks. Again, until the poor man stilled at last and the stake was well sunk into his chest—yet he had shed not a drop of blood. Staring down at his contorted features, I could think of nothing but Jeffries as I chose the largest, thickest blade from among the tools and went about the grisly business of separating the head from the torso.

It was horrid work; sickening work, and I cannot bear to describe it in detail here. Most sickening, though, was the abnormally bright gleam in V.'s eyes as he watched me perform the task.

And then the time came to deal likewise with Frau Mueller. For modesty's sake, I lowered my eyes and averted them as much as possible when placing the stake between her breasts. I prayed that she, unlike her unfortunate husband, was truly dead; after all, had not V. forbidden Zsuzsanna to continue drinking because the girl had died?

Reassuring myself thusly, I struck again—and wept aloud as she, too, came to life and screamed as heartrendingly as her husband had. I knew then that V. had intentionally deceived me for some terrible purpose.

"How unfortunate," he whispered, when it was over and both bodies had been decapitated. "It seems they were both alive. But how could this be?"

I could only look on him with hate. Did he expect that, having once shed blood, I would be broken and do whatever he bade? "I have done what you asked," I said heavily. "Now take me to my wife."

"Very well," he replied, and conducted me to a doorway hidden behind the throne. This opened onto a dark narrow passageway, which led to a heavy wooden door, from behind which came, very faintly, my wife's agonised cries. V. put his hand upon the door, then hesitated, and turned back to face me, half smiling.

"You have performed admirably, Arkady. There is but one more small thing. I have an unexpected visitor who according to his letter has been waiting in Bistritz since dawn for my caleche to arrive. But Laszlo was indisposed this morning" —and here his smile widened—"and now is even more so. Could you . . . ?"

"I cannot leave Mary! And I have not slept in days—"

V. gave a gracious nod. "In the morning, then? After you have had time to sleep? Only this one small thing, and then you may remain with your wife as long as you wish . . ."

I heard the threatening undercurrent in his tone. At that moment, I could scarcely bear to stand listening to my wife's groans, could not bear to think of anything keeping me from her side, knowing that she was so close by, and so I agreed wearily, "Yes, yes, of course—I will go in the morning."

"Excellent." V.'s smile widened again to reveal teeth; he turned and pushed open the door.

The chamber beyond was windowless and small, and like its owner, full of glitter edged with decay—festooned with cobwebs, limned with dust, but magnificently appointed with golden candelabra, cut crystal, and a great canopy bed draped in gleaming gold brocade. Dunya sat at the bedside on a velvet stool, and when the little chamber-maid glanced up at us, her gaze went blank, vacant upon meeting Vlad's.

I shuddered, unable to hide my disgust and dismay at the revelation that V. had used her to betray us. He saw my expression, and the ironic smile returned to his lips. "I will leave you now to your privacy on this remarkable occasion," said he, and left, closing the door behind him.

On the bed lay my struggling wife, her golden hair damp and dark with sweat, her face flushed bright with effort. I went at once to her and took her hand, and we wept together.

"We cannot trust her," Mary said tearfully, in English. "Her neck . . . I have seen her neck."

She did not so much as glance at Dunya, who sat beside her with the most innocent of expressions, unable to follow our conversation. "He has bitten her?" I asked softly; Mary nodded and bowed her head, overwhelmed by grief.

Soon the pains began again in earnest. I wished to do something to help, but apparently my dismay at seeing her in such agony added to her distress. And so I sat just outside the doorway, where she could see me and be reassured by my presence, but could not glimpse my tormented expression.

For a few moments, when her labour grew intense and she and Dunya were distracted, I slipped downstairs to learn that the doors leading out of the castle have been bolted from the outside.

So I sit outside my wife's elegant prison, writing it all

down on the perfumed stationery I discovered within the room.

God help me, I am twice a murderer. And we are prisoners, with no hope of escape.

❧13❧

The Diary of Arkady Tsepesh

21 APRIL, MID-DAY. ADDENDUM ON SEPARATE PARCHMENT.
Exhaustion at last overtook me and I slept in the hallway with
my impromptu diary upon my lap until the grey morning
light filtered through the open door. Heart pounding with
fear, I leapt to my feet as I recalled our circumstances, then
dashed into the room where my wife was confined.

The child had still not been born. Mary was so worn and
pale, her lips so grey, that I was frightened. Dunya, her face
somber with concern, said Mary must not be moved at all for
fear she might bleed to death. This I believe to be true and not
some suggestion put into her mind by V.; a glance at my poor
wife confirmed it.

Even so, I asked Dunya how much longer the birth might
take. She shook her head and opened her mouth to speak, but I
could not hear her reply for my wife's sudden anguished
groans.

The sound caused tears to fill my eyes, for it seemed she
was crying out because of the misery I had caused her, bringing her here. Dunya saw my distress (Poor child. The horror of
it is she is still herself, with a good heart; I do not think she is

even aware V. controls her), and immediately ordered me to fetch more pain-relieving herbs from the kitchen.

I hesitated to leave Mary; but I had heard the servants' whispered claims that the *strigoi* slept by day. Certainly, this was V.'s custom, and so I felt Mary was safe—at least, for the moment.

Grateful to be of help, I went downstairs, and en route discovered that the main entrance had been unbolted and flung open sometime in the night. The morning sky was grey, filled with ominous clouds; the air smelled of imminent rain. Beyond, near the front steps, awaited horses and the caleche. The sight brought both gladness and dread: gladness, because here was a chance at escape; dread, because I remembered my promise to retrieve the new visitor from Bistritz.

I stepped down into the courtyard. The horses were rested and groomed, despite the fact that every servant had disappeared from the castle. As I stood staring at them in wonder, I felt pulled in four directions by varying impulses.

First, I wished to flee, to carry my suffering wife down the stairs and gallop off with her in the caleche, despite the danger to her; second, I wished to go to Bistritz to warn the visitor to return from whence he came.

Third, I wished to go to Bistritz, retrieve the visitor, and deliver him into V.'s hands—knowing it would purchase the safety of my wife and child. What was one more death when the Muellers' blood was already upon my unwitting hands?

Yet if the legend was true that the vampire slept by day, then I needed do none of the foregoing—only to kill V. as he slumbered. I knew the method, and had the means.

I made my decision just as the soft sunlight began to burn through the mist, which hung low to the ground. When it seemed that the white swirls beside me grew solid, I judged it a *trompe l'oeil* born of exhaustion, and paid it no mind until I heard a familiar, agitated voice whisper:

"Kasha . . . !"

The horses snorted nervously and stamped.

I glanced up. Zsuzsa stood, clutching the wispy white cerements of the tomb about her like a cloak of fog. She seemed younger, a woman of barely twenty years. Her body was still straight, still perfect, still possessed of unearthly beauty, yet in the light of day, her supernatural radiance was dimmed. She approached with movements graceful but so entirely human that sorrow clutched my throat. I stared into eyes striking and full of allure, but no longer distant and predatory; a hint of their golden lustre remained, but the dominant hue was soft brown—the colour of my dear, dead sister's eyes.

Her cheeks were wet with tears.

"Oh, Zsuzsa," I whispered, and closed my eyes. When I opened them, the vision remained. I swayed, suddenly dizzy.

"Kasha," she said urgently, and caught my wrist; I shivered at her cool touch, and saw that she, too, shuddered—at the sight of Ion's crucifix, which I had drawn with my free hand from my pocket, and displayed in my open palm. She recoiled at once, as if my skin scalded her like vitriol. "I have been waiting for you to venture where *she* cannot hear. Kasha, I must talk to you at once! We must save you—you do not know what he plans! But let us go into the shadows; the light pains me."

I straightened, unsteady; she gestured as though to help, but was forced by the crucifix to keep her distance. Together we walked into the shadow cast by the castle, and there she reached out to embrace me—then dropped her arms, helpless in the presence of the cross. Yet I sensed no attempt on her part to mesmerise.

"Kasha," she repeated, in a low voice that shook with desperation. "I know that you were there last night. You saw me feed—"

"I saw you kill a woman," I said.

Her lids lowered. She did not meet my gaze, but there was no trace of guilt in her voice, her expression as she said, "Yes, but I had no choice. You cannot imagine the hunger, the pain; I was not myself. Not myself at all, but I am what I am now, and I cannot change it. I do not say these words to entice you, but because I mean to help: Kasha, you must let me bite you. You must let me make you as I am! It is the only way; otherwise, what happened to poor Father will happen to you!"

I raised the crucifix and held it before her face, wondering at its effectiveness—so the peasants' tales are all true!—and wishing I had thought to use it last night, to save Frau Mueller from the creature standing before me. She grimaced and drew back, raising her hands as if she feared I might strike her, but she showed no anger. "Go back," I commanded. "Go back to him, monster. My sister is dead."

She let go a single bitter sob, but stood her ground, though clearly the proximity of the cross tormented her. When she had gained some measure of control, and wiped her eyes with the edge of her burial clothes, she said, in as determined a voice as I had ever heard the living woman use, "I *am* your sister, Kasha. Yes, I am undead—but I am still Zsuzsa. You must understand; Vlad has always been as he is, a cruel tyrant. Death and immortality have changed him—and me—but little. Do you not wonder why I have come now, in the morning, when you have never seen him?"

I had no answer to this, for in fact I was amazed. My silence brought her faint satisfaction.

"He can move at day, if emergency demands it," she continued, "but the light is very uncomfortable, and he does not like it, for his powers are greatly reduced. He *must* rest for a portion of each twenty-four hours, more when he has fed, and so he chooses most times to rest at day. But I fed and rested last night; and I appear before you now at the time when I am most vulnerable, as a sign of trust. Oh, I am still stronger than you, and I could try to control you—but I will not. Arkady, you must listen and believe!"

Her tone was one of anguished sincerity; and I could not deny that she was not attempting to hypnotise me, as she had the night she first rose. And so I asked, "Listen and believe what?"

"The truth." Her face contorted with pain. "He does not love us. Oh, Kasha, he has never loved us! I thought, when he came to me, that he did so because he had feelings—but it has all been a lie. He controlled me then, he made me feel and believe things, and even when I drank his blood—"

Here, she lost her composure and lowered her face into her hands and wept; her dark hair, free now of any trace of silver, fell forward from beneath her white veil. After a time, she raised her face and continued, in a shaking voice, "When I drank his blood, I knew all that he knew. I learned then the terms of the pact—"

"The covenant," I said.

"Yes. I learned everything about it then; but he still controlled me, and forced me to forget what he did not want me to know. He thought—his arrogance knows no bounds!—he thought I would be so grateful to him for my immortality that I would continue to be his slavishly adoring little Zsuzsa, that once I rose as *strigoi* and remembered everything, I would still love him. Perhaps he thought I would become as heartless as he! But you are still my brother, and I am still Zsuzsa, even though changed. I still love you, Kasha, and cannot bear to see him use you so.

"He made me *strigoi* because my worship of him appealed to his ego; and so, in his hubris, he decided he would appease his hunger, silence my opposition to his desire to go to England, and have an immortal partner who would forever revere him as the *voievod.* You see, he has surrendered control of me— he does not know my thoughts, does not know where I have gone. It is part of the bargain he struck, in order to break the covenant and make one of his own family *strigoi.* He could not do so without paying a heavy price, for to make one of his own a vampire meant the soul would be trapped eternally between Heaven and Hell, so the Devil cannot have it; so he chose that, once I rose as undead, he would forfeit his ability to enter and control my mind. He was that sure of my loyalty."

"Bargain with whom?" I interrupted, but her eyes narrowed at this and she could not seem to bring herself to answer, but continued rapidly.

"And so I remembered none of the truth of his pact when I was changing, before I died, because he still directed my thoughts then; and when I rose from my coffin, I could think of nothing except the horrible hunger. Only after I had drunk the woman's blood and rested was my mind clear enough to think; and then I was horrified for your sake. Our poor father suffers in Hell now, in *his* place! Vlad could have saved him, could have done for him what he did for me—trap my soul upon earth; but instead, he made sure he would suffer eternal torment! Do not think he kept his teeth from Father's neck out of kindness! And he will do the same to you—entrap you, force you to commit crimes out of your own free will. You should hear how cruelly he laughs when he speaks of sending you to Bistritz to see the *jandarm.* He delights in your torment; it is all but a game to him, watching your growing dread as you realise the truth, bringing you to the edge of madness in hopes of breaking your spirit . . ."

I closed my eyes, thinking of Radu's letter: *He is like an old wolf who has made so many kills he grows bored and must find new pleasures; destroying innocence is one of them . . . This entertainment remains fresh for him, for he can only enjoy it once a generation.*

"The Muellers," I said abruptly as I opened my eyes, realising that V. had killed Laszlo in order to force my complicity. At Zsuzsanna's quizzical glance, I added, "The visitors. He tricked me into driving stakes through their hearts before they were dead; tricked me into murder, when I thought I was only preventing them from rising as undead."

"You did not kill them," she said, with such certainty that I believed her. "I felt the girl die."

"But she screamed—"

"As the undead do, when they are destroyed." I felt a relief so deep my eyes filled with tears; but my sister shuddered at the thought as she added urgently, "Have you harmed anyone else? Brought anyone to the castle, knowing what Vlad was, and what he would do to them?"

"No."

My sister clapped her hands in a childlike gesture of glee. "Then perhaps it is not too late! Perhaps there is no need yet to make you one of us! You have committed no mortal sin yet. He tried to deceive you into thinking you have already done so, and that therefore future crimes will not make any difference."

I shook my head and said, in a tone filled with irony, "Whether it was sin or not will make no difference to the authorities in Vienna. They will know only that I wielded the stake and knife—"

"Kasha, I do not speak of anything so unimportant as the *jandarm* in Vienna! I speak of the pact, the covenant! Your eternal fate!"

For an instant, we stared at one another, each realising the other did not understand.

I spoke first, softly. "I know about the covenant. Dunya spoke to me of the one he has with the villagers, for their protection; and V. himself explained the agreement he has with our family: the eldest son's service in exchange for the family's protection and wealth."

"Oh, no," said she, in a whisper so harsh it cut through the air between us, cut through my heart as easily as V.'s dagger cut through a child's tender skin. "Then you know nothing of his true covenant—with the Devil.

"Your soul, Kasha. Yours, and that of your father, and his father before him. The soul of the eldest surviving son of each Tsepesh generation: that is the gold with which he purchases his immortality."

⊹⊹⊹ ⊹⊹⊹ ⊹⊹⊹

Zsuzsa told me more, in a low voice that shook with horror as we stood in the castle's shadow. After V. had escorted me to my wife's side, he had returned to the inner chamber and turned on Zsuzsa in a fearsome rage, screaming that she had betrayed him.

"He accused me of bewitching you," she wept, "of entering into my own pact to set you free from his control."

"It's true," I said. "He no longer controls my mind. Not from the moment you rose from the tomb . . ."

She nodded sadly. "Vlad meant to entangle you further, to tie your child to him with the blood ritual before returning your will to you. That is why he was compelled at the last moment to abduct Mary—to bring you and the child to the castle, since he could no longer mentally summon you here. But I suspect he was tricked by One even more evil and cunning than he. Perhaps the price of my will was not enough payment to break the covenant and make me *strigoi;* perhaps yours was needed, too . . . for he threw me from the inner chamber, and his wrath was so frightening that I have not yet returned. But I lingered near the outer door, and I could hear him shouting at someone—something—inside."

I thought of the black altar at the head of V.'s coffin and shuddered. My mind still could not believe, could not comprehend, but my heart accepted Zsuzsa's words. For if something so heinously evil as V. can exist, there must surely be a Devil.

"Zsuzsa," I whispered, as the realisation dawned. "He has asked me to go to Bistritz, to retrieve another visitor . . ."

"Kasha, you must not go! If you deliver a victim into his hands, then he has won—and your soul is lost."

"Then help me kill him! He is asleep now, and vulnerable—"

She jerked her face towards me, and her eyes gleamed not with gold, but with the dull, angry red of dying embers. "Do not speak of such a thing again! How can you ask—"

"He is a murderer a thousand, a million times over, Zsuzsa! You said yourself you no longer love him."

"No," she said slowly. "No . . . I do not love him. I despise him for what he has done to you and Father, for how he has misled me. But I came to you because I wish to see no one harmed. Not even him."

"But he might hurt Mary!"

She lowered her beautiful face, with its faint rosy blush, stolen from Frau Mueller's cheeks—and sighed in reluctant admission. "Yes . . . he would do anything to corrupt your soul—would kill your wife, your child (so long as you live to sire another). But he will not harm you, not as long as you remain innocent."

I lifted my head, my heartbeat quickening as another, more powerful revelation presented itself. "And if I die uncorrupted . . . ?"

"He would be destroyed."

"Zsuzsa!" Forgetful of the crucifix, I seized her hand; she drew back with a small cry of pain. "Zsuzsa, you must promise me, then, that you will explain everything to Mary and see to it that she and the child are well—" I reached for Father's revolver, hidden beneath my waistcoat.

She threw out her arm to stop me, wincing as our flesh touched. "No! It must be an innocent death, Kasha. If you die by your own hand, or with your complicity, your soul is forfeit, and the covenant upheld."

I knelt before her. "Then kill me!"

She averted her face and stared for a moment at the sunlight dappling the forest before she whispered, "This life is grotesque . . . yet too beautifully strange for me to abandon, Brother. I have powers, abilities, beauty I never dreamed of in my pathetic little human life. Do not ask me to surrender it so soon . . ."

"Zsuzsa, I don't understand . . ."

She drew in a breath and turned back towards me, her perfect features marred, twisted by inner turmoil. "If you destroy Vlad, you destroy me."

I looked into her eyes and knew then that she still loved V. as much as she hated him; that I would get from her no help beyond that she had already offered. Indeed, I saw in those eyes the dawning of regret.

Abruptly, she added, "Flee, Kasha. Flee. Stay alive, for the baby's sake, and see it is taken far from here. Because the moment it is born, Vlad will tie it to him with the blood ritual . . . unless you prevent him."

And she disappeared. Not subtly, not gradually, backing into the shadows, but as abruptly as my brother's small spectre had vanished before my eyes in the forest. One moment I stared at the image of my radiantly lovely sister; the next, at the grey morning and the tall, distant shapes of trees.

I did not linger, but went back inside the castle, located the pain-relieving herb Dunya had requested, and delivered it into her hands.

Mary's torment is constant now; surely the child will be born soon. I can no longer bear to wait, writing and listening to her suffering.

I must take action.

14

The Diary of Arkady Dracul

DATE UNKNOWN. NIGHT. Eternity has passed since last I wrote in this journal; but let me begin at the moment I left off.

Mary's cries grew so desperate that I ran into the room to comfort her, dropping the diary upon the night-table beside the bed. When they subsided I did not remain, but took my place again in the hallway, waiting until I was certain both women were too distracted to notice my departure; and then I slipped silently down the dark, claustrophobic corridor, past the stone entry, back into V.'s outer chamber, which housed the throne and the theatre of death.

I had already passed through the room twice that morning, each time hurriedly, with eyes averted. This time, I entered and carefully noted my surroundings.

The air seemed stale, lifeless, heavy with death and the sorrows endured there. To my left, the great throne sat unoccupied; before me, the velvet curtain was still pulled back to reveal the strappado and other implements of torture. The cleaver which Laszlo had hurled had been carefully replaced in the carving-block with the other tools of the butcher's trade.

I walked behind the table on which Herr Mueller had

lain and pulled the largest, thickest blade from the block, then chose a short, sharpened stake and the heavy mallet. Thus armed, I headed for the innermost sanctum. That door stood slightly ajar as well. I nudged it with the toe of my boot, and heard it swing open with a groan like that of a dying man.

I was surprised that V. trusted me enough to leave the door unbarred; I thought of Zsuzsa speaking indignantly of his arrogance. He had let her glimpse his heartlessness, yet his egotism could not permit him to believe she would not still adore him. Was he so foolishly sure of my love, as well, that he feared no betrayal?

I entered. Again, the smell of dust and faint decay. I moved immediately to the larger of the two caskets, set Laszlo's knife silently on the floor, and, with stake and mallet in one hand, opened the coffin's lid with the other.

It lifted easily, without resistance, and in the instant it rose, my heart momentarily ceased its beating in response to the purest, coldest wave of fear I have ever known. Yet it was oddly exhilarating, like standing in the breaking waves of an arctic sea, and I knew in that instant I would not shrink from my task.

I pushed the lid fully back, and peered in the dimness at the scarlet lining, worn and showing the clear impressions made over countless years by the weight of head and torso upon the fabric.

Empty.

A man's distant voice, unfamiliar and oddly accented, broke the stillness.

"Hallo-o-o!"

The sound so startled me the mallet and stake dropped from my hand and clattered against stone. My heart pounded furiously; had Zsuzsanna regretted her confession, and, realising that she and V. might soon be destroyed, gone at once to warn him?

I hurried into the outer chamber, scarcely seeing the unveiled theatre of death.

"Hallo-o-o!"

The call grew louder, more insistent; with a start, I real-ised it echoed off the interior walls of the level below. A stranger had entered the castle.

I directed an agonised glance at the entryway that led to my wife's genteel prison, from which her cries issued unceas-ing. I had no desire to leave her in Dunya's untrustworthy company, especially now that I was uncertain of V.'s where-abouts; nor could I ignore the stranger's summons—for I knew, with unhappy certainty, who called.

I hurried from the chamber and dashed down the spiral-ing staircase. Near the main entryway, I chanced upon the stranger, who had just begun to climb the stairs. We stopped several steps apart, I above and he below, to study each other.

He was a tall, heavy-set bespectacled man with fair, thin-ning hair, a florid complexion that showed beneath his goatee and moustache, and light-coloured eyes. From his dress I took him to be well educated and from the upper classes; from his demeanour, I took him to be thoughtful and steady. At the sight of me, he recoiled, almost losing his balance on the stairs —then recovered with a nervous smile and said, in strangely accented German:

"Forgive me for arriving unannounced, but I have my own carriage and wished to arrive as soon as possible."

For a moment, my wits left me; I did not speak. My expression must have alarmed him, for he asked hesitantly, "This is the castle of the prince, Vlad Dracula, yes?"

"Yes," I said, when at last my mind returned. "Yes, it is, but you must leave swiftly, sir—at once!"

His pale eyebrows met in a furrow above his spectacles as he gazed up at me; with mild indignance, he straightened. "But I am Erwin Kohl, his invited guest! Surely he must have spoken to someone of my arrival—"

"Indeed, sir," I replied, more cordially as I regained my poise. "And we are sorry that no one was able to meet you at

Bistritz, for the very reason you must now leave: There is illness in the castle. Terrible illness."

Still frowning, Kohl narrowed his eyes and tilted his head as he scrutinised my face; I knew at once from the kind intelligence in his eyes and expression that this was a man of keen perception.

I also knew that he sensed I was lying.

He lifted an eyebrow; beneath his disbelief, I saw a glimmer of concern. "Who is ill? Perhaps I can help . . ."

"Everyone," I said, descending a step towards him, "except myself."

"It might explain the absence of servants," he whispered to himself, then said aloud to me, "And the prince . . . He is ill, too?"

"The prince is most afflicted of all." I advanced another step closer; my tone grew strident. "Sir, many have died! For your own safety, I must ask you to leave at once!"

I uttered those words with genuine panic and frustration, for I meant them utterly, and I believe he knew it. He should have reacted with fear and departed with alacrity, but to my dismay, he straightened and stood his ground, then set his jaw, tilted his chin slightly upwards, and in those subtle, stubborn gestures, I saw my defeat.

He was determined to remain—for a reason I could not fathom.

"It does not matter. Let me see the prince." His voice was velvet over stone: soft on the surface, flint-hard beneath.

"No. You must leave *now.*" I quickly descended the remaining steps towards him and took him by the shoulders, thinking to turn him around and lead him down the staircase and out the castle. But he was a larger man than I, and resisted. We scuffled clumsily, halfheartedly—both of us clearly neither men of violence—with the outcome that he stood two steps above me, holding a pistol in his steady hand.

"Take me to the prince," he said again, and aimed the weapon carefully at my forehead.

I gazed up into his eyes. They were pale blue, rational, the eyes of a compassionate man. I did not judge him capable of cruelty; yet he seemed to have reached a level of desperation that matched my own.

I sat down on the step, put my elbows on my knees and my hands to my eyes and laughed until tears came, thinking, *Now he will shoot me, and the covenant will be broken and my family saved.*

The alleged Mister Kohl did not fire, but stood quietly in the face of my hysterical mirth, perhaps as surprised by my reaction as I had been by his.

I glanced up and demanded with faint irritation, "Well, kill me then, and be done with it." I fell silent, then, realising that urging my own death might constitute suicide, and fulfill Vlad's pact.

With a quizzical expression, the stranger asked, "Who are you?"

"Arkady Tsepesh, his great-nephew." I laughed again, a sharp, humourless bark. "Or rather, his great-great-great-great-grandson, many more times removed."

"You must take me to him."

Once more, I tried to laugh; it emerged a sob. "Would that I could; he has hidden himself." I lowered my voice to an urgent whisper. "He is a murderer—worse than a murderer. That is why you must leave at once! Please . . . I beg you! Go! You are not safe!"

Behind his spectacles, Kohl's eyes widened with amazement; that emotion soon gave way to trust. Yet he remained, stubborn and immovable upon the stairs, with the revolver still pointed at my head. "I believe you," he said calmly. "And I have no wish to harm *you.* But I must insist—"

"*Domnule! Domnule!*"

Dunya hurried shrieking down the stairs, dark hair streaming from beneath her scarf, bright red smeared upon her linen apron. So agitated was she that she failed to react to the odd tableau of Kohl standing with pistol aimed at me as I crouched two steps below. In German, the language she shared with her mistress and had no doubt been speaking all the past night and morning, she cried, "Come and help! The child is turned and I cannot move it! She is bleeding—! I am afraid they both will die!"

The tears and panic in her eyes were genuine. Without a thought for the gun barrel pointed at my forehead, I rose and pushed my way past Kohl; V. and all the demons of Hell could not have held me. Dunya and I ran up the stairs, through the inner chamber, back to the elegant prison, to Mary's side.

The bed linens were stained crimson, and my wife swooning and so frightfully pale I deemed her dead until she stirred and groaned. I sank to my knees beside her and took her cold hand. She was in such blind misery that she did not recognise me, and I was in such misery of my own—helpless as I looked upon my grey-lipped wife—I gave no thought to the stranger, did not realise that he had followed, until I heard his voice behind me saying to Dunya: "Keep her warm, and press *there*. I shall return at once."

Even then, I listened to his words but did not truly hear them. Dunya unquestioningly obeyed the stranger's orders, sobbing softly as, for the first time in my life, I prayed. I am not sure whether I prayed to Mary, my father, or God, or some abstract Good; but I know that the utter desperation of my heart rent the veil between this world and the world unseen, and allowed me to reach through and touch the hem of Something—a force—very real, very alive.

I offered my life, my soul, if only my wife might survive at this moment, if only my child might be spared his father's fate. I prayed there might be Good in the world, that It might be strong enough to conquer the Evil that had ruled my family; I prayed the blood legacy might end with me.

So absorbed was my soul in its petition that I never noticed the stranger's departure or return. I only know that at last a large, looming shadow fell over Mary's pale face; I glanced up, fearing V. . . . and instead saw the stranger, standing like a great blond bear at the foot of the bed, his jacket gone, his shirtsleeves rolled above his elbows. Dunya had kept candles burning in the windowless room; tiny flames danced, reflected in his spectacles.

"I did not mention in my letter I am a physician," said he, setting a large black doctor's bag upon the bed. "I can perhaps help." He bent low, and with a discreet manipulation of the sheets, examined my wife by touch. "So. It is true, the babe is turned. But we shall right him . . ."

He set to work. It happened soon after: Mary's piercing cry, followed swiftly by the child's, and then the stranger held up in his huge hands my slick and bloodied child.

"A son," he announced, and we grinned at each other with unrestrained delight, as though we were not strangers, but old, dear friends sharing in this joy; as though he had not minutes before held a pistol to my skull.

My son. My tiny, angry, wailing son.

My wife fell at once asleep while her unexpected physician tended her. I sank into a nearby chair and wept at the beauty and horror of the event.

When the stranger had finished and washed his hands in a basin, he turned towards me, wiping his hands upon a towel, and said in a low voice, "The child is small, but healthy. He is early, no?"

I nodded, and drew a shaking hand across my eyes.

"No doubt the mother has suffered some recent shock."

I shot a dark glance at Dunya, who had finished bathing the child and now wrapped him tightly in blankets, for I wished to be able to speak freely to this stranger, but dared not in her presence. The doctor saw, and seemed to detect my reluctance, though he smiled at Dunya as she handed the clean child over to him.

I nodded quickly, so that Dunya did not notice.

He tucked the child into my dozing wife's arm and said softly, "She is young and strong, but she has lost a dangerous amount of blood. She will need a great deal of care."

Mary stirred then, and found the baby in her arms; and the smile she graced us both with at that moment shall remain my sweetest memory. "His name," she whispered to me. "What shall be his name?"

"Stefan," I replied. "For my brother."

"Stefan George." She said it slowly, savouring the sound.

"A handsome name," the doctor added, beaming. Mary started weakly at the sight of a stranger; but I started at his words, for the three of us had just conversed in my wife's native tongue.

"You speak English," I said.

"Yes. There is something you wish to say that you do not want the girl to hear?" Still smiling, he nodded at the child as if he had just paid the proud parents a compliment.

I gazed down at my red, wrinkled, beautiful son. "She is in league with the prince; he will know, now, that you are here. Your life is in great danger. You must leave at once—"

"And what of you and your family?" The stranger leaned over the child and proffered a large thick finger, which little Stefan gripped fiercely. "It would be unwise for your wife to travel. But this place . . . I have seen what horrors lie in the room that leads here. You seem kindly people. Am I to abandon you here?"

I knew at that moment my prayer had been answered in the form of this man, who had saved my wife and might now save my son.

I looked at him with hope. "Perhaps you can help." I stood and walked towards the doorway, leaving Mary with the child. I had no desire to dim her happiness at that moment.

Kohl seemed to understand; he smiled at my wife, and said in German, "The boy is no doubt hungry, madam. Let me allow you a few moments' privacy to feed him."

He followed me into the hallway and drew the door closed behind him.

I said in a low voice in English, "Why are you here?"

The stranger hesitated; his expression revealed that trust

warred with suspicion. "First: I must know why *you* are here. What leads a man to the home of a murderer, even if he be kin?"

"We are his prisoners," I said, with no attempt to hide my misery. "As you will be, if you do not leave. He has threatened my wife and child, hoping I will be broken and assist him in evil." I raised a shaking hand to my eyes, blotting out the sight of the stranger; wishing I could blot out the memory of what I had just revealed.

The stranger sighed deeply and said, "My father visited this same castle twenty-five years before."

I lowered my hands and met his gaze. "And disappeared."

Grief flickered in his eyes before he looked away. "Without a trace," he said grimly. "I was of course but a boy at the time. The last letter we received from him was postmarked from Bistritz, the day before he was to visit your great-uncle. For years, my family attempted to reconstruct what befell him —but we were thwarted at every turn. No one would help us; neither the police in Bistritz, nor local government. We spent an enormous amount of money on solicitors, even a private detective, attempting to track him down. The lawyers were unsuccessful; and the detective himself disappeared and was not heard from again.

"At last my poor mother surrendered, and gave up hope, for it was clear that he had been the victim of foul play and that some sort of conspiracy surrounded his disappearance. I, too, gave up searching—until dreams of my father pleading for help so disturbed me I could no longer ignore them. I have vowed to avenge him. And so, in desperation, I journeyed here, and have learned much from kind-hearted locals. I have heard many, many stories, some quite fantastic; but all indicate that your uncle is a murderer many times over. I have no doubt but that my poor father was one of his victims."

"All the stories are true," I said grimly. "Even the most fantastic of them . . ."

Kohl released a startled laugh. "Certainly not! They

say . . ." He lowered his voice. "They say he is a vampire. A drinker of men's blood. You seem an educated, intelligent man. Surely you do not—"

"Her neck," I told him. "Examine the girl's neck."

"You are joking," he said, with less conviction, and gave a smile that faded slowly as he examined my face. "It is impossible."

"Yes, impossible . . . and true."

I said nothing more; merely stood in silence until, at last, Kohl turned and knocked upon the door, waiting until Dunya called that it was safe for him to enter.

I watched in the open doorway as he again examined my wife and child, speaking cheerfully to both of them in German; his gaze fell upon the papers, covered with my scrawl, which lay on the table beside my reclining wife. Perhaps he saw something disturbing there, for his expression darkened briefly. And then he smiled again, and turned to Dunya, saying: "Young miss, you seem very drawn! Are you sure you are not ill?"

She blushed and stammered, "No, I am simply tired," but he waved away her response and insisted she open her mouth, that he might look at her throat, "for there has been an outbreak of diphtheria in the region." Deftly, he touched the glands in her neck, managing to lower the collar enough to see the incriminating marks.

"Good, good," he murmured, with a composed expression, but his spine stiffened slightly in reaction.

I stepped into the doorway and said for Dunya's benefit, "Herr Kohl, let me show you the guest quarters, and assist you with your luggage. No doubt you will wish to rest."

"Ah." He turned, his pale eyes still bright with astonishment, and followed me out into the corridor. When we were a far enough distance not to be heard, he said, "It is not conclusive. The marks might have been made by an animal . . ."

I held my tongue and led him into the great outer chamber, past the throne. He beheld it all with wide eyes, shaking his head in disbelief.

"I saw it before, when I followed you to your wife, though I scarce could believe my eyes," he whispered. "What sort of monster . . . ?" He pointed over at the unveiled theatre of death. "And that is no doubt where—"

He broke off, unable to continue. I put my hand upon his shoulder, understanding too well his sense of horror and loss.

After a moment of silence I said, "Come."

I led him into the inner sanctum where the coffins stood, their lids still opened to reveal the imprints of bodies upon crimson silk. Beside them on the floor lay the stake, mallet, and knife which I had dropped. Kohl looked on the scene and the black altar with an expression of horrified wonder but did not speak.

"He sleeps in the day, just as legend says," I told him. "Normally here, but he has hidden himself—somewhere on the castle grounds, I am sure.

"I intend to destroy him. Your call interrupted my search. Will you help?"

Kohl's gaze, of uncommon intensity, met mine at once. "Yes."

I gave a joyless smile. "It matters not to my pride whether you believe that my great-uncle is a vampire, or an entirely human monster; but I must insist for your own safety that you take this and wear it. Your gun will provide you no protection in this house."

I handed him Ion's crucifix, which he hung round his neck without hesitation. "And you?" he asked.

"I am currency to him," I said. "He will not harm me."

Kohl looked askance at this, but I did not explain. We equipped ourselves with the stake, mallet, knife, and a lamp, and began the hunt.

For the next few hours, we went through the forty or fifty rooms—painstakingly, slowly, looking beneath beds, in cupboards, pantries, closets, stables, wine cellar, everywhere that might afford V. and Zsuzsa a resting-place.

Outside, the clouds blackened and thundered; at last the storm arrived, with a gusting wind that pelted water furiously against the windows, a fitting backdrop to our hunt. After a thorough search of the upper levels, we made our way down to the cellar and discovered, beneath a layer of dust so thick we almost failed to find it, a door which led to a staircase. These stairs in turn led to an entire series of subterranean catacombs, dug out of damp earth and layered with cobwebs. I half-expected to find the bones of martyred Christians, but the first few chambers were empty, save for the rats that scurried at our approach, and a thriving beetle population: the edges of the beam cast by my lamp seemed alive with small, dark crawling creatures.

But I sensed we neared the objects of our search; and so, I think, did Kohl, for his expression grew ever more taut. Keeping the lamp lifted high, I strode with him through chamber after chamber. The ground sloped slightly downward, and I had the sense of going deeper and deeper into the earth, the air growing danker with every step.

Then we entered a long, narrow corridor that stretched into endless darkness. Suddenly, Kohl touched my shoulder and said, "Look!"

I followed the direction of his gaze, and saw, to my left at the edge of the lamp's wavering light, cubicles each the size of a large closet, carved from the earth. Within were rotting wool blankets, tin cups, bowls, chains, an occasional wooden stool . . .

And each was sealed with iron bars and rusting padlocks. Cubicle after cubicle, a dozen, perhaps, in all. A prison.

"*Gott im Himmel,*" Kohl whispered.

"Of course," I murmured. "When the snows close the Borgo Pass, no more visitors can come; but he still must feed . . ."

Was this, too, to have been my task—to fill his prison in autumn, that he might sup at leisure over the winter?

We turned our faces from the horror and somehow managed to keep moving. The cells at last ended, and the tunnel itself terminated in an abrupt earthen wall laced with the dying roots of trees and nests of small animals. At the foot of that wall was a large trap door of wood bound with thick bands of rusted metal and studded with iron spikes.

I ran to it, set the lamp on the ground, and took hold of the large metal handle with both hands. Kohl dropped our weapons and joined me, and together we pulled.

But the door was bolted fast from the inside, and the outside bound shut with a thick chain attached to a long spike driven into the hard ground; no creature could pass through that portal by any means less than supernatural.

I took the mallet and pounded the wood, but it was petrified, like pounding rock. I could not so much as leave a dent. I tried smashing the chain, with equal success, and then tried driving the stake between earth and wood as a lever; this too failed. When I was spent, Kohl did his best to smash and then pry the door open, but after a frustrating half hour, we surrendered and returned the long, winding way we had come.

"He will rise at sunset," I told my companion. "You must leave well before then, or your life is forfeit."

"You and your family must accompany me, then," Kohl insisted. "It is dangerous for your wife to travel, but it seems a far greater danger to leave her here."

I agreed—simply to avoid argument, though I intended to stay and delay V. from following for as long as possible. It was already late afternoon; I explained that V. would rise at sunset, so that we would only be able to get a couple hours' head start. Swiftness was imperative.

"Then there is the matter of the chamber-maid, Dunya," I said. "Vlad knows all that she knows; and if she is awake and unrestrained when we depart, he will know through her when and in which direction we left. If there is some way to render her unable to do so—"

"Leave it to me," Kohl responded firmly.

We returned to my wife's prison to find the baby still nestled in her arm, and papers in her lap; Dunya sat attendance at bedside. My wife looked up, and our gazes locked; I saw that she held back tears. As I neared, and stood at her bedside opposite Dunya, I saw that the papers were covered with my handwriting—Mary had read my diary entry about Zsuzsa's revelations.

I lowered my eyes from that stricken, knowing gaze, heartbroken to think I had again caused my wife such misery. Neither of us said a word because of Dunya; we did not have to. The tale was told by Mary's loving, horrified eyes.

Kohl stepped beside me and said cheerfully to Dunya, "Young miss, you seem very tired and pale yourself. Go and sleep. I can watch your mistress."

She lowered her eyes shyly, embarrassed at having been noticed, but her voice was resolute as she answered, "No, sir. You are a guest of this house. It is my duty to stay awake and help my mistress and the baby."

Kohl considered this, then nodded indulgently. "Well, then, let me give you a tonic to make you strong."

For a moment she brightened, and seemed on the verge of glad acceptance; and then her eyes dulled in the same horrid manner they had when she had seen V., and her expression shifted to one of suspicion. "Thank you, sir, but I am strong enough."

He shrugged and said good-naturedly, "As you wish. But I shall prepare a tonic for your mistress," and set his bag upon the credenza at the wall nearest the foot of the bed. His back was to us, and neither I nor the others could see what he was doing; and then he turned towards us, smiling, and walked swiftly up to the side of the bed where Dunya sat.

She suspected nothing, but was studying with concern and puzzlement her tearful mistress. Kohl leaned over the bed as if to administer some drug to Mary, but at the last instant turned and clapped a handkerchief over Dunya's nose and mouth.

She rose at once to her feet, and released a muffled cry; above the handkerchief, her eyes were wide with indignant surprise. But within seconds, they closed, and she sagged, unconscious, in Kohl's strong, solid arms.

"Do not hurt her!" Mary cried. "She cannot help what has happened." In her distress, she clutched my hand, and at last allowed the tears to flow; I cried, too, and we wept for a time while Kohl softly set the sleeping girl upon the floor.

He returned swiftly to Mary's side, and soothed, "She is unharmed; she will merely sleep for some hours."

"Mary," I said, "you and the baby must go at once with the doctor. It's the only hope I have of keeping you safe."

"You cannot stay!" Aghast, she struggled to sit; the sleeping infant in her arm stirred. Kohl gently but firmly guided her back against the pillows.

"If you read that"—I nodded at the papers piled in her lap—"you know that he will do nothing to harm me. I can distract him until you are safe. When the time is right, I will join you."

Despite her weakness, she spoke fiercely. "Knowing your life is no longer in danger is little comfort; he will stop at nothing to corrupt you, and more than your life will be lost."

I ran a hand over her hot forehead and smoothed back her damp hair. "Mary . . . you are no longer safe with me."

"Perhaps not," she said. "Perhaps he will kill me. I no longer care what becomes of me, so long as I am with you. But I won't lose both my husband and son.

"Vlad knows that he has no power over you save through me and the baby. You won't be able to hold him here; he will go after us at once—for only so long as we are alive and in his reach can he blackmail you.

"I cannot let him destroy you because of us. You must accept this; you must be brave. You are my husband and I will not abandon you. I will remain with you until you are free of the curse."

I turned my face away from her, unwilling to let her see the grief there, for I knew what she said was true. If I sent her and the child away together, V. would follow—with, I feared, terrible consequences. It mattered not whether I accompanied them.

But the same horrors would befall them if they remained.

There seemed no solution to our little family's plight. Even so, at that moment, revelation descended: I saw with magical clarity what had to be done, though I could not bring myself to give it voice, knowing the unspeakable pain it would inflict on the one nearest my heart.

Yet she was strong; I turned back towards her as she said with bitterly poignant sweetness: "But we both want our son to be free. I believe God sent this man to deliver our son from evil. I trust him." She nodded at the stranger as she spoke, her pale face radiating such serenity and grace that he was clearly moved, for he knelt at her side and gazed on her with unmasked admiration.

"Madam," he said, and laid his great broad hand upon the small frail one she used to hold the child. "May I prove worthy of that trust. Your courage is remarkable; only name what you require, and it shall be yours."

"Will you help us?" she asked, echoing the question I had asked him in the *strigoi*'s inner sanctum.

And again Kohl promptly replied, in his unwavering bass voice, "Yes."

Thus were our fates decided. I could do nothing but kiss the palm of my wife's hand, and grip it tightly as we made the plans that broke our hearts.

+I+   +I+   +I+

Within the hour we had abandoned the castle, taking with us only the most basic necessities in the event we survived. I directed the stranger to the north, while we took the more obvious escape route to the southwest, towards Bistritz. By then it was late afternoon; the rain had ceased, but the air was damp and cool. Dark clouds still filled the sky, transforming day into the gloom of premature twilight. The tall trees were hung with raindrops, recalling another time, another Stefan. I had dreamt of my brother on my re-entry into this dark forest; I thought of him now as we fled. And of Shepherd, whom we had trusted, but who proved to have the heart of a wolf.

I drove the caleche, Father's Colt tucked beneath my waistband as protection against wolves. Mary lay behind me in the passenger's seat, reclining on pillows and covered by wool blankets, with a small swaddling bundle held tenderly at her breast.

We had but an hour before sunset. By then the stranger would cross running water, which Mary told me rendered the vampire unable to follow, save in his coffin or at the slack of the tide.

But because of our chosen route, my wife and I would not reach the nearest stream for some two hours. It was a danger we willingly accepted, so that the other carriage might be safe.

Still, I was seized by the same panic I had felt twenty years before, as a five-year-old running through the rain-drenched forest in search of my brother. I calmed myself by calling out to Mary. I feared she might begin to haemorrhage —a possibility the stranger had warned of, but for which he had also provided instruction.

She answered weakly, but with encouragement that all was well. And so I drove, forcing the horses as hard as they could go, grimacing at each bump in the uneven roadway and glancing over my shoulder at Mary, who bore it all in silence, but was pale and tight-lipped with pain as she clutched the bundle more tightly to her bosom.

After a time, the forest gave way to village—where I gave one final glance at Masika Ivanovna's little house and the church graveyard—and then to forest again as we headed towards the Borgo Pass. Soon the sun set, and the winding sand road narrowed until we were closed in by darkness and the black shapes of trees and distant mountains. The moon rose, limning the rain-kissed branches with silvery light.

The night brought with it more fear; I sank into the same suffocating panic I had experienced when trapped blindly with the horses and snapping wolves in the midnight forest.

Silence. All silence, save for the laboured breathing of the horses and the rumble of the earth beneath the wheels. We rode thus for the space of an hour, until I dared hope we might make good our escape.

And then: a howl. Distant at first, then closer, and joined by another. And another. And another.

I snapped the reins and cried out to the frightened horses to go faster, faster, knowing that it was all for naught: the salvation-giving stream lay another half hour to our west.

Still I drove, praying that the other carriage had already found deliverance by water, praying that our sacrifice should not be in vain.

The howls neared. I drew Father's revolver. As if evoked by that very action, the wolves emerged from the darkness in all directions. A pack of six rushed the caleche, attacking the screaming horses with an urgent ferocity that made Mary and I cry out as one.

At the same time, I felt pity for them, knowing that they were but V.'s pawns, as I had been—but pity could not supplant the instinct for survival. I fired, forcing my hand not to tremble, for there would be more wolves than I had bullets. Indeed, I killed one cleanly, as it caught hold of a shrieking horse's leg, only to watch two more snarling creatures spring from the darkness to take their fallen comrade's place.

And then the focus of the wolves' attack shifted from the quivering horses to us. As my bullet struck a yelping second, yet another emerged from the darkness and leapt up into the passenger's seat where my wife lay.

Fear and instinct rendered me mindless. I turned with

preternatural swiftness and pulled the trigger in the split second before the animal sank its teeth into Mary's neck. It died
with a rattling sigh, its slavering jaws open wide for the kill,
and fell to her feet as she rose speechless with shock, the bundle pressed tightly to her. With revulsion, we pushed the dead
creature from the carriage.

Of a sudden the wolves ceased their attack. For a few
moments they paced, whining softly, then crouched in the
moonlight like silent grey sphinxes encircling us, their ears
pricked with an odd, restless expectancy. The horses—trembling and bloodied, but none seriously harmed—stamped and
neighed fretfully. I set the gun down upon the driver's seat
beside me, knowing the remaining bullet in the chamber
would prove useless against the evil to come.

From out of the brooding darkness, a thin column of mist
sailed out of the eastern sky, crossing over our heads and settling in front of the caleche, just within the circle of wolves.
As we watched, the mist, asparkle with glints of unearthly
blue and rose light, began slowly to solidify and take on the
form of a man, until at last V. himself stood before us.

He was young, raven-haired, possessed of the same dazzling, leonine beauty I had witnessed in the Impaler when my
father had led me to his throne, and in those piercing evergreen eyes shone mocking contempt. At the sight of their
master, the animals whimpered, and lowered their chins between their paws in unhappy obeisance.

"Arkady," he said—softly, but his voice filled the entire
forest. "I had not taken you for such a fool. Did you truly
believe you could escape me?"

He moved towards the carriage—not by walking, but by
simply looming larger in my field of vision—and stretched out
his hand towards Mary, who sat, pressing the white woolen
bundle to her heart. "Give him to me. Quickly! My patience
was long ago spent."

My eyes at once sought Mary's, and we gazed at each
other with secret triumph in the midst of our fear. She stood,

and with an expression of such intense loathing as I had never before seen, hurled the bundle from the carriage at the wolves, shouting: "You will never have my child, monster! Never!"

V. let go a gasp. Before he could come to himself, the nearest wolf, startled and yielding to instinct, had sunk its jaws into the soft child's blanket and shook it as though wringing a rabbit's neck. The act revealed the blanket to be empty of content, and the creature, after sniffing it with puzzlement, sat on its haunches with the blanket between its front paws.

V. turned back to stare at us, his face gleaming in the moonlight like white-hot ash, his eyes blazing with a fury that could never be assuaged. "Harlot! Deceiver!" he screamed, his lips twisting to reveal sharp teeth. "Do you think you are indispensable? If not your child, then that of another woman's —by your husband!"

And then his rage went cold, and a cruel, sensual smile played upon his red lips. "Mary, pretty Mary," he crooned, as though reciting a child's rhyme, and suddenly he stood upon the passenger's step. "Hair of gold, eyes of sapphire. You think you can deceive me, hide your baby from me; but the truth is carried on your blood. I have only to taste it . . ."

And he reached a finger towards her, as if to caress the skin beneath her chin. She recoiled, falling back against the seat.

"No!" I begged. "I will do anything—*anything* you ask. I will go to Bistritz at once, bring you a victim, help you dispose of him, have other children by other women—whatever you require. Only let her live!" I uttered those words with complete sincerity, for I no longer cared what became of my eternal soul, so long as my child and wife were safe. Now that I knew little Stefan's escape was achieved, I was willing to do whatever V. bid to save Mary's life. This I had been prepared for from the moment we fled the castle—but I could not confide it to Mary, for she would never have accepted it.

V. drew back and smiled with pleasure at this; but Mary's

mouth fell open, and she cried, "Arkady, you mustn't: your soul will be lost, and it will never end! He will hunt Stefan down!"

And with swift, sudden sureness, she reached forward and took my father's gun.

V. threw back his head and laughed with arrogant delight as he spread his arms, offering himself as a target. "Go ahead, my dear: Fire! Fire! And see what good it will do."

And my brave wife fired. Mary, my soul, my saviour, my beloved murderer.

Less than a second passed before the remaining bullet struck my chest, but in that fleeting instant of time I saw my wife take aim, and looked up into her eyes. Those eyes held such love that the evil surrounding us seemed to fade into unimportance; and I smiled at her with adoration and utter joy, for I knew my life had not been cursed but blessed, blessed to have loved one who would stain her own soul to save mine.

I had not been able to speak to her of ending the covenant by taking my life, for to have done so would have amounted to suicide, and victory for the *strigoi.* I could do no more than leave the journal entry where she might find it, and read it; and then pray she would have the strength to do what was necessary.

She did not disappoint me.

The impact hurled me backwards from the carriage, against the horses, down amongst the wolves. The pain grew, consuming my heart, my lungs like a raging fire, but it mattered not, for my bliss, my triumph, were greater. I stared up at the black velvet sky and saw that the stars had disappeared . . . and knew this was not night, but the sweet darkness of approaching death.

Silence enveloped me. The world receded as, grateful, drowsy, I sank further into bliss. An eternity—or perhaps only an instant—passed.

The pleasurable stillness was rent by the screams of horses, the thunder of hoofbeats, the rumble of wheels. And in the midst of these, a horrified cry—muted, seemingly distant, yet when I opened my eyes, I beheld V. kneeling over me, wailing in terror.

He bent low to embrace me, gathered me into his arms—and pressed his lips to my neck, softly, tenderly, as a lover might.

I groaned, tried to struggle, but my mortal wound rendered me unable to so much as avert my head. I prayed (not with words, for I was too weak to petition with aught but my heart) that death would take me first, for even as he lingered over my neck, vision failed, and all became consuming blackness. I felt joy, victory in death, for I knew the horses had bolted, taking Mary with them. God had heard my petition: my son and wife were safe.

Yet in the midst of the blackness came a small pricking pain, less intense than the fire that filled my torso, but bright and sharp and silvery, like moonlight upon water. I felt a surge of anguish—yet that wave of emotion, ere it passed, turned sweetly sensual. My moan of dismay became one of pleasure; the agony in my chest faded, forgotten, and I yielded to the intoxicating sensation of my life blood flowing out to meet his.

I felt his deep gratification; and I felt my own thoughts sailing towards him on that crimson flow:

The memory of Kohl; each detail of his broad florid face, his rounded nose, the sparseness of his pale golden hair, the gleam of pale blue eyes beneath his spectacles.

Mary's tears, and mine, as Kohl solemnly swore to us that he would raise our child as his own, should we not survive.

These memories faded, and I knew nothing but my own pleasure. With a final burst of strength, I raised my arm and clutched the back of V.'s head, pressing him deeper into my flesh.

And then my arm fell, and blackness descended utterly. It was the instant of most profound ecstasy I have ever known; even now I cannot write of my own death, cannot recall it, without a thrill of pleasure, without the desire to return once more to that infinite moment.

+I+ +I+ +I+

When I woke it was night, though I could see as day. I was alone, in the family tomb, lying in the open coffin from which my sister had risen.

I went to the castle, finding that I needed not travel on foot, but could cast my essence upon the air, and move like the wind.

V. and Zsuzsa were gone; no doubt the coward knew I am now as strong as he, and will gladly destroy him. Of my darling Mary, I could find no sign.

I go now to search for a mortal who will free me with stake and knife, and end the covenant. If I can only die innocent, without tasting of human blood, without taking a life . . .

But the hunger! The hunger—! I thought when I first rose it would drive me mad. I went into the forest and chased down a wolf, and suckled at its neck like a newborn.

It tasted foul, but it calmed me a time, permitting me to record the ending—and strange new beginning—of my life. But it is not enough! Not enough . . .

+I+ +I+ +I+

God, in Whom I had put no faith, help me! I do not believe in You—did not, but if I am to accept such infinite Evil as I have become, then I pray infinite Good exists as well, and that it has mercy on what remains of my soul.

I am the wolf. I am Dracul. The blood of innocents stains my hands, and now I wait to kill him . . .

+I+ +I+ +I+

I have killed a man. I went in search of my own destruction, but the hunger overtook me, and I drank—drank, and found it the most divine nectar.

⊰323⊱

I am corrupt. I have tasted blood and will do so again, with relish. I dare not seek my own end now, for my tarnished soul will fulfill the covenant, and purchase V.'s continued immortality.

V. will learn of this, and seek to destroy me.

And my son! He will pursue my son . . .

I may be *strigoi,* one of the Devil's own—but I swear that Mary's loving crime shall not be in vain. I will see even this great Evil turned to Good, for love's sake. I possess the vampire's powers, and shall use them all to see V. destroyed. He has created a foe as mighty as he.

And I shall not rest until I find my darling Mary, and my son, and protect them both from V.'s wiles. My son, who I pray never learns what became of his father.

Go swiftly, little Stefan. May your heart remain pure, and may you find solace in the love of strangers, and a name not your own . . .

I am the Wolf. I am Dracul.
my hands, and now I
in Whom I put no faith
in You — did not, but if
evil as I have become, th
s well, and that it has
my soul I am the Wolf.
innocents stains my
kill him ... God, sin
ne! I do not believe in
accept such infinite
then I pray infinite
his mercy on what rem
self. I am Dracul. The Bl
ends, and now I wait.
put no faith, help me
did not, but if I am to ac
have become, then I pr
ell, and that it has